Flat out, the Bluebird hurdled trees at 375 mph. They'd have radar tracking, missiles locking on. But at this height the smallest judgment error would prove fatal anyway – he was flying into the fierce sun's sinking eye.

Chequers' tall chimneys and steep gables grew from the trees. A tic started tugging beneath the pilot's eye. Click to manual. Leap a last line of sentry-beeches. Once again he was a young man fighting over the inhospitable South Atlantic.

Everything was as promised. For a slow-motion second he studied the galloping group, spotting the Prime Minister's distinctive white mane leading the field. They were well short of the refuge offered by an arched Gothic doorway. As he pressed the release button, the pilot saw a Latin motto picked out in grey stone against the red brick of the house – *IUSTITIA TENAX*.

About the author

Former journalist Fid Backhouse now works as an advertising copywriter, having set up his own creative studio in an old village maltings in 1989. He has one son and lives 'beside the shop' in North Suffolk with his wife, three springer spaniels and two cats. *By Other Means* is his first novel.

By Other Means

Fid Backhouse

CORONET BOOKS
Hodder and Stoughton

First published in Great Britain in 1997 by Hodder and Stoughton
A division of Hodder Headline PLC
First published in paperback in 1998 by Hodder and Stoughton
A Coronet Paperback

10 9 8 7 6 5 4 3 2 1

ISBN 0 340 70726 7

Printed and bound in Great Britain by
Mackays of Chatham plc, Chatham, Kent

Hodder and Stoughton
A division of Hodder Headline PLC
338 Euston Road
London NW1 3BH

For supportive family and friends, and yet to be published writers who also believe that lightning will strike. Sometimes, it does.

PROLOGUE:

20–21 August

Nettlesmere, Suffolk

He'd driven to rural Suffolk to satisfy himself that the murder weapon was ready. It was, and the die would soon be cast.

The Prime Minister had to go. Derek Minton-Briant's government was choking Britain, but nobody seemed willing or able to restrain the authoritarian Premier. So the PM and his lackeys could hardly complain when determined people were forced to consider a radical solution.

After months of careful planning, the time had nearly come.

To a casual glance, the Bluebird looked like any other light aircraft, standing on oil-stained concrete at the back of a cavernous World War II hangar, blue-and-white paintwork sheened by the glare of overhead lamps. But the twin-engined plane was potentially lethal. The stocky pilot explained his modifications with craftsman's pride and the agitated enthusiasm of a fanatic.

There was no weakening of the embittered aviator's resolve, just eagerness to do what must be done. After they had run through every aspect of their meticulous plan for the hundredth time, the man from London left the assassin to his inner demons. They would not meet again.

His official Jaguar bumped across the wartime airfield, which looked very peaceful. Concrete runways had long vanished, replaced by cultivated fields running away to an encircling horizon of dark pine trees. A faded red windsock hung from its pole beside the grass landing strip, but otherwise there was little evidence that young Americans had once pounded the Third Reich from here.

But they had. He stopped briefly beside a polished granite memorial at a country crossroads, set against a copse of trees. It showed a mighty B-17 bomber bursting headlong through chains above a bold message – *FORTRESS FOR FREEDOM*. The agony and achievement of the 388th United States Army Airforce Bomb Group between June 1943 and August 1945 was faithfully recorded: 306 missions; 8,051 sorties; 191 aircraft lost; 222 enemy aircraft destroyed, 526 killed or missing, 801 prisoners. A wilted wreath of flowers showed someone remembered.

This was another sort of war, but one more deadly flight would originate from Nettlesmere Field – and hands would again join across the ocean to free Britain from tyranny. As he drove away, leaving behind memories of men who fought and died for a better world, he started whistling *Rule Britannia* – somewhat tunelessly, but with great verve.

San Antonio, Texas

Maria Martinez was frightened. That was nothing new. Fear lived close by, ready to spring when a door slammed or someone gave her a second glance. Sooner or later they would discover her secret and send her back, to her father's anger and mother's tears.

This was worse. The man said he would hurt her if she didn't do as he asked, and she believed him. There was something cruel in the way he stroked her cheek with rolled dollar bills, barely brushing the skin. He spoke again, the voice gentle.

'You understand what to say, Maria, what you must do?'

She clenched her hands until fingernails bit the palms, lapsing into Spanish without realizing she had done so.

'*Sí, señor.*'

The man's dark eyes held hers. He thrust the notes into the hip pocket of her tight jeans, allowing his gloved hand to linger. When he stepped back she rocked, as though released from a physical embrace.

'You're a pretty girl. Let's keep it that way. Remember, we know where your brother is and who you are. Say anything or screw up and we'll trash the both of you. Do this right and I'll see you after with another grand and that gen-u-ine Green Card I just showed you. You ain't got no choice, honey, so be a winner.'

He turned and left the small room as suddenly as he had arrived. It was as though she had been with a dangerous animal, felt hot breath on her face. Maria threw the dead-bolt and leaned against the door. Soon she could no longer feel fluttering in her chest.

She took out the money, went to her narrow bed and sat on the patterned blanket. Carefully, she smoothed nearly-new bills against rough fabric until they lay flat. Fear temporarily forgotten, she counted the ten banknotes twice, savouring their smooth texture.

Maria decided to send them home, then realized this was not possible. Her mother would worry there was no good way her daughter could earn so much in so short a time. Such a fortune was more than they expected in a whole year, even from someone who had met person-ally with one of only two Next Presidents of the United States.

Governor Patrick Stark nodded as the ancient Congressman worried hell out of the Welfare Program. The Candidate composed his face – attentive, alert, involved – leaving most of his mind free to wander.

Running for the world's greatest office was a lonely race. He sometimes hated clutching hands which reached for the magic, movers and shakers who wanted their piece, losers who stared with hope on naïve faces. His own slick team weren't much better. They put him in mind of NASA technicians servicing a shuttle – offering total commitment with not one detail overlooked, but nothing personal. All that mattered was the mission.

No problem. He'd been doing the job for thirty years, and wouldn't want things any other way. What if he could count true friends on the thumb of one hand? He had thousands of influential acquaintances and the power game gave him a buzz – especially with a nine-point lead and the first Tuesday after the first Monday in November less than eleven weeks away.

Nights were more complicated, because his thoughts turned to forbidden territory. He and Ella had lived a charade for years. If he hadn't acquired a coming-man label, they would have divorced. But she played by Washington rules. Their joint career demanded the perfect public marriage, so they delivered. Stark valued Ella's loyalty and political savvy, but physically they had drifted apart.

'Hell, no!'

After two or three trips around the Welfare block, Congressman Elmer Farris ran out of gas with a final splutter. Patrick Stark clapped him on the shoulder and stood up before the old bigot could refuel.

'Well said, Elmer, well said. Couldn't have put it better myself. Now if you'll excuse me I must get back to the room. Big day tomorrow.'

Tomorrow was always a big day. Farris jumped up, body language dynamic, telling people he mixed with serious players and got things done for the electors of South Texas. The Congressman grabbed Stark's hand, cracked his wrinkled face and showed every cent's-worth of gleaming bridgework.

'Great to talk again, Pat. We're going all the way to the White House this time. Yes sir, we surely are.'

Farris spoke loudly, for the benefit of video cameras behind plush rope which kept the news people away – but not too far away – from his intimate head-to-head with the main man. He held the smile, along with Stark's hand, until reporters tired of shouting questions.

The Candidate waited patiently, his expression open and sincere.

The man had driven fifty miles after leaving Maria Martinez, just to use a pay-phone on the wall of a sleepy Texas gas station. He was pathologically cautious, detouring off Interstate 81 to make the call. Not that he expected to be followed. Who knew he existed?

Peeling off leather gloves and flexing big hands, he watched the skinny kid sponging the windshield of his Ford – maybe hoping for a dollar tip, perhaps itching to shut up shop so he could join the gang at the drugstore. Little hustler probably wanted both. He checked his Rolex then made the connection, hearing a click as the recording machine came on line.

'Martinez looks solid. We may get lucky. If not, there's a shot lined up in Houston. After that nothing until San Diego.'

Weekly report filed, he hung up. The American Dreamer was still busy – this time with the air line. The man looked at the pump, pretending not to notice a squeaky-clean windshield. Gas came to $17.50. He gave the boy four fives and told him to keep the change.

The man moved off towards Laredo and the Mexican border. He took the old road, to check for company. But the rearview revealed no following lights in the darkness. A few miles down the arrow-straight blacktop alongside the main highway, he rejoined Route 81 near Devine.

Turning back north, he headed for San Antonio at a steady fifty-five. He never had and never would receive a traffic citation.

In the service kitchen's staff room, Maria Martinez sat by the phone, watching the clock. Next door in the kitchen Candy was joking around with Randy, the good-looking short-order cook from Del Rio. They had a thing going. Maria envied their right to have fun.

The mesmeric digital display flicked from 01.13 to 01.14. Less than fifty minutes before Room Service finished and she had to face reality too awful to contemplate. The man would return, eager to hear her mission was accomplished, ready to give more dollars and the paper that would make her a person. She wanted that Green Card more than anything in the world. If the call came, she would do what must be done. If not, perhaps the man would let her keep the thousand dollars as promised.

She had compromised over the money, mailing two bills to her mother on the way to work. The letter explained she had put in extra hours because a Next President of the United States was staying at her hotel along with many television crews and reporters. Maria had seen Patrick Stark, been alone with him, spoken to him at length. He was a fine man who admired her looks and liked her a lot.

The truth was less dramatic, but a girl had her pride. When she served coffee, the tall man with white-blond hair and suntanned complexion glanced up from a mess of papers and said, 'Thank you, no cream.' In the short time before he looked down she registered the seriousness of his blue-grey eyes. They noticed her where many did not.

He reminded her of Robert Redford, who featured in old movies she watched on television to improve her English. Maria never switched to the Spanish-language channel, because she did not intend to remain a double-shift wait-ress on minimum wage for ever.

She imagined the stir her news would produce back home – father playing the big *enchilada* as he spent the dollars on imported beer to impress *compadres* from Mercado Juárez, mother telling with pride the letter's contents to women who would be encouraged on behalf of their own lost ones. All things were possible for those who made the short but difficult journey to *el norte*.

Patrick Stark closed his briefcase on the morrow's speeches. A retentive memory had also logged choice facts, meaningful statistics and personal snippets that might impress the right people. He'd done enough. The adrenalin surge of campaigning carried him through unremitting days, but he needed quiet night hours.

The Candidate lay back on the davenport, pushing out long legs. He found himself thinking about a Washington party, years before, where he'd been nailed by a French novelist called Pierre Something-or-other.

Stark recalled the man perfectly. Short, mid-forties, plump, olive complexion, over-long oily brown hair, tinted specta-cles – even a whiff of garlic and black tobacco on pun-gent breath. The writer's theory was simple: Creativity is inspired by sexuality, serving as a higher outlet for that basic instinct. Scratch any artist, and you find a man channelling above-average sex drive on to canvas or page.

When he had interrupted with a mischievous 'What about women, my friend?', Pierre misinterpreted the question. His reply suggested womankind's contribution to Great Art might be summarized on the back of a food stamp.

'Women, M'sieur,' said Pierre with no vestige of humour, 'are what one must 'ave when one 'as written a perfect sentence, for release and reward. I personally 'ave 'ad thousands.'

That was when Ella arrived. She pronounced the tongue-twisting name perfectly, laid an intimate hand on the creep's arm and confided that Harvard were looking for a visiting European Literature professor. When she pointed out the Dean, the Frenchman's bushy eyebrows went into orbit. Making no attempt to excuse himself, he hurried away with a sharply exhaled 'Ahhh'.

Later, in bed, Ella laughed until tears came as he replayed the conversation, mimicking Pierre's Chevalier accent. Afterwards, they made love. Strangely, he remembered little about their lovemaking, then or at any time. There had been many women since Ella. But nothing serious, and lately nothing at all. Whatever his desires, Pat Stark was too close to triumph to risk headlines that could blow away presidential ambitions like smoke in the wind.

He lit a Marlboro, inhaling deeply. Another weakness Stark kept to himself, ensuring he was never photographed or seen in public with a cigarette. Seven seconds later, nicotine hit his brain. He once used three packs a day, and cutting back was harder than renouncing sins of the pecker.

Maybe Pompous Pierre knew something. Stark wondered whether, if you substituted politics for creativity, the end result was the same – demanding work followed by acute need for sexual activity. He felt stirring tumescence in his groin. If only Ella were around. They no longer slept together, but she was the one person he could communicate with intimately, distracting desire for physical release. But Ella was in Washington, guarding home base. He neither knew nor cared if she took discreet lovers. His wife put her emotions into getting him to the top. If she used sex, it was for light relief.

Stark glanced at his wristwatch. Well over an hour into another day. Time for sleep, that great eraser of troubled thoughts – providing sleep would come. He reached for the phone. A malted milk might help. Perhaps that attractive Mexican-American girl who served morning coffee would be on duty. Those kids had to work all hours to make an honest buck. Personally, the Grand Old Party's tough line on repatriation distressed him.

But he was a politician, and he never let inner reservations inhibit his platform performance. Until burgeoning underclasses developed muscle, nobody gave a damn.

Back in San Antonio after his discreet date with a telephone, the man was about to steal a Stark campaign vehicle. Months ago, he had targeted the blue Buick sedan used as a runaround – obtaining a duplicate key by making like a car hop outside an armoury in West Virginia, where The Candidate was addressing seven hundred members of the American Legion.

A staffer delivering baseball caps bearing the legend *PAT STARK – THE VETERANS' FRIEND* was behind schedule, terrified cameras would roll before the headgear was filled by patriotic heads. He surrendered his vehicle without question, because these things were taken care of. When the Buick was turned over to the parking lot attendant, the man had the wax impression he needed and nobody the wiser.

He walked down into the hotel basement. A guard sat in brightly lit isolation at the foot of a concrete ramp, attended by the flickering colours of a portable TV. Otherwise, the garage was deserted. The man pulled down a white Stetson hat, shadowing his face. A waste of tradecraft. The booth potato didn't even notice him heading for the wheels, in their reserved slot alongside The Candidate's black Lincoln Continental.

The man used his clean-cut key and slipped into the driver's seat. The motor started first time. He drove slowly towards the exit. The guard glanced up, raised the pole and waved him through. Travelling uptown, he was just another set of moving lights. Stopping outside the girl's building, he studied the run-down street. It was a chicano neighbourhood with plenty of people around to eye the smart Buick, despite the late hour. Anonymous behind tinted glass, attention suited him fine.

When a gap appeared in foot traffic the man emerged, crossed the broken sidewalk and slipped the rooming-house lock with a charge-card. The girl's door was equally obliging.

Inside, he prowled, touching a plastic crucifix above the bed, opening a painted closet to inspect cheap clothing and a fibre suitcase. There was money in the toe of a leather boot. Dumb, but he wasn't her keeper. A tiny bathroom yielded hotel soap, flannel facecloth, toothbrush and paste, Walmart own-brand cosmetics, an unopened pack of sanitary towels.

He sat on the bed, feeling no impatience. If the girl didn't come home, he'd find her.

An hour later, Maria Martinez stepped down from a trash-fouled white VIA bus with cheerful rainbow flashes. The ease with which she handled a Next President of the United States had been surprising. Perhaps her mother was right – men *were* fools, if you let them think they called the shots. This awareness gave confidence.

She felt like a game show contestant one question away from the big prize. And she had the answer. She could tell the man what he wanted to hear, convince him she spoke the truth. Her proof was more than a stained skirt and the blouse she had ripped. He would believe, be satisfied, hand over money and the paper that meant freedom.

She would take the Greyhound to California. There would be no movie producer to discover her and turn her into a star. But she could take a job where she might be noticed. Men found her attractive. With fluent English and a quick brain, it should not be so difficult to find someone. If she liked him, where was the harm? She would make a good wife, had something to give most American girls did not.

What pleasure, returning to Juárez in triumph, married to a rich *americano*! She could summon family to the Hotel Del Prado, show fine clothes and expensive luggage. She would buy a meal at Quinta Anita, give her mother a beautiful lace shawl and father a crisp hundred from an alligator pocketbook, like over-tipping a waiter to show money didn't matter. There would be small but carefully chosen gifts for the others.

Close to her house, catcalling spoiled the dream. Three leather-jacketed boys sat on a wall, smoking grass as they watched the world float by. Maria knew who they were. Two brothers and their cousin from Sabinas – unemployed wetback garbage who shared a room on the next block. When they did this before, she had dropped her head and hurried on, provoking obscene remarks.

This time, she stopped and looked into their stupid faces. It was enough. They got up and sauntered away, combing their hair and arguing about what to do next. When she saw the shiny blue car outside her apartment, Maria was not afraid. She was beginning to understand how men could be handled.

He heard her outside, humming an unrecognizable tune. A key turned. The man did not rise from the bed. She stood in the doorway. The previous day's frightened mouse had changed – her pose was almost bold, the expression less submissive. Her accented voice was knowing.

'You gonna blackmail Stark for political favours, right?'

'Come in, Maria, close the door.'

Martinez hung her coat behind the door and perched on the single armchair. He noticed a faint damp patch staining the front of her powder-blue uniform skirt, a missing top button and torn buttonhole on the white blouse. She ran a hand through raven-black hair, then tossed her head. He took a recorder from his fawn windbreaker and set it on the bedside table, already sure. But he had to check.

'Tell me how it went, Maria. If the story sounds good, you get what I promised and I'm out of here. But I want the truth. Even if things didn't work out like we planned you still get to keep that thousand bucks, just for trying.'

The girl watched hungrily as he took out money and Green Card, laid them on the coarse blanket and started the machine. She began to speak, without hesitation. He let her tell it her way.

'At first I didn't think he was gonna call down. It got to be late and I was worried he wouldn't come through. There were other orders, but I asked Candy to fill them. She's the girl I work with. I said I wasn't feeling good with stomach cramps. Candy helped out, she's real friendly. Then the phone goes around one-thirty and it's him, hot malted milk for Suite Twelve-seventy.'

Martinez dared to tease by making him wait. He humoured her. No reason why she shouldn't enjoy the small triumph.

'You logged the order, like I said?'

'Always the first thing to do, for the tab, that's the rule. So I take the drink up on a tray with a napkin and some chocolate chip cookies, case he's hungry. I knock and he calls out "It's open" so I go on in. Mr Stark's on the couch but he gets up. He's wearing grey slacks and sport shirt, white socks, no shoes. He smiles and points to the table. I go to put the tray down . . .'

She stopped, covertly assessing his reaction. Her performance was fluent. She was telling the truth, but he prompted – a co-conspirator letting her see he was totally convinced.

'The drink goes all over him, you start crying, right?'

'Right. He looks real angry when the milk goes down his shirt and pants. I guess it was pretty hot. He takes off the shirt and tries mopping up with the napkin, then sees my tears. He isn't angry any more. He says, "Hey, don't cry, no harm done, I won't tell a soul." I cry some more. He doesn't know what to do so he grabs me, real clumsy, pats my back. I stop crying. My skirt's getting wet from his pants. He doesn't try anything, just sits me down on the couch.'

She paused, small breasts rising and falling, the tip of her tongue visible between even teeth. No wonder Stark was tempted.

'I blurt out the whole thing, how I'm illegal and my brother's been caught and is waiting to be shipped back and how I'm frightened they'll get me too and how my father will beat me for sure. I start crying again, real tears. They came easy. He sits beside me, tells me not to worry, nothing bad will happen. Then suddenly he's all over me . . .'

The story faltered. The man anticipated hesitation, would have been suspicious of anything else. He nudged.

'So he screwed you. Happens every day. How was it?'

She answered reluctantly, her delivery flat.

'Everything was quick. I don't remember, exactly. I tried to fight but he was strong. Afterwards my skirt was up around my waist and my blouse was torn and his shirt was open. He didn't even take his pants off. He told me to keep quiet or they'd send me back and anyhow nobody would believe my word against his. He made me clean up in the bathroom then said go home without talking to anyone.'

'Did you?'

'No . . . yes. Candy saw me in the rest room. Maybe she guessed what happened, or thought my stomach cramps were bothering me. The shift was nearly over and she said she'd cover, so I left.'

'How do I know you're not lying to me, honey?'

The man made his tone friendly. He looked into eyes bright with tears. She answered in a whisper.

'Stark has a brown mark on his chest, shaped like a bird.'

He stopped the recorder, got up and looked down at her.

'That he does, though he don't shout about it. I guess he likes the world to think he's just perfect. You done good, real good. Thank you, Maria, our business is finished. For the record, I have to tell you blackmail ain't it.'

The man reached out a reassuring black-gloved hand to pat her shoulder.

A few miles and whole world away in Castle Hills, David Turrow's phone went at 6.27 a.m., beating the alarm by three minutes. San Antonio's hot-shot First Assistant DA found the clock but failed to silence the insistent electronic sound. He worked things out. Opening gummy eyes, he groped for the phone. Keeping the right company could be hell, especially when it meant drinking too much imported wine. Debbie rolled away with a groan, pulling covers over her head.

'Turrow. Who the hell is this?'

'I'm down the morgue. We got a dead one here, a nice-lookin' Mexican kid. Or she was. Battered and strangled. Found in a dumpster uptown less than an hour ago. Anonymous tip. We sent a blue-and-white and there she lay, still warm. I'm takin' charge myself.'

The First Assistant DA recognized the voice – Lieutenant

Richard Schneider of the San Antonio Police Department, sounding more cheerful than the barbaric hour or down-beat message should allow. Turrow struggled to comprehend the policeman's angle.

'You got a dead Mex, so what? I'll be in the office by eight-thirty, same as always. Call me then if there's something you need.'

Irritated by three minutes' lost sleep he hung up, sat on the bed edge and knuckled itching hair. Goddam cops, always elevating drama into crisis. Schneider especially liked to needle him. The laid-back senior detective made no secret of his contempt for the lawyer's abrasive approach.

The phone sounded again, sparking Turrow's anger. He snatched it up and made like a dummy in a cheap TV drama – speaking before he knew who was on the line.

'Shit, I thought I said to leave it.'

When it came, the voice was nothing like Schneider's.

'Mr Turrow? Charlie Hecht, City Editor of the *Light*. We've spoken before. I just got word on the Martinez killing. Any comment?'

David Turrow jolted to full consciousness. He switched on the voice used to impress anyone who could damage him.

'Sorry, Charles, nothing at this point. Call me in business hours and I'll be happy to supply any information I have.'

He hung up for the second time in under a minute. Pulling on Debbie's robe, Turrow padded downstairs to fetch his organizer. Back in the bedroom, he found and punched the number, tapping his knee while he waited.

'City Morgue.'

'David Turrow from the DA's Office. You got Schneider there?'

'Sure do, sir. Saw him going into the autopsy room and he ain't come out. Hold on, I'll transfer you.'

His wife turned over and muttered something like 'Is it morning, lover?' in a sleepy voice. Before he could think up a crushing reply Schneider came on, sounding none too friendly.

'Yeah?'

'What the hell's going on? I just had the *Light* asking questions, I guess it's about your girl, so what's so goddam special that the papers are on the case before I am?'

'Tried to warn you, Dave. Kid's provisionally ID'd as Maria Martinez. Worked at the hotel where a citizen with ambitions to be Commander-in-Chief is stayin' right now. Handled Room Service for his floor. Want me to go on, or have you woke up?'

Turrow understood Schneider's earlier good humour. It was shit-hits-fan time. The first Assistant DA was gripping the phone tightly, and made an effort to relax.

'Thanks, Dick, you did right to call. Sorry I was short. No press briefing. There's already been a leak, so stall. I don't want a media circus here. As of now we're in no-comment mode. I'll be with you as soon as I can. Called the DA yet?'

Schneider snorted.

'You kiddin'? That roadrunner would tell me to tell you all about it and remember an urgent appointment out of state.'

'Right. You down there for a while?'

'Only till I get the Medical Examiner's preliminary report.'

'Wait.'

David Turrow replaced the phone, calculating implications he didn't like one bit. He looked aggressively at his wife. Debbie was sleeping peacefully, an arm outflung into his space.

DAY ONE:

Thursday 5 September

Vice-Presidential Special Adviser Vernon Lustbader came out of his waterside cabin and looked at the angry fall skyscape above Vandercook Lake. Sure as night followed day, something always came up. Or more accurately in this case, down.

He needed this vacation in Michigan after months on the campaign trail. A neighbour had called by earlier to leave groceries and milk, lighting the old Vermont Vigilant wood stove and setting a chipped enamel coffee pot to brew. A soft-action rod waited in the barn. The flat-bottomed Jon-boat was ready on shore. And twenty thousand carp were out there in cold, clear water waiting to be stalked.

Not for Lustbader Florida bonefish or native gamefish. He preferred those immigrant descendants of five sickly *Cyprinus carpio* who survived passage from Holstein, Germany, in 1872. But the carp would remain unmolested. For a while, leastways. The threshing beat of General Electric turboshaft motors grew louder.

He walked towards the meadow to meet the helicopter. The Vice-President's Sikorsky swept over the trees and dropped neatly, door unfolding as engines settled to idle. Lustbader blinked. The mountain had come to Mohammed, and come unaccompanied by Secret Servicemen.

Errol Tidyman bustled down the steps. The Vice-President looked like a catalogue shot designed to shout 'Successful

African American'. He wore hand-tailored Scottish tweed that emphasized his trim figure. A triple-pointed handkerchief peeked from the breast pocket. His shirt was white silk, the tie blue wool. Mirror-polished brown brogues completed the ensemble.

Refusing to bow beneath decelerating rotors, he strode over and thumped the shoulder of Lustbader's check jacket with playful force.

'Vernon, great to see you. Surprised?'

'Nothing you do much surprises me, Errol.'

The two men went back to the cabin in easy silence. Lustbader poured black coffee and they sat at the plank table.

'Social call, Errol, or have you come by for the fishing?'

'You know me, old buddy. Business before pleasure seven, maybe eight days a week. This place clean?'

'Swept for electronic ears when I arrived. Unless some reporter is under the log pile we're off the record. So what crazy notion have you come up with this time?'

Tidyman smiled the smile that had illuminated a nation, teeth flashing against ebony skin.

'You're quick, Vernon, always were. Came to work for me 'cause you saw sooner than most you'd be throwing in with the next President. But that ain't enough. We're going to show the small guys they voted a team that gets results. And one in the crotch for those goddam WASPs and their TV networks who're badmouthing my ability to get on top of foreign relations. Tell me, when were you last in London, England?'

Lustbader swilled coffee round his mug, studying the vortex.

'So that's it. You aim to put the Special Relationship back together, neutralize their hostile UN veto and free up foreign policy options. Nice idea, Errol, but way off base. Those Brits will never step on to the ball park, even supposing we do win. Last time I looked you were trailing seven points. That's a distance of ground to pull back inside two months if Stark's wheels stay on.'

'We'll win. I'm already thinking second term. And believe me when I say they'll play. I've been doing groundwork. Very private, very promising. I need you to close the deal. Details

on the way back to Washington. Lock up this shack and
let's get mobile.'

'What's to lock up for?'

Lustbader rinsed mugs under the faucet and picked up
an overnight bag he hadn't unpacked. He followed the
Vice-President out. The sky was clearing from the west.
Down on the lake, carp were starting to roll. It was a great
afternoon for fishing.

Nothing stirred in the Chiltern Hills. Honeysuckle and clematis crowded the twin lodge gates of Chequers, smothering
intricate ironwork that barred a long-disused approach to
the Prime Minister's country residence. The scent of an
English autumn was fragrant on still air.

Inside the brick-and-flint lodge cottage, Corporal Terence
Seymour lit a cigarette and settled his stocky body in the
swivel chair. Sophisticated electronics seemed insignificant
beside moted sunlight striking through the diamond-pane
window.

Seymour blew smoke at a bumble-bee dashing against
the window in clumsy pursuit of freedom. The motorcade
would start its forty-mile dash to London within the hour,
leaving him to pursue Joy Christie's most desirable possession. Sweet Sixteen and never been more than fondled,
he felt sure. He planned a walk in empty beech woods – arms
circling waists, hips bumping, senses heightening. As the
sun fell behind the hill they'd find a mossy bank he knew
well, and this time . . .

Because his daydream was reaching a climax, an amber
light on the corporal's console flashed unheeded for fifty-five
seconds. A minute too late, Seymour returned to work.
Dropping into practised routine, he smacked the alarm.
Response from the house was instantaneous.

'Control to Alpha One. Report. Over.'

He recognized the measured voice of General Forsyth,
who *would* be on duty. Forsyth had the knack of being
around when things happened. Seymour thought the nas-
tiest word he knew, but didn't make the mistake of uttering
it.

'Alpha One to Control. Distorted contact on ground-to-
air. Over.'

'Control to Alpha One. Report plot development, this channel remains open. Out.'

Watching fluid green light patterns with guilt-inspired intensity, Corporal Seymour didn't speculate. Every alert was serious, even if the outcome was a rookie pilot from Wycombe Air Park fluttering towards summary clipping of new wings. When he was sure, he told Control, the lilting accent of his native Wales suddenly pronounced.

'Alpha One to Control. I now have positive contact, repeat positive. Low-flying light aircraft, bearing one-ninety, range eleven miles and closing. Computer predicts a pass one mile to the south of Chequers exclusion zone. Over.'

'Control to Alpha One. Report any status change immediately. We are moving to Condition Red, repeat Red. Out.'

Lieutenant Innes answered, which was surprising. Not like Forsyth to delegate to a pipsqueak graduate entrant. Control's acknowledgment had hardly died in his speaker when the unknown aircraft made a sharp northward turn.

Field Marshal David Chandler sat in a shaded corner of the top terrace. He was giving the tea party on the Chequers lawn only half his attention. The Security Minister felt tired and vaguely uneasy – open space, no cover, risk. As Head of Intelligence, he had reason to worry.

Last year a nineteen-year-old had been spotted by a security patrol in a nearby coppice, pushing a clip of brass .303 cartridges into an old Lee Enfield Mk 1V service rifle. That dangerous young man had drifted away from a group of students on one of the public footpaths criss-crossing the Chequers estate. His vantage point overlooked Prime Minister Derek Minton-Briant in a deckchair enjoying morning sun, marmalade on toast and Sunday newspapers.

The would-be assassin had been reading headlines through his Sniperscope when the patrol leader shot him dead – hearing a reflex snap as the bolt flew forward, smashing the firing pin against a dead percussion cap. But the next round functioned perfectly in a subsequent ballistics test and the lad knew his terrorist literature. The bullet-tips had been drilled, mercury dripped in and points resealed with wax.

Derek Minton-Briant was lucky to have kept his head. Yet the PM, mindful of his patriarchal image, always refused to acknowledge the dangers of office. 'These are my people,' Derek would say when personal security came up at meet-the-media sessions, head jauntily cocked for the cameras. 'What can I have to fear from my own?'

When the young radical provided a pointed answer, news of the incident was suppressed so the fiction could be maintained. Chandler massaged aching temples. Might be an idea to spend a week at his house in Hampshire, for the early partridges or late sea trout.

On the barbered lawn below, Derek Minton-Briant was dominating an attentive gathering with pugnacious small talk. Lately, the man had become more interested in the privileges of office than exercise of its responsibilities. Sad, but matters couldn't be allowed to slide much further. Derek should plan for the succession, as he himself had. Nobody was immortal or irreplaceable, though the PM rated himself highly on both counts.

Then Chandler smiled, finding relief from sombre thought in Minton-Briant's confident laugh. You had to admire the old ringmaster. He was manipulating the great African statesman and President Julius Awami would soon be dancing on his hind legs. Despite a formidable personality, the Living Legend was physically insubstantial – a desiccated charcoal-suited black stick topped by a deeply lined face and iron-grey hair. He was sitting comfortably as liveried servants fussed round, crustless cucumber sandwich in one claw and teacup in the other, nodding judiciously in response to a whispered aside from the PM which set him above his colourful entourage in their tribal robes.

Colonial threads still trapped President Awami in a complex web, despite formative years at Moscow's Patrice Lumumba University, an extended sojourn in white man's prison on Robben Island and the acclaimed achievement of majority rule. Residual illusions would surely subside when the President got home and tried to explain cuts in the Federal African Republic's life-giving aid package. But for now he could bask in the warmth engendered by life membership of the élite confederation of world leaders.

Chandler was distracted by brisk footsteps on granite

flagstones. He glanced up to find General Robert Forsyth beside him.

'Important, Bob? I'm feeling a bit off colour.'

'Unidentified aircraft threatening the exclusion zone.'

His deputy's reply was terse, but Chandler prevaricated.

'Not one of your efficiency exercises, I suppose? No, or you'd hardly be here. Some idiot incapable of handling a topographical display unit, then?'

'A check through Air Traffic Control shows authorized aircraft accounted for. We have a maverick.'

'How long?'

'Less than a minute.'

'Christ, I'll pull the PM.'

Field Marshal Chandler scrambled from his chair, stumbling slightly on rheumy legs. The younger man ran towards the house, chased by a faint murmur of high-revving propjet engines.

Prime Minister Minton-Briant was in his element. President Awami was mesmerized by his resource-saving charm. Nearly time to knee him in his tiresome country's bulging groin. Field Marshal Chandler approached at an ungainly lope.

'Prime Minister . . .'

The breathless interruption ruined a tale from the PM's fondly remembered days as scourge of the Party. Minton-Briant released a crab-like grip on the President's upper arm, a rush of colour suffusing his square face.

'I'm conducting important negotiations with President Awami and his distinguished colleagues. We're not to be disturbed, even by you.'

The uniformed Intelligence officer straightened, breathing now controlled.

'Security, Prime Minister. No argument.'

The PM had spoken from pride. Despite recent differences, Chandler was too good a man to trouble him without reason. For all that, the retreat was grudging.

'What is it?'

'Unidentified aircraft. You must take shelter. Now.'

'Naturally, if the safety of our guests is in question we must heed your advice. Mr President?'

The surrender was gracious. Two great but elderly leaders of men rose from the tea table without haste, as befitted one another's dignity.

Flat out, the Bluebird hurdled trees at 375 mph. They'd have radar tracking, missiles locking on. But at this height the smallest judgment error would prove fatal anyway – he was flying into the fierce sun's sinking eye.

Chequers' tall chimneys and steep gables grew from the trees. A tic started tugging beneath the pilot's left eye. Click to manual. Leap a last line of sentry-beeches. Once again he was a young man fighting over the inhospitable South Atlantic.

Everything was as promised. For a slow-motion second he studied the galloping group, spotting the Prime Minister's distinctive white mane leading the field. They were well short of the refuge offered by an arched Gothic doorway. As he pressed the release button, the pilot saw a Latin motto picked out in grey stone against the red brick of the house – *IUSTITIA TENAX*.

The Bluebird bounded free of its lethal load. A violent roll set him on deception course. The twin-engined plane shuddered into a steep climb, jinking like a woodcock to avoid ground fire. When the explosion's violent turbulence caught up, the sturdy aircraft rode the storm. The pilot dived back to treetop height. Picking up the London–Aylesbury rail line, he turned north, scattering trippers on Ramble Route 17. One fired a broadside from his motordriven Canon, securing photographs that would be seen around the world.

Less than six miles away, VTO Harrier jump-jets rose into the air at Halton airfield, electronic noses sniffing for a flying fugitive.

General Robert Forsyth wasn't tempted to rush outside. His place was the underground control room, equipped to act as Britain's brain in times of war or civil insurrection. Swallowing to clear ears still popping from blast waves that slammed into him as he ran for the elevator, Forsyth reached his command console. He keyed the emergency code, contacting Alpha One as pre-programmed instructions flowed on to his screen.

'Control to Alpha One. Over.'

'Alpha One to Control. Standing by. Over.'

Bolshie little sod, Seymour, but reliable.

'Control to Alpha One. We've been hit from the air. Do you have a bearing? Over.'

'Bloody haven't. He headed south-east but the bastard's vanished. He's down, or tree-hopping again. Over.'

'Keep calm and keep trying. Out.'

Someone shouted a question.

'HQ on Screen One. Will you take it?'

'Hold London, I'll need time with them. Tell the Duty Officer to assemble Department Heads for telebriefing.'

Forsyth breathed deeply and looked round the brightly lit bunker. A dozen duty staff looked back. He swallowed. His throat was dry, though his voice hadn't wavered.

'Acknowledge my orders, then get on with it. Innes, double upstairs, see who's alive, tell my chopper pilot to wind up in case there are casualties to lift out. Find out what happened then straight back with a first-hand situation report.'

'Sir!'

The young lieutenant departed. Forsyth issued a stream of instructions, wondering if anyone survived the explosive tea party.

'I saw the aircraft. BA Bluebird. Notify Halton. It went away to the south-east and may be down. If they've got contact on military radar, fine. If not try civilian Air Traffic. Order a helicopter sweep for wreckage.'

'Sir!'

'Find out if we put up enough fire to disable that plane, check security videos, ask why the Patriot battery on the southern perimeter didn't take him out.'

'Sir!'

'Maximum response under Condition Red procedures – seal M-routes, cover airfields, stations, ports. All in the book. Cut HQ into the loop so they confirm under priority codes from London, or Police Central will waste time checking back. Got that?'

'Yessir!'

'Talk to Media Section at HQ, Colonel Granger. I want an all-channels public service flash at five-minute intervals for the next hour. People should watch for low-flying planes and contact local police if they see any. Nothing released on the attack. Then bring down every Bluebird on the nearest field. No, make that all light aircraft.'

'Sir!'

The tasked operatives bent over terminals and a babble of urgent conversation filled the room. So much for the most pressing needs. Forsyth called for coffee, then switched in London.

'Copy this most grave situation report, HQ. General Forsyth at Chequers Control. There has been an assassination attempt. A bomb delivered by light aircraft caught the Prime Minister's party outside the house. Minton-Briant may be down. To permit rapid response it is necessary to invoke Standing Order Nine, repeat Nine. I have assumed command in the absence of Field Marshal Chandler, who may also be dead or injured . . .'

Forsyth briefed senior Intelligence executives, shoulders slumping with involuntary release of tension. Five minutes had elapsed since the attack.

Consciousness struggled back. Field Marshal Chandler awoke to infernal noise. Strange motion. Eyes not registering. Pain. Horrifying memory returning. Screaming aircraft blocking sky, underbelly glinting fish-white. Metal cylinder detaching, falling. Running. Shouting 'Down'. Crashing into a rose bed. Thorns. Blackness.

Pricked arm, medics on the job, stretcher case. Irritating tickle at back of throat. Don't fight, play by the book. Backwards from five, try for zero. Five, four, thr . . .

The Security Minister slid into chemical oblivion. As she crouched over him, hypodermic gun in hand, the nurse from Chequers Medical Unit thought he'd died. But a fluttering neck pulse confirmed the stubborn presence of life within.

It was a short flight to Stoke Mandeville Hospital. David Chandler reached theatre within nine minutes of the explosion. Little more than manual dexterity was needed to repair his injuries. When they finished, he had more than two hundred microsutures in non-life-threatening wounds, many superficial.

But surgeons could do nothing to repair the damage inflicted by the jagged shard of shrapnel that sliced through the right bicep before destroying the Field Marshal's eyesight.

Every tenth second took the Bluebird a mile nearer safety. He had not failed. Even if they found him, his work could not be undone. But his feint fooled the interceptors. Tuning the radio across bands of commercial chatter, the pilot passed a monotonous order for light aircraft to land and found a fragment of military communication.

'Purple Cygnet to Purple Swan. Vectoring on assigned patrol corridor north of London Gatwick Airport. Visual contact negative, radar negative. Will maintain watch at Angels Nine. Over.'

'Purple Swan to Purple Cygnet. Message received and understood. Commence fresh sweep on bearing . . .'

The conversation faded into static. He was cheered by gung-ho jargon, the nervous tic beneath his eye stopping as abruptly as it came. Streaking over dark fenland fields and market gardens south of Spalding, he made the course correction that took him out over Holbeach military bombing range. Rocking the Bluebird's wings, he crossed the coast. Someone would remark, remember and report.

Leaving the Wash for North Sea proper, the pilot switched to auto. Unclipping his face mask, he lit a cigarette and glanced at the instrument panel. The digital timer had logged 995, 996, 997 seconds since he pressed the release button.

Unaware that the flying fox had slipped his hounds, General Forsyth eased out of the hunt as Intelligence Headquarters assumed direction of the search. Activity in Chequers Control subsided as London cut in, machine mating with machine. He sipped coffee. Time to analyse, evaluate, plan.

Switching on his desktop TV, he caught the public service flash. Viewers weren't missing much. Transmission returned to Denis Dimbleby, hosting his *Skeleton in the Cupboard* series – a leading opiate of the people.

Forsyth registered incoming reports. Air force pilots were logging nothing but false alarms. An abject message was relayed from the south perimeter. The spares-starved Patriot missiles had been fired – two malfunctioning on launcher, the rest looping no further than Home Farm. Rare Highland Longhorn cattle, property of the nation, were no more. Lieutenant Innes hurried from the elevator. Hushed conversation died. The junior officer's report was concise, delivered with the staccato precision of hard-held emotion.

The Prime Minister was dead. President Awami, his entire delegation, three Chequers domestic staff – also dead. Field Marshal Chandler – injured, condition unknown, airlifted to hospital. Outer fabric of Chequers – severely damaged. Forsyth relayed the body count to Headquarters. As he finished, Innes slumped against a computer console, head in hands. Nobody despised his weakness.

The unthinkable had happened, suddenly and violently. The old order had perished. What now?

Spray flew. The Bluebird bounced, then belly-flopped. The pilot stepped on to a blue wing, dragging the survival pack after him. Compressed air hissed and an orange boat blossomed. Pushing out the dinghy, he abandoned the murder weapon. Resting on plastic oars, he watched as a small charge breached the lower fuselage. The plane faced disaster with dignity, settling slowly. But the end was quick. Tail fins cocked high and followed heavy engines into a cauldron of bubbles.

The pilot didn't have far to go. Ahead, a deserted gas platform towered above moderate swell, awaiting scrap tenders with massive indifference. After five minutes' erratic paddling, he reached a slime-green ladder which ran down into milky depths and up to the sky.

Hanging one-handed, he took a Beretta 6.35mm automatic from the side pocket of his battered leather flying coat and thumbed down the safety. The tiny pistol cracked through the clip, stitching an uneven eight-hole pattern in rubberized fabric. Unable to argue with lead weights, dinghy reluctantly followed plane.

His eyes swept the seascape. No floating traces. He started the long climb – pausing frequently, arriving on the platform with aching limbs and searing lungs. Dereliction surrounded him. Brown-streaked doors hung open and rusted deck machinery confirmed that no metal could withstand corrosive North Sea atmosphere. Generations of gulls had passed, leaving their mark. Some still mewed and swooped around the intruder to their lonely domain.

The utter bleakness appealed, matching his mood. Perhaps it would have been better if retribution had visited, destroying him before new dead faded into myriad sad memories already inhabiting his mind.

The girl came in quietly, but the closing door betrayed her. Since the explosion's distant thunderclap and flurry of following activity, dialogue with Control had dried. Corporal Terence Seymour's instruments only registered search helicopters, and his thoughts turned inwards.

Would there be any comeback on his delay in reporting that first contact? He couldn't know if Control had picked up the damning discrepancy. No, they wouldn't nail him. Stupid buggers didn't know their arses from their elbows. He'd also been wondering when he'd see Joy Christie. Now he struck out that thought, spinning his swivel chair to face her.

'Hello, gorgeous. What brings you here in duty hours? You know the rules. Wouldn't want to get me into trouble, or is that the idea?'

Seymour regretted the words as he uttered them. Joy was in no mood for banter. She stood against the rough white wall, mutely appealing for help. He half rose, uncertain how to respond.

'What's the matter, love, what's wrong?'

His eyes fastened on her heaving housemaid's blouse. He bit his lip. Hardly fair to ask if she fancied a cuddle. She dissolved the dilemma, coming forward with a rush that knocked him off balance. They almost fell. Clinging tightly, Joy mumbled into his chest.

'It was horrible, Tel. I was in the study, see. One minute I was dusting the coffee table and the next thing there was this terrific bang outside what broke the windows and knocked me down. There was glass all over the parquet and in the Persian rugs and I had this ringing sound in my ears.'

He tightened his arms, squeezing a torrent of words from her.

'I ran out to see what was happening. Men were shouting

and there was this big hole in the ground and smoke
everywhere. I went to have a closer look, then trod on
something.'

She trembled, and he experienced a shameful erection.

'It was an arm. No body, just a hand and a black arm with
a big gold watch on it. I wanted to be sick but wasn't and
ran up to my room. Then I didn't want to be on my own so
I came here.'

Awkwardly, Seymour supported her lolling head.

'Don't worry, you're safe. Duty Officer's too busy up the
house to do his rounds, shouldn't wonder.'

As he soothed her, he realized he was right. They would
be undisturbed. Joy became dead weight, trauma purged.

'Come on, love, lie down for a bit.'

He backed her to the divan used by relief oppos on early
shifts, helping her down. He knelt and stroked tangled hair.
Her plump face became calm, eyes fluttering shut amidst
streaked make-up. Tentatively, he undid the blouse's top
button. Joy's final snuffle suggested she needed comfort-
ing. Seymour managed the remaining buttons without
fumbling. She didn't protest. Hardly able to believe his
luck, he cupped her breasts, then pushed the lacy bra up
and over. They were the stuff dreams were made of.

After a brief struggle with prudish panties, he loosened
his belt and freed himself. He rolled on to the divan, jamming Joy against the wall. Scarcely pausing to get his
bearings, Seymour thrust forward.

He was so surprised by her deft assistance and the slippery ease of conquest that he ejaculated the moment she
slid eager hands inside his trousers and hooked sharp nails
beneath his buttocks. He buried his head in her shoulder
and lay still, growing small in mind and body. Joy pushed
him off. She rearranged her bra and spoke in a tone that
cut through pride like a wire slicing cheese.

'You blew it, Tel.'

Terence Seymour was just thinking it was the worst day
of his life when he became aware of Lieutenant Innes in
the doorway – clipboard in hand, a riot of emotions on his
youthful face.

The Prince Regent's official Rolls-Royce was lapping up

miles. The titular Head of State's lazy afternoon at Windsor Castle had been destroyed by a peremptory summons to an emergency Cabinet meeting in London. To deaden the blow, George was murdering a bottle of Scotch.

He was in a foul mood. Hunger for life's succulent flesh was hard to satiate, hampered by the need for discretion. Position and status were fine, but a few old Rembrandts on the wall hardly contributed to the practical pursuit of pleasure.

The Prince Regent scowled, remembering the Fabergé egg fiasco. He'd smuggled the gaudy trinket out of Windsor Castle and placed it with a Second Secretary at the Dutch Consulate. Not his fault the idiot tried to smuggle it out in hand luggage instead of using the diplomatic bag. Spoilt everything.

He banished the unpleasant memory, fumbling American *Vogue* from a leather briefcase which contained a sachet of cocaine, rolled dollar bill, small Coca-Cola mirror and single-edged razor blade. The cover girl was sensational. Cornflower eyes, wide mouth, neat nose, neat figure, tumbling blonde hair. He moistened his lips. Unlike some clothes-horses he'd known, Beth Highsmith was better in real life than on the page. She'd been introduced at a Buckingham Palace garden party earlier that summer and he couldn't dislodge her from his mind.

George meant to have her, body and soul – though he'd settle for body. Tricky. He had no appetite for another lashing of prime ministerial rage, sure to explode if the killjoy was told his Prince Regent was rogering a photographic model. And Minton-Briant *would* be informed. Iscariotism was rife.

As the Roller floated along elevated M-route 4 towards London's heart, police outriders fell in, guiding them through a priority lane at the final roadblock on Cromwell Road. Lost in sensual fantasies, George was oblivious to progress.

Only when the big car swung round Parliament Square did he face journey's end. He detested the thought of a Cabinet meeting. He'd been anticipating a serious drinking session before the flap started, with the PM occupied playing God at Chequers – doubtless with perfection born of long experience.

Government bored George to tears, and Minton-Bloody-Briant frightened him rigid.

In the Confidential Communications Room at Chequers, General Robert Forsyth decided to spoil Cabinet's year. He'd allowed the politicians time to assemble at 10 Downing Street, then added thirty minutes to escalate tension. He activated the video link.

Faces – white against dark panelling in the Cabinet Room – snapped into focus on the wall-sized screen. They looked subdued but restive – suspecting much, knowing nothing. He'd made sure of that. The PM's assassination would have a volatile effect, and Forsyth meant to keep Intelligence at centre stage. Cabinet Secretary Harry Higgins was forced to ask a collective question.

'What's happening? There are armoured vehicles on Westminster Bridge and I've been trying to raise Chequers for nearly an hour.'

The rotund civil servant tried to sound masterful, fooling nobody. Forsyth checked his wristwatch before answering bluntly.

'I'm sorry to inform you that exactly seventy-six minutes ago the Prime Minister was killed by a powerful bomb dropped from a light aircraft. President Awami and his entire delegation also died. We're still picking up the pieces. Literally.'

They were riveted – faces disbelieving, stunned by the enormity of what they were hearing. Forsyth resumed decisively.

'Field Marshal Chandler survived but is incapacitated. As Deputy Head of Intelligence, I assumed command of the search operation under Standing Order Nine. There can never be complete protection against a determined attack of this kind, but I initiated an intense hunt for the aircraft and took certain other precautions.'

Without their master, the cardboard bastards were pilloried by uncertainty. Hardly a crisis manager amongst them, which was why the sly old divide-and-ruler chose them. But they'd rush into the vacuum soon enough. The Intelligence general continued with suitable gravity.

'If Minton-Briant was the primary target, the assassination may signal civil unrest or coup attempt. Our priority must be maintenance of stability. I require official confirmation that I have acted properly in pursuit of that end.'

Forsyth sat back and waited for them to panic.

Despite peeling paint and littered debris, conditions in the rig's radio room were tolerable. An air-bed nestled beside food boxes, bottled gas lamp, portable cooker and battery television. The homing device that guided in the Bluebird had gone over the guardrail outside. More evidence that would never be uttered.

Empty instrument sockets stared from one wall as the pilot made coffee, switched on the TV and lay down on the bed. Reception was good enough to relay a request for sightings of low-flying aircraft. They'd be lucky, unless someone happened to be visiting Davy Jones.

He lit a fresh cigarette from an expiring stub. John Wayne rode on to the screen. The Duke represented fantasy days when right beat wrong and ready sixguns answered every problem. He remembered the Latin motto at Chequers. *IUSTITIA TENAX*. Hold on to justice? Trust in justice?

He extracted a photograph from his wallet. Mary would have been forty-six now – a warm, mature woman with children, grandchildren to come. *His* children and grandchildren. *His* wife, loving and loved. Her beauty was animated by fond memory. The snap had been snatched by a Nikon-plated hustler on their last holiday, catching Mary's spontaneous smile. That night, under burning tropical stars, they made love beside the Indian Ocean with the urgency of youngsters, lying entwined as inquisitive water crept up to lick away the sweat of passion.

When he destroyed the things carrying memories of their life together, he tried to burn the picture. Couldn't. Was she the reason? If she were alive, would Minton-Briant be dead? Surely greater justification was required? Not a tooth for a tooth, but an eye for an ideal. *IUSTITIA TENAX* – rough justice, but justice none the less.

With melancholy insight, the pilot realized he *had* done it for her, or more truthfully himself. Could Mary's death have stemmed from flawed character rather than an insensitive system? Was his stubborn adherence to lost love a mark of self-delusion?

For the first time, he could ask taboo questions and try to answer honestly. At least he might find peace now the lonely, grievance-ridden years were avenged.

The temperature was rising. Deputy Premier Ken Stanley watched as the Intelligence general cooled down flustered Cabinet members. Forsyth was fielding outbursts about further attacks, the American menace and violence on the streets. Stanley couldn't join in. He was suffering a physiological reaction – tightness of the chest and disorientation which distanced him from the others.

For all his faults, Derek Minton-Briant held Britain together while tension stalked the international jungle. Fast-breeding humans, irrational nationalism, intractable ethnic conflicts, impossible aspirations, economic rivalries, planetary resources going into overdraft. But Derek created stability for fifty-five million people.

Autocrat? Of course. Regeneration was impossible without vision, determination and ruthless application of socialist principles. The hogs of capitalism had wallowed too conspicuously, and few tears were shed when they fell. United Kingdom plc, with a majority government shareholding on behalf of the people, proved perfectly capable of doing business without them. True, unbridled individuality had to be sacrificed in favour of tight social control, because no government could allow itself to be destroyed by perennial public expectation that ever-increasing services should be provided in return for ever-decreasing individual contributions.

But the rewards were great, shared, real. They reshaped a class-ridden society that had failed its majority and created a single nation fit for the new millennium. It was as simple – and complex – as that.

The magnitude of their social engineering gave Ken Stanley almost sensual pleasure when he awoke every morning. Without fail, remembrance of their achievement was his first awareness of each new day.

Derek led as they snaked up the ladder of power, showing patience and sure judgment. Like Winston Churchill, he was waiting when the call came after decades in the political wilderness. At moments of supreme crisis, ideology scarcely matters. What counts is the emergence of a dynamic leader – a man for the moment, ready and able to accept the challenge.

Ken Stanley smiled, and realized it wasn't a nostalgic salute to the good old days. He might have come to terms with a supporting rôle, but circumstances had changed. He swerved his mind to Forsyth, studying the wall-mounted screen through narrowed eyes.

The thirty-nine-year-old general was David Chandler's heir apparent and looked the part – green uniform with simple silver insignia, alert face dominated by penetrating hazel eyes, square chin, a sprinkling of salt in close-cut light brown hair. He sounded good, too, speaking with authority and confidence.

Force and power were insatiable bedfellows, and he who controlled Intelligence commanded force. General Forsyth could be a valuable ally, or an enemy to reckon with.

Watching Forsyth tire of the game and call Cabinet to attention, Ken Stanley knew his forty-year political career would culminate in control of a nation's destiny.

Two floors below, in Number 10's well-appointed kitchen, the Prince Regent was playing truant. George had been unable to resist a few hands of stripped-deck draw poker with old adversaries – the pastry cook and underchef. Life could be looking up, if below-stairs gossip meant what he thought. George drew a third nine and looked up slyly, every inch a disappointed man about to be overcome by bravado.

'Go on, son, opener's bet.'

The fresh-faced underchef studied his hand.

'I'll go a score, squire.'

George snickered unpleasantly.

'Your two tenners and up six more. Yes, could make sense. Unexplained panic but the PM ain't here, you say? Interesting. Can't think he'd miss the party without good reason. Seeing me? Full house, nines up.'

George allowed himself to hope that Minton-Sodding-Briant might be dead, deceased, out of his hair for good. Or better still paralysed after a massive, agonizing stroke. He scooped up the pot.

'Sorry to quit while I'm ahead, but duty calls. I'd better toddle up and see how the land lies. All right, one more hand.'

His three kings lost to the pastry cook's club flush. George took the reverse with equanimity, though it consumed his winnings and every penny he started with.

'Anyone beating four kings deserves everything he gets. I'm off to give the politicos the benefit of wisdom distilled from centuries of constitutional monarchy, as embodied in my good self.'

Still chuckling, the Prince Regent set off for the Cabinet Room.

He'd indulged them long enough. Forsyth tapped with his pen. Cabinet members snapped to attention like squaddies on parade.

'Please! I have asked for your support. I need a decision before operations are hampered. Police chiefs can start ignoring Intelligence directives unless Standing Order Nine is extended. I understand the need for checks and balances, but at this moment the scales must tilt in favour of effective security.'

Home Secretary Godfrey Cornwell shook his head. He was responsible for the police service and Forsyth's demand challenged his authority. Cornwell was youthful by Cabinet standards, with a strong power base derived from the support of Party activists. The others looked uncomfortable.

They were experienced in government's hidden workings, but lacked match practice in any game bar follow-their-leader. Forsyth mentally reviewed Intelligence files that chronicled the élite's peccadillos. There were pressure points he could use in almost every case. Except Ken Stanley's.

The Deputy Premier was over sixty – but abundant lank hair surrounding a domed forehead, drooping moustache and world-weary bloodhound's face combined to make him ageless. In his youth he'd been involved in everything from gay rights to troops out of Ireland, not forgetting internecine Party strife.

There were other old comrades in Cabinet, like the bald-as-a-coot former miner's leader who ran Energy with lots

of table thumping and little acumen. But none the late
PM had trusted like Ken Stanley, though their relationship had been deteriorating. In search of easy popularity,
Minton-Briant had been ducking tough decisions on the
stagnating economy, while Stanley had been promoting
painful recovery policies.

Ken Stanley's chin rested on interlocked hands and his
eyes were closed. Forsyth feared no man, but was wary of
this one. As he thought the thought, intuition was validated. Stanley came to life, delivering a question with the
subtlety of a wounded rhino breaking cover.

'Let's be clear. You're asking us to leave you in charge of
Intelligence, with *carte blanche* to operate as you think fit.
Correct?'

Forsyth faced the charge without flinching.

'The PM's dead and an aircraft with sophisticated wea-
ponry suggests rather more than the infamous lone assassin.
Your Security Minister is incapacitated. In his absence I'm
required to take charge of Intelligence.'

Unexpectedly, Stanley smiled.

'Not losing time bidding for the family business, then?'

Forsyth answered with asperity.

'So I'm Field Marshal Chandler's son-in-law. Not relevant.
I'm a professional. It's sophisticated work. Intelligence is
good at it, I'm good at it.'

Stanley's smile broadened.

'And you haven't thought about inheriting David Chandler's seat at this table?'

Forsyth wasn't intimidated.

'You may not like the fact, but you need me. The security
operation *must* bring results. Intelligence is the tool for the
job. Use anyone else and the mess will be horrendous.'

'Nice try, General, but you don't dispute Cabinet's right
to assess the position differently?'

Before Forsyth could deflect Stanley's well-aimed dart,
there was a noisy interruption. The Prince Regent arrived,
speaking loudly to the Deputy PM as he walked towards
his chair.

'Point made, Ken, we know you make granite look soft
under that cuddly exterior. Now, will someone please tell
me what's going on?'

Sweat popped on Forsyth's forehead. The old politician had learned his trade in a rough school, graduating with honours.

He'd achieved his objective, and Ken Stanley was pleased. Sensible to give Forsyth a taste of steel, silly to skewer him. He struck an attentive pose as discussion began with a contribution from the Cabinet Secretary.

'General Forsyth has a point. If we don't crack down, who knows where this awful business might end?'

Harry Higgins was first overboard. He had acute instincts for the stirring of a new tide. Others clutched the prospect of action like drowning men finding a life-raft instead of a straw. Except Home Secretary Godfrey Cornwell, who fiddled with his pencil, staring at a virgin notepad. Stanley left them to it. Less than three minutes later there was consensus in favour of Forsyth, who hadn't said another word.

'Ken?'

Impatience further marred the Prince Regent's dissipated face. What a sight. Undernourished. Pouches under the eyes. Fleshy lips that were simultaneously moist and slack. Receding chin. Thinning fair hair. The beginnings of a paunch. George had been at school with Forsyth, though you'd never guess by comparing them now. The connection might explain the Prince Regent's foray into the political arena. Might. Ken Stanley mistrusted obvious explanations. Ignoring George, he nodded pleasantly.

'You're decided, then. However, I remind you the Constitution demands my signature on the document our friend wants, along with the Prince Regent's. As it happens I concur, with one proviso. I propose a time limit of forty-eight hours on General Forsyth's authorization. By then the position regarding David Chandler might be clarified and we can reconsider the whole matter.'

Everyone would agree. They might be frightened, but weren't fools. Studying the screen, Stanley analysed Forsyth's strong face. The Intelligence officer had remained impassive throughout – arguing his case with conviction when necessary, gazing down his nose at them when it wasn't. David had chosen well, son-in-law or not. Stanley looked at the camera.

'General, you find that satisfactory?'

'Yes.'

'Then I so move. All in favour please show.'

They were, each confirming with nod or murmured affirm-
ative – even Godfrey Cornwell, though he was the last to give
in. Stanley kept his expression neutral.

'Despite Godfrey's agonized expression you'd better minute that as unanimous, Harry. Prepare the necessary
paperwork. You have your two days, General.'

'I'll be in touch.'

It seemed Forsyth had no further time for politics or
politicians. He faded off screen as Cabinet Secretary Harry
Higgins hurried through the Greek Doors to set newly oiled
wheels spinning. The meeting disintegrated into disjointed
conversation.

Ken Stanley remained aloof, active brain racing ahead.

Police chiefs received and absorbed Cabinet's orders. So
much for the influence of Godfrey Cornwell, their man
in the highest place. Reluctantly, they started deploy-
ing resources as instructed by Intelligence, until a safe
rationale for prevarication could be devised.

A round-up of undesirables commenced. Nothing was
announced, but fright scorched through the nation. Nobody
would give a neighbour the time of day. Children were
snatched from play areas by anxious parents, unjustly
scolded and sent early to bed. Doors were locked, though
an Englishman's home was no longer a castle.

But the country was used to dropping the portcullis.
Every foreign correspondent in London was invited to a
news conference at the Press Association off Holborn Circus. Each was excited. Perhaps Britain's brave new world
was finally unravelling.

Speculation bounced off pastel walls as the briefing
hall filled – curiosity turning to puzzlement as canned
music came round for an encore and the podium remained
deserted. Then anger, when the *New York Times* London
bureau chief tried to leave, only to be turned back by armed
policemen. The aristocrats of international news gathering
belatedly realized they'd been suckered.

Authority's knee-jerk desire to muzzle the media was

undermined by the CNN correspondent. The New Zealand-born veteran of Baghdad assessed the situation more swiftly than most. He locked himself in the Ladies' Room and filed via satellite phone. His speculative transmission ended in mid-sentence with the sound of a splintering door.

Special Adviser Vernon Lustbader watched the end of CNN's dramatic live report from London in the library of Vice-President Errol Tidyman's Washington house, wondering about his mission to England.

Despite a glib promise at the cabin, Errol hadn't told him much during the flight back from Michigan. Or since. The Vice-President killed the sound, licked a speck of dressed crab from a pink fingertip and wiped his hands on a linen napkin.

'Beats the hell outta slumming it down at Martin's Restaurant. Build the man another coffee, Lulu.'

Lustbader watched the young woman's graceful approach. Errol's sister stooped and refilled his cup, which rested on a low mahogany table made in England when George III was on the throne and off his trolley. Lustbader's club chair was comfortable; the light lunch had been exceptional.

'Thank you kindly, Louise.'

She went on to serve her brother. They made a handsome pair. Their father must have been some character. The Reverend Benjamin Tidyman had lived through nine hellfire-and-brimstone decades, four wives and fourteen children. Including one Vice-President of the United States, two pro footballers and one Oscar-winning actress successful – and confident – enough at twenty-nine to back-burn her career for a two-year presidential campaign.

Louise Tidyman was the most attractive woman Lustbader had ever seen. Not only for striking African-American looks, nor the compelling way her slim body moved, but also because her face had a luminosity you couldn't explain in words – or take your eyes off. She made a good executive assistant, too – perceptive, imaginative, efficient. Lustbader liked her a lot.

He looked around, considering the epic journey from clapboard shack outside Shreveport, Louisiana to flat-fronted town house in Washington, DC. The room was tastefully furnished. Like any Georgetown library, the books behind glass doors were leather-bound. The place lacked ancestral oil paintings, but dozens of framed photographs substituted. The whole Tidyman clan was there, down to the latest great-niece.

In one, old Pa Ben was waist-deep in some creek, plunging a white-robed child-woman beneath muddy waters for the good of her soul and the glory of the Lord. In another, Errol stood tall on graduation day thirty years ago, daring the world to get in his way.

It tried, without success. The Vice-President's business empire grew from astute exploitation of a flamboyant orator's rising reputation as the acceptable face of black aspiration. Lectures, books and television supplemented income from a radical New York law practice. When he accumulated capital and contacts, Errol Tidyman set about proving that blacks could wheel and deal alongside the best.

He made the point over two decades of rapid expansion into information technology, real estate, manpower services, ethical manufacturing, retailing, distribution, energy management. Despite jealous sniping, Errol was an honest American – which admittedly meant he didn't miss many tricks. Nowadays the family ran Tidyman Inc. with help from the best corporate talent money could buy, while Errol played politics. Louise's melodic voice broke the reverie.

'Hey, my face may be a shade over-exposed for the Historical Preservation Office's liking, but I sure know what's expected of a gal in Museumtown. You menfolk chatter among yourselves.'

She gathered dishes on to a lacquer tray and headed out, hips swinging provocatively. Lustbader's eyes followed. When the door closed, Errol smiled wickedly.

'You're long in the tooth for that, Vernon. I got something more exciting in mind for you.'

Lustbader read the bones. Tidyman wanted reassurance on something already decided, but meant to travel the scenic route. The Vice-President stood by the window, pulled closed velvet drapes apart and talked at the street.

'Q and A. What does it take to elect a Democratic President in this great country of ours? One sentence.'

'A few dollars, no lovers past or present willing to dish the dirt, sound liberal policies at home, good fiscal track record, foreign policy somewhere to the right of Hitler's, the promise of change.'

The Vice-President tired of the street scene, dropping the drapes and pacing deep-pile carpet manufactured at a Tidyman Inc. plant in Gainesville, Georgia.

'I buy that. Next, what did it take to saddle the Brits with that lousy left-wing government of theirs? One sentence again.'

'The Right stopped delivering the feelgood factor, split over Europe, lost an election and got blown away by a mob that tore up the old rule book and wrote a new one.'

'Okay, so where're those crazy lefties at now? Give me the big lecture.'

The scenario was starting to unfold. Lustbader's interest quickened.

'People are unhappy. The economy's shaky, but the opposition can't come back, assuming there is any. Those guys hijacked the goddam island, dismantling the old system in favour of their own self-perpetuating model. We may not like him, but that Minton-Briant's one hell of an operator. He's elevated centralized control to an art form. Easily done. There's a tradition of official secrecy and governments of both shades that meddle with every aspect of society.'

Pausing by the photograph of his father, the Vice-President touched the old hell-raiser's grainy image.

'If the British Government fell?'

Lustbader shrugged eloquently, every inch the intellectual college professor he'd so recently been.

'Big if, but the Brits wouldn't shed tears. Politics used to run in cycles over there – a decade of what's in it for me, a counter-balancing decade of social conscience. That's one of the reasons they never got their economic act together. Pressure's building as living conditions deteriorate. They're good and ready to change lanes but like I said, that's not an option.'

Moving away from his father's memory, Tidyman perched on the library steps, losing interest in America's confused ex-ally.

'How long have I been campaigning for top spot? Forget

the first hundred years, I mean lately. Six years, eight, ten? Tell me what's going for us on this fine September afternoon.'

Lustbader played along, checking off plus factors on the fingers of one hand.

'You're Vice-President in a half-popular administration. The President's ill-health means you've had more responsibility than your average Veep. Your profile's high. History proves a Vice-President can be elected. With ethnic voter registration at an all-time high you start from a solid base-line. You've got style, the opposition's duller than Chesapeake Bay in a mid-winter squall. We've got cash in the bank, polls are moving in the right direction, albeit slowly, we haven't made mistakes.'

'Sounds promising. Against?'

'You're blacker than the ace of spades and lots of people hate niggers. Stark's campaign isn't faltering, you still trail. There's a perception Republicans would do better overseas. The days when we controlled the UN are starting to look good. Joe Public is tired of foreigners who let us fight their battles, grab handout money, freeload on our expertise, build things we want cheaper than we can, sell them back, throw us out of work and spit on all we stand for by way of dessert. Voters want America to start kicking ass again.'

Tidyman drew up his legs and hugged them with blue-shirted arms, rested his chin on raised knees and switched on the charm that made you believe, even when your head knew different.

'And just suppose I could deliver something around Inauguration time that makes Smokin' Joe Public feel real good in that department?'

'What Inauguration? You haven't said anything that makes me think we'll get that far, Errol.'

The Vice-President stood up.

'Hell, Vernon, you don't listen. I've got the election covered and that ain't what we've been talking about. You heard me up at your cabin, I'm already thinking second term.'

General Forsyth watched the floodlit bull's-eye landing pad growing as his helicopter sank through the dusk towards

New Centre Point, the Intelligence Headquarters building on London's Charing Cross Road.

Colonel Anderson Kyle was waiting on the roof. The two men walked away, a study in contrasts. Forsyth's short hair was scarcely ruffled by down-draught from twin rotors and he looked as though he'd just put on a fresh uniform, but hadn't. Kyle's Afro formed an explosive halo round his head and he was wearing crumpled field fatigues that looked slept in, but weren't. Forsyth was tall and well built. Kyle topped him by a head and forty pounds, all muscle. Forsyth was lightly tanned, Kyle the coffee colour inherited from a West Indian father and Scottish mother.

They were colleagues and friends. When engine noise diminished, Kyle shouted a question.

'Want to talk?'

Forsyth felt like an automaton with the batteries running down.

'My office, half an hour.'

The express lift stopped at the sixtieth floor. Leaving Kyle to go down to Control on the thirty-fifth, Forsyth headed for his suite, which doubled as occasional living quarters. His PA had left for the night and the place was deserted.

Forsyth had a large corner room. Apart from Sally Sayers' work station in reception outside and a beechwood conference table, the office looked like a designer residence – white walls, spotlights, abstract sculptures, avant-garde paintings, steel-and-leather chairs. Two glass walls gave panoramic views south over the river and east past St Paul's Cathedral. Forsyth loved the lighted city blazing up through darkness and never closed the blinds.

After mixing a Campari soda, he walked through to his study bedroom. One wall was devoted entirely to *Rain, Steam and Speed – The Great Western Railway*, a Turner on loan from the National Gallery. Forsyth could relax just by looking at the blur of merging colours and dynamic movement. He did so, before undressing and taking a shower. Needle-point hot water banished fatigue. Afterwards, he donned casual clothing and carried his unfinished drink through to the main area.

He telephoned Stoke Mandeville Hospital. News of Field

Marshal Chandler's blindness shocked Forsyth. He liked the old man. And his absence would have political repercussions for Intelligence. As he hung up, Kyle bustled in with a file under one arm. The big man nodded.

'Don't quote me, boss, but that's a distinct improvement. Had me worried back there – you looked almost fallible.'

'You're a minute late, Andy.'

Four and a half hours had passed since the attack at Chequers.

Forsyth's damp hair was slicked down above interrogative eyes. He must have showered, sluicing away uncharacteristic signs of stress Andy Kyle had noted earlier.

'Sorry, boss, Control's a bloody madhouse.'

'Hardly surprising. How's your hunting instinct tonight?'

'Thirsty.'

Forsyth went to the fridge and underarmed a lager.

'Denmark's finest, shaken not stirred. Ten seconds to sink it.'

As Kyle caught the can, he saw Forsyth hadn't taken a fresh drink, instead toying with a slice of lemon from his empty glass. He drank the beer in one long draught, crushed the can in a powerful hand and hit the waste bin first time. Forsyth's tangible concentration didn't unsettle Kyle, who admired his superior's ability to focus. He began his report.

'Nothing on the Bluebird. The registration mark lifted from the Chequers security video was a dupe. The real GA-3923 belongs to the Highlands and Islands Development Board. It's been inspected by local police. Sitting on the tarmac at Stornoway covered in bird shit, waiting for spares. The chopper sweep around Chequers was useless. We're widening the search area, but he got away.'

'Sighting reports?'

'Thousands. The computer *wunderkinder* are running them against logged flight plans to eliminate legitimate aircraft, providing I keep a boot up their backsides.'

Kyle lifted a size twelve. The corner of Forsyth's mouth twitched.

'We may get something when interrogations get under

way, but I'd guess the usual suspects have nothing to offer. If you'll settle for gut feel, Minton-Briant's only the beginning. There's more to this than some maniac with a chip on his shoulder. Gut feel's about all I *can* offer. Still, we must try to deal in facts. I've brought stacks of data. Interested?'

'Doing jigsaws is your business. Just find that pilot before this gets out of hand.'

Forsyth dropped a lifeless sliver of lemon into his glass.

The report lacked substance, but Kyle wouldn't have missed anything. Amongst other attributes, he was the best investigator Intelligence possessed. He'd been Forsyth's staff college tutor and would have stagnated there if Forsyth hadn't been impressed, remembered, rescued him when he had the clout. It was hard to be non-white and beautiful in Establishment eyes.

Once in London, outstanding ability brought swift promotion. After a late start, Andy Kyle was nearing the apex of the Intelligence command structure, though still only forty-six. By the mysterious alchemy that decides these things, he and Forsyth had become the men to watch.

Now Kyle waited patiently. For all his rough good nature and quirky humour, there could be a quality of stillness about him, like a hunting cat that has spotted prey. Forsyth watched for a moment, reminded of the man's mental and physical strength.

'I trust your gut reactions, Andy. This is too slick for a loner. We must be dealing with a new group, but until they move again or we nail that pilot we're impotent.'

'We'll keep trying. What about practicalities?'

'I'll approve Media's bulletins for release. Time to put the wondering world out of its misery. Should catch the late evening news. After that I'll see Department Heads individually then clock off until first light. All sorts of people will be trying to collar me, but I need thinking time. Keep them off my back. If anything breaks, tell me. You know where I'll be.'

The matter had never been discussed, but Kyle did know. Forsyth fetched him another lager.

'A couple more things before you rush back to Control.

Chandler's in a bad state. Multiple shrapnel wounds and the poor sod's been blinded. So I take temporary command. Any internal difficulties there?'

'You're heir apparent. Bound to be some who try and advance their own careers, mind. You know who they are. Might be sensible to get Chandler's endorsement as soon as possible.'

'I will. Meanwhile I want you running Intelligence day-to-day. I need someone dependable at my back while I deal with the politics. I'm promoting you to brigadier, which should give you the necessary clout.'

'Great, I need the money.'

If Kyle was pleased, he didn't show it. Forsyth phrased the next item carefully.

'Chandler wanted to centralize security forces under his ministry. He felt the existing structure with its in-built rivalries would fail in a crisis. Ironically, Minton-Briant refused to grasp the nettle, yet our response to his murder may suffer in consequence. Police chiefs will try to sabotage our efforts out of sheer bloody-mindedness, and they won't be alone. The future of Intelligence is on the line.'

Kyle finished his beer, watching Forsyth as he drank. The scrutiny was disconcerting. Kyle got up and dropped the can in the bin.

'Two out of two. Must be my lucky night. You're right. Without Minton-Briant and the Field Marshal protecting our interests in Cabinet we could be in trouble. We're their Praetorian Guard, but the politicians fear us. Unless we deliver Ken Stanley might push you out. Or Godfrey Cornwell could shaft the pair of you. That cunning little pederast wants to be PM.'

The big man planted both hands on the table and leaned forward before continuing.

'For millions out there Minton-Briant's death will be a nine-day wonder. Their lives won't change. The machine will grind on, steered by a few old men who're scared shitless someone will try to prise their hands off the levers of power. And they're sustained by an army of bureaucrats who're doing very nicely out of the deal. That's us, in case you didn't recognize the self-portrait.'

Forsyth was normally acute, but for once wasn't really listening.

'The Thinking Detective? It'll never catch on. I'll come down with you.'

They walked to the lifts in silence.

The Vice-President's Special Adviser had given up on the hidden agenda. If Lustbader waited, Errol Tidyman's plans would become clear. Meantime, it was business as usual. He peered through half-moon spectacles at the briefing folder.

'Daughter by the third wife's called Shari-Belle, only child, spoiled rotten, sixteen years old. She'll be there. The old man's convinced she's the best thing to hit ballet since Pavlova, but the kid has a weakness for candy and must be twenty pounds overweight.'

'How much is Big Daddy good for? We need ten mil for the final TV push, and I still reckon us short a dollar.'

The Vice-President had a mind like a mainframe. He could probably state the net worth of his majority holding in Tidyman Inc. down to the last dime.

'Twenty grand, with a little help from Shari-Belle, who loves your smile and thinks you're *so* virile. Say two thousand to each of the PCAs who'll be canvassing.'

'An even quarter says he kicks in twice that, Vernon.'

Lustbader held up his hands in mock horror.

'Sucker bet. I've seen you in action at fund-raisers before.'

They'd spent the afternoon discussing campaign strategy, ending with a rundown on the day's major event – dinner followed by lavish entertainment for the richest Democrats inside the Beltway. Tidyman was endorsed by big show business names, many of whom would be performing at the Willard Hotel that evening.

But something bigger was going down. The Vice-President always had three things scheduled for each space in his calendar and wouldn't normally waste hours chewing the fat. Hell, it was a first. Lustbader studied the boss, then made his play.

'You're up to something, Errol.'

He was rewarded with an innocent smile.

'Always knew you had a twenty-four-carat brain concealed under that thatch of college professor white hair, ol' buddy.'

'Don't old-buddy me. We have a deal, remember? You tell me everything, I don't get shit on my shoes. But something stinks. Don't drop into that trust-me routine, either.'

Tidyman's face became serious.

'I do have reason to believe there may be a change of government in the UK, a change for the better. Look . . .'

While he was choosing words, his sister came in.

'Phone, Errol. The big man from NSA.'

No telephone was allowed into the library. The Vice-President bounded to the door. Before Lustbader's antennae stopped quivering, he returned.

'NSA have just evaluated the latest signal traffic from England. Their Prime Minister was just terminated. Wham, bam, dead as last year's Thanksgiving turkey.'

Lustbader couldn't believe it.

'Derek Minton-Briant?'

'How many Brit PMs do you know? Thought your grasp of world affairs was A1, Vernon. Bomb attack at his country place, details sketchy. We better hit Eighteen Hundred Pennsylvania Avenue. To hell with the fundraiser.'

Lustbader saw the light.

'So that's it.'

The Vice-President showed rare anger.

'Hey, you don't think I had anything to do with this? No way, man, no way. I may've known something was going down, but had no idea Minton-Briant would be hit.'

The older man was unimpressed.

Photographic models can read, though Beth Highsmith's choice might have been atypical. She lay on a yellow sofa engrossed in *Germinal*. It was beyond belief that European life was once as stark as Zola's hell on earth. Mahler's First played, haunting music complementing the novel's harsh imagery.

Her apartment was a top-floor Chelsea studio with angled ceilings. Designer fashion originals jammed a commercial garment rail. Piles of paperbacks elbowed stacked compact discs. A video machine squatted on a cupboard overflowing with tapes, beside an unloved TV set. Someone had etched a leering face with question-mark topknot on the dusty screen.

She yawned. Nearly tomorrow. Closing her book, she went to the tiny kitchen and made herb tea. Then she filled a glass with ice, adding Campari, soda and a slice of lemon.

He probably wouldn't come. He was always busy, she was often away. The casual arrangement suited them. She undressed, put on a robe and sat at her dressing table. Pulling a brush through springy fair hair one hundred times before bed was a ritual followed since childhood. The face in the mirror looked fine, even without make-up. A while yet before the professional nightmare of visible ageing stared mockingly back.

Slipping naked beneath the goosedown quilt on her Victorian bed, she relaxed completely, drifting towards sleep. She didn't hear her lover enter the room, and the pleasant tenor voice startled her.

'Drinks on the house?'

General Robert Forsyth stood by the bed, Campari in hand.

'Bob, I didn't expect you.'

'Then why the drink?'

'Oh, just because.'

Beth giggled. He put the drink down, hung his suede coat over the back of a chair and started to unbutton his shirt. She drew the quilt under her chin, enjoying slithering movement over sensitive nerve ends. Forsyth sat on the bed to remove his socks, the bumps of his spine prominent beneath taut skin. He slipped in beside her and whispered a confession.

'I need to be with you.'

She stroked his hair until she felt him relax. He'd talk when he was ready. Beth wasn't really interested in his work. But she knew how to listen, and make quirky observations about her day in the fashion trenches which amused him.

Eventually, they drifted into gentle lovemaking, which went on for a long time. The final intensity still amazed and delighted them both.

The graveyard shift in Intelligence Control was bedlam.

Anderson Kyle prowled restlessly, peering over shoulders and asking unnecessary questions. When his presence started unsettling the night staff, he reluctantly retired to his sanctum.

The wall clock marked time. Kyle random-checked incoming data on his desk system, but the diversion palled. He picked up the phone and nagged for an answer on aircraft sighting reports. Head of Processing was only thirty-one, but his department was mainstream. He cheerfully announced that miracles were upstairs. Processing was on the top floor.

Welcome distraction arrived in the shape of Colonel Joe Granger, a busy little body whose nickname was Goebbels. He regarded the sobriquet as a compliment. He ran Media, which watchdogged the nation's reading and viewing. Under Standing Order Nine, a proactive role was assumed by Intelligence. Granger thrust back narrow shoulders and spoke crisply.

'Sorry to bother you. General Forsyth's press announcement went out, but now it's been translated into single syllables for the *hoi polloi* problems have crawled out of the woodwork. Could you take a look? The papers are screaming for permission to roll the first editions.'

Kyle smiled at the man's enthusiasm.

'Time's one thing I do have. Let's go down.'

The Media staff had linked with computerized newspaper systems, vetting pages as they were made up. High-pressure inkjet presses wouldn't run until every word had been seen and approved.

Granger stopped beside a member of his team – a slim woman whose dark head was bent over proofs. Kyle recognized her. They had enjoyed a brief but lusty interlude the previous autumn. When you worked his hours, you mixed business and pleasure. Granger put a hand on her shoulder.

'Alison has the titillating job of looking after the *Sun*. Show us that dodgy lead.'

She handed over the front-page proof, a slow flush climbing her neck. Kyle noticed, Granger didn't. A huge *PM: BLOODY SLAYING!* screeched above a black-edged colour portrait of Minton-Briant. Below, a top-heavy nymphet in see-through black negligee was captioned *PAGE 3 – SAMANTHA COVERS UP TO PAY HER LAST RESPECTS*. Granger's bony forefinger stabbed the lead story.

'Para two, sentence one, "Derek Minton-Briant rode roughshod to power". The phrase "rode roughshod", fair comment or slander?'

Kyle answered without hesitation.

'Leaving aside the tricky question of whether you can slander a dead man in print, our late great leader's reputation is sacrosanct.'

'Just what I thought. Tell the night ed to lose "rode roughshod" and substitute "was elected", Alison. I hope he doesn't make a scene. Odd characters, these newshounds. They hate us interfering, but what on earth do they think we're here for? Thanks, anyway.'

Granger hurried off in search of fresh verbal atrocities. He should have handled the matter, but Kyle didn't mind – the diversion killed a few minutes. Something might have happened in Control.

When he got back, nothing had.

In San Antonio, seven hours back across the time zones, David Turrow and Lieutenant Schneider of SAPD were separated by the First Assistant DA's well-organized desk. It wasn't far enough. The lawyer's temper was on a one-second fuse. During the two weeks since the Martinez murder he'd taken heat – mostly from people he couldn't afford to ignore, all aimed at keeping the Stark connection quiet. He had to bury the investigation or climb out on a limb and wait for chainsaws to get busy.

Their after-hours conference had stalled. They sat in morose silence. The grizzled police lieutenant lit a cigar, wreathing his head in smoke. The DA hated the habit.

'Those things give me a headache. God knows what they're doing to you.'

'No stogie, no brainwork. Got anywhere to stash the ash?'

Turrow produced a Bud ashtray from a drawer and skidded it across. Schneider sat back, leathery face impassive. Turrow knew the worldly-wise cop was enjoying the situation – watching him struggle, waiting for a fumble. He looked up sharply, ready to take on the world.

'Let's run through this again. Maria Martinez served a hot drink in Pat Stark's suite around one-thirty and left ten minutes later. The Candidate says she spilled the drink over him and burst into tears. He comforted her. His pants and shirt were messed up so he sent them to be cleaned, then went to bed. End of story. The Secret Service log confirms timings, but nothing's proven, right?'

Schneider nodded wearily. They'd churned the same words dozens of times. Turrow wasn't deflected. He'd understood where they were headed days before. Now he was ready to journey. He resumed his review.

'The Paretsky girl says Martinez was hyped up and left work without finishing her shift. She went home on the bus and hassled with the Sanchez clan, then nothing. Room turned over, strangled body found in a dumpster after a phone tip, informant never traced. On track so far?'

He kept needling, but Schneider was only biting on his cigar.

'So you read the reports. I'm impressed.'

The DA didn't react. He needed the lieutenant on his side.

'Those Sanchez boys we're holding on dope charges were the last people to see her alive, but neither of us thinks they're killers. They give her lip, period. They also claim to have seen a late-model Buick outside her building.'

They were getting there. Schneider joined in.

'They ain't wrong about that. We got confirmation on the car, which don't belong in the area. And the blue Stark Buick was out and about that night, though they deny all knowledge. Then there's eighteen hundred bucks hidden in her room. Where did a maid get that sort of cash? This don't make sense, unless . . .'

Unhelpfully, he stopped. Turrow slammed in.

'Unless we try the one theory we've been dodging all week?'

The cop nodded.

'Stark's had zipper problems. Martinez is upset after spillin' the drink, maybe blurts out she's illegal. He's tempted, makes a pass. The girl struggles and he comes to his senses, pushes a wad into her hand, tells her to keep stumm and shoves her out the door.'

Turrow took up the story, voice suddenly sceptical.

'Stark wonders if she'll put the bite on, or blab to reporters. He sends someone to find her address, get after her, threaten her with deportation. She won't play. So that someone – say an over-zealous aide – shuts her mouth. Tries to make it look like a neighbourhood killing, just another dead Mex and who gives a shit? Jeezus! Far-fetched, even for Texas.'

Turrow was originally from New York. Schneider laughed.

'You said it, not me, but the car and the cash mean we gotta consider the possibility. No neighbourhood killer misses money. Stark's been open about his end, but knew we'd tie him to the girl. But it ain't altogether straight-forward. Why risk movin' her? Hotels are used to these casuals vanishin', and Stark could've been long gone before the body was found.'

Turrow frowned.

'The anonymous tip, plus the fact the press were on the killing so quick. Anything there?'

'Plenty of good citizens don't like to be seen puttin' their hands up, and even I wouldn't claim the PD's watertight.'

The DA fiddled with his black-and-gold Parker Duofold pen and asked a question to which he already knew the answer.

'What do you need to put this show on the road?'

'Stark's Buick. If it *was* used to move the body, we get to ask searchin' questions. If not, everyone's happy. That vehicle's out of state. Talk to people who can get it back into my lab. No fuss. We've kept the lid on so far. Say we must eliminate the Buick and that'll be end of story. See if they play ball.'

Turrow considered the implications, but not for long.

'Let's do it. I'll make some calls in the morning. But for Christ's sake don't let this leak. We're messing with heavy artillery here. Billy Ray Brandon may have turned this over to me, but that doesn't mean he isn't interested. That SOB watches my every move.'

For once, Schneider seemed appreciative. He disliked District Attorney Brandon, a good ol' boy who owed favours all over town and whose agenda was not confined to impartial dispensation of criminal justice.

'Thanks, Dave. I know your ass is in a sling, but someone killed that little girl. I'm not about to forget that. Anyway, inside a year I'm retired and the only thing I'll be huntin' is quail. I got nothin' to lose. You're somethin' else, so I sure do appreciate what you're tryin' to do here.'

Dick Schneider mashed out his cigar.

DAY TWO:

Friday 6 September

In Beth Highsmith's Chelsea apartment, the telephone assaulted General Robert Forsyth. His body was tired, but his mind wouldn't sleep. He reached from the bed to silence the mobile phone before his lover woke.

'Rise and shine, *mon général*. It's morning and yesterday was no nightmare. It actually happened.'

Andy Kyle sounded bright. Forsyth counter-attacked.

'You're a heartless bastard.'

'Not true. I checked my pulse *and* the marriage lines first time you cracked that. The run of aircraft sightings against logged flight plans is through, for all the good it does.'

'Meaning?'

'He's long gone. Witnesses saw the plane north-east of Chequers, so the southward dash was a feint to draw the Air Force. Various intermediate reports, but the last confirmed sighting was at Holbeach, fifteen minutes after the attack.'

He stopped. Forsyth didn't disappoint him.

'Holbeach, up on the Wash? That means the North Sea and . . .'

'Those industrious American trawlers.'

Kyle stole the punchline. Though the North Sea no longer contained fish in commercial quantities, Spanish-flagged US boats – top-heavy with scanners, dishes and radio masts

– still landed a valuable catch, harvesting European electronic intelligence around the clock. Forsyth was tempted by the obvious conclusion.

'Must be a chance he homed to those boats. Several Cabinet members suspected American involvement. The CIA has done crazy things, but I can't believe they'd pull a stunt like this. Still, we'll kick the idea about later. You were right to call.'

He dumped the mobile. The heating hadn't come on and chill seeped through windows misted with condensation. Forsyth dressed quickly, then went to the bed. Beth's eyes opened. He kissed the tip of his right forefinger and touched the corner of her mouth.

'Your country needs me.'

She nodded wisely, and was asleep when he returned with a synthetic sable coat from the clothes rack to spread over her.

It wasn't far to Forsyth's house near Cheyne Walk. He walked, deciding to pick up his car later. London was stirring. Early traffic was on the move and streetlamps snuffed out erratically with the growth of day.

Turning off the embankment, Forsyth reached his front door. The whine of a police hydrofoil carried from the river as he punched the entry combination. He stepped into the hall. A wall-lamp converted from a nineteenth-century gas fitting burned in reproachful reminder of his conjugal indifference.

He turned off the light and went through to the kitchen. Alex had left sandwiches under an upturned china basin, scrawling a felt-tip message on the work surface – *THOUGHT YOU MIGHT BE HUNGRY*. Suddenly, he was. After eating, he made tea and coffee and carried steaming mugs to the master bedroom on the second floor.

His wife lay on her back, an arm and breast spilling from a nest of bedclothes. Even with her chestnut hair in a tangled mess she was handsome, but desire was buried in the rubble of a collapsed marriage. He set the tray on her dressing table, went through to the *en suite* bathroom, showered and shaved.

The impending scene couldn't be postponed. He shook

her exposed shoulder. Brown eyes opened, blinking in unfocused confusion, their contact lenses in a tiny container on the round Victorian chamber-pot cupboard that served as a bedside table.

'It's early, but I must go back to the office and wanted a word. Here, tea.'

She stretched out an obedient hand, pushing herself upright against the pillows with the other, before pulling a crumpled sheet over exposed breasts.

'So why bother to come home?'

'You knew I would, otherwise why the sandwiches? Besides, we must talk.'

'Talk? Since when do we bloody well *talk*? You've been out screwing again, haven't you? Don't deny it, I know you have.'

'Listen, Alex . . .'

Fully awake now, she reacted angrily.

'Listen, Alex, listen, Alex. Why the hell should I? That bitch can do the listening, whoever she is. Do you realize we haven't made love for seven months?'

'Very few people can do it for that long, even in their prime.'

Crashing through self-control, his retort skidded out. She dropped her mug and hit his shoulder with a wild fist. Tea soaked the sheet. It was fortunate the liquid had cooled. Her anger broke. She started crying – hopeless snuffling he could scarcely bear. He sat on the bed and held her until tears were spent.

'Alex, before I go there's something I must tell you.'

She looked up, startled. This dialogue wasn't in the script. Forsyth realized from her expression that she assumed he was finally leaving her. He blurted clumsy words.

'We had a security incident. Your father's been blinded.'

Moist eyes blinked rapidly as she tried to switch from one stressful idea to another.

'Why him?'

'Sheer bad luck. Caught the edge of a bomb meant for the PM. Minton-Briant was killed. Others too. At least David's alive. Apart from his eyes, he isn't badly hurt.'

He took her back into his arms with a flash of powerful emotion and held her tightly.

'I'm sorry, Alex, truly. I know how close you are. This isn't easy for me either. I'm fond of the old devil, too.'

Although he was needed elsewhere, Forsyth stayed with his wife until she became calm.

Deputy Premier Ken Stanley hadn't slept, spending the night in the large living room of his official residence at Somerset House, beside the River Thames at Waterloo Bridge.

He'd stared over the reflective river for long periods. Watched Derry the piranha perform his nightly cabaret in the tank on the bookcase, ingesting a frankfurter an inch at a time. Studied photograph albums that chronicled a long political career. Remembered good times and bad, highs and lows, faces and places.

He'd always known this exhilarating moment might come. But there was a ghost to lay. Poor Derek. Clinging to power might not be a characteristic unique to the elderly, but advancing years certainly emphasized the addictive properties of unbridled authority. Stanley regretted the anger with which he'd responded to the PM's behaviour in recent months.

Derek Minton-Briant was the flame that illuminated free-market darkness – sometimes flickering, never extinguished. *His* were the principles uncompromised by decades of ridicule. *His* the coup bringing control of the Party after general election victory. *His* the will that smashed barriers obstructing the long march of social revolution. If anyone had earned the right to enjoy a few golden years, it was Derek.

The components of their Ten Year Plan had been discussed often enough – some publicly, some in private. Crippling disease called for drastic surgery. Abolition of the House of Lords was easy on the basis of a manifesto pledge, but suspension of the five-year election rule precipitated a crisis that nearly brought them down. When the Queen refused to sign enabling legislation the new administration tottered, despite obedient parliamentary support.

Trouble was provoked on the streets, a State of Emergency declared and a clampdown imposed on hostile media. The House of Windsor was forced into abdication. They and theirs were rounded up, rushed to RAF Brize Norton and deported, carrying the clothes they wore and a thousand years of tradition. King and government in exile still sat in Canada, plotting a second Carolean restoration.

Derek's most brilliant ploy had been the appointment of a Prince Regent, instead of declaring a republic. Links between Royal Families old and new were tenuous, but no matter. Cabinet's edicts could be validated both by Parliament and Royal Assent, giving a veneer of legality under Britain's unwritten constitution.

A worm of self-contempt wriggled in Ken Stanley's mind. Perhaps they had grown old and complacent together. Whatever happened to the clarion ideal? That was about improving the lives of ordinary people.

But *he* hadn't forgotten. Everything they set out to achieve had flooded back – sharp and unequivocal, charging him with resolve and energy. Leaving Memory Lane, he walked to the videophone. His night had been well spent.

Ken Stanley knew what must be done, and how.

General Robert Forsyth's working day started as it meant to go on. At her work station in reception, Sally Sayers was looking less composed than usual. She waved a telephone.

'Cabinet Office. I'll switch them through. All hell's broken loose.'

He stepped into the office. Apart from a dusting of haze which a climbing sun would soon burn off, the familiar London panorama looked much the same as it had two mornings ago, before the fateful Chequers trip. He took off his uniform jacket, sat down and selected the phone with a flashing light.

'Forsyth.'

'We've been on hold for three minutes. I assumed you would be available at all times.'

The cultured voice of Cabinet Secretary Harry Higgins was pained.

'Really?'

'Yes, really. It *is* after seven. Can you make a Cabinet meeting at three-thirty? Mr Stanley's insistent that you should be present.'

'I'll be there.'

He rang off before Higgins could become tedious. Sally buzzed. 'Colonel Kyle's here. And Ken Stanley's just been on. Asked you to return his call as soon as possible.'

'Send Andy in, get Stanley when we're through.'

The door crashed open. Kyle strode in, handed Forsyth a mug of coffee and collapsed into his favourite chair like a falling factory chimney.

'Morning, boss. Must rest these tired bones, the dog-watch has knackered me. Sleep well?'

A flicker of eyebrows robbed the question of innocence.

'No, some idiot kept phoning. Those trawlers?'

'We'll never prove anything one way or the other. But we're narrowing the Bluebird's origin, only thirty left to clear. The explosive was American. Our esteemed police colleagues have started checking qualified pilots. One thing we *do* know is that this bloke knew how to fly an aircraft . . .'

For a man who'd worked twenty-three straight hours Kyle was remarkably animated, hands moving expressively as he made each point. He'd probably taken a shot. Forsyth stopped the flow.

'I meant what I said last night. The search operation's down to you. Your promotion will be posted this morning.'

The two men had always been separated by rank and background. Yet their professional relationship was close – a colleague worthy of absolute trust was beyond price in the introverted world of state security. The need for support was unspoken, but Kyle responded.

'We'll get there, Bob.'

Forsyth steepled his fingers.

'I hope so. This is about power. Who's after it, who gets it. But someone's operating outside the rules and Intelligence might end up on the losing side. That makes me nervous. We could speculate all morning, so let's not worry *who* they are for now, but think about what they're hoping to achieve. Make sense?'

Kyle spread his arms, unable to repress natural humour.

'As much sense as anything. Control have probably cracked the case, so I'd better dash back to grab the credit.'

The intercom buzzed and Sally came on.

'The monarch, God save us. I tried to stall him, but he

made a scene. Insisted you'd want to talk, and I thought he might be right for once.'

'Put him through. When we finish, get Ken Stanley.'

Forsyth picked up the phone and turned to Kyle.

'Happy?'

'As a London cabbie with piles and laryngitis.'

He ambled out with a clenched-fist salute. Forsyth returned to the Prince Regent. He'd been expecting the call. They never got on well at school, but the fiction of youthful camaraderie might suit them both.

The Prince Regent had mourned the PM's demise with Bollinger '92 and should have been snoring off the effects. Instead, he was galvanized by instinct to strike while the corpse was hot. After kick-starting his system with a stiff Bloody Mary he telephoned the Acting Head of Intelligence, General Robert Forsyth – an old school acquaintance he hated, because he'd been better at almost everything. After dealing with a silly girl, he made the connection. Forsyth's voice was neither friendly nor hostile.

'George, what is it? I'm busy.'

'Too busy for an old school pal trying to do you a favour?'

George simulated goodwill. Forsyth had doubtless been waiting for the call. Clever sod always was two steps ahead, even at school. The Prince Regent continued blithely. 'This isn't a social call, dear boy. You know me – never socialize before the midday gun. I can't pretend to be sorry about Minton-Briant. Miserable bugger made my life hell. He was worse than a nagging wife. Not that I've ever had one of those, but I imagine the grief factor is similar.'

He waited to hear how the vindictive overture was received.

'Go on.'

Forsyth sounded non-committal – encouragement enough.

'I'm no political animal, Bob. My penchant is for the quiet life. Wasn't easy to come by with our prudish PM heaving me up on the cross and banging in the nails personally. No parties. No booze-ups. No birds. No bees. No friendly games of chance or fun wagers. Positively none of the harmless pleasures a man needs to keep sane in this dreary world.'

'Life must have been unbearable. But things might change.'

'I hope so. As Prince Regent, one shouldn't undervalue oneself. All those constitutional powers! In theory, anyway. But isn't that the point? The biggest rubber stamp in the history of human duplicity. Left to myself I would have settled for the earldom and a fortune safely stashed abroad.'

He paused again, but the Intelligence general said nothing. George went fishing.

'Unfortunately old Pater's judgment left something to be desired. Two legs or four, made no difference. So no fortune and I'm forced to work as a government king-pin, pardon the pun. Which leaves me cold. Not interested in politics. I'd rather have twenty grand and enjoy one good night out at the Golden Fleece Casino.'

George hardly waited for his gaudy lure to settle before tweaking it across Forsyth's nose.

'Nobody knows how things will work out, who'll take over and so forth. Me, I don't give a damn, providing I'm free to do what I do so well, which is nothing in particular. Anyone underwriting that would secure my unswerving support. I'm sure you appreciate how much that support's worth in these uncertain times.'

Although he hadn't risen, Forsyth hadn't darted away. George thrashed confidently on.

'What's the world coming to if friends can't see each other right? Whoever takes over as PM requires Intelligence support, yes? But Cabinet might not like a bright chap like you having too much clout. Ken Stanley could give Intelligence to that nice Godfrey Cornwell.'

He jammed the phone against his shoulder, fixing another Bloody Mary as temptation worked. Forsyth's voice became almost friendly.

'Quite a speech. It's also quite a lot of money. You're a real chip off the old blockhead. But you always were a chancer. Weren't you found fondling a housemaster's daughter behind the rifle range, while the other fourth-years were combing biology textbooks for basic how-to information?'

The Prince Regent felt a tug of triumph. The lure was taken, the hook set.

'Not true. She was fondling me, if memory serves.'

Forsyth ignored the boast.

'I have contingency funds. A messenger could deliver to Palace Mews before the sounding of that midday gun.'

George drained his glass, but his old school buddy hadn't finished.

'Two tiny points, George. It's important that we find Derek's assassins before they strike again, and such matters are best left to the professionals.'

'My sentiments exactly. Made that very observation to Cabinet yesterday. Delighted nothing's transpired to change my view. Rest assured, you can count on me. The second?'

'You didn't by any chance feel strongly enough about Minton-Briant to have contributed to his last rites?'

'Certainly. But regrettably I lack the stomach for violence. The only bottle I've got is an empty magnum of Bollinger. Twenty big ones before noon, you said?'

'I did.'

'Splendid, I'll wait up.'

George rang the bell and ordered a large snifter of Remy Martin from Bagley, his po-faced butler. After tragedy, triumph.

The Acting Head of Intelligence was a chess player. He extracted a cassette from his communications console. A classic king's pawn opening. Sally Sayers came through.

'Ken Stanely. He wants to use video.'

A matt-black security mask slid down the video screen, revealing the Acting Premier. He was in his apartment, sprawling on a red chesterfield, dressed in frayed jeans and crumpled shirt. Over his shoulder, a stubby fish watched malevolently from a bubbling tank. Forsyth touched the record button.

'Morning, General. Caught any assassins lately?'

'We're doing everything possible.'

'No need to go stiff-necked. I have confidence in your abilities and you have the balance of your two days, though I've called another Cabinet meeting this afternoon.'

'I heard.'

They were like arm wrestlers taking first measure of an opponent's strength. Then Stanley relaxed, sincerity sweeping over him. He was a good politician. No wonder he'd opted for video. He continued, observing Forsyth closely,

his richly textured nasal voice an instrument of persuasion
played to perfection.

'History's mostly about people who were in significant
places at significant times and seized their opportunities.
People like us, Bob. It's people who shape events, make
history.'

'By strange coincidence I've entertained similar thoughts.'

'Coincidence? Surely not. Nobody could accuse Intelligence of failing to understand how society works, or the
ways power may be gained and used. Perhaps we should
have a chat before Cabinet, weave another strand into life's
rich tapestry. One o'clock, here at my place?'

'Why not?'

Stanley picked up his remote control.

'Until one, then. Replay your tape. Should give food for
thought.'

Forsyth's screen went blank.

The chess player would have liked time to analyse Stanley's
gambit, but the clock was racing. Forsyth had moves of
his own to make. George's sweetener was easy. He spoke
with Head of Covert Operations, specifying an open card
for £20,000 with a record of expenditure to be kept.

There were other preparations. He asked Communications to install a secure video link to Field Marshal
Chandler's hospital room, then dropped by Control to see
Andy Kyle. His deputy was worrying interrogation reports,
scratching wiry hair as he alliteratively muttered about
mastering the monster that was the manhunt. Forsyth
listened, offered words of support and left.

He visited every Department Head in turn – discussing
the contribution required of each, calming fears, spreading reassurance, asserting authority. A natural leader, he
understood that time must be found to boost morale before
a big offensive. When he got back, Sally Sayers was defending the command post with vigour.

'Various police chiefs have been pestering. Don't think
they had anything worth saying. Hope not – I put them off.
Godfrey Cornwell called. Him, I promised you'd call back.
The link to Stoke Mandeville is being tested. They expect
Chandler to be awake soon. Coffee?'

'Thanks. Then order flowers for my wife, delivered to the house. When testing's finished, put the hospital through.'

Forsyth went into his room and wiped business from his mind. Alex had been sleeping when he left. Flowers might make the waking easier. They had been deeply committed once. In love. How could something so vivid have faded?

'Contemplating the end of the civilized world as we know it? I've ordered red roses for Alex. The hospital's holding. You can pick them up on video.'

Sally set down coffee. She looked very attractive in white blouse and knife-edged black trousers. Chandler's room appeared on screen. A house surgeon was waiting. His patient was about to emerge from post-operative sedation, but would not be fit to talk rationally.

Forsyth studied the Security Minister. The swathed object on the bed looked more like a mummy than his father-in-law. The only visible portions were nose, mouth and a square of skin above the heart. Wires looped from chest-taped electrodes to a monitor. The green blip pulsed reassuringly. A plastic tube protruded from Chandler's nose and another vanished into his left arm.

A nurse came in. Forsyth recognized her as a member of the Chequers medical team. The doctor's respect for authority struggled with concern for his patient. He issued rapid instructions.

'Another bottle of dextrose, three grams potassium chloride. Four-hour flow. Check the IV tap's clear. Vibro-massage for three minutes, then run the diagnostic tape over to the lab.'

Forsyth watched with fascination. He liked competent people who exercised different skills. When the young doctor was satisfied, he turned back to camera.

'The nurse will stay until he regains consciousness. Before you talk she'll administer ice chips to ease his throat, but don't expect miracles. He experienced severe trauma, though he's in fair shape for a man of his age. You've got five minutes, and that's pushing his luck.'

He left with a lingering backward glance. Welcoming thinking time, Forsyth watched the nurse's deft movements. Imperative that Chandler should understand what was required of him. She attracted his attention.

'Sir, he's waking.'

Wondering how much to tell the old man, General Forsyth prepared to brief his superior.

As Field Marshal Chandler regained consciousness, Vernon Lustbader was awaiting take-off from Washington's Andrews Air Force Base. He disliked flying, having survived an accident when a Cessna came down in the Arizona desert. Time had done little to heal pre-flight nerves, though he trusted the 89th Airlift Wing absolutely. His ordeal wasn't long delayed – Air Force Two's Pratt and Whitneys were working into howling frenzy.

Despite the Vice-President's candour, his final briefing had been unsatisfactory. Tidyman admitted intriguing with a highly placed Brit over a number of years, but maintained he knew nothing about the PM's assassination. Still, it made sense to exploit the situation, and Lustbader had reluctantly agreed to play his part.

He was bound for Ireland, maybe England after that. One question remained unanswered. Reversal of a hostile British UN Security Council veto would give President Tidyman's administration a terrific boost. But how was Errol going to win the election?

Lustbader was curious, but some things you work out for yourself. The 747 started to roll. Feigning relaxation, he studied his *Wall Street Journal* without reading a word. With nobody to see, the effort was wasted. Other than himself, two Secret Service guys playing gin in the back and fourteen crew scattered about, the huge airplane was eerily unpeopled.

Which didn't make the going any easier.

An Environment Ministry reconstruction team had made Chequers their own. Corporal Terence Seymour stepped over snaking compressor lines as yellow JCBs shunted debris. The house was a mess. Scaffolding was up, the roof was half stripped and most windows were out.

Seymour was on a high. Control hadn't noticed his delay in spotting the Bluebird, and no way would Innes report his extra-curricular activities. Face scarlet, the wordless wimp had turned and fled. Joy's pique was something else, but she'd soon find he could do the business. Outside the staff canteen he ran into Sergeant Geoffrey Hackett, the oppo in charge of Patriot batteries. Seymour draped an arm round the morose Yorkshireman's shoulders.

'Bad luck, Geoff, can't win 'em all. Look on the bright side. Not every anti-aircraft ace can claim to have shot down a whole herd of cows. Could be a *Guinness Book of Records* job. What's on the lunch menu – well-charred beef and Yorkshire pudding?'

Seymour skipped aside, avoiding the sergeant's lunge. Deprived of physical recourse, Hackett blustered.

'If you'd done your job we might've stood a chance. Bloody plane'd been and gone before we even knew the sodding thing was coming. Bog off before I have you, you Welsh cocksucker.'

Seymour swaggered into the canteen and ordered hamburger with double fries. He was early for the meet with Joy Christie. His eyes idled round the room, stopping when they reached a straining Environment Ministry tunic, fully occupied by a foxy-faced, copper-haired woman in her late twenties. She was alone, returning his stare as he hurried casually towards her.

'I'm Terry Seymour. You're new here. Came in with the repair squad, did you? I must give you the guided tour.'

'I may be new, Terence, but do I really look that green? I've heard about you. Fancy yourself rotten, they say. My name's Liz Pike, and I like eating small fry like you for breakfast.'

She grinned boldly, showing slightly crooked teeth. Swelling with excitement, Seymour plonked his hamburger on the table and sat down. Pike touched his sleeve with a vermilion nail.

'Down, boy. Don't mind my asking a personal question on our very first date, but is that child by the door anything to do with you?'

Seymour turned his head, libido deflating. The expression on Joy Christie's face was not pretty.

Forsyth's driver took four minutes to get from New Centre Point to Somerset House. The gateman ran his card through a scanner, recording the visit. A guard remained in a booth beneath the entrance arch, Heckler & Koch MP5 clearly visible. Forsyth could remember when the sight of a policeman with a submachine-gun was shocking.

His Rover crossed the central courtyard to the River Thames frontage of Chambers' classical eighteenth-century building – once the national Registry of Births, Marriages and Deaths. Forsyth passed through a final security check and walked up to Ken Stanley's apartment on the second floor.

Stanley answered his door – he'd always refused domestic staff. He steered his visitor to a living room overlooking the river. He settled Forsyth on the chesterfield and gestured at his unusual pet, which rose lazily in the tank and emitted a bubble.

'You're familiar with my friend *Serrasalmo piraya* by reputation, General, though not I trust in the flesh. I keep a piranha to remind me that politics can be dangerous. Little chap's called Derry, after you-know-who. But that gentleman has been consigned to the filing cabinet of history. Speaking of which, any thoughts since we talked?'

Forsyth didn't reply, and Stanley wandered over to a chromed percolator.

'Milk, sugar?'

'Neither.'

Stanley handed over a mug bearing a youthful representation of the late PM, placing a twin on the arm of a chair that was his favourite, judging by interlocking rings that stained the leather surface. He sat down, scratched an ear and leaned forward expectantly. They considered who should begin. Forsyth volunteered.

'History? Riveting subject, though I always thought it came in book form. But you think we might make some here and now.'

'A man who calls a *schwarz* a *schwarz*. I like that. Any progress with the investigation? Someone's doing some heavy-duty deceiving. Me, you, rogue Cabinet members, Africans, Americans, dissidents. Even our respected police force. Plenty of prime suspects.'

Forsyth picked up his cue.

'But mystery killers and their intentions are not our main interest.'

'Very true. Neither of us is prepared to trust anyone until the facts are known, but we can still co-operate. Don't get me wrong. I mean to see Derek's murderers punished, just as you mean to catch them. But we can't achieve anything unless we're in a position to do so.'

Stanley raised his coffee, offering Forsyth an opportunity to contribute. He declined, so the Acting Premier put down his mug.

'Call it politics, pragmatism, what you will. I'm going to be Prime Minister and you mean to defend Intelligence interests. Nothing incompatible there, nothing at all. Unless you try and stop me.'

He thumped the arm of his chair. The coffee in his mug jumped, washing down Derek Minton-Briant's transfer-printed face. Then Stanley laughed, aggression extinguishing. The change of tone was extraordinary.

'Why be pessimistic? I'm sure we can reach a mutually beneficial understanding.'

Forsyth nodded judiciously, though qualifying his response.

'You certainly need Intelligence support. Your position isn't strong. Apart from Minton-Briant's killers you could face sniping within Cabinet. If they don't come to life, Cornwell will. The man wants to be PM, has lots of clout. We could handle all that, but where's the *quid pro quo*? The best deals involve give as well as take, Ken. I can call you Ken? In private, naturally.'

The Deputy Premier radiated satisfaction.

'Ken's fine, but don't lecture me, I've been playing this game for forty years. If I get your support, you'll be con-firmed Head of Intelligence with Chandler's Cabinet seat to follow. Besides, what's your alternative? No compromise leadership candidates will emerge. Me or Cornwell, take your pick. Nobody else fits the bill, with your boss out of contention. I know who I'd rather be doing business with. Cornwell's always hated your secret army.'

The thrust was humorously delivered. Forsyth stared at the older man, surprised by Stanley's casual reassignment of Chandler's status.

'You're dangling the Field Marshal's position like a juicy carrot and expecting me to behave like a half-starved donkey?'

Stanley looked at him in disbelief.

'Don't come the loyal number two. I've been there. We're useless without ambition. I rediscovered mine, you never lost yours. Be realistic. David isn't fit to fight the Intelligence corner. He'll *expect* you to take over. That's why he picked you, promoted you over more experienced men, why you got to marry his darling daughter.'

He studied Forsyth keenly.

'Come on, Bob. He saw something in you. Developed it against the day he couldn't carry on. That day has come. Like I said, history is made by particular people in particular places at particular times. The place is here, the time is now. And we're the people.'

The old power broker sat back and finished lukewarm coffee.

His meeting with the Intelligence general had gone well. Ken Stanley was a master of the delicate double-dealing that sustained politicians. Unblinking ability to renege on solemn undertakings went with the turf. Deals were made to be broken, but when both parties benefited in roughly equal measure, political pacts could be durable.

This should be such an arrangement. Minton-Briant and Chandler had worked an identical set-up for years, with a little give and take. Chandler giving, the PM taking. That was as it should be, could be again. He put down his empty coffee mug, watching Forsyth do the same. The man was nobody's fool – glancing up sharply, decision made.

'You're right, I don't trust anyone. But I'm inclined to trust your proposition, because it splits in your favour. You run the country, I get to do my job. Big deal. Not that I have a choice. You know I can't let Intelligence lose out to Cornwell. You've found a partner. A good one, if you keep our bargain.'

Forsyth stood up. Stanley remained seated, a half-smile warming his lived-in face.

'I love a good cliché, superb verbal shorthand. D'you know where "going to the wall" comes from?'

The question surprised Forsyth, who misunderstood.

'Firing squad?'

'No, this isn't an unsubtle warning. Dates from medieval times when there were no seats in churches and the peasants stood through interminable Latin gobbledygook. Except the lame and sick, who were allowed to sit on benches along the walls. Winners don't go to the wall. See you in church, three-thirty sharp.'

Forsyth nodded, composure restored.

'Cornwell's dreams don't stop with destroying Intelligence, Ken. He wants what you want, but we'll help you avoid that wall. The firing-squad kind.'

Stanley beamed at his new partner.

'I've been locking horns with young stags like him for ever and here I am. See yourself out.'

Ken Stanley went to the window and gazed across wind-lashed water. The flood tide was running, silent and strong.

As Forsyth ran downstairs to his waiting car, he passed an apartment one floor below Ken Stanley's. Had the occupant been aware of the general's visit to Somerset House, he would have been very interested.

But Stanley's rival was lying in a sunken bath, and the information wouldn't reach Home Secretary Godfrey Cornwell until he emerged. The bath was an ideal place to think, free from interruption. He savoured the warmth that suffused his body – a glow owing more to raw excitement than hot water. Just one more hurdle.

Not bad for a bus driver's son from Battersea. His old dad was a trier, mind. Bought the council flat, made inspector on the buses, brought up his child single-handed. The wife and mother took a minicab ride out of their lives when Godfrey was two. He had no memory of her.

His mother was never mentioned. So when Godfrey was nine, he asked. His father had held him tightly and said, with infinite sadness, 'She's dead, son.' It was the only close physical contact Cornwell could remember between them. Within a year the old man was dead himself. Cancer. Or a broken heart. Only then did Godfrey discover the truth.

He was fostered by a divorced aunt, a decent soul whose contribution began and ended with her charge's practical well-being. Aunt Jess could never fathom the emotional

needs of a determined loner motivated by ambition beyond
her comprehension.

Politics fascinated him. His father pontificated about
rights and entitlements, inequality, sharing and caring –
long before Godfrey could understand such things. When
he could, they didn't interest him. Politics was not about
ideology, but power. Without conscious thought, his egocentric drive found focus.

He left school at sixteen with no qualifications. Aunt Jess
supported him as life became a whirl of protest marches,
action groups, ecological crusades, public and private meetings, lobby campaigns, unpaid research for MPs and union
officials, a controversial speech entitled *Power to the People*
at Party Conference – oratory that drew prolonged cheers,
incurred the leader's wrath and put him firmly on the
left-wing map.

At twenty-seven, he was elected to Parliament. Now,
inside another ten years, Godfrey Cornwell was sitting in
Cabinet as Home Secretary. He was the most able scion
of a rising generation of partycrats, the first to attain high
office, their leader. He had not been alone in anticipating
that he would succeed Derek Minton-Briant when the time
came. Unfortunately, it had come too soon.

Awkward, but not disastrous. Cornwell had been unbeaten
in an amateur boxing career spanning forty-nine middle-
weight bouts. Losing wasn't in his lexicon. Now he was
about to do something the good Lord – had there been one
– put him on earth to do brilliantly.

For nearly five minutes, he hadn't thought about tough
in-fighting that lay ahead. Remembering where he came
from fed confidence that he would get where he'd always
been going. Odyssey complete, Cornwell stepped from the
tub. He examined his body in the full-length mirror. Flat
stomach. Hard muscle. No flab.

He dressed quickly and picked up the bulging Filofax that
never left his sight. Familiarly known as *God's Bible*, the
leather covers concealed thousands of names and numbers: those trusted to co-operate for advancement of the
cause; others who helped if the price was right; some
whose indiscretions could be used to compel compliance.
Together, they formed a unique army.

He exploited them to further his aims, applying a simple philosophy. Godfrey Cornwell never forgot a friend. Or forgave anyone who crossed him.

For Mary-Jo MacInnes, as for many a good reporter, morning wasn't prime time. But as a junior *Washington Post* political specialist she wasn't expected to be late for work, despite a growing reputation.

She didn't make it by an hour. Not that it mattered. The newsroom was bereft of senior eyes. Dropping her shoulder bag, she fell into her chair, set plastic coffee-to-go on the cluttered desk and prised off the lid with chewed thumbnails. She raided the bag, coming up with a crumpled pack of Pall Mall Lites. She'd give up tomorrow.

After three pulls she was ready for the coffee. After six more, she booted up the computer. The screen greeted her with a *Welcome to Macintosh*. She blew smoke at the grinning cartoon face, then shut down. No point. She'd been set for fifteen minutes with Errol Tidyman the night before, at the Willard Hotel, but he hadn't showed.

Some Ivy League gofer had stood up and explained that the Vice-President was unavoidably detained by quote affairs of state unquote. At 2 a.m. she split, leaving showboating stars of stage and screen trying to keep the party going. Their grandstand play had fallen flat without the main attraction. At a grand a pop, the high-toned audience expected to squeeze the main man's flesh.

She'd given blood to get that interview, finally coming up with an angle that fitted campaign strategy and might have made a good piece. Sure, she'd been promised a reschedule. Tidyman knew her through previous interviews, said he liked her work.

She thought about chasing, then decided to check the mail. Wrestling with eel-like spin doctors was a second-cigarette job. The envelope was three down the pile, the first that looked to be anything but junk. Typed, mailed from San Antonio TX, marked *PERSONAL*. She slit the flap, looked inside, turned the envelope and shook. Small newspaper clippings fluttered to the desk.

She removed a folded paper that stuck. The typed message said *I KNOW WHO RAPED & KILLED THE KID, BUT*

THEY'RE COVERING UP. As she finished reading the clip-pings, the phone went. It was Managing Editor Douglas Diehl, sounding a tad exasperated.

'Where the hell are you and where the hell do you suppose everyone else is? While you've been sleeping in someone finally got around to blowing away the British PM. Haul your sweet ass into conference now, that is if you can spare a minute, and put out that cigarette. You know the rules.'

She dunked her Pall Mall in the coffee and dropped the sodden butt into the waste bin.

'I respect and admire you too, DD. Remind me to ask for your autograph, like on the bottom of last month's expenses. I'll be there.'

She stood up, flicked at rebellious curly brown hair, pulled down her sweater and shoved back her shoulders. Maybe something could yet be salvaged from the day.

Brigadier Anderson Kyle sat in Control at Intelligence HQ, sparing little thought for power-seekers and brokers, though his investigation could influence their struggle and its final outcome.

A good line of enquiry was emerging. Derek Minton-Briant's official diary lay open at yesterday's date. One more day in the ordered existence of a Very Important Politician was divided into 288 five-minute sections, each accounted for.

Many were accompanied by human detail. Breakfast seg-ments, by way of example, bore the admonishment *Coffee & toast ONLY (official lunch, tea AND nine-course dinner to fol-low!)*. The entry pencilled alongside thirteen sections from 1530 to 1635 read *Tea on lawn with FAR delegation if fine (otherwise green drawing room). NOTE: President Awami's second wife = Betty.* Kyle shuffled facts like dominoes, seeking a fit.

Fact. The assassination required resources and organiz-ation, wasted unless the PM's vulnerability was guaranteed. Conclusion. The bombers were confident of hitting the target.

Fact. Since an abortive attempt on his life by a student sniper the PM's schedule had been ultra-secret, circulated only on a need-to-know basis – Cabinet Office, security services, close colleagues. Conclusion. The bombers had access to restricted information.

Fact. Diary entries suggested the hour-long tea party was the only occasion for a month either way when an air attack could succeed. Conclusion. The bombers knew when Minton-Briant would be exposed.

It pointed to conspiracy and betrayal. Whether ideologically motivated, paid or participatory remained to be seen. But if the third option panned out, the culprit must be at the highest level. Satisfied, Kyle breathed deeply.

Catching and skinning moles was a speciality of the house.

General Forsyth numbered himself among the power brokers. Driving back from his encounter with Ken Stanley, he projected ahead to the Cabinet meeting. Nobody liked Intelligence – at best regarding the organization as a necessary evil, at worst with outright hostility.

Prominent in the latter category was Godfrey Cornwell, who might be able to do something about his antipathy. The Home Secretary could call on influential friends in a bid to dominate the new government. But politicians were natural-born compromisers. If sufficient force were exerted, Cornwell would bend.

Providing Ken Stanley delivered on their deal, the alliance should be invulnerable. But would Stanley come through? He was using ringcraft acquired over countless rounds of political sparring. He might draw back, fearing further strengthening of Intelligence.

Suppose Stanley held parallel discussions with Cornwell? The crafty old campaigner might bribe his rival with the promise of an influential number-two slot, leaving Intelligence isolated. Cornwell wouldn't refuse. He would still be young when his turn came.

The Rover arrived back at New Centre Point. Forsyth abandoned speculation. Too much was happening, and maintenance or advancement of Intelligence influence wouldn't be easy. The organization's pervasive powers were the product of a special relationship between Minton-Briant and Chandler. One was dead, the other maimed. As he entered his suite, Sally Sayers looked up from her screen.

'That pushy Andy Kyle wants a quick chat – "most urgent" were his exact words.'

She indicated the corner unit provided for waiting visitors. Kyle occupied the whole thing – head resting peacefully on a crooked arm, knees drawn up, breathing slow and deep. Forsyth examined his slumbering deputy.

'Throw a bucket of water over the brute and send him in. Any chance of sandwiches?'

Forsyth went into his office.

Kyle heard Sally Sayers emerge after delivering a lunch tray. He feigned sleep. Sally knew better.

'Rise and shine, big fella. Boss wants you five minutes ago.'

He opened his eyes, treating her to a soulful stare.

'But do *you* want me?'

She leant down and brushed fluff from his shoulder.

'Only your poor tired body. Keep the dirty mind.'

He uncoiled, rose to his feet and ambled into the sanctum. Forsyth gestured at the laden tray.

'Grab a bite.'

Kyle carried the sandwiches to his usual chair, anticipating a pause. Forsyth had a habit of organizing his thoughts before speaking, but this time began immediately.

'Urgent, you told Sally.'

A prawn and mayonnaise sandwich was arrested in mid-air. Kyle reluctantly replaced it on the plate.

'We, *I* overlooked something. The PM's schedule was classified. Yesterday, for one hour and five minutes, he was exposed to the very danger which materialized. I've checked his diary. Only time in eight weeks he was vulnerable to air attack. Tell us something?'

'High-level security leak? With a plan like that they had to be sure of catching him in the open, which means an inside source.'

They shared a moment's silent contemplation. Kyle broke it.

'But was the source a major player? Could be some clerk selling secrets for an overseas bank account, sex, a promise of US citizenship. Still, something's festering. We didn't hear a whisper. Intelligence is supposed to abort creatures like this, yet we're facing a full-grown monster that's killed once and may kill again.'

Forsyth looked at his subordinate, inviting him to finish what he'd started. After a moment, Kyle did continue.

'How can some freak blow away the PM? We think we're good, but we've been fooling ourselves. We keep things tight, mop up dissidents, penetrate government departments, build files on everything that moves and a lot that doesn't, keep those crafty foreigners at arm's length. But we've never faced a serious challenge. When we do . . .'

Forsyth held up a hand – simultaneously commanding officer and tolerant friend.

'These things happen. What's really bothering you?'

Sharp, was the boss. Kyle decided to speak frankly.

'This is different. I sense a player out there who's several moves ahead. I smell corruption, a power play, surprises. We've lost control, and control is everything in our business. Sorry, but you did ask.'

Kyle picked up his prawn sandwich and bit into moist bread.

Satisfied by his subordinate's forthright declaration, Forsyth lowered his hand.

'We're up against clever people. Ruthless people. But they rely on anonymity. How long will they last if we expose them?'

Kyle seemed unimpressed.

'As a statement of the obvious, that's brilliant. What are we beavering away to achieve, if not exposure of the conspiracy?'

The big man was getting irritable. Forsyth abandoned the discussion.

'You're tired. Go away and sleep, and that's an order. Then start looking for their inside track. Then maybe we can deal with them. Now move. I must brief Chandler before the Cabinet meeting.'

Forsyth asked Sally Sayers to raise the Field Marshal's room at Stoke Mandeville. Kyle sat tight.

'What does that mean, "*maybe* deal with them"?'

After the briefest hesitation, Forsyth answered – best be sure that Kyle was under no misapprehension.

'My priority is Intelligence. If our influence can be increased, fine, but the essential thing is to make sure we don't lose ground.'

Kyle was ahead of him.

'You're throwing in with Ken Stanley?'

'Our loyalty must go to the man best placed to support our objectives. Ken and I have already made an arrangement. We back him for Premier, help him stay there and make sure he rewards our contribution. I can envisage circumstances where our interests might not be served by exposing conspiracy.'

Kyle absorbed the implications of Forsyth's statement, then asked a supplementary.

'Like if Stanley himself was involved?'

'We're committed to him. Besides, he'd never deal with Yanks, however disillusioned with our late PM.'

'They're involved. So who *is* playing footsie with them?'

'You tell me, Andy. You've been to the States, know the way they think. They trade with anyone who delivers what they want, surely? Their State Department hated Minton-Briant. They'd like to destabilize us as an end in itself.'

The brigadier rejected the proposition.

'Two holidays and an exchange year studying the operating methods of NYPD hardly qualifies me as an expert, Bob. Even so, that idea sucks. Oh, they'd like to bloody our nose. Their pride's been bruised, but they're in the middle of a presidential election. The incumbent's a sick man and there's nothing in this for him. As of January he's out.'

'Who'll win the election?'

'Bet on the Republican. The black candidate's good but Stark's looking stronger. The President wouldn't get into this to help Tidyman's election chances. He was forced to accept him as running mate for his second term, and since his illness Tidyman's been grabbing too many headlines. No love lost there.'

He stopped, aware of Forsyth's impatience. Kyle heaved himself out of his chair and plodded towards the door.

'You're right, the best thing I can do is catch some sleep.'

As the door closed, Forsyth was already talking to Sally.

'Have you got Chandler?'

Her voice sounded a warning.

'The call you asked for's on hold, the party in question is not available. And you have a visitor. The Home Secretary.'

Forsyth was startled. If nothing else, Cornwell had nerve.

Concealed behind a copy of *California Hot Car*, Godfrey Cornwell listened to the PA. Bright girl, keeping the destination of her master's call to herself. He rose, reaching the door as Forsyth emerged and sweeping past him into the office. Fifteen-love. When Forsyth caught up, he thumped his arm.

'General, congratulations on your sudden elevation. I felt sure you'd want to discuss the security situation. We should consider a joint positional statement for Cabinet this afternoon.'

Forsyth closed the door and indicated a chair.

'I'm surprised you got into the building, but take a seat.'

Fifteen-all. When they had settled, Cornwell attacked.

'I can be blunt, General Forsyth. We don't know one another well, because we've been on opposite sides of the fence. Let's put that behind us. Together with many colleagues, I feel the national interest will be ill served if Ken Stanley becomes Premier. He's too closely identified with the old way. That won't do. Minton-Briant went soft, lost sight of things he was supposed to believe in. Things *you* believe in, perhaps?'

Thirty-fifteen. He waited at the net for a response. Forsyth returned the bullet serve defensively.

'Sounds like politics, something you'll sort out among yourselves. How does that concern me?'

Neat return. Volley, then.

'Answering a question with a question? First-class debating technique, but don't play the innocent. We're talking power here, and you're interested. Chandler's removal from the game gives you influence. So which way are you going to point Intelligence?'

Forsyth was a hard man to dominate. He rallied with gusto.

'You can be blunt, can't you? That's a rhetorical question, not a debating ploy. I'll also speak my mind. I'm new. I'm Acting Head for two days, after which I can lose the position on Cabinet's whim. I'm trying to oversee a manhunt and uncover a possible plot to destabilize Britain. I care about Intelligence. What do you expect me to do?'

Thirty-all, but Cornwell felt strong. Nothing more satisfying than being stretched by a worthwhile opponent.

'You'll fight hard to get the best deal for Intelligence. And yourself, because you're the right man for the job. None of us gets into this thinking we're losers. So how will you tackle your complex task?'

Forsyth smashed fiercely.

'We're not fools, or losers. Who's calling the shots under Standing Order Nine? Your boys in blue do what we tell them. As for my task, I do have a strategy, but unholy alliance with you forms no part of it. Considering traditional antipathies, you must be desperate.'

Thirty-forty. Rattling good stuff. Cornwell put on his Cheshire Cat look, radiating more confidence than he felt. This was one tough player. Try a swirling lob.

'Understanding, perhaps. Alliance, no. We could never accept that. Alas, your strategy's also predictable. Ken Stanley all the way. Why else were you with him earlier? Well, he has a fight on. If I become PM I'll destroy Intelligence. If not, we can be patient. My turn will come. There will be life after Stanley, but you won't enjoy it if you throw in with him now. Why make a powerful enemy?'

Cleverly judged. He kept up the pressure, continuing smoothly.

'Rivalry between police and Intelligence has always been keen. I won't insult you by suggesting you'll prosper mightily under me and mine. Our first task will be implementing the plan promoted with such enthusiasm by Chandler. It is important to centralize security, but under my ministry. Stay neutral and there will be a decent rôle for you. I always look after my friends.'

Deuce. And that was where the score would stick. Forsyth was unimpressed by threat or promise, standing up to show the meeting was over. He sounded amused.

'If I were a poker player, I'd say you were bluffing. See you at Cabinet.'

Cornwell rose abruptly, unable to prevent annoyance tightening his face. He forced a lazy smile.

'Tennis is my game nowadays. I knock a few balls around every day. We might play a set some time.'

Forsyth ushered him through the door.

'I prefer something more cerebral, like chess. Besides, I'd hate to get into a game I might lose.'

Reluctant to concede the last word, Cornwell threw out an oblique comment.

'There are tougher games then tennis, Bob. More subtle than chess. We're more or less of an age, you and I. Perhaps it's time we showed yesterday's men what we can do.'

He left, softly whistling the melody from Elgar's cello concerto in E minor.

Douglas Diehl of the *Washington Post* – universally known as DD to his face and 'Dealer' behind his back – surveyed the best newspaper talent a managing editor could wish for. He looked around the table, passing two Pulitzers on the way. The faces were focused. He summed up.

'I don't like relying on CNN for information any better than you do, but there's nothing we can do until London Bureau gets a handle on this. The situation over there is confused. But we know their PM's been taken out, so a mother of a power struggle's getting under way. This'll run and run. Okay, those of you on the story get going, I want more than this morning's file obit. That's all.'

Electronic notebooks snapped shut and the conference room started to clear. Diehl rubbed his eyes. It had been a tough meeting, but he loved every minute, always had. The place emptied, except for MacInnes, who sat there fiddling with an unlit cigarette. Mary-Jo was prepared to break most rules, but even she stopped short of smoking during conference.

'Mind if I don't smoke, DD? I'm trying to give up.'

She lowered her head, parodying the respectful subordinate. Diehl folded his arms and tried to look severe. He liked the kid, even when she was firing cruise missiles through his authority. Mary-Jo had a rare way with words and inborn instinct for an angle, but that wasn't it – so did most of his staff, some of whom he respected professionally but didn't care for personally.

He pretended he warmed to her because she was the

sort of independent and talented young woman who could
have been the daughter that – with three sons when he
always hoped for a girl – he never had. But the truth was
different.

With passionate commitment to the search for truth and
pit bull tenacity, she reminded him of his own formative
days as a reporter in Chicago. Whilst revelling in the pivotal
job that had climaxed a distinguished career, Douglas Diehl
envied Mary-Jo's ability to get out there and do the job
– sometimes in outright defiance of restraints older and
wiser heads like his sought to impose. She exploited this
weakness ruthlessly.

'Okay, hit me.'

He braced himself for some outrageous proposition. She
smiled, face suddenly vibrant.

'You know my Tidyman interview blew out?'

'I heard. Hardly surprising. Don't suppose I'd've given you
the time of day either, with the President hospitalized and
State climbing all over my back. You'll catch up with him.'

'Yeah, well it's bound to take a few days to reschedule
and there's something else I'd like to follow up meantime.
You'll like it, means me going to Texas and getting out of
your remaining hair.'

He ignored the comment, which no other staffer would
have dared make, and reached for papers she slid along
the polished table top. He speed-read the newspaper clippings, lifted them, studied the anonymous sentence beneath,
reread the clippings. He looked up into Mary-Jo's determined
eyes.

'This is it – illegal alien who worked at a hotel where Pat
Stark stayed murdered by person or persons unknown,
plus an unsigned note from some mountain oyster looking
to help his man's election chances by smearing the opposition with help from a gullible reporter?'

'Killed when Stark was actually there, DD. Maybe he even
met her. It's not much, but I've got a hunch there's a story,
maybe a big one. I want to follow up. You know I don't make
brickbats out of straw.'

She went quiet, knowing enough not to over-ice the cake.
Diehl weakened.

'Three days, Mary-Jo, then we review. Keep me posted.

Phone me at home over the weekend if anything comes up. And don't fly first class this time, you know the rules.'

Mary-Jo MacInnes was up and running almost before the words were out of his mouth.

The nurse's voice contained a hint of Irish brogue. David Chandler had been told she came from the Chequers Medical Centre but couldn't put a face to her.

'Your office wishes to speak to you, sir. General Forsyth. Shall I be switching him through?'

Chandler felt annoyance. Why couldn't they leave him in peace? He stamped on the negative emotion. He'd be the first to complain if Bob kept him in the dark. In the dark – that was a good one.

'Please. Would you go outside to guard the door? Make sure nobody sneaks in while we're talking.'

'There's two fellas out there to do the guarding, but I'll be around if you need me. You can talk now, they're on screen.'

He waited until the door shut out any curious ears.

'Bob?'

Wrong. Another female voice. Competent, sympathetic, reliable. Strange how quickly one started compensating with other senses.

'Sally Sayers, sir, General Forsyth's PA. I'm putting him on.'

He remembered Sally. Attractive girl.

'David, how are you?'

This time the voice was familiar, reassuring. Chandler tried to answer cheerfully. Important to support Bob all the way.

'I'll live, reluctantly. How's Alexandra?'

'Haven't been in touch since I broke the news. I'll get home when I can, but she'll cope.'

Chandler was too professional to spare more than a passing thought for his daughter.

'What's happened since you briefed me?'

'Plenty. I've started shaking things up, along the lines we discussed. But more advice wouldn't come amiss.'

'I suppose Stanley and Cornwell are already fighting to the death? They're the only leadership contenders, unless there's some sort of fudge, but it'll get messy. How's everything looking?'

'Stanley's favourite. I met him after we talked, at his request, pledged full support. Not sure he's trustworthy, but what's the alternative? If Cornwell gets in he'll demolish everything you've achieved. Cocky bastard was in this very room a few minutes ago, treating the whole thing like a crazy game and trying to intimidate me. I've fixed the Prince Regent, though.'

Chandler's tiredness vanished. This was the stuff of life – and by God he was still alive. Capable of kicking.

'Good. Never underestimate George's constitutional role. You must keep him sweet at all costs, even if it sticks in your throat. What did Ken promise?'

Bob was uncomfortable – betraying himself with hesitation that Chandler found transparent and rather touching. But his number two replied without dissemble.

'Your job, for starters. Plus the Cabinet seat if you're unable to return. Sorry. But he needs me. I only hope he'll play straight if he gets in, run with an arrangement like yours with Minton-Briant. Once he's secure, he might dump us.'

Chandler offered reassurance.

'I think not. No doubt he's feeling on top of the world, but the reality will take some getting used to. He'll feel more comfortable with you protecting his rear. Trust him. And don't feel guilty about grabbing what you can. Personally, I mean. I'll be back, or not. Until that's resolved minding the shop is down to you. You're doing fine. Any progress on the assassination?'

'Nothing concrete. I've promoted Andy Kyle to brigadier and put him in charge of ops, to free me for the main task. There's a strong suggestion of American involvement, linked back into our own government circles, perhaps at top level.'

'Don't take any action which might jeopardize long-term Intelligence interests. Keep up the pressure and see what flushes from the coverts. Then we can start shooting.'

'Honestly!'

Chandler smiled beneath his bandages.

'I know you'll handle yourself properly, but I'm getting

frustrated, lying here like some damn vegetable. When do things come to a head on the political front?'

'There's a Cabinet meeting this afternoon. If everything goes to plan Stanley will get the leadership and I'll be confirmed Acting Head of Intelligence. Providing Cornwell doesn't jam his monkey wrench into the works.'

'Don't worry about Cornwell. Ken's a street fighter. Young Godfrey will have to wait, if granted the privilege.'

Forsyth sounded pleased.

'I hoped you'd say that. Look . . .'

'Work up to the navel and rising fast? Understood. You get off. Call again after the meeting. I'll be bored out of my skull here. Can't even have a piss – I'm drained through a tube.'

Chandler stirred restlessly. Waiting would be hell.

The building with the famous black door had hosted many momentous meetings since 27 September 1735, when Sir Robert Walpole first crossed the threshold of his new official residence as First Lord of His Majesty George II's Treasury. But the walls of Number 10, Downing Street retained no remembrance of world-shaping decision-making.

The bit players congregating to create contemporary drama had little interest in the past. Derek Minton-Briant was yesterday's Prime Minister, and there were plenty of those, as massed portraits above the staircase dado rail confirmed.

They arrived in ones and twos, well before the scheduled start of the Cabinet meeting that should formally nominate the fifty-seventh Prime Minister to occupy Number 10. Some congregated like pawns on the chequerboard foyer floor. Others drifted along the high corridor to the anteroom where they habitually gathered, waiting to take ordained places around the long, lozenge-shaped Cabinet Room table when the PM arrived.

On this occasion, bolder Cabinet members marched straight in, making a forceful statement. Nothing was fixed any more. Not yet.

There was no sign of the stars as Cabinet Secretary Harry Higgins fussed around. He didn't encounter Cornwell or Forsyth, while the central position at the table – reserved

for the PM – remained empty. Even the boldest did no more
than glance at the twenty-second chair – the only one with
arms, its back to the white fireplace.

The likely occupant was sitting in his stationary car, along
the Embankment from Westminster Bridge. Ken Stanley
was rereading a tattered first edition of *Animal Farm*, waiting for Higgins to phone from Number 10 to tell him everyone was there.

By accident or design, Home Secretary Cornwell and Intelligence General Forsyth arrived in Downing Street simultaneously. At six outriders apiece, the result was a high-
scoring draw. They nodded curt acknowledgment and went
into Number 10, where Harry Higgins greeted them with
relief.

'There you are. Not plotting together, I hope? Go on
through.'

The bureaucrat scurried ahead, entering the Cabinet
Room at a brisk trot and vanishing into his sanctum,
pulling the Greek Doors shut.

Forsyth's place, usually filled by Field Marshal Chandler,
was to the left of the prime ministerial chair. Cornwell's
location was opposite, within the prestigious central third
of the table. The rivals' stern demeanour discouraged more
than token greetings from Cabinet members. Sporadic conversation faded. Higgins bustled back and sat down.

'The Acting PM will be with us shortly.'

His place, as Cabinet Secretary and head of the Civil
Service, was at the Prime Minister's right hand. That left
empty three seats – two of them Ken Stanley's. The one he
normally used, directly opposite the PM's, would remain
vacant. The other, reserved for the holder of the highest office, he would surely occupy. It was anyone's guess
whether the third – the Prince Regent's – would be filled.

Tension crackled as the nation's most powerful players
waited for the leading man to make his entrance.

'Apologies for the delay. I've been reminding myself of the
pitfalls awaiting those who would be King, though fortunately we're not animals.'

Without amplifying his cryptic remark, Ken Stanley walked

to the vacant PM's seat. He stood behind it, running a finger along the worn red leather chair-back. He made no attempt to sit down. When he spoke again, his nasal voice was decisive.

'I know what you're going through, because I'm thinking and feeling it too. Shock at Derek's brutal murder. Uncertainty. Apprehension. Ambition and fear. Anxiety that our achievements may be at risk, our hard-earned positions too. We're all human . . .'

He glanced around the table. Stanley had always been capable of turning on the charm. Now, with power to influence their destinies, his presence was hypnotic.

'But I also say this. We have a solemn duty to ensure that the conduct of national affairs proceeds without disruption. In view of the need to act decisively, I recommend that you appoint me Party Leader and Prime Minister, as the Constitution specifies. End of simple proposal.'

Stanley was a master of timing. He let the frisson run its course, then continued before murmuring became a hubbub.

'There's one proviso. I have no wish to be dictatorial, so we must return to a rule abandoned after Derek had been occupying this chair for a year or so. The one saying our leader should be subject to annual reselection by Party Congress.'

There was silence, invaded by the evocative *Dead March* from Handel's *Saul*, as a military band on Horse Guards Parade started rehearsing for Minton-Briant's state funeral. Cabinet was stunned. The proposal was constitutionally sound, but every member had expected to play an impressive part in the selection process, even if the result was never in doubt.

The hiatus was destroyed by the crash of the Cabinet Room door. The Prince Regent had arrived for his walk-on role as Head of State. Without looking at him, Ken Stanley issued a curt instruction.

'Sit down, say nothing, put up your hand when everyone else does.'

With a glare an angry cobra might have envied, George did as bid. While he settled at one end of the table, as far from the centre of influence as a man could be, General

Forsyth offered the first reaction to Stanley's pre-emptive strike.

'Speaking for the Security Minister, I feel the suggestion has merit. Intelligence is concerned about public order implications of a lengthy handover period, apart from any encouragement offered to the PM's murderers. They must be hoping to destabilize government. I'm mandated to put Field Marshal Chandler's full weight behind this logical proposal.'

Face expressionless, Ken Stanley nodded gravely – the gesture of a man who must agree with the wisdom of another's reasoned judgment. Others were less certain, suffering the agonies of schoolboy swains who want to declare themselves, but remain silent for fear of an awful gaffe. Godfrey Cornwell had no such reservations, asking the question they all wanted answered.

'And the portfolios and status of the people in this room?'

Stanley was waiting in avuncular ambush.

'Unchanged, Godfrey, with the exception of my own and the Security Ministry, which depends on David Chandler's recovery. We must also appoint a new Deputy Premier. Lightning may strike twice, though that would be a poor reflection on our much-vaunted security services. One dead PM is bad, two would be careless.'

Harry Higgins finished writing on his pad and spoke, a sure reader of rattled bones.

'I think we should vote, unless anyone has any constructive comments.'

None materialized, so he read out scribbled words.

'The motion is that Kenneth Stanley, our Acting Premier, should take up the post of Party Leader and Prime Minister forthwith, subject to reselection by Party Congress on an annual basis. All those in favour please show.'

Forsyth's hand beat Stanley's by a fingernail. After slight hesitation, more arms levitated. Within seconds, every hand was raised except the Home Secretary's.

'Against?'

Nobody. Even Cornwell was unwilling to go that far, though he sat with folded arms, clearly displeased. He stated his position with determination.

'It's irresponsible to display this indecent haste. Our

loyalty is to Party first, country second. We must convene a Special Congress to establish the Party's wishes. I require this objection to be minuted.'

Stanley shook his head sorrowfully. He walked round and stood behind Cornwell, resting his hands on well-tailored shoulders. The seated man twisted uncomfortably. Stanley's voice was mild.

'You're going off at half-cock, but we can put that down to inexperience in one of tender political years. I naturally intend to submit my appointment for approval by Special Congress. We will then recall Parliament to confirm the decision. I assumed something so obvious would go without saying.'

Outmanoeuvred, Cornwell reluctantly nodded. Despite partial attainment of his goal, he was unable to prevent anger at his humiliation from showing. As the new Prime Minister returned to stand behind his chair, Higgins jumped up.

'Congratulations, Ken. You can count on our loyalty and support in the difficult months ahead. Thank goodness we didn't take all day to reach the right decision.'

The Prime Minister ignored the hand extended by Higgins, instead addressing the meeting. He let them see he was moved.

'Thank you for your confidence, which gives me strength at this critical moment in the affairs of our great nation. I shall not abuse your trust. There is much to accomplish. Derek's work goes on – we must build on his fine legacy. That is both our challenge and our duty. So, to other business . . .'

Stanley had completely dominated proceedings. Apart from his contribution, debate had involved only three other speakers. It was a political *tour de force*.

He pulled out the Prime Minister's chair and sat down.

The Cabinet meeting was not prolonged. General Forsyth gave an update on the search operation, refusing to speculate on the identity, motivation or possible intentions of the killers. Brief discussion on practical aspects of the leadership change followed. Then, without dissent, Cabinet accepted Stanley's proposal that the Deputy Premiership be left open until it became clear if Field Marshal Chandler was a candidate.

Stanley recommended that Forsyth should remain in command of Intelligence and have the Security Ministry's Cabinet seat on an *ad hoc* basis until Chandler returned. With Cornwell sulking, this was approved without a vote.

The meeting ended with agreement to meet regularly until the crisis stabilized. Godfrey Cornwell was first away. Remaining Cabinet members collected in fluid pools which spilled into the anteroom and flowed down the passage beyond. In contrast to earlier reticence, they were suddenly verbose.

The new Prime Minister went into a huddle with Higgins, who agreed to have the former incumbent's possessions removed from the apartment at the top of the building. Ken Stanley meant to live over the shop.

General Forsyth spoke with the sullen Prince Regent, assuring him no refund would be claimed though he had yet to earn his fee. George's moment would come. Teeth shown, Forsyth was next out, after interrupting the PM's conference for a handshake. No words passed, or were necessary.

As he departed, the hovering Arts Minister swooped on Stanley. She was a handsome woman, who experienced a sudden career change when, as an actress of some notoriety, she met the newly bereaved Minton-Briant and acquired a sudden passion for politics. Forsyth wondered if she was hoping to pass on with other prime ministerial privileges. She might be disappointed.

The file on Stanley was ambivalent on the subject of sexual proclivity.

Increased vigilance by police patrols failed to focus attention on the house. It was truly unmemorable – one of a hundred thousand Siamese twins that wandered out along London's arterial highways in the 1930s, semi-detached dreams for a long-vanished lower middle class secure in the straitjacket of superior servitude.

Number 372 presented a raddled face to the disinterested world. Its rising-sun gate was setting. Dirty traffic film coated windows and crumbling pebbledash. The privet hedge dividing pavement and garden was unkempt. A postage-stamp lawn was uncut. The entrance porch hadn't protected the front door's peeling paintwork.

One of the least desirable components of the state's property portfolio, it was accidentally acquired and improperly documented when the spinster whose parents bought the new house for £395 in 1933 had died intestate.

Four men occupied the front room. They were silent, apart from ritual comments that accompanied their card game. Overflowing ashtrays on the coffee-cum-card table – and frequency with which the men looked across at automatic rifles and ammunition cartons stacked beneath the bay window – testified to tension.

The telephone rang. Boredom was destroyed in an instant. The leader threw down his cards and rose from the torn vinyl sofa. He walked to the rear kitchen, passing plundered provision boxes, a litter of empty cans and stacks of unwashed washing up.

He knew what he would hear after lifting the wall phone. Only one person was aware of Number 372's unofficial tenants. Nevertheless, he felt a jolt of excitement when he heard the identification code – the melody of *Rule Britannia*, whistled somewhat tunelessly but with great verve.

Wedging the telephone against his shoulder, he began jotting detailed instructions on a small notepad.

It was the first serious glitch. Patrick Stark had been inclined to shrug the Martinez business off. But he'd changed his mind when Ella dropped everything and jetted to California. If his wife thought it a serious matter, the matter was serious.

They were in conference, leaving nervous staffers in the adjoining suite to await their decision. Some things were best dealt with in the family. He had recounted the facts one more time, and Ella cross-examined.

'You didn't leave anything out of your statement to San Antonio police, anything at all?'

The Candidate had, but didn't think it was important.

'Only that I took off my wet shirt and put on a robe. That cop Schneider had a mean look and I figured bare flesh might not sound too good, so I kind of overlooked that. The kid saw my chest. Big deal. She's dead and I'm the only one who knows what went down.'

'That's the whole thing?'

Ella was giving him a final chance to tell a different story. She wasn't concerned about his morals, but rather damage limitation. He had no need to lie.

'That's all, Ella.'

'So why the heat over this goddam car? I don't like it.'

'Witnesses saw a similar vehicle outside the Martinez girl's apartment house around the time of the murder. They have a guard who claims our Buick went out of the garage. He got it wrong, or saw a different car. Unlucky coincidence.'

His wife wasn't convinced.

'One coincidence is two too many. You're sure none of our team was involved?'

'Sure I'm sure. The guys swear they were in the hotel all night. I believe them. Besides, there's only one car key, held by Chuck Woodward. It never left his possession. We're in the clear. The cops want to eliminate the Buick, just like they said.'

Ella lectured him as though he were a five-year-old.

'I know what those dirty-minded people are thinking. That hot-as-mustard First Assistant DA plans to run next time around and wants headlines. His investigation's stalled, so he decides you had a work-out with the girl, she squealed foul and we shut her mouth. He gets elected, you don't.'

Stark replied indignantly.

'Not only didn't I touch her, but none of our people knew she'd been in my room, where she lived, anything about her. The guy's chasing shadows, and I say give him the goddam car. If you're still bothered we can have that sedan scrubbed cleaner than a new pin before releasing it, but let's bury this and get on with winning an election.'

Ella agreed, reluctantly.

'I hope you're right. The papers haven't made anything of it yet, barring small items in the San Antonio dailies. Same with local TV, nothing on the networks. If we don't oblige it'll only increase that DA's suspicions.'

Stark was relieved the problem was solved.

'I've used all the clout I can muster to keep this Turrow

in line. He's started hinting at a cover-up. Called again this morning, twice. So let's get him off our backs before he has an excuse to go public.'

Ella got up, put a friendly hand on his shoulder.

'I'll tell Chuck to make the arrangements, but something still feels wrong.'

The Candidate watched his wife all the way to the door, unease rekindling.

Displeased but not downhearted by failure to advance his cause at the expense of Intelligence, Godfrey Cornwell contacted the Cabinet Secretary and asked for a meeting with the new PM, on a delicate matter. Harry Higgins interpreted the hidden imperative.

Within an hour, Cornwell crossed the garden of Number 10 in deepening twilight and was admitted at the rear door. Ken Stanley received him in his new sitting room on the top floor, pointing the Home Secretary to a chintzy armchair. Stanley smiled his charming, cynical smile.

'Sit yourself down, Godfrey, tell me what's eating you.'

Wasting no time on social foreplay, Cornwell did both.

'A neat afternoon's work, Ken, very neat. But it won't stick. You can't get away with bulldozing the Party aside. Or me. I'm their man.'

The PM appeared unruffled.

'Quite the soapbox orator, Godfrey, as ever. But you're not addressing your Young Pioneers or a sycophantic meeting of police top brass. You have clout with the membership, granted, but Special Congress meets in one week and delegates hate rocking the boat. This time, I think you'll find the Party's behind me.'

Ritual sparring concluded, Cornwell allowed his voice to convey conciliation.

'Suppose we split the pot eighty-twenty in your favour? Me, I'll settle for the Deputy Premiership. My people will find that acceptable. They'll see it as modest reward for their man and a check on Intelligence. Chandler and Forsyth have their wings clipped but not so they're humiliated, you're firmly in the box-seat with everyone beholden to you. Sound good?'

The new Prime Minister rubbed the side of his nose

with a blunt forefinger, making a few seconds in which to formulate a response.

'You want my job, Godfrey. If I give you enough rope you're clever enough to hang me. However reasonable your proposition, the outcome will be to purchase time. Time which you could use against me in furtherance of your personal agenda.'

The ticking of a brass carriage clock on the mantelpiece was clearly audible. It tinkled the hour, echoed by the deep voice of Big Ben from nearby Parliament Square, striking eleven times. When the Premier continued, it was as though he were thinking aloud.

'Chandler may be down, but Intelligence isn't out. Forsyth's tough. He could damage me. Later, I may take a different view. But right now I can rely on them. You'd also be a valuable ally if I could trust you. But can I? It's the sort of fascinating equation that makes our work so stimulating.'

Cornwell sensed progress.

'I've just told you how to have your cake and eat it. Go against me and you might finish up with a bare plate. I'm young, I can afford to wait. But you only get one shot.'

The two men talked on. When the Home Secretary eventually left, once again using the back entrance, it was almost midnight. Nothing had been settled – but the fact the PM had discussed his proposition was enough.

As he breathed cold night air, Cornwell felt euphoric. Stanley appreciated how much pressure could be brought to bear by the Party. After reluctant analysis, he would give in. Once he'd done that, he wouldn't last six months.

Cornwell didn't consider himself long-term shit-eating second-best material.

Godfrey Cornwell's assignation with the Prime Minister hadn't gone unnoticed by Intelligence watchers. They'd been in place five minutes after the meeting was arranged, alerted by an inside man at Downing Street. General Robert Forsyth paced his office at New Centre Point, considering their report. Following a storm, everyone scrambled for windfalls, the biggest heap falling to the toughest scrapper.

If Cornwell ripped through the PM's defences, Stanley would crumble. Forget old friends and allies. Fight for survival. Withdraw the support needed to nourish Intelligence. Then the Home Secretary would move to destroy his rivals. Power was exercised through the system. With access closed off, Intelligence influence would wither.

As David Chandler had observed when they talked earlier, Intelligence had to support the new PM by every possible means – fair or foul. The Field Marshal's contribution had been shrewd and helpful, but something was missing.

In the end, Chandler had fallen silent, turning his head on the antiseptic hospital pillow, away from a video camera he couldn't see. In that gesture, Forsyth found understanding. His mentor was reacting against his own emasculation, coupled with awareness that the future direction of the powerful organization he had created lay in other hands – Forsyth's.

Comprehension was frightening. For the first time, General Robert Forsyth felt the loneliness of command. He put down the surveillance report from Downing Street, served himself a generous Campari soda and went to his study bedroom, where he lay down.

He stared at his luminous Turner for a long time. Then, thinking about everything and nothing, he dozed off.

DAY THREE:

Saturday 7 September

At dawn on the second day following the attack, fatigue struck Brigadier Anderson Kyle. He'd been running Control for thirty-seven hours, obeying Forsyth's order of the previous afternoon only when concentration collapsed.

Whilst he lay in a dead slumber, life ticked on. Despite official edicts that normal life should resume forthwith, Saturday commuters and shoppers were delayed by painstaking police identity checks.

Morning telecasts and papers were full of Ken Stanley's elevation, lauding an outstanding political record, fine personal qualities and the reassuring continuity implicit in Cabinet's unanimous decision. It was widely reported that ratification of the appointment by Special Party Congress and Parliament would be a formality.

At Intelligence HQ, there was negative fodder for breakfast. The killer plane's origin remained obscure. British-registered Bluebirds were eliminated, leaving only export models. Interrogations revealed nothing more than a dusty web of dissenters, already well documented.

Kyle had asked to be called after two hours, but the Duty Controller let him sleep on. If asked, he would have justified the lapse by saying his superior was exhausted. In reality, he was unwilling to abandon his pivotal role.

Kyle's respite was brief. At nine he was gently awakened by an orderly. He was wanted upstairs in fifteen minutes.

Muttering incoherently, he rolled off the cot, sluiced his face in cold water and found his uniform fatigues. They had been sponged and pressed while he slept.

There was barely time to visit Control, acquaint himself with current status and make his meeting with Forsyth.

Beyond the lake, Dromoland Castle stood solidly in a girdle of trees, its grey stone tower illuminated by morning sun. Vice-Presidential Envoy Vernon Lustbader ran a hand down the steel shaft of his club. Waiting for the call from London was hard, despite a wealth of leisure activities and the comfort of the historic hotel's best suite. It was too early for golf, but fresh air appealed after a sleepless night.

In theory, the mission was straightforward. He would table a fat deal in the hope that the cash-starved Brits would react like hungry hogs. But there was more. Lustbader endlessly tried to fit jigsaw pieces together without a finished picture to work from. Errol Tidyman had a hidden agenda, but he couldn't fathom it.

His emotions were pulled between desire for Errol to win and the hurt of not being trusted with the truth. Most of all, he hated the possibility that hope invested in Tidyman by himself and nearly half America might be a bad speculation.

Without commitment, he waggled his four iron and addressed the smug white ball. Watched by an impassive Secret Service agent who was acting as caddy, he sliced his shot. The ball flew left towards the lake, dropping into deep rough. That made twenty-seven, and he was still two hundred yards short of the fifth green.

Lustbader plodded after his errant drive. He should have tried the trout fishing.

As Kyle ran into Forsyth's outer office, Sally Sayers glanced at her Cartier wristwatch. Kyle consulted his Omega.

'Sorry, Sal, but that electronic toy is a minute fast.'

'Or your clockwork antique's a minute slow. Now go, you're ninety seconds late.'

He found Forsyth leaning against the picture window, hands flat against armoured glass. Kyle walked over and stood beside him, taking in the miniaturized city below. Forsyth turned.

'Impressive, isn't it? Best view in London. Your promotion is official, Brigadier Kyle. I'm also appointing you my acting deputy. It'll put the odd ambition out of joint among ranking senior officers, but you're well respected.'

When Kyle replied, his voice lacked its customary flippancy.

'Not bad for a snotty kid from Notting Hill. My ol' daddy would never have believed it. He slapped me when I opted for the constabulary. Not done, in those enlightened days of brothers versus pigs. Old devil hardly spoke to me for years.'

Forsyth moved away from the window.

'Let's talk. We need to find new angles, can't let things stagnate.'

Kyle reached for the telephone.

'I'll make my excuses.'

'No need. I had Sally tell your Duty Controller to hang in there. He seemed rather pleased.'

'I hope nothing happens.'

'He's been told to disturb us if anything does. You won't miss a thing, Sherlock. Tell me how it's done.'

He mimed a long nose. Kyle laughed.

'Elementary, my dear Forsyth. I'm concentrating on the leak that fingered Minton-Briant, which means treading on eggshells. We can't roar over the hill or we might find our Little Big Horn.'

'Custer let his heart rule his head. He split his forces and attacked without thought. But not all generals are so reckless.'

Forsyth went back to the window. The panorama was coming into sharper focus, morning mist dissipating as an orange sun climbed above the City of London skyline. When he continued, his voice was sombre.

'What's really happening out there, Andy?'

Watching the Acting Head's silhouette against the bright window, Andy Kyle felt alive. Adrenalin was a great antidote for fatigue. The stress of unexpected command had got to Forsyth, but confidence and drive were returning fast. Turning decisively, he confirmed Kyle's perception.

'A quick summary. Things went well in Cabinet. I'm

confirmed Acting Head. We have an understanding with Ken Stanley and I'm assuming his appointment as PM will be ratified. But Cornwell's working on him and has leverage. We must protect Stanley's position to safeguard our own.'

'So what's new?'

'When we spoke I more or less suggested we should support Stanley and hope for the best. Now, I think we must go on to the offensive. Suppose we assume that Minton-Briant's murder was part of some as yet obscure plan, then extrapolate. There will be more terrorist acts, or not. Discount the former until something happens, leaving an interesting question. What if the assassination was not the overture, but the main work?'

Kyle's turn had come.

'Big if. But we should look for those who wanted the PM neutralized as an end in itself, or stood to benefit when he was removed.'

'Like?'

'The Americans. They have the logistical capability and wanted him out of the way for ideological reasons. They hated his politics, disliked him personally. They've mounted similar operations elsewhere, though nothing as ambitious as this.'

The Acting Head played devil's advocate.

'But would they chance the leadership passing to an even more radical PM?'

Kyle couldn't fault the logic.

'No. They would need reason to suppose that the new set-up will be to their liking. So we look at winners on the domestic front and wonder if they're in with the Yanks. Ken Stanley has already benefited. Godfrey Cornwell might. Beyond them, your guess is better than mine.'

With the thinnest of smiles, Forsyth got to the point.

'I like your analysis. Pure hypothesis, but we have to start somewhere. Press on with the investigation. If you find you're straying into sensitive areas, take personal charge on the ground.'

At times, Kyle could be acute. Arranging his face into a mask of crocodile dismay, he proved it.

'Don't tell me. You want full-scale operations targeting Stanley and Cornwell, in case one of them is implicated.

But if anything goes wrong, you don't know anything about it.'

Forsyth leaned forward.

'We need insurance. A production number will do nicely. But tread carefully, I'd hate to lose you. Use your new authority, but nothing in writing and definitely nothing copied to me.'

Returning to the window, Forsyth distanced himself from the instruction. Before Kyle could react, Sally Sayers buzzed through. Developments in Control. After a rapid telephone exchange, Kyle gave Forsyth welcome news.

'We're on the move. Sheldon may have been found.'

'Donald Sheldon, the CIA's blue-eyed boy?'

'The very same. The location of a possible safe house came out of last night's interrogation reports, a derelict terraced property in East London. Just a whisper, but local police were told to run an infrared scan. The house is occupied, so the good lady of the night who placed Sheldon there could have heard the right sweet nothings.'

The Acting Head responded enthusiastically.

'If the Americans *are* involved in this, Sheldon must know something.'

Kyle was up and moving, with agility that belied his bulk.

'This could be the break we've been waiting for. I'll motor up to Control before something goes wrong.'

He was gone before Forsyth could delay him with a reply.

Harry Higgins was at his desk in Number 10, staring gloomily at a varnished wooden plaque with gold lettering positioned in the centre of his desk. The admonition was simple: *THINK!*

The Cabinet Secretary was thinking all right, mind darting round like a trapped rat. He was at his best within the orderly structure of government – pulling bureaucratic levers, pushing departmental buttons, coaxing a response from the ponderous machinery of state. But complacency had evaporated in the aftermath of assassination.

There was a knock on his office door. After a moment of mental paralysis he got up, walked over and admitted Alan Forbes, his executive assistant. Higgins noted sharp creases in the young man's pinstriped trousers with irrational irritation. This prig was acting as though nothing was wrong. The prig spoke.

'There's a message coming through from the White House on the secure line. Marked for PM's eyes only.'

Higgins regarded him frostily.

'You do know there's been no direct contact between the two leaders for more than three years?'

'No mistake. May I have your authority to decode? It carries a "Most Urgent" tag.'

'No you may not. I'll handle this.'

The Cabinet Secretary went to his wall safe, located behind a large framed photograph of Minton-Briant in overalls and hard hat, posing with black-faced miners. Ken Stanley wouldn't have the same presence, but Ken it would soon be. He presented his palm for examination. The lock burped contentedly and the steel door swung open.

Higgins removed a floppy disk. He closed the safe and led Forbes along to the Private Office. The communications operator looked up.

'Message complete, sir, ready for decoding.'

Higgins handed her the disk.

'Get on with it. Use security mode.'

The woman's machine gobbled the disk. She moved the cursor and clicked her mouse. With a five-second sigh, the printer ejected hard copy in a sealed envelope. Higgins took it, along with the code disk.

'Clear the memory and acknowledge receipt. I'm going up to the PM.'

Brigadier Kyle was staring at him with concentrated venom. The Deputy Controller stood rigidly to attention. In his eagerness to earn points, he'd made a fundamental error.

He'd asked Police Central to arrange a watch on the house in Bow. It seemed a sensible precaution, until he was informed that they were mounting a full search-and-arrest operation. With glory to be had, the police weren't waiting for Intelligence. As a result, it was too late to deploy an élite Special Intelligence Service squad with the skills to make such a difficult snatch.

Sheldon was violent. His psycho-profile suggested he

might take his own life if cornered, rather than submit secret knowledge to chemical interrogation – probably taking several hunters with him. Highly developed survival instincts honed by Langley training made him testing quarry. A police operation lumbering into place would be better than a personal alarm call. Kyle finally spoke, very quietly.

'The information in Sheldon's head is vital. If he's in that house and we lose him, I'll break you into little pieces.'

The ex-Deputy Controller started shaking, devoutly hoping that his angry superior wasn't thinking in terms of physical violence.

Donny Sheldon twitched curtains, studying the street for the fifth time in as many minutes. He was a sallow man of medium build with greasy brown hair, greying at the temples. His seedy appearance was valuable, camouflaging the real man. He was nervous.

Every time he had tried to make a contact since the Prime Minister's killing, security units had preceded him. He hadn't experienced such intense activity in six years as the CIA's Field Director (UK). It was never easy to operate under cover, but this was something else.

His network was disintegrating under the police sledge-hammer, wielded with ruthless accuracy by Intelligence. Even when he found contacts who had escaped arrest, Sheldon had been greeted with furtive rejection. People rated liberty above a cause, or those cash payments that made life easier. Worse, his cover was eight weeks old and many of his agents were under interrogation. Some knew his cover name, one or two the location of this safe house.

Once more, he looked out. The short dead-end street was populated only by a perambulating couple with a shiny new baby carriage, turning into courtyard garages opposite. Sheldon's glance swept over them, pulled back. Beneath denim trousers, the man was wearing polished official-issue boots. Other small inconsistencies clicked into focus.

The brick wall of the raised railway embankment forming one end of the cul-de-sac magnetized small truants, drawn by its potential as a target for their soccer ball. They were atypically absent. Sheldon had also noted that two old men

spent most mornings working on a vintage Ford Anglia outside one of the lock-up garages. But apart from the suspect
couple, the courtyard was deserted. The sun shone, but the
pram's waterproof flap was up, perhaps hiding emptiness.

His sixth sense became neuralgic. Snatching a pre-
packed holdall, he left the front bedroom, went down a
short flight of stairs and into the upper part of the back
extension. The window was covered with corrugated iron
sheets which leaked daylight round rusty edges, providing
an ideal observation point.

Sheldon knelt and studied a long wedge of overgrown
back gardens, formed by the high railway embankment
on one side and shuttered backs of houses on two more.
The untidy ground was completely enclosed, his street
completing the boundary.

Nothing moved, save a lean black-and-white tom cat
slinking along the top of the yard-high brick wall of the
garden four down, at right angles to his own tiny patch. As
he watched, the animal approached a wild-sown sycamore
tree which grew against the wall.

The gardenwise feline went rigid, shredded ears flatten-
ing, then turned and fled in an explosion of energy. And
the American knew there were men beneath the sycamore,
concealed by the wall.

Sheldon opened his holdall. It contained the uniform of a
Metropolitan Police inspector, blued Colt automatic pistol
with sound moderator and one box of .32 ammunition. He
changed into the uniform, hoping he wouldn't suffer the
irony of capture because the outfit lacked regulation boots.
He put the loaded weapon into his tunic pocket.

He went down through semi-darkness to the kitchen.
Sheldon had removed six-inch nails that once secured the
back door, before oiling stiff hinges and fitting a bolt to
discourage prowlers. He eased the bolt free, listening for
the next train – the embankment carried the main line out
of Liverpool Street Station.

Within a minute, Sheldon heard a distant rumble. He
threw back the door and stepped out, raising his voice to
compete with the advancing train.

'You men by the wall. Stand easy. Officer coming through.'

He crossed rubble-strewn ground, climbing low garden

walls. If they'd got marksmen in the deserted houses, Sheldon would be dead within half a minute. The awareness didn't distract him. He'd been living dangerously for a long time.

Police riot helmets and cautious faces rose above the wall, suspicion fading at the sight of an officer. Mentally rehearsing a London accent, Sheldon reached the wall and leaned casually against it.

Two constables brushed dust from flak jackets and blue uniform trousers. They had radios clipped to breast pockets and held Enfield service revolvers. Sheldon spoke quickly, distracting them from the threatening radios.

'Would you believe another false alarm? Some old tramp dead to the world in a haze of meths. Should be a law against it. Still, you better stay put. The order to stand down hasn't come through.'

They accepted his authority, lowering their weapons and sentencing themselves to death. He whipped out the Colt. The double plop of the silenced automatic was overwhelmed by the thundering train above. The second man managed to get his revolver to waist level. But no further.

The American crouched behind a rusted water tank for a few seconds, then climbed the wall. He'd chanced a fatal high-velocity bullet from the houses, and called right. He propped the dead men against the wall in a parody of vigilance. For every winner there must be losers.

Sheldon stayed ahead of his dangerous game by shading the odds. He made for the far end of the waste ground, following his midnight path of a month before. After smashing the back window of an abandoned newsagent's shop, he'd jimmied open the street door, resecuring his emergency exit by kicking wooden wedges underneath. He emerged into the shadow of a Victorian railway bridge. Close by at the road junction, a police motorcycle patrolman sat astride his machine, diverting traffic.

He walked around the sharp corner hiding the entrance to the street he'd just left. Invisible from the safe house, a crowd had gathered – held back by uniformed police, keeping a passage clear for patrol cars. Two marksmen were carrying cased rifles up steep steps into a house along the terrace to the right, watched by an Environment

Ministry crew summoned to open the boarded-up property. Bureaucracy could be beautiful.

The sharpshooters must have reported back when they were in place, covering the now-unsafe house's rear exit. The lead car jumped forward on smoking tyres. Seconds later, the crump of an automatic eight-gauge using SSG cartridges – an awesome passkey – suggested nobody was standing on ceremony. Sheldon strode over to the patrol-man, who was edging his machine forward. He stopped when Sheldon tapped his shoulder, straightening at the sight of a senior officer whose face was a study in urgency.

'Thank God you're at your post. Come on, off that bike. I need it. There's been shooting and he escaped over the railway. Run and find the Super, tell him Inspector Heller has driven round to co-ordinate things in Malmesbury Road.'

Despite an authoritative performance, Sheldon once more had police discipline to thank. The man climbed off and heaved the bike up on its stand, leaving the engine running. It would take a couple of minutes to find the officer in charge, who probably wouldn't want to talk to him – until someone realized what had happened.

Sheldon pushed the machine off its stand, stamped into gear and twisted the throttle. The bike slewed on its axis and surged away, blue light flashing. Turn right. On through barriers barring four-wheeled traffic. Into Grove Road, up towards Victoria Park.

Clean away. The emergency safe house, known only to him, would be uncompromised. As Sheldon wondered where to ditch the bike he cornered too fast, and a child's discarded ice cream settled things. The front wheel skidded and the Triumph Bonneville dropped on to a footrest, spin-ning away in a vicious Catherine-wheel of sparks.

In the eyrie at Number 10, Ken Stanley roosted in the armchair he had adopted as his own, Washington message in his hands. He hadn't spoken for several minutes. From a precarious perch on the edge of the sofa, Harry Higgins watched uneasily. The Prime Minister finally shared his thoughts.

'A special envoy rushes across the Atlantic at the behest

of Vice-President Tidyman and sits in Ireland hoping for our call. But you wouldn't think there was much to discuss, so what's going on?'

Ken Stanley put the Cabinet Secretary on the spot. Higgins rose to the challenge. There was nothing he liked better than worrying a tricky political conundrum into submission.

'Puzzling indeed, Prime Minister, when you remember the two governments have hardly spoken for three years. Must be a motive for the sudden volte-face, but what? Paying respects to the new man? Sounding you out to see if policy will change? Offering cash for concessions?'

Higgins rubbed his eyes, seeking a solution. Stanley interrupted cheerfully.

'Don't blow a fuse, I didn't expect you to come up with the answer. No way of second-guessing the Yanks. But I know how to find out.'

The plump little man looked hunted, assuming the PM was privy to undisclosed information. Stanley put him out of his misery.

'Let's have the bugger over and ask him. See to it, will you? Lay on a discreet plane to fetch this fellow from Shannon. Keep Intelligence and police in the dark for as long as possible.'

'No difficulty with the aircraft, but the security services have ears pressed to just about every wall, floor and ceiling in the corridors of power. Do you want Lustbader's file?'

'And hand the news to the secret servants on a platter?'

'On my way. I'll get back to you when everything's arranged.'

The Prime Minister – eyes hooded – watched him go.

Brigadier Anderson Kyle charged past Sally Sayers' protests into Forsyth's office.

'We've caught Sheldon.'

His boss displayed rare excitement.

'He *was* in the house you pinpointed, then?'

'Yup. Going by the name of Oscar Heller. Killed two policemen and stole a patrol bike before they even hit the place, but we got lucky. He crashed in Hackney. He'll wake up with sore elbows and a nasty headache. He's downstairs, fully sedated.'

Kyle turned and ran, knowing Forsyth wouldn't be far behind. Ten minutes later they were in Medical, standing beside Sheldon's bed while they waited for the drugs to bite. The Intelligence doctor looked up from his needle.

'A nice cocktail, gentlemen. Stimulant to counteract the sedative, plus a concoction of my own to loosen that stubborn tongue. He should be receptive in a few seconds. His eyes won't open but he'll hear you, understand questions and be capable of rational answers.'

Sheldon shifted uneasily, as though crossing from oblivious slumber to a disturbed dream state. Sweat slicked his sallow face. The white-coated doctor bent close.

'Donald, you've had a motorcycle accident. No bones broken. I'm your doctor. You can trust me. There are friends here who have questions, so your work can continue. You must answer truthfully. Will you do that for me?'

The bandaged head moved obediently. The doctor stepped back.

'All yours, but I can only give you five minutes. The medication is unpredictable. Any longer and he may suffer permanent memory loss. I'll wait outside. Stop if his behaviour pattern becomes abnormal, or he shows signs of waking.'

Kyle flipped open his notebook at prepared questions. Forsyth started a portable recorder. The time restriction meant many areas would remain closed, but five minutes would give them a start. Kyle employed the light tone of a friend making conversation.

'What do you know about Minton-Briant's murder, Donny?'

'Killed. Killed by a bomb. Knew something was going down.'

Despite slight slurring, the answer was prompt.

'You knew he was going to be killed?'

'Not exactly, no.'

'What d'you mean, "not exactly"?'

'They never tell me anything.'

Kyle and Forsyth exchanged puzzled glances. So much for the script. Sheldon was the CIA's top UK field operative, and had to be aware of any Company involvement in the PM's assassination. Kyle pressed him, initiating a rewarding burst of question and answer.

'Come on, Donny, was CIA responsible?'

'Not sure.'

'Explain.'

'They tell me nothing unless it directly concerns me, in case I'm caught, made to talk. Waste of time, I'll kill myself first, you'll see. They'll never take me alive. Never.'

Kyle touched Sheldon's shoulder reassuringly.

'No, Donny, I don't suppose they ever will. Why d'you think your bosses might be involved?'

'Langley's played around with the idea. But when it comes to it they never sanction. Maybe they grew some balls at last.'

'Would they involve you in a decision like that?'

Sheldon didn't reply immediately. Kyle's instincts told him not to force the pace. He glanced at Forsyth, who nodded, trusting his judgment. They were rewarded with an outpouring of resentment.

'They keep me in the dark. Need to know. Think I could be caught, made to talk. I'm the errand boy, gathering their precious information from my network. If they terminated Minton-Briant I'd be the last to hear. Should've been warned, nearly cost me my head. I'll have words to say when I catch up with those bastards.'

Time was ebbing. Questions flowed fast.

'Could you find out for sure?'

'Maybe.'

'How?'

'Ask my contact.'

'Who is?'

'Head of Station, London. Mendlebaum. Cultural attaché. Works out of the Embassy in Grosvenor Square under diplomatic cover. Can always fix an emergency meet.'

Kyle and Sheldon were trading question and answer like punch and counter-punch. As his wristwatch timer buzzed, Forsyth stopped the bout.

'Time's up.'

Kyle looked round in frustration.

'Three more questions, just three more.'

'No. Don't risk damage. Just tell him.'

It was a sound order. Kyle turned back to Sheldon.

'Fix the meet, Donny, talk to Mendlebaum. You have a

right to know. And wipe this conversation out of your mind.
Okay?'

Sheldon replied through clenched teeth.

'Damn desk jocks. I could've been killed.'

As Kyle repeated his commands, Sheldon's arm jerked.
He rolled on to his side, pulling the sheet over his head.
Forsyth opened the door.

'Doc, he's waking. All yours. Come on, Bob, upstairs.'

The doctor hustled in, fluid arching from his eager needle.

The Buick came to San Antonio draped in a sealed car
cover. The SAPD transporter had made a round trip to Los
Angeles. Two drivers shared their cab with a Stark aide on
the return journey. His job was to stay by the vehicle and
observe every move until the police were through, then drive
it back to California. Nobody much doubted which was the
most important task. This arrangement had been proposed
by Ella Stark, the smart-as-a-cookie First Lady in Waiting.

Lieutenant Dick Schneider chewed an unlit cigar, looking
sour. No smoking in the garage. Besides which, he didn't
like the idea of working under outside scrutiny. But Turrow
had reluctantly approved the deal. At least the damn car
was here. He nodded at Ella Stark's poodle, who was trying
to find somewhere to lean that wouldn't deposit grease on
his lightweight Farrah suit.

The Buick's blue paintwork shone under powerful lamps
and the interior was squeaky-clean. They had the damn
car valeted before parting with it. Schneider watched the
fingerprint team go to work before the forensic examiners
made a start.

If anything showed up, legitimate users would all have to
be printed – more paperwork, more arguments with snotty
Stark people, more hassle he didn't need, just to eliminate
some kid down at the valet service. Police work could be a
pain in the butt. Schneider pushed sliding doors apart and
slipped outside. He found a matchbook, firing up the cigar
at the second attempt.

Cop's intuition was still suggesting the Buick would point
him at the truth.

After analysing the Sheldon interview, they had decided to

implant a micro-transmitter under the American's scalp
and let him run, after reinforcing the subliminal instruction
to contact CIA Station Chief Norman Mendlebaum.

It meant passing on the opportunity to sweat out the
names of Sheldon's agents, but small beer could be mopped
up later – Sheldon would be rearrested when he'd served his
purpose. For the moment, Intelligence were more interested
in linking the CIA to Minton-Briant's assassination. As the
scam neared completion, Forsyth and Kyle were working as
an operational team, setting larger matters aside. Kyle was
buzzing.

'We must avoid arousing suspicion. Escape and pursuit
must be realistic or he won't go within two hundred miles
of Mendlebaum. Sheldon's proved he can run rings round
the police. So we set them to guard him, with instructions
not to damage him under any circumstances.'

Forsyth offered a word of caution.

'Waking in hospital may seem suspicious, but Houdini
couldn't escape from New Centre Point. No problem with
the transmitter?'

Kyle screwed a finger into the side of his head.

'Being implanted now, next to his injury. No way of
detecting the thing, it's tiny. Range is short, but I've laid
on full surveillance. Doc reckons three to four hours before
Sheldon regains consciousness. They're about to transfer
him to hospital. I'll brief the police and leave them to guard
him in their own inimitable style. Anticipate fireworks from
mid-afternoon.'

Forsyth wanted to respond to Kyle's enthusiasm, but
found himself replying almost pompously, wondering as he
did so if his long-established relationship with the dependable officer who was also a friend might become a casualty
of command.

'Get on with it. I shouldn't have got into this loop. Too
much happening on the political front. Come back here
when Sheldon's in place and I'll update you on some intriguing news. Send Sally in as you go.'

Kyle was already moving. Forsyth went to his picture
window. He spoke without looking round.

'I've just had a report from our man in Downing Street.
Get a file from Records, US Government Section.'

He turned. His PA was waiting, pencil poised.

'We're looking for a Vice-Presidential Special Adviser by the name of Lustbader, Vernon Lustbader.'

With calls held, General Forsyth had lost track of time. Rousing himself, he threw down the concertina of computer print-out he'd been holding. It brought US Vice-Presidential Special Adviser Lustbader to life, right down to shoe size and a penchant for Scandinavian classical music. The man seemed too good to be true.

Old Boston banking money. Family friend of the Kennedy clan in their golden days. Second-in-class Yale law degree. Advocate of liberal causes, starting with passionate defence of Vietnam draft dodgers. Law professorship at Mid-Western university.

And the rest – one wife, struck by chronic arthritis aged forty, leading to incapacity and premature death. Never remarried. One son – live-wire civil rights attorney who, surprise, graduated fourth in class from Yale. Unexpected emergence two years back from self-imposed exile to become the most influential counsellor to Vice-President Errol Tidyman as he began his presidential run.

But even if he won, Tidyman was not a man the British could do business with. The ideological canyon was too wide, and deep, to contemplate a crossing – unless the left-wing British government reneged on everything it had stood for under Derek Minton-Briant.

So what was Tidyman's senior adviser doing in Ireland, *en route* to London? People like that didn't rush across the Atlantic on spec. Lustbader was a man of integrity, trusted absolutely by Tidyman. And this major player was about to have a secret meeting with Prime Minister Ken Stanley.

Donald Sheldon remembered dropping that brute of a bike. Aching head and throbbing elbows confirmed the memory. His eyes registered an angle between white ceiling and green wall, broken by a rectangular air-conditioning grille. He swivelled his head. No one else was in the room. Metal cabinet flanked tubular bed, TV set against the wall, oxygen and service outlets above the bed.

Hospital. Encouraging, yet he couldn't believe an unconscious man improperly dressed as a policeman – lying beside a bent government-issue motorcycle – had been overlooked by the security forces. His sixth sense whimpered. Before he could speculate further, a woman spoke outside the door in a chirpy Cockney voice.

'Fancy anyfink, Sarge?'

'What you offerin', pet?'

Sounded like a Geordie. Sheldon was an expert in English dialects, and guessed at Newcastle.

'Choice of tea or coffee. What did yer 'ave in mind?'

'That'd be telling, gorgeous.'

'Who's in there, anyway? Must be someone a bit special, wiv a big strong bloke like you mindin' the door.'

'Should be two of us, but my oppo's been waiting nine months for an X-ray on his bad back. Only went and chatted up a tasty radiographer, didn't he? He's having it done now. Or making his back worse if he's just having it, crafty sod.'

Sergeant and tea lady rattled on. Sheldon lost interest. Whatever the reasons, they'd been negligent. Escape monopolized his thoughts. The room was windowless, with a clear observation port in the door's frosted glass. When it came, the idea was simple. If the air-conditioning grille were removable, he could squeeze into the duct beyond and vanish into thin air. Sheldon slid out of bed.

Feeling dizzy and slightly unsteady, he moved the TV. The set's spindly legs quivered, but he managed to climb on top. Working a corner of the grille loose, he ripped it away with no more noise than the tiny clatter of a dislodged screw hitting the floor. Suggestive laughter from beyond the door reassured him.

A steel cross-member halved the aperture, preventing entry to the dusty secret passage. He climbed down and reconsidered a negative option. They should have known he would never surrender information, or suffer long-term confinement in a prison cell.

Death held little terror. They had flirted too long for him to fear its embrace. Method was the problem. It was tempting to draw the guard and force him to shoot, because this offered a remote possibility of escape. Reluctantly, he

discarded the notion. A non-fatal wound could result, or
the man might summon assistance.

The bed covers were artificial fabric, impossible to tear
into useful strips. His hand strayed to his throbbing head.
A second later, he had his method. The head dressing
was crepe, strong enough to support his weight. Swiftly,
Sheldon unwound the bandage.

Amateur hanging wasn't the swift death trap offered by
a professionally manipulated rope. He wondered if self-
strangulation could be accomplished without alerting the
guard.

The Acting Head of Intelligence was in a dangerous mood.
Brigadier Kyle listened intently to Forsyth's taut briefing
on Special Envoy Lustbader, confirming an American connection suspected from the beginning. Kyle refrained from
comment. Only someone who knew him well would have
divined Forsyth's agitation. The signs of stress were pale
complexion, slightly flared nostrils and compressed lips.
When he spoke, the voice was clipped.

'Lustbader's no Administration hack. He's committed
to Tidyman, who badly wants to be President. Suppose
this isn't a sanctioned US government operation, but free
enterprise? Could be timed to produce a payoff before
the election. Britain back into the fold, with all that
means in terms of prestige? Voters would love it. And
a Vice-President can always find people prepared to do
the dirty work.'

Kyle underlined the thought.

'Hence Sheldon's ignorance. Unless Tidyman has the CIA
in his pocket, they wouldn't be involved.'

'Precisely. And suppose Ken Stanley's his man? Nothing
adds up unless Tidyman knows he'll end up with a friendly
government here. I thought Stanley's pitch in Cabinet was
a bit slick. He'd probably been rehearsing for weeks.'

For all Forsyth's suppressed passion, Kyle knew the the-
sis was speculative.

'It's a shot in the dark, Bob, but dicey if you're right.
Pardon a mixed metaphor, but you recently spent time
explaining that our wagon is hitched to Stanley's star. So
what can we actually do?'

A streak of anger flashing through his composure, Forsyth answered aggressively.

'We stay cool, maintain an appearance of absolute normality. You just look for evidence against Stanley and leave the rest to me.'

The meeting was at an end. Innocent or guilty, Kyle didn't envy the PM. General Forsyth made a dangerous enemy.

Suddenly, thoughts of suicide seemed histrionic. Donny Sheldon knotted the bandage, testing the wide loop to make sure it couldn't slip. Outside, the guard was trying to close the sale. His low voice droned on – words unintelligible, intention plain.

Sheldon scrambled on to the television set, earlier unsteadiness gone. Measuring carefully, he tied the bandage to the exposed cross-member of the air-conditioning aperture. He slipped the makeshift halter over his head. Facing the room, he hyperventilated, grasped the bar with both hands and lowered himself until the cord pulled tight.

A kick toppled the TV. The crash was gratifying. Sheldon released his handhold, bracing neck muscles as the bandage tightened. Soon, he became disorientated, beginning to fight the noose.

The door opened. A handgun crept into the American's blurring vision. The guard anticipated a ruse, but not this one. Hastily holstering his pistol, the sergeant unfolded a lock-knife and rushed forward. He reached up and cut the bandage. As it parted, he dropped the knife and tried to support Sheldon's dead weight with both hands. He failed, half lowering and half dropping the inert body.

'Shit.'

As an epitaph, it proved prophetic. Sheldon took a tearing breath, rolled and bounced upright, knife in hand. Before the sergeant could recover, his head was jerked back. Steel sliced the jugular.

The policeman's life haemorrhaged away, a spreading stain on his blue tunic. Sheldon lowered the twitching flesh. He knelt by the corpse in a charnel odour of blood and voided bowels, heaving lungs recovering. Extracting the corpse's holstered revolver, he spun the cylinder. Apart from the chamber under the hammer, it was fully loaded. Opening the door, Sheldon stepped into the corridor.

The woman, incisors nipping a full bottom lip, was awaiting her intended lover's reappearance. She was a generous blonde, marginally past her sell-by date. A carmine mouth opened to scream. The heel of Sheldon's right hand snapped against her jaw. She collapsed, narrowly missing the tea trolley.

He walked down a deserted corridor. The floor had probably been cleared in his honour. A staff room provided sanctuary, plus clean socks, coverall and doctor's cap to cover the head wound. Discarding bloodied pyjamas, he washed at the sink. After a moment's rest, Sheldon shredded a towel and soaked a strip in cold water, wrapping it around his bruised neck. He dressed quickly and assembled a pile of sheets.

A young uniformed copper sat by the lifts, chair tilted against the well, absorbed in a paperback. He barely glanced at a pile of laundry with legs entering the lift.

On the ground floor, Sheldon dumped the sheets and surveyed a seething entrance foyer. Neither persistent attention-seekers nor harassed reception staff showed any interest as he headed for the exit.

Two policemen lounged outside the main doors, watching an ambulance collecting elderly day-patients. Sheldon walked out boldly – a worker with an honest day's toil completed and hot meal waiting, along with slippers and the evening paper.

They almost believed him, but after fifteen yards a shout pulled him up. As Sheldon flashed out his pistol and spun-turned, he expected inimical gun muzzles. Instead, the guards had their weapons on their shoulders. From the age of nine, his marksmanship had earned prizes when the carnival came to Des Moines. Two years later, the owner of the shooting gallery started giving him a ten spot to stay away. Then the Company taught him to shoot properly.

One of the men took a pace forward, the other turned to run. Sheldon dropped into a marksman's crouch and shot the dangerous one in the chest, seeing the bullet strike above the left breast pocket. A second later, he hit the runner in the lower spine. He watched them drop. Kill or be killed, winners and losers. Somewhere, somebody screamed.

When neither man stirred, Donny Sheldon turned and trotted to the waiting ambulance.

Now they'd put the San Antonio business behind them, the campaign was going like a dream. Even Ella seemed pleased. Yesterday's speech to an audience of San Diego shipyard workers had been well reported. The Candidate had talked on foreign relations for the hundredth time, and the story just got better with the telling.

Tidyman was weak in that department, and newspapers and television knew it. They were hitting his opponent hard, giving Pat Stark the sort of boost the deepest war chest couldn't fund. When he won the election, President Stark would have a lot to thank the friendly media for.

Today, he was addressing two thousand of Silicon Valley's finest. Their California Casual looks were deceptive. Between them, these laid-back technocrats probably earned more hard currency in a year than a medium-sized country.

The Candidate raised and shook clasped hands above his head in the traditional salute, and they responded. He held his pose while the nerds let off steam. Stark loved playing a crowd, soaking up the heady brew of cheering, enthusiastic shouts and piercing whistles.

He dropped his hands. Noise tailed away into anticipatory silence and waving placards stilled. He smiled at the multi-coloured sea of faces and prepared to tell them what they wanted to hear.

Nothing, but nothing, could stop him now.

Following Minton-Briant's assassination, General Robert Forsyth had done his duty. But the likelihood of treachery in high places had been a watershed. As he finished shuffling heavy guns that could support an offensive strategy, should suspicions of Prime Minister Ken Stanley and the Americans be justified, Forsyth felt a surge of energy.

Calling in the Prince Regent's marker, he'd arranged a select dinner party for that evening. George had reluctantly agreed to play host at Windsor Castle. Army, air force and navy bosses had been equally obliging. Already irritated by politicians deciding everything behind closed doors, Forsyth's veiled hints of chicanery in high places piqued their curiosity. After checking with one another, they accepted his invitation.

All of which should make for an interesting gathering. Forsyth was confident of making the case for decisive action and swinging the forces chiefs behind him – professional military types rarely had the luxury of choosing the winning side before hostilities commenced. His videophone bleeped. It was his deputy. Kyle's deep voice was cheerful, his coffee countenance sardonic.

'I know you're incommunicado. But I managed to outflank Sally. Told her I had news which couldn't wait and that I'd kill myself if she didn't put me through.'

In spite of his pumped-up mood, Forsyth was amused.

'And she resisted temptation? I trust it's good news.'

Kyle leered and adopted a brown-sugar voice, though his tone quickly reverted to normal.

'Sho' is boss man, we's winnin'. Sheldon's busted out. Terminated three plods in passing, so he'll hardly suspect a set-up. Made off in an ambulance complete with siren, flashing lights and four bemused senior citizens. The monitoring device is working perfectly. When I listened in he was singing *Can't Get You Out Of My Mind*. Not true, but it's a good line.'

'We wait for him to contact Mendlebaum, yes?'

'Tomorrow, maybe. He'll need time to arrange a meet. We've linked field receivers to Control so we can monitor the operation here.'

Forsyth moved on.

'Can you free up this evening, if the Sheldon thing develops as you expect?'

Kyle's expression suggested he couldn't imagine what might be more important than pursuit of Minton-Briant's assassins.

'I suppose I could get away, providing the Duty Controller can reach me. Why?'

Forsyth spoke impatiently to the screen.

'Politics. Minton-Briant's killing has created volatility, dangerous instability. Probably the intention. But however you read it, the result's a power play we can't ignore. We're being dragged into a fight for the survival of Intelligence. As my deputy, it's your duty to care about that too. I really . . .'

The look of astonishment on Kyle's face pulled him up short. He made an effort to loosen up.

'Sorry, you know what I'm driving at. I want those killers, but I'm also concerned about protecting our backs.'

Kyle was offended.

'I'm on your side. Which is what this little outburst is about, of course. Don't worry, I'll back you, however dirty the fight. But I can and will pursue my investigation. With respect, you're overlooking the need to produce results for Cabinet.'

When Forsyth remained silent, he continued cheerfully.

'To ask my simple question one more time, what's with tonight?'

'You get a decent meal. Exclusive dinner party at Windsor Castle. You, me, forces chiefs, George. Give you a chance to meet the military and provide a second opinion when I hit them with the fact that Red Ken may be playing footsie with the Yanks.'

Kyle made an interrogative statement.

'You're planning to neutralize Stanley, despite the fact there isn't a shred of real evidence against him.'

'Not necessarily. I don't know what he's up to, but we can't take any chances.'

Kyle dutifully agreed, though Forsyth noticed an irrepressible quirk at the corner of his mouth.

'Hell no, we're selfless and public-spirited people. So what's the plan?'

'Call for me here at six and we'll go down to Windsor together. See to the transport arrangements and liaise with forces chiefs. Sally has the contact numbers. George must be in a car on his own. I don't want our scheming Prince Regent talking to anyone. Insist we travel in convoy and organize some protection.'

'Will do, but we're not seriously going after Ken Stanley?'

It merited consideration.

'We can't rely on our new PM's good intentions, Andy. He's had at least one session with Godfrey Cornwell. At best the cunning old sod's playing the field, at worst he's trying to sweep aside potential opposition in one hit, with violent help from across the water. Look, we can discuss this later in the car.'

Forsyth broke the connection before Kyle could ask further questions, watching his own reflection replace the older man's quizzical image on the dark screen.

Godfrey Cornwell's first action upon elevation to Cabinet had been to order a whirlpool bath. The speed with which it had been installed at the Home Office building in Queen Anne's Gate provided gratifying confirmation of his new status.

He did a lot of thinking in that bath. Now, with a lazy big toe, he moved the hot-water lever, admitting a slow jet of scalding water. He sighed with satisfaction as fierce heat soaked into him, then snapped his fingers.

His personal assistant looked up from the file he was studying. Alec Ambler was twenty-eight, possessing a massive IQ and academic qualifications to prove it. And – though of small stature – he was also attractively made, with a muscled physique, intense blue eyes and glossy black hair.

Godfrey Cornwell had spotted Ambler's multi-faceted potential when the lad addressed an election meeting in Truro. After that, Cornwell had taken an interest, hiring him after he completed a research degree at Exeter University.

Alec Ambler's adult drives were devoted to his dynamic master. He opened a cedar box and extracted a Havana cigar. He removed the moist torpedo from its silver tube, stripped the band and cut the end with a penknife. Striking a match, he allowed the sulphur to burn off and rotated the cigar tip to ensure an even burn. Ritual over, he passed the Romeo y Julieta to Cornwell. After a long draw, Cornwell exhaled slowly, smoke mingling aromatically with steam.

'So, Alec, you've completed a straw poll.'

Ambler imparted totals in a voice that retained a West Country burr.

'Forget the Parliamentary Party. If it gets that far we've lost. They'll back Stanley two to one. But Special Congress is another matter.'

'How will delegates split?'

'I reckon forty per cent for us. Stanley can only count on twenty-eight, no more than twenty-nine. Don't-rock-the-boaters, mostly, plus personal friends. That leaves a quarter undecided, but we're strong.'

Cornwell blew smoke at the tiled ceiling before replying.

'The old fool's forgotten the hard work we've put in on these people.'

He moved, creating hot counter-currents which swirled round his sensitized body.

'Some people never learn. Remember how Derek Minton-Briant grabbed power?'

Alec Ambler grinned in anticipation, transforming his serious countenance. He knew his part, eagerly delivering the opening lines.

'I was there, Godfrey. The Party won a great general election victory and I voted. Before you could say "social reform", Congress threw out the Islington window-dressing and elected Minton-Briant as Party Leader, *ergo* Prime Minister. The old lot didn't dream they were vulnerable, though Minton-Briant had been cultivating the rank and file for ever.'

Cornwell tapped cigar ash on to the carpeted floor, then laughed. It wasn't a humorous sound.

'Who masterminded that oh-so-slick operation, Alec?'

'Kenneth Stanley, Godfrey. No less a man than Kenneth Stanley.'

'Precisely. Our new Prime Minister. But what did Derek and Ken forget to do as the years rolled by and lazy feet crept further under the table?'

'I'm sorry to say they didn't pay much attention to the rank and file any more.'

'Absolutely correct. But who *did* bother?'

Ambler clapped his hands.

'Clever old Godfrey!'

'Not so much of the "old", but right in one. Nobody's worked harder than me to build a power base in Congress. Especially not Ken Stanley. Oh, he thinks they love him dearly, but he's living in the past. His kind have gone, mine have come. He hasn't bothered to get out there, cultivate the grass-roots. But I have. Come Special Congress day Ken is in for a nasty shock.'

'Very nasty. You're going to grab his shrunken scrotum and twist his balls off.'

The notion appealed to Cornwell.

'Yes, I may do just that. He had a chance to co-operate. I wasn't greedy, was I? Told him I'd wait my turn in the interests of stability and unity. What happened? Nothing. He thinks he can make it with the support of those mercenary swine at Intelligence. That shows more than a modicum of fatally flawed judgment, in my humble opinion.'

He lowered the glowing cigar into the bathwater. It hissed and died. He tossed the corpse to Ambler, who deftly caught it. Cornwell submerged his unacclimatized arm, savouring the exquisitely painful rush of heat.

Back in Control at Intelligence HQ, Brigadier Anderson Kyle made arrangements for the Windsor trip, before instructing his new Duty Controller to keep him informed on the Sheldon surveillance.

Despite the tantalizing potential of Donny unchained, the search operation had stalled. Kyle removed piles of paper, pushing them into an overflowing cupboard and jamming the door shut. Then he placed a notepad on the empty desktop and sharpened a pencil with his pocket Buck knife – a souvenir of his first American trip years before.

He had decided to ignore the larger canvas and focus on one small detail of the composition – the assassin's aircraft. Kyle made notes in tiny, neat handwriting.

The plane was a British Aerospace Bluebird, built only in the UK. Indigenous Bluebirds had been eliminated. There had been a few export sales to distant Third World countries, none reimported. But the fatal flight did not originate abroad. He stared at his pathetic summary. Aircraft don't materialize from thin air, yet one very solid aircraft appeared above Chequers, so unless someone had built one in their garden shed . . . *Built one!*

The missing Bluebird must have been assembled by British Aerospace. He hurried out and found the Duty Controller, thumping a large fist on the nearest VDU to emphasize the urgency of his order. The display juddered and the screen went blank. Kyle didn't notice.

'Get the Chief Executive at the British Aerospace production plant. That's Weybridge, I think.'

The elimination process had used a list of Bluebirds supplied by Central Aircraft Registration, which might not be comprehensive. He returned to his office, and the Controller came through with commendable speed.

'Chief Executive's called Coppel, but he's on sick leave and I can't raise him at home. Do you want Wheatley, the General Manager? I tracked him to the nineteenth hole at Wentworth. He's holding.'

Kyle took the call. The golfing plane-maker sounded unfriendly.

'What is it?'

'Mr Wheatley? As you've gathered, this is Intelligence. We need your help on a national security matter. Are you proposing to answer my questions?'

The voice became peevish.

'Let's get done, if it can't wait till Monday.'

'Correct me if I'm wrong, but doesn't your operation have Grade One security classification?'

Wheatley's manner became less confident.

'That is correct.'

'Then follow procedure and call me back on the Intelligence Headquarters number in your security directory. Ask for Brigadier Kyle. Consider yourself fortunate I'm not the unauthorized person I might have been.'

'But I'm not in the office.'

'I know. Call your weekend duty officer and get the number. No hurry. Finish your gin and tonic, tell a couple more dirty jokes. Just be back on this line in one minute, using a phone where you can't be overheard.'

The parting shot was salutary. A return call came seconds after Kyle had alerted the Controller to expect it.

'Wheatley again, Brigadier. I'm in the club secretary's office, it's quite private.'

'You know we're looking for the Bluebird used in the Prime Minister's assassination?'

'Yes indeed, your people have already enquired. Super aircraft. Very versatile. Not the sort of publicity we're looking for, but we wouldn't have wanted it to be a Cessna, would we?'

'Don't piss me about. Can a new aircraft leave your assembly line without Central Aircraft Registration knowing about it?'

'Absolutely not. One of their inspectors is responsible for quality approval during construction as well as final certification, and no aircraft can be flown without his say-so. Even for test purposes. The rules are strict.'

'Rules can be broken. And are.'

The man's previously arrogant composure was decaying.

'Not in this case, Brigadier, I promise you. Records covering every plant are channelled through Weybridge. You can't misplace a single nut without the computer logging the loss. As a Grade One establishment the system has to be tamper-proof.'

Despite negative feedback, Kyle wouldn't give up.

'I hope you're right. But I suggest you double-check those records. We won't be pleased if you've misled us, intentionally or otherwise. The one sure fact is that you manufactured the Bluebird in question.'

'I can only repeat that aircraft aren't allowed off the production line without certification.'

Kyle glanced at his wall clock. Nearly time to collect Forsyth, and this was going nowhere.

'We'll leave it for now. Telephone me personally if you come across any useful information. You have the number.'

'I do, I will.'

Wheatley was relieved, hoping his initial indiscretion wouldn't prove damaging. Kyle decided to keep him on tiptoe.

'Your performance thus far leaves something to be desired. You presumably hope to enjoy a comfortable retirement.'

He hung up.

After a lengthy session with Cabinet Secretary Harry Higgins, the PM had retired to his private apartment. There was much to ponder. Apart from the mysterious American saga, he was facing problems on the home front. His intelligence-gathering was efficient, based on a network of friends, contacts and colleagues.

Godfrey Cornwell was trying to subvert Special Congress

and overturn his appointment. He'd also heard about General Forsyth's covert meeting with forces chiefs, scheduled for that very evening. Ken Stanley felt like sandwich meat.

Fortunately, the young were predictable. Rushed along by dynamism, energy, their desire to take the world by storm. Misled by misplaced feelings of invulnerability. Well, patience and subtlety could still combine to teach young upstarts a lesson. Could, and would.

The Home Secretary was going so fast he might trip over his own arrogance. Cornwell was relying on assiduous cultivation of Party activists – the hard cases who attended every branch meeting, voting *en bloc* and regarding themselves as the true custodians of radical socialism. They loved Cornwell. But would they risk their cosy niches?

As for General Forsyth, any attempt to bite the hand that fed him could cost him his teeth. Maybe he was getting overheated by proximity to real power, perhaps he was genuinely concerned with fanciful notions of conspiracy in high places. But he would need a friend. Antipathy to Intelligence permeated the Establishment.

It wasn't feeding time, but he found a frankfurter. Derry the piranha observed the unexpected offering suspiciously – remaining motionless as the sausage hit the gravel bed of the lighted tank in a puff of silt. Greed triumphed.

The fish darted down for the kill.

When the call came, the occupants of Number 372 were variously engaged. An adrenalin high generated by their excursion to suburban Surrey had subsided, suppressed by the inexorable return of tension.

One man was upstairs, lying on an unmade bed. Bone-weary, he couldn't sleep. Instead, he thought about his girlfriend. She was inside for six months after propositioning a plain-clothes Vice Squad officer behind King's Cross Station. But absence made thinking about what they'd do when they got back together all the sweeter.

Another drank beer in the front room, watching sports results on television. He'd already demolished one six-pack. The third sat on the upstairs toilet, essaying the *Daily Mail*'s quick crossword. He strained periodically, more in hope than anticipation. That was how a job affected him.

Their leader was making a cheese roll in the kitchen. He answered the phone before the second ring and listened to *Rule Britannia*, whistled somewhat tunelessly but with great verve. Action time.

When he went to brief his men on the new assignment, all three had congregated in the curtained front room. He noted with approval that they were checking automatic rifles and filling carry bags with ammo. They would need all the firepower they could muster.

Corporal Terence Seymour had sought sanctuary in the lodge cottage. As he dragged on a chain-smoked cigarette, he allowed indignation to seep through him. Joy Christie had recovered from her bad experiences during the air attack with remarkable rapidity. They'd just had their first row. One quickie and the girl was behaving like a wife. Fishwife, more like. Just because she'd caught him passing the time of day with Lizzie Pike in the canteen.

Who'd've thought Joy had a temper like that? And her bleeding language! He hadn't enjoyed his retreat from the canteen, especially the broad grins of Sergeant Hackett and his mates from the Patriot batteries, as the sergeant's thumb ground graphically on the table-top.

Easy come, easy go was always best with women. It would be Lizzie Pike's way, for sure. He'd got nothing against strong women who knew the score and went for what they wanted. Compared with her, a moaner like Joy was nothing but trouble.

Time to make a move. Lizzie was back with the Chequers reconstruction crew, but she'd casually mentioned that she carried a mobile phone, strictly for business purposes. Given him the number. Confided that she'd be free in a couple of hours.

Joy only had herself to blame.

Vernon Lustbader's frustration was a memory. A flurry of communications activity had opened the way forward, and the Prime Minister of Great Britain would see him. An aircraft would pick him up at six the following morning.

He was scheduled to fly into Northolt, a military field to the west of London, then be driven to Downing Street. Immigration formalities would be waived, allowing unrecorded access to the United Kingdom. Practical arrangements finalized, he used the secure satellite link to raise Tidyman in Washington. After a brief delay, he was in contact.

'Ol' buddy, how goes it?'

The Vice-President's reassuring voice boomed into the luxurious hotel room. Lustbader turned down the volume.

'Good work at your end, Errol, everything's fixed for tomorrow morning. Any late instructions?'

'Nary a one. Gotta go, I'm into a heavy lunch with that dinosaur who doubles as chairperson of the Senate Finance Committee. Hominy grits and fried chicken in my honour, can you believe that? Make the play, Vernon, just like we agreed.'

Without warning, the link was broken. Lustbader looked at the mute transceiver with reluctant admiration. You didn't get within a heartbeat of the Presidency by laying cards face up on the green baize.

They collected the Prince Regent from his large apartment in the former Royal Mews off Buckingham Palace Road and the convoy was complete, standing in line astern on a carpet of exhaust smoke. George's Rolls slipped into place behind the lead vehicle, a Panga armoured car with twin machineguns, smoke launchers and whip antenna – one of a small fleet of ex-army vehicles kept by Intelligence for riot control.

Next came an air force staff car carrying three armed forces chiefs. Must have been tough deciding which service should supply the transport. Then their own Rover – Forsyth in the back, Andy Kyle up front. Another khaki Panga brought up the rear, a dozen motorcycle outriders flanked the line. Kyle found the spectacle impressive. Forsyth did not.

'Bit over the top, isn't it? I wanted this Windsor meeting under wraps for an hour or two. That's why I chose an out-of-town location. No chance, with this lot grinding through Central London for all to see.'

Glancing around, Kyle issued a mild rebuke.

'Protection you said, protection you see. I can always stand down the AFVs and bikes.'

With an impatient shake of the head, Forsyth sat back against leather upholstery. He looked tense. The meeting's outcome was obviously no foregone conclusion.

'Don't bother. Stanley and Cornwell probably knew about the whole thing ten minutes after you made the arrangements. Let's go.'

Kyle raised his hand mike.

'Convoy Leader to Escort Leader. Move out. Follow Security Route Two. Over.'

He rehung the mike and fastened his seat belt. The lead Panga jerked forward on fat tyres. The escort leader's helmeted and goggled head swivelled watchfully above an open turret hatch as they followed off. Despite an earlier suggestion that the journey would provide discussion time, Kyle's superior didn't want to talk. As they passed Brompton Oratory, Forsyth fell asleep.

Kyle tried engaging their driver in conversation. The man made brass monkeys seem loud. Armstrong was Forsyth's regular chauffeur – an unarmed combat specialist whose security clearance was the equal of Kyle's.

The convoy forged on, restricted to the speed of the elderly armoured cars. They reached the pulsing artery that was M-route 4. Dreary suburbs passed – a negative introduction to Britain for travellers being driven into London from Heathrow Airport.

The airport exit came, went. Traffic thinned. The convoy slowed as the first blue-and-white sign for Junction 6 appeared. They would join the expressway for Windsor – past those famous Eton playing fields, over the divided River Thames and into town on Maidenhead Road.

As the lead Panga slanted down the exit road, Kyle checked his clipboard and glanced at the dashboard clock. Three minutes ahead of schedule. Ever watchful, he noted an ancient Nissan on the slip road's hard shoulder, bonnet up. Two outriders accelerated ahead to block the roundabout, awarding them right of way. The armoured car slowed, drew level with the stalled vehicle. Behind, the convoy telescoped. Incredibly, Kyle saw the Panga start to flip sideways. The flash of the exploding Nissan seared his eyes.

When sight returned, the AFV lay on its side, upper wheels spinning. George's Rolls was swerving through a spreading pool of blazing fuel, the staff car skidding in its wake. Armstrong braked hard, stopping short of the inferno.

Kyle was snatched back by the locking safety belt, aware of Forsyth's body slamming into the back of his seat – a cruel awakening. Outside, percussive gunfire hammered like pneumatic drills. The Rover took bullet strikes, security glass starring.

He realized the radio mike was in his hand. Beside him, Armstrong was calmly inserting a clip into a short Uzi machine-pistol. Kyle hit the transmit button.

'Convoy Leader to Panga Two. Smoke, give me smoke.'

The message got through. Or the commander of the second armoured car knew his business. Kyle heard the double crack of a grenade launcher. Gunfire intensified. From a distance – attackers. Close by – surviving escort. Dense white smoke eddied round the Rover, obliterating Kyle's vision. Eerie peace, disturbed only by the guttural sound of a well-set fire. The smell of burning asphalt invaded the vehicle. Eternity tiptoed by before the radio crackled, spoke.

'Panga Two to Convoy Leader. Hostile elements have ceased firing and appear to have withdrawn.'

The offside door flew open and Armstrong was out, Uzi in hand. Determined attackers could be taking advantage of confusion to get among the convoy. Kyle gathered thoughts, communicated them.

'Panga Two, call Windsor Police, summon assistance. Get them to throw up roadblocks, ten-mile radius. Stop everything. We'll need ambulances, helicopters. Notify Control at London HQ.'

'Will do, Convoy Leader.'

After the laconic reply, the radio went mad. Kyle looked around. Forsyth pulled himself up on to the back seat, asking a disorientated question.

'What's happening?'

He opened his door. Kyle reached back with a restraining hand.

'Stay put, Bob, I'll find out.'

Kyle stepped into the road, slammed his door, felt a fresh evening breeze on his face. Dusk. Classic killing time. That same breeze exposed the killing ground – snapping away smoke, carrying the ululation of distant sirens.

Of the Nissan there was no sign. The lead Panga had burned. A puckered road surface smouldered, testifying to the fire's brief intensity. George's Rolls-Royce stood in the roundabout, staff car rammed up its back end. Uniformed men crouched behind the coupled cars – dismounted motor-cycle outriders holding handguns, pointed up at the main carriageway.

The surviving Panga crawled down from the rear, stopping beside them. For the first time in an otherwise undistin-guished career, the AFV had seen real action – bright metal showing through drab paintwork where bullets had hit, the remains of blackened dust patches round the muzzles of ventilated machinegun barrels indicating traffic had been two-way.

Its commander was an Intelligence lieutenant, grime streaking a face scarcely old enough to be exposed to adult life, let alone street warfare. The youngster shouted down from the squat turret – his voice, by way of contrast, mature and confident.

'Messages sent and acknowledged. The attack came from the motorway, on the bridge. When they broke off, I sent a couple of bikes to close the westbound carriageway. Pande-monium up there. Should I recce? The gunmen are probably long gone, but you never know your luck.'

He was excited by the firefight. Kyle responded sharply.

'This isn't a bloody training exercise. We've taken casu-alties. Your mates in the lead AFV, for starters. Get on with it.'

Unabashed, the commander gave his chest mike a quiet instruction. After a crunch as the unseen driver located reverse gear, the armoured car backed up the slip road. Forsyth's chauffeur-bodyguard hadn't watched the brief exchange – eyes wandering restlessly in search of residual danger.

Forsyth was still dazed. A bruise was starring his right temple, livid against chalk-white complexion. Kyle looked at his trusty Omega. Less than five minutes from beginning to end. A well-planned pro hit. In, out and he was prepared to wager, clean away.

Two police cars arrived, coming round the roundabout the wrong way on protesting tyres and stopping by the Rolls, blue lights turning brightly in gathering gloom. If the cacophony of sirens was anything to go by, they'd be the first of many.

The Prince Regent was first to rat – striding up to the Rover, shaking with rage. Or delayed reaction to fear. He didn't approach Forsyth, who saw him coming from his back-seat refuge. Instead, voice high with indignation, George gave Kyle an angry message.

'Tell your boss he can keep his stupid deal. I nearly got killed down there. He had no right to drag me into this.'

Without waiting for a reply, he turned and marched off. They watched him all the way back to his Rolls which, apart from a dented rear fender, was undamaged. George climbed in and slammed his door. The Roller shot forward, shepherded towards Windsor by a police car. As Kyle stooped, Forsyth lowered his window.

'I heard. Miserable creature, isn't he? We'd better find the Joint Chiefs, see if they're still with us. In the land of the living, I mean. They certainly won't want to be associated with our cause.'

The forces chiefs had survived. They were in animated conversation with a police superintendent beside their battered staff car. They fell silent as Forsyth approached, Kyle at his side. Any curiosity they may have felt about the Intelligence proposition had vanished. Forsyth had lost them, at least for now.

The military men glanced at one another. Air Chief Marshal 'Shorty' Lecomber, string-bean tall, elected himself spokesman.

'Don't bother about us, we'll be fine. The Super here's been kind enough to offer a car and proper escort to get us back to town. Safely.'

Sarcasm cracked. Admiral of the Fleet Clive Forester nodded vigorously. The army's Chief of Staff, Field Marshal Jimmy Jones – not noted for subtlety – added a tart postscript.

'Intelligence? More like bone-headed incompetence.'

He glowered. With the merest incline of the head, Forsyth offered a courteous answer.

'It might be wise to reserve judgment. This attack gives added weight to matters I intended to discuss this evening. These matters must still be addressed.'

As a damage limitation exercise, it left much to be desired. But Forsyth hoped tiny seeds of uncertainty had been sown, which might yet germinate.

Pondering problems was wearying the Prime Minister. Easy enough to pose questions, but there were too many unknown factors to make the effort of seeking answers worthwhile. His new apartment at Number 10 seemed increasingly confining.

He ordered his car. The phone buzzed back before he could don his tweed jacket – the senior house detective, enquiring what his plans were so escort details could be finalized. Ken Stanley didn't intend to be accompanied by anyone but his driver, and terminated the discussion by putting down the phone. Suddenly, he felt a whole lot better. As he reached the downstairs lobby, Higgins accosted him. The security team had enlisted the Cabinet Secretary's support. Stanley waved him aside.

'I want to be alone for a while. Don't bother me unless World War Three breaks out.'

He left Higgins hand-wringing in the doorway of Number 10, scrambled into the car and gave his driver the destination. Playing truant did wonders for morale. The journey passed swiftly as they raced retreating daylight and lost by a nose, reaching the Chequers guardhouse as dusk was deepening towards night.

Stanley stood on the top terrace, looking out over the grounds. The crater excavated by the explosion that killed Derek had been filled, but the house was in bad shape. Reconstruction work had finished for the day and he had the place to himself.

Despite everything symbolized by the damage, the PM relaxed completely as he leaned on the stone balustrade, watching a silhouetted tree against a luminous horizon.

Two people moved through the gardens below, talking quietly. Stanley couldn't distinguish any words – just the man's quick-fire tone and the woman's amused responses. They came up the steps beside him, arm in arm, too absorbed to see the silent observer. Handsome couple, both in uniform, the woman taller than the man. A mass of copper-red hair escaped from her jauntily tilted cap, catching the last light.

'You won't say anything, Lizzie?'

'Me brag about my conquests, Terence?'

Stanley felt like an eavesdropper – there was something illicit about the relationship, judging by the few words he overheard before the man saw him and called a warning in a voice indubitably Welsh.

'You'll be in trouble if they catch you here, boyo. Restricted area, see, on account of the building's not safe.'

The Prime Minister smiled – at anonymous human contact, and the contradiction implicit in the couple's own presence. Or perhaps that was the point. They expected to have the place to themselves.

'Thanks for the warning. I won't be long. Sleep tight.'

The woman made a quick riposte in a pleasing contralto voice.

'He should be so lucky.'

The Welshman would have his hands full with her. They passed on along the terrace. Stanley's perception was uncluttered as he drank the atmosphere of the place where Derek died.

It lacked sinister ambiance. He was not surprised. The ghost was laid. Derek Minton-Briant was no more than a memory. In this place, where so much had been discussed and determined, it was easy to understand that history paused for no man. Merely accepted each when the time came, as a meadow absorbs the droppings of cattle to enrich the pasture for generations yet to come.

The Reverend Benjamin Tidyman looked sternly down on two successful members of his brood. The photograph had been taken on the occasion of his ninetieth birthday, but strength of character was still plain to see. Born of freed slaves, he'd lived to see a world where his own offspring could become business multimillionaires or make it big in movies.

Vice-President Errol Tidyman sipped ice water, relaxing in his Georgetown library after a lunch date with the elderly Southern gentleman who chaired the Senate Finance Committee. The food still sat heavily on his stomach. He grinned up at his half-sister, who was sitting on the arm of his chair.

'Grits and fried chicken, Lulu, can you believe that? But speaking of chickens, maybe we should start counting some. The election's going to turn our way and Vern's about to do his thing over in England. One-two, buckle my shoe.'

Louise ruffled his hair.

'I like Vernon, but he won't be happy if he ever gets to read the unedited script.'

'He's a good man, if a mite principled for this business. Don't worry, he'll stay on the team.'

They sat in companionable silence, enjoying these few minutes together. Brother and sister were close, despite the wide age gap. He was the second wife's firstborn, she the last wife's afterthought. Such bonding was not unusual amongst those who start at the bottom of the pile. If you don't trust family you can't trust anyone. If you can't trust anyone you still rely on family.

The supper party for local Party branch chairpersons from the London area was going well. Godfrey Cornwell flitted attentively, sharing his vision of a better Britain with each guest. They loved every word.

The Home Secretary didn't mention Special Congress, votes, power for the taking. No need. Everyone present was a political capitalist. They'd invest where the return was greatest. Alec Ambler entered the crowded drawing room, waiting by the door until Cornwell joined him. The PA pitched his distinctive West Country voice so it wouldn't carry to straining ears.

'That nice General Forsyth's had a spot of bother. Thames Valley Police report, just biked over marked "Minister's Eyes Only". I didn't think you'd mind if I peeped. Forsyth was sneaking off to Windsor with the Prince Regent and Joint Chiefs, but a funny thing happened on the way to the castle.'

Cornwell was suitably intrigued.

'And?'

'They were shot up. Rather badly. No top-line casualties, mind, we didn't get *that* lucky. The police haven't got a clue who did it and I don't suppose Intelligence have either.'

'Do go on.'

'Would that I could, Godfrey. But save for saying that the PM's gone missing, I know no more.'

'Stay with it, Alec. I'll reveal all to our guests. They'll be flattered, knowing they're among the very first to be trusted with this sobering news.'

Ambler unobtrusively touched the back of Cornwell's hand.

'There are at least a dozen cautious types here who haven't committed their Congress vote. Now, I think we can mark them down as ours.'

'I'll also use it as an excuse to boot them out. We need to talk. I must say, the possibilities are appetizing.'

Cornwell turned, gravity saddening his expressive face.

After the attack, Intelligence had become guests of the army, retreating to the radio room at Windsor's Victoria Barracks. The body count was surprisingly low – all three crewmen from the Panga which took the full force of the car bomb. Two motorcycle outriders had minor bullet wounds. Various cuts and bruises had been suffered as the convoy braked violently in the opening seconds of the attack.

The assailants had sped away along the westbound carriageway of M-route 4, leaving hundreds of cartridge cases on the flyover. It seemed they had done no more than discharge a few magazines apiece before fleeing – *they* because the number of spent rounds suggested several gunmen, inflicting maximum damage for minimum risk.

A short, violent assault on senior Establishment figures had changed everything, for the second time in as many days.

Physically, General Forsyth was feeling better, apart from a nagging headache. But the surprise attack had wrecked more than the dinner – his plans were in ruins. That much had been obvious before he left the ambush scene.

He'd sent a message to Intelligence HQ in London, summoning a helicopter and asking them to brief Cabinet Office on the attack. It wouldn't be easy to convince Stanley that the Acting Head of Intelligence, forces chiefs and Prince Regent had been planning a quiet Saturday night social gathering.

Forsyth then spoke with Field Marshal Chandler, telling the old man what had happened on the Windsor road and mentioning the imminent arrival of US Special Envoy Vernon Lustbader. When Chandler started asking questions, he cut him off.

The army operator watched warily from his comms console, thinking the angry Intelligence general might explode. Driver Armstrong had seen it all before, and sat impassively by the door, Uzi across his knees.

Forsyth walked – fists clenched, eyes unfocused. Up seven paces, turn. Down seven paces, turn. Up seven paces, turn.

Ken Stanley's interlude at Chequers had served a dual purpose. He had not only interred the lingering influence of Derek Minton-Briant's powerful personality – but had also reminded himself that it takes more than one shoulder to turn a heavy wheel.

He told his driver to head for Stoke Mandeville Hospital, a few miles down the road. A shoulder was needed, and he knew where to find one. Easy to forget David Chandler's strength, simply because he wasn't around. But he existed still.

As they travelled along deserted country lanes towards the main road, the car phone sounded. Despite his rude request for privacy, Stanley hadn't expected to remain incommunicado for so long. Inevitably, it was Higgins. When the Cabinet Secretary blurted out details of the attack outside Windsor, Stanley knew the interruption was justified. He said so, with gruff friendliness.

'Hardly World War Three, Harry, but veering in that direction. Thanks for letting me know. I'm on my way to David Chandler, but then I'll head back to town.'

Intelligence were protecting their own. Stanley's car was

halted at the hospital gates by a pair of tough-looking oppos in the public green uniform of the nation's most secretive service. They were manning a temporary barricade of coiled razor wire on X-frames, with anti-vehicle spikes across the central aperture.

If the guards recognized their visitor, they gave no sign. One radioed, the other watched from a 20mm mobile cannon – ready and able to punch armour-piercing shells through the car's toughened bodywork. The operator swivelled his lethal weapon on its D-ring until Stanley was looking down the muzzle.

A Land Rover arrived at speed from the main building, pulling up behind the barricade. An Intelligence captain jumped out. After one quick glance into the car's interior, he came easily to attention.

'Sorry, but you weren't expected and we must take every precaution. I assume you're here to visit Field Marshal Chandler. If you drive down, I'll call ahead and have someone show you to his room. He'll be pleased, he's getting restless.'

One of his men moved the spikes. Stanley's driver rolled forward. A plain-clothes man was waiting in reception. Without speaking, he led off along antiseptic corridors. The only sound was the squeak of Stanley's rubber soles on buffed floor tiles. When they reached their destination, his guide knocked and opened the door. The inside guard laid down a newspaper he'd been reading aloud.

'A visitor, sir. Call if you need anything.'

He left. The patient turned his bandaged head, sniffing the air like a gundog. Stanley stepped into the room, closing the door behind him.

'You can't smell a rat then. Must be losing your touch.'

'Ken!'

Stanley took the chair vacated by the Intelligence minder. The seat was still warm.

'Sorry I haven't contacted you before.'

Chandler snorted.

'But now the aggro's biting back, and you feel the need for a shoulder to cry on? Don't worry, you're not the only one. Young Bob's been on the blower a couple of times. He's feeling the pressure too.'

Stanley nodded ruefully, realizing even as he did so that the gesture was lost on his companion.

'I just nodded. You're right, except I was thinking in terms of that shoulder being hurled against the wheel. You always could read me. How much d'you know?'

After a moment, Chandler replied. His measured voice was reassuring, reminding Stanley of many crisis meetings over the years when the canny operator's counsel had prevailed.

'You mopped up the top job before anyone could break wind, much less ranks. Sound move. Left to themselves Cabinet would have argued for a week, fought for a month and finally got it sorted next year. That nonsense is best left to the Curia. You've also made a deal with my lad – more or less an extension of the old arrangement, he tells me. So what's the problem?'

'Same old David. You know more than that, but you'll lie there while I dig my own hole, then watch me fall in.'

'Hardly watch, Ken.'

The reply contained no self-pity. Stanley's flicker of amusement was extinguished, his apology forestalled by an impatiently shaken head.

'I can still think. Submitting to ratification by Special Congress may have stampeded you over the first fence, but could backfire. Cornwell has influential friends. You underestimated him, didn't you?'

Chandler paused, turned towards the companion he couldn't see.

'I must speak frankly, Ken. Deal or no deal, my people are beginning to wonder what you're up to. They're uneasy about the contact with this American envoy. That's putting it mildly.'

Stanley interrupted, voice rising indignantly.

'Don't give me that crap, David. Your deputy's already having second thoughts about our agreement and don't think it's because he believes I've thrown in with the Americans. He's on some sort of power trip. You know I'd rather starve than sup with those bastards.'

'Then why meet with Lustbader? You can't blame Bob for being suspicious. Something's rotten somewhere.'

'I want to find out what the Yanks are up to. But your promiscuous son-in-law has jumped into bed with forces chiefs and that bloody Prince Regent. They were all set to cosy up at Windsor this evening, when that rotten something you mentioned had a crack at them. I see an impending gang-bang, with me getting screwed.'

Chandler scratched the knot of white hair crowning his head dressing.

'I heard about the shoot-up. All the more reason for Bob to cover the angles. I've taught him well. Make no mistake, his first loyalty is to Intelligence. He's afraid we'll lose out if Cornwell sneaks in. Bob will fight anyone who threatens our organization, and I'll back him.'

Stanley was not placated.

'Intelligence was created to safeguard the status quo, not promote its own self-interest.'

He received a sharp reproof.

'Derek made Intelligence powerful to reinforce his own position. But he's gone and we expect our share. We're a force in the land and won't be short-changed.'

Ken Stanley stopped feeling like a Prime Minister.

'What do you have in mind, David?'

'Intelligence must have a say in the future of this country, Ken, a big say. By "Intelligence" I mean me. I may be sidelined, but Bob acts as my eyes, my right arm. Don't blame him for this.'

Stanley sighed. They were old verbal sparring partners.

'So you throw me to the wolves?'

'You know damn well I'm suggesting the exact opposite. We stand or fall together. Don't even consider cracking under Cornwell's pressure. Don't treat with the Americans. Hold the line and we can stop Cornwell, together.'

'Together?'

The Security Minister sank back on banked pillows, a crooked smile showing beneath encircling bandages.

'You don't really suppose I'll vegetate here for long? Bob's doing a grand job, but this is uncharted territory for him. You and I will sort this. Together.'

Stanley felt tangible relief.

'That's what I wanted to hear. Partners, then.'

Chandler shook his swaddled head reprovingly.

'Not just partners – *equal* partners. If you have any more worries, give me a call. Bob's a good lad, but prone to over-enthusiasm. I'm glad you came, before you got yourself into real trouble.'

For years, the country had been run by three powerful old men. Now there were two.

After dark, the helicopter had come to lift him from the abandoned North Sea platform. Beyond the fact they were landing at an airbase, the pilot had no idea where he was. Germany, probably. When he asked, the winchman shook his head and pointed to his earphones.

A limo was waiting. He was hustled into the vehicle, which moved away from the helipad, turning on to a well-lit concrete road. His attempt to make conversation with the driver, a gum freak, was also ignored. They stopped at the back entrance of a utility block.

An officer in USAF uniform stepped forward, took his arm and hurried him into the building. They walked along a windowless corridor. The officer showed him into a functional room – bed, wardrobe, table. A varnished bookcase contained worn paperbacks and a mint Gideon Bible. There was a Norman Rockwell print on the wall. An internal door presumably led to the bathroom.

'There are clothes in the closet, your size. You should find anything else you need in the bathroom, right through there.'

The attractive light voice went with clean-cut looks. After taking in the room, he turned to the young man.

'Am I a prisoner?'

The officer looked surprised.

'You're our guest, though you must remain within this building. I understand we're into a security situation here. I'll call back when you've had time to freshen up, escort you to the Officers' Club for a meal.'

He departed. The pilot wandered over and studied the Rockwell – a cheerful Uncle Sam, flying through the air with three aircraft trailing behind, grinning like he owned the world. Must have had the gift of foresight. Late 1920s or early 1930s, to judge by the planes. Above his signature, the artist had made a dedication: *To my good friend Bob*

Savago – a tiny place in history, long after Bob was gone and should have been forgotten.

Would he be remembered by name? The pilot hardly thought so. His future held nothing but anonymity in a foreign land.

The men returned to Number 372 one by one, the rising-sun gate squeaking to mark each arrival. They had locked untraceable American weapons in the boot and abandoned their car in the ill-lit station car park at Amersham, the furthest extremity of the London Underground network.

They'd journeyed from Windsor through back roads, with one moment of gut-tightening shock when a police patrol passed at speed, forcing them into the verge. But the car accelerated away and disappeared round the next bend in an on-off blaze of brake lights.

After a rattling journey lasting forty minutes, each in a separate carriage of the uncrowded silver train, they had disembarked at Baker Street, to make their way home by different routes. The last man arrived at eleven, after walking from Manor House on the Piccadilly Line. He brought Greek takeaway for four.

They gathered in the small front room and wolfed kebabs, toasting their safe return with beer from the fridge. There wasn't a combat scratch between them. The best anyone could offer was a cut finger, sustained when changing the magazine of his M-60 in the heat of battle. When the beer was finished, their leader addressed them briefly.

'You did well. Now get some sleep, there's more work to be done before we're through.'

Vice-Presidential Envoy Vernon Lustbader lay on the suite's jumbo bed, hands behind his head, listening to a CD from the small collection of favourites which travelled with him.

Sibelius didn't turn everyone on, but Lustbader had always been drawn to his work. The First Symphony soared through the lofty bedroom, appealing more than one of the austere later works. It reflected the composer's fears of the threat posed to his native Finland by Imperial Russia.

As he did every day, Lustbader remembered his wife. Thoughts of Amy no longer unsettled him. Many women died young across the USA each year, every one with parents, kids, husbands, lovers, workplace buddies. Someone had to grieve – you just never expected it to be you. But they'd had good years together and death brought release. For Amy, from crippling pain. For him, because he found her suffering hard to bear – not least because she never complained.

That he'd hidden for the next fifteen years was understandable, and he harboured no regrets. But now he was back. Reservations about Tidyman's activities were on hold. It was worth recalling why he joined Errol in the first place.

The man was America's best shot at acute problems attendant on the switch from global superpower to embattled trading nation. Like every great empire, the United States was discovering that when you reach and bestride the summit, there's only one way to go – and sooner or later go you must. But his country could adjust with dignity, rediscover caring values muddied in the fight to retain supremacy. The USA could still deploy vast resources for the good of all its people.

If Errol Tidyman was cutting corners to get where he could do something about that, so be it.

She was deep in a tiny tapestry depicting a sailboat in stormy sea. Needlepoint was therapeutic medication for malignant boredom. Her involvement in intricate cross-stitch was so complete that the telephone took a while to attract her attention. She set down the stretcher.

'Alex Forsyth.'

'Alexandra, remember me? I'm calling from my death-bed.'

'Dad, how are you? I wanted to visit, but Bob said I should leave the patient alone until he recovered his good humour.'

'That son-in-law of mine doesn't want to share you. Can't say I'm surprised. Let's disappoint him. How would you like a house guest for a few days?'

'Great! D'you really mean it? When? I'd love to have you!'

She bubbled with enthusiasm.

'Steady on, old girl. I'm discharging myself. Hospital

makes me feel even older and more miserable than I am, but I don't want to go back to my place. I need time to find my feet.'

Her father sounded stern, but was putting it on. She'd seen through him when she was six and twirled him round her little finger ever since.

'I'll air the spare room. There may even be a bottle of champagne somewhere. We'll drink to the future.'

'Why not? I'll call when final arrangements are made.'

She suddenly felt happy.

'It'll be like old times, when we were together after Mum died.'

Her father chuckled.

'Not quite. I won't be able to catch you and put you across my knee when you misbehave.'

The *Washington Post* had come to town. Mary-Jo MacInnes handed the keys of her airport rental to the valet, gift-wrapped in a dollar bill. It made sense to follow in Candidate Stark's footsteps. She threw some plastic on the registration counter and looked around the soaring foyer. The Texas granite floor, rounded balconies and potted palms were impressive. Assorted people – all loaded, if her room tariff was any guide – were sitting around in cosy corners wondering which mall to plunder next.

Formalities complete, she fought off a bell-boy and rode the elevator up the tower. She had the evening to plan some moves and tomorrow to get the feel of the place, because she wouldn't catch the law in action before Monday.

In the room, she threw lightweight luggage on to the rack, went to the bathroom and freshened up. She studied a face that was familiar but not familiar. After twenty-nine years, Mary-Jo MacInnes sometimes wondered who she really was, or if she even knew the person who looked defiantly back from the mirror.

Whatever else, she was a reporter. She went back to the bedroom and took the press clippings from her briefcase. Five inches of newsprint weren't a great reason to fly half-way across the country on a weekend, but there was a story. Stark always did look too squeaky-clean.

Mary-Jo would follow her instincts through a brick wall.

Luckily, she had delivered often enough to have a boss who
also respected them, however much he complained about the
bottom line. She reviewed anonymously-supplied information
that had initiated the expensive trip. A Mexican girl murdered,
an illegal alien who worked at the very hotel where Candidate
Stark – and now Reporter MacInnes – was staying.

No news value in that, which is why the Stark angle only
made two sentences in the original story, thrown in by some
local hack padding out nothing to make nothing. The other
clippings reported that the girl's body would not be released
for burial until family was located, then that three Hispanic
men were being questioned about the killing. There was no
mention of charges.

That alone would not have attracted her. Neither would
the unsigned one-line note hinting at a Stark connection,
though that was more intriguing. The world was full of
crazies who sent anonymous letters designed to smear
personalities, from preachers to the President himself. The
Post got fifty a week, most finishing in the trash.

What brought her here was an off-the-record telephone
conversation with a Stark aide she'd been working on for
months, woman to woman. The girl had confided that one
of their campaign cars had been shipped back to San
Antonio at the DA's request. The comment betrayed a
college graduate's inexperience of the dog-eats-dog world
she'd moved into.

She opened up because Mary-Jo hinted at rumours of
a Stark link to a hot murder case. The kid threw in the
car because she was sure forensic examination would put
them in the clear, and hoped to stall press interest before it
developed into an orgy of speculation. She would have been
better advised to have kept her mouth tighter shut than a
Texas dirt farmer's wallet.

Mary-Jo MacInnes flipped open her Power Book and
started making a list. Sunday, she'd look around the neighbourhood where Martinez lived, maybe talk to hotel staff.
Monday, she'd start in on cops and legal eagles, and have
fun watching what happened now a vixen had sneaked into
the henhouse.

Godfrey Cornwell rose from his chair and wandered. No

external noise penetrated Somerset House. He stopped at the window, looking down at Waterloo Bridge. A police Land Rover crawled over from the South Bank, indicator blinking left as it moved into the lane above the underpass.

'Let's sleep on it, Alec, we're going round in vicious circles.'

Alec Ambler set down pencil and notebook, which contained a shorthand record of their discussion. Quitting wasn't his style.

'The Americans must be in on this, Godfrey, and I still think the PM may be involved. Suppose the Windsor attack had succeeded? With General Forsyth and the Prince Regent out of the way, together with forces chiefs, who but Stanley would have gained?'

The Home Secretary turned from the window.

'You may be right. Forsyth's his own man. He's our generation, Alec, not theirs, a potential threat. They must know I met him, but can't be sure he told me to piss off. Stanley and Chandler will stick together and fight like deranged demons to hold what they have. Come on, this is going nowhere. Bed.'

Ambler studiously ignored Cornwell's attempt to end the conversation.

'If Stanley's responsible for tonight's attack, we have a clear idea of his agenda. If there's a hit list, you're on it.'

Throwing his arms wide, Cornwell dropped into the parody that always embarrassed the younger man – a ploy used when he became impatient with his PA's persistence.

'Oi veh, can't she stop worrying for half a minute? So what's to happen before morning?'

He stopped, squatting beside Ambler and placing a hand on his knee. When he continued, his voice was devoid of caricature.

'You're right. Call the office, get them to send extra men over. The best we've got – Diplomatic Protection Unit. If we have to sleep, we may as well sleep soundly.'

The two senior Intelligence officers returned to London by helicopter, leaving Armstrong to drive the Rover back. The night was still, their flight passed smoothly. Forsyth's headache intensified. From time to time he glanced across at Kyle, who seemed exhausted – head falling to his chest before jerking upright again.

When Forsyth saw the floodlit landing pad at New Centre Point, he remembered the last time he'd seen that yellow-and-black bull's-eye, on his return from Chequers after the assassination. Was it really only two days ago? Seemed more like a month, a bloody year. In the lift, Forsyth finally broke silence.

'All right?'

'I'll live.'

A grey tinge undermined Kyle's brown complexion. Forsyth replied sympathetically.

'We both need sleep. I'll get my head down for a few hours. Why don't you make sure Sheldon's still on the leash, then do the same? Let's meet for breakfast and start fresh. Seven o'clock, my office?'

The lift stopped. As Forsyth stepped out, Kyle fired a question after him.

'No way could those gunmen have hurt anyone with assault rifles, we were all in toughened vehicles. If they wanted to kill principals, they only had to wait until one of our cars was beside their bomb. Instead, they used it to take out the escort. Why?'

Fortunately, a closing door saved Forsyth from the effort of coming up with an answer. On reaching his outer office, he listened to a message tape full of routine stuff. Taking paracetamol and coffee through to the main room, he sat down.

A second later he reached for the mug, and found the drink was stone cold. He rubbed his eyes, looked at his watch. Well after midnight. The headache had gone.

The thermometer beside the kitchen door told David Turrow the temperature in San Antonio was retreating into the low eighties, but said nothing about humidity that sucked him in as he stepped from the air-conditioned house. He surveyed the beautiful people surrounding his pool and dotted around the three-hundred-gallons-an-hour lawn in animated groups.

A shimmer of mingled heat and smoke from the electric barbecue suggested *fajitas* would soon be served. One of two uniformed maids brought in for the occasion wheeled a salad cart past with a muttered 'Excuse me'. The other circulated, topping up drinks and dispensing fancy appetizers by the handful.

She reached poolside. An intern from Baptist Medical Center whose girl went to aerobics class with Turrow's wife tried for bourbon and branch. The medic had been lounging in an inflatable 1953 Chevvy parked on the water. As he reached up for the tray, the Chevvy reversed into mid-pool. The man went with a big splash – surfacing with a Rebel yell, holding his glass aloft before taking a swig of chlorinated water. A few people looked and laughed.

Their monthly party was going great guns. The movers and shakers were switched on by each other's high-voltage company, but David Turrow didn't feel like joining in. He had mixed feelings about these gatherings at the best of times, and tonight was anything but the best.

Turrow caught his wife's eye and smiled brightly. Debbie raised her eyebrows in acknowledgment before turning a sleek blonde head back to the owner of a computer publishing house. He was down from Austin for the weekend to discuss spending big promotional bucks, many of which would finish up in Debbie Turrow's business account to support a lifestyle to which it was easy to become accustomed.

The First Assistant DA's eyes flicked to his power-hungry boss and Congressman Elmer Farris, forming a huddle of two beneath a blue lamp that zapped any insect foolish enough to eavesdrop on a doubtless meaningful discussion about their contribution to the better future of mankind. With luck, a frazzled corpse might drop into an iced vodka martini.

Billy Ray Brandon had wangled an invitation and turned up with his old golfing buddy Elmer Farris. They steered him into the den and cross-examined on the Martinez killing. They hadn't come right out with it, but when Brandon wrapped up with a casual 'Sorta nuthin' case I always like to see dealt with quickly and quietly, Dave', Turrow got the DA's drift.

In case he didn't, Congressman Farris had told some rambling joke about a monkey with a cork up its rear end which filled with shit for three months, before it decided to remove the obstruction. The punch line went, 'You shoulda seen that dumb ape's face when it tried to put that goddam cork back.' The two good ol' boys cackled happily, watching him with unblinking reptilian eyes. Turrow resented the pressure, but couldn't ignore these guys.

Now, he was about to receive another uninvited guest. The babysitter fetched him to take a call – which proved to be from Dick Schneider's car phone. The SAPD detective was coming over. Sounded like trouble, but he'd soon know. The grizzled cop was leaving I-10 at Castle Hills, a minute from the house.

Turrow went outside to meet him, putting on a 'this better be good' expression out of habit. The detective may have been impressed, but didn't show it.

'My people have been at that vehicle all day. You better back me when the City starts bellyachin' about overtime. They found human blood and hair samples in the trunk. Ten gets you five it'll match. That Buick was used to dump Martinez after the killin'. Awkward, huh?'

David Turrow stared at the partygoers, who were stampeding in the direction of perfectly charred beef and chicken. Sometimes he longed to be out of this life his ambitions had chosen to pursue – back in New York, behind the counter of his old man's deli like the smart kid working towards college he once was. But the block was torn down and his parents had relocated to a sunshine retirement complex in New Mexico.

'I think you just wrecked my entire future, you sonofa-bitch.'

'Any time, Dave, any time. I'll be in touch. Have yourselves a real nice party, now.'

Lieutenant Schneider turned and slouched back the way he came.

He lay on his cot, but sleep wouldn't return. Eventually, Forsyth called for a car. It was a relief to escape from Headquarters. He didn't hurry the Jaguar through empty, neon-bright streets. The drive to Beth's took ten minutes. Forsyth parked and walked up silent staircases to her studio. Despite a strip of light beneath the door he used his key. Like the last time, she might be in bed.

Inside, he stopped. Mournful blues was playing – Bessie Smith, a favourite when they relaxed together at the end of a day. Beth had company. A tall man sprawled in an armchair. One hand balanced a drink on the chair arm, the other casually tapped in time with the music. Beth sat cross-legged at his feet. She smiled a greeting, but Forsyth was disconcerted. Her guest had sun-bleached hair, a tanned face and powerful body which gave him the look of a professional golfer. Whatever his line, he radiated the assurance of a high achiever in the prime of life. Beth got up, came over and kissed Forsyth's cheek.

'Bob, meet Greg. We're doing a session at the Tower of London on Monday, for *Paris Match*. You've heard me talk about him, we work together a lot. He's one of the best, when he bothers.'

Forsyth looked at the photographer, who was unwinding from his chair.

'The Australian?'

The man's accent answered the question.

'Good to meet you, mate. Greg Browne. I'd like to say that I'm here strictly on business, but that isn't quite true.'

He glanced at Beth before going on.

'I reckon Europe's the only place where you can enjoy a civilized conversation. Look, the last thing I want to do is shove in my paddle where it isn't wanted. We can finish off tomorrow.'

Forsyth shook his head. The Australian was attracted to Beth and he hated the idea. He wanted Browne out – out of the apartment, out of Beth's life – but his reaction was contradictory. He found masochistic pleasure in a civilized reply.

'No, don't let me interrupt. I just dropped by for a quick nightcap, but I've got a busy day tomorrow. I'd better go.'

Turning his back on Beth's puzzled expression, he went. Outside, hating himself, he sat in the car, watching her building. But the photographer didn't emerge. In the end, Forsyth started the car with a savage twist of the key and drove home.

After garaging the Jaguar, he walked through the yard and entered the darkened house. Why this unexpected,

irrational need to own another person? His relationship
with Beth wasn't like that.

He went straight upstairs, unable to summon the energy
to fix a drink, and looked in on his wife. Impossible to discern her familiar features in the indirect illumination from
the landing light. Forsyth felt a surge of tenderness. Just
lately, he'd been treating Alex as a problem. On impulse,
he undressed and slipped into the double bed instead of
going to his own room. She shifted position, but didn't
waken when he stretched out an exploratory hand to touch
her hair.

His hand moved to her back, and he lightly traced the
line of her backbone with the knuckle of his index finger.
She shivered. He pulled her to him, buttocks soft against
his groin. One hand went to her left breast, the other turned
her head. Urgently, he kissed her waking mouth. Her nip-
ple hardened. He couldn't hold back, and she responded
quickly. In two frenzied minutes, they found simultaneous
release.

Forsyth rolled free, ignoring Alex's moan of displeasure.
He lay on his back, staring at a ceiling he couldn't see.
His wife snuggled against him, flinging a warm arm across
his chest. He remembered how fulfilling their lovemaking
used to be. The last time he tried, three months ago, he'd
been pleasantly intoxicated. And an abject failure. That
humiliation, at least, was now expunged.

But he cursed his weakness. Satiated, he couldn't understand the compulsion that had possessed him. Alex spoke
sleepily.

'Bob, was that good for you?'

'You know it was.'

'Me too. I was beginning to think we'd never do it again.
Not like that.'

'Well, we did. Now go to sleep.'

'Guess what? Daddy's coming here for a while. That's
good, isn't it?'

She turned over and obediently fell asleep.

DAY FOUR:

Sunday 8 September

Another day, new possibilities. General Robert Forsyth had overslept, arriving at New Centre Point to find an urgent message waiting in reception. CIA man Donny Sheldon had broken fast. Forsyth went directly to Control. As he arrived, the room filled with the bustling noise of a railway station. The sound issued from a speaker on the command console. The fresh-faced Duty Controller looked up.

'He's arriving in Nottingham. Spent the night near Chalk Farm. Left at six and contacted the US Embassy on a pay-phone. There was a coded exchange and he headed for the station. Must've fixed a meet. Mendlebaum set off for Nottingham shortly afterwards. He's waiting in a house off Castle Boulevard. Brigadier Kyle's flying up there now.'

'Excellent.'

Forsyth was fully revived. Sleep had arrived unexpectedly, just as he became convinced it never would. The speaker spoke.

'Purpose of journey?'

Sheldon had reached a police checkpoint.

'Visiting a sick relative. The mother-in-law.'

Sheldon's reply was weirdly distorted by the implanted transmitter.

'Where's the missus, then?'

'Tucked up in bed with the milkman. Hates her old mum more than I do and it's my bloody turn. Fancy a grape?'

'Not likely, they give me the runs. Okay, chum, rather you than me.'

Control hummed with street noise – car engines, a loud motorcycle, impatient horns. The sounds faded. A large-scale city map was on screen, a red blip indicating their unwitting informant's position. The Duty Controller whispered a comment, as though Sheldon could somehow hear.

'He's cutting through to Castle Boulevard along the canal bank. It's a fair walk to Mendlebaum's safe house.'

Forsyth merely nodded. Sheldon started whistling, stopped. They heard his distorted voice again.

'Anything?'

'One small perch and three gudgeon, but I've only started an hour since.'

The reply was in the flat local accent. Creating mental pictures was fascinating. Forsyth saw brown canal water and the patient fisherman with an array of expensive equipment, spending his Sunday outwitting fish he promptly released.

'Good luck, then.'

'I'll need it, now the sun's on the water.'

Another whisper spoiled the picture.

'The fisherman's one of ours. We got a team in position as soon as we knew where he was heading.'

Traffic noise returned as Sheldon reached Castle Boulevard, but it was ten tense minutes before a bell sounded faintly – long, short, long. The speaker crackled expectantly. A security chain rattled.

'Donald. Upstairs. We can talk there.'

Norman Mendlebaum's greeting was hardly effusive. Muffled footsteps climbed creaking stairs. The listeners waited eagerly for the Judas speaker to start talking.

Sheldon had made his home run, little realizing that Intelligence was sitting on his shoulder like a patient vulture.

The CIA men settled in a drab first-floor living room. A 1930s sideboard leaned against one wall. Foam intestines spilled from an old sofa. A battered armchair and imitation teak coffee table completed the furnishings. It wasn't the sort of place where you'd want to live.

'Why have you broken procedure?'

The CIA Head of Station's Brooklyn voice contained a sharp edge that cut through Sheldon's aggressive intentions. This wasn't the moment to pour out his resentment at being kept in the dark.

Norman Mendlebaum was a round-faced, overweight diplomat with the day's beard already shadowing heavy jowls, but he had presence. Sheldon disliked him, though respecting his professionalism. Defensively, he outlined recent events. When he finished, Head of Station rebuked him.

'That doesn't explain why you used the emergency contact routine. You should've stayed in the Chalk Farm safe house until arrangements to lift you were made. If I've been compromised, Langley will have to pull me too, assuming I'm not expelled first. That would be dandy.'

Sheldon thought hard. His head was beginning to throb. Mendlebaum was right. This visit breached elementary security. The failure to come up with a satisfactory answer rekindled anger.

'Since Minton-Briant was terminated, everything's changed. My network's collapsing. Dozens of contacts have been taken and the rest are running scared. Years of hard work, down the tubes in three goddam days. What am I supposed to do?'

Mendlebaum raised a cautionary finger.

'You're losing it, Donny. Get a grip. That assassination may have been unexpected, but we must still turn it to advantage.'

Sheldon looked curiously at his handler.

'So that little number wasn't down to us? I thought . . .'

'Donny, you're not paid to think. You run an information-gathering network. That's valuable, though there's more to our work than that. The aim has always been a friendly British government, but we've never been talking bullets-and-guns revolution. This isn't some banana republic. Drop a bomb on their PM from a great height? No way.'

He sensed Sheldon's reservations, continuing persuasively. The senior man had an over-developed sense of his own importance.

'We've got sympathizers here. If there's a shake-up at the top, which looks a sure thing, we may come out well. Our friends could advance, move into positions of greater influence. Once supporters in the media are able to start telling the British people the truth, then change becomes inevitable.'

Feeling light-headed and physically nauseous, Sheldon switched off. He'd been lectured on Company policy before. Mendlebaum's peroration rolled on, but he couldn't be bothered to listen. He was a field agent. There was only one way to counter the bad guys, and that was with direct action. Wars weren't won with fancy words.

He turned his attention to a semi-comatose bluebottle which was crawling along the coffee table, wondering if Mendlebaum would still be gabbing on when the fly reached the precipice and had to make a decision.

A jumbled kaleidoscope of half-remembered images crowded into his mind, just beyond identification, analysis, understanding – eager faces bending close, fast questions, hesitant answers, quick instructions, subconscious apprehension. He felt dog-tired, and experienced an intense longing to see the white frame-house on North Waterburt Street where he grew up.

He struck savagely. Shocked by the lightning-fast movement and sharp slap, Mendlebaum stopped talking. Sheldon studied the smeared corpse of his victim, then flicked the fly's remains on to the faded floral-pattern carpet.

The pilot of Vernon Lustbader's Gulfstream V banked the sleek aircraft as they came in over the Welsh coast, affording a panoramic view of towering cliffs pounded by surf. The Vice-Presidential Special Envoy was moved by the rugged spectacle. Wild, lonely places appealed to him. He even forgot that he hated flying. A cheerful English voice boomed through the cabin speaker.

'That's Ramsey Island and St David's Head on your right, with St Bride's Bay beyond. We will now climb through the cloud base to twelve thousand feet, at an airspeed of six hundred knots. ETA at London Northolt eleven hundred hours.'

The aircraft levelled in hazy blue infinity, panoramic Pembrokeshire vanishing beneath cumulus clouds. He watched the plane's shadow dashing across the white floor below, thinking about his meeting with the newly appointed Prime Minister.

If Errol was in cahoots with this Ken Stanley, Lustbader was willing to play the hand, just like the Veep asked. He'd worry about Vice-Presidential knowledge of – and possible involvement in – the murder of a British Prime Minister later.

Brigadier Kyle's helicopter set down beside the boating lake in Nottingham's University Park, far enough from the CIA house to prevent engine noise from carrying. A car was waiting, and an Intelligence lieutenant briefed him as they drove. The Special Intelligence Service unit from Hereford was in place. Team leader Roger Nolan had already finalized plans. City Police had been told of the operation, but ordered to stay away.

After a short drive, the Range Rover went round Abbey Bridge roundabout, under a flyover and into the gravelled rear car park of Dunkirk Fire Station. The SIS assault team had commandeered the crew relaxation room, providing a secure base within a hundred yards of the scruffy terraced property in Cloister Street containing the CIA men.

Captain Nolan was rehearsing his six-man team. A diagram of the target house was pinned up, marked with felt-tip to indicate possible entry points. Kyle greeted the SIS officer.

'Hello, Roger, how's that MG you're restoring? Pre-war TA isn't it?'

He knew many Intelligence personnel and not only remembered names, but also personal snippets which made each feel special when they met again.

'I can't quite match the original paint colour and still need to find a new tonneau cover, but otherwise she's ready to roll.'

'You must give me a ride one day. All set?'

'Ready as we'll ever be.'

The radio monitoring Sheldon's implant microphone was turned down, but it was still possible to hear the CIA men arguing. The assault team stood up, reached for equipment and shuffled round the littered table towards the door. Kyle had a final word.

'Alive, Roger, especially Mendlebaum. Embarrassing if we blow away an innocent cultural attaché.'

Nolan shrugged eloquently and followed his men out. Kyle didn't make the mistake of wishing him luck.

Donald Sheldon stopped contributing. His sixth sense had woken up. Mendlebaum couldn't see the nose in front of his face, let alone smell fear. But he'd never been hunted. That didn't stop him going on like a true zealot.

'We're what Agencyspeak quaintly describes as "humint". Since Gates turned Langley upside down, forty billion dollars a year has been buying Uncle Sam information. That's why you were put in here. You've done your bit, but I'll tell you something else. Gates had a sign right behind his desk, saw it myself. Know what it said? "As a general rule, the easiest way to achieve complete strategic surprise is to commit an act that makes no sense or is even self-destructive."'

He found himself thinking about that. Before he could make much sense of it, Mendlebaum continued eagerly.

'Don't you see? We may not have planned Minton-Briant's killing ourselves, but the effect's the same. We have the advantage of surprise, and it's up to us to make . . .'

Donald Sheldon could never be sure if he heard him say 'the most of it'. The room's twin sash windows shattered, showering glass. Mendlebaum started to get up. Sheldon's hand moved faster than his conscious mind. The revolver liberated from the hospital still contained three rounds. Before his Head of Station was fully upright, the pistol was coming free.

Sheldon registered his chief's shocked expression – open mouth, rolling eyes. He didn't pull the trigger, but somehow the hammer snagged. The gun discharged. Mendlebaum's head jerked as a nickel-jacketed .38 slug entered his forehead at maximum velocity, mushrooming slightly as tissue and bone slowed its onward journey.

The heavy Station Head collapsed, mutilated head rolling against the younger man. Sheldon fought desperately to clear the gun, swing the muzzle on himself. He never got close. Stun grenades went off. Sheldon lost movement in his limbs. Hooded men came fast. Someone was on top of him, pinning him to the sofa.

Sheldon was aware of the revolver being pulled from his

hand, weight lifting from his chest, the thud of a body hitting the floor, smooth plastic against his wrists, clicking ratchets, low voices. All he could think about was Mendlebaum. In life, the man had irritated him intensely. In death, the brash New Yorker was a patriotic American who worked hard for his country.

In the end, they'd been arguing about nothing.

The Gulfstream made a smooth landing, turned and taxied back up the concrete apron. It stopped alongside a low prefabricated building with a World War II look about it. Lustbader's armed protectors were first out, eyes darting around the bleak military airfield.

Two cars were waiting, each with uniformed driver. Beyond the perimeter, traffic was light on Western Avenue, which Lustbader hadn't travelled since the 1970s, when he did an exchange professorship at Oxford University. He went down the steps, flanked by the Secret Service.

The first car's driver explained he would take them to Downing Street. In the interests of low profile, there would be no escort. However, the vehicles were armoured. Lustbader thanked him and climbed into the Jaguar's comfortable back seat. One of his guardians joined him, the other got in up front. The second vehicle contained four people – British security, decoys to confuse would-be assailants or both.

As they drove out of the airfield, he noted that the aircraft guarding the gate was a Tornado. In his day, it had been a Supermarine Spitfire – or was it a Hawker Hurricane? Perhaps he'd never known, but registered a Battle of Britain-style fighter in passing.

He became lost in returning memories. He'd spent time in England, loved the place. Dinner parties. Challenging conversation. Walking beside the River Isis. That wonderfully relaxed social confidence only European countries seemed able to achieve. Whatever happened to all those people he'd lost touch with?

He'd even been to Number 10 before, when Maggie's love affair with Ronnie was at its most passionate. Lustbader attended a gathering of American academics, businessmen and freeloaders of the international influence circuit, convened to advise the Prime Minister on the intransigent US attitude to stalled GATT talks.

His own advice had been limited. The PM's bluff press secretary introduced Lustbader. His twinsetted mistress produced a charming smile and a question.

'Professor Lustbader, what does your country really have to fear from European farmers?'

Lustbader's contribution had not been impressive, because he paused to select meaningful words. Before he chose them, the Iron Lady began a forty-five-second lecture on encouraging free markets worldwide, the desirability of level playing fields and benefits of unfettered trade between great nations. She concluded with a firm handshake and a crisp 'Most interesting, Professor', before sweeping off to the next expert.

They'd arrived. As the Jaguar turned into Downing Street, Lustbader recalled the encounter with self-deprecating amusement. Hardly his finest hour. Perhaps this time would be different. Perhaps not.

Nothing had changed. An identical policeman reached over to knock twice as his car stopped by the same black front door. The entrance hall was as he remembered. Now as then he was surprised that there was no overt security check, and that he was allowed to carry his briefcase into the building unopened.

But this time there was no photographer waiting to pose him in front of the marble mantle with the PM. A small, overweight man with centre-parted hair bustled forward. He took Lustbader's free hand with both of his.

'Harry Higgins, Cabinet Secretary. Welcome to London. Perhaps your chaps would be kind enough to surrender their weapons. We'll look after them for you. The men, I mean. The PM is waiting and I'll take you up. He's most interested in what you have to say.'

The Vice-Presidential special envoy grinned.

'Don't bet on it, buddy.'

The neat little political bureaucrat managed to look both startled and alarmed. Lustbader lowered his voice and dropped a friendly hand on Higgins' pinstriped arm, which stiffened at un-British contact.

'I meant no disrespect. But the last person who said those

words to me in this building wasn't the least bit interested
in what I had to say. Okay, Mr Secretary, take me to your
leader.'

Ken Stanley had been notified that the special envoy's car
was arriving. The PM waited a few moments before going
down. He timed his descent from the private apartment
to perfection, coming into the first-floor drawing room as
Lustbader sat down on one of two matching velvet sofas.

The American was forced to stand up again to shake
hands. It was the sort of technique for asserting superiority
politicians adopt without thinking. As Lustbader held the
handshake, something about the set of his mouth suggested he'd seen through the gambit and was amused. He
released Stanley's hand and spoke easily.

'Prime Minister. I must congratulate you on your appointment and thank you on behalf of Vice-President Tidyman
for agreeing to meet with me at such a difficult time.'

'Sit down, Vernon, there was no need to get up. And
forget the Prime Minister crap. Ken will do nicely. Harry
will take notes. Neither of us wants any misunderstand-
ing, I'm sure.'

They sat down – Stanley and Lustbader facing one another,
Higgins using an upright chair. Stanley had intended to
occupy the higher chair, but having taken the American's
measure decided the ploy would be wasted. The Cabinet
Secretary placed a small recorder on the low table. A green
light indicated spools were turning, capturing conversation.
Stanley raised eyebrows.

'No problem with the recorder, I hope?'

Lustbader produced a miniature Sony from his briefcase
and set the machine beside its twin.

'Thought you'd never ask. This is purely an informal
exploratory meeting, nothing from us in writing. But I
am empowered by the Vice-President to make suggestions
which may be of interest to your government.'

Ken Stanley let the bait lie. Instead, Higgins asked a
question which – despite fancy packaging – was tough and
direct.

'Forgive me, Special Envoy, but are we to assume Vice-
President Tidyman is acting with the full knowledge and

approval of the President, and if so can you expect us to consider any proposition from an administration with only months to run?'

Stanley watched Lustbader's reaction closely. His first impression was confirmed. The man was a damn good operator, weather-beaten face betraying nothing.

'As you know, the President has been unwell for some time. Vice-President Tidyman is in day-to-day charge. You may assume this approach carries the full weight of the US government. In addition, it is our strong belief that our presidential campaign will be successful.'

Higgins probed a nerve.

'But surely the opinion polls tell a different story. Patrick Stark is leading by the proverbial street. Where would that leave us, if we accepted anything offered by your man?'

Ken Stanley made a mental note not to underestimate the Cabinet Secretary. He might seem timid, but Harry's mind was scalpel-keen. The special envoy was unfazed.

'Please believe there are sound reasons for assuming that Errol Tidyman will become President. We can deliver.'

The pleasant smile that followed this bland statement was too much. Aware that his face was flushing, but not caring that undiplomatic anger was showing, Ken Stanley stared into the American's washed-out blue eyes. They met his unflinchingly.

'This offer – would it include substantial loan guarantees, access to technology needed to expand our Atlantic oilfields, covert financial support if we agree to compensate American companies whose assets were taken into social ownership, even an air base or two made available to the US Air Force as evidence of resumed friendship, that sort of thing?'

Lustbader's smile broadened.

'You've peeked at my script, Ken. So, can we cut a deal? No need to rush, but our great nations used to be best friends, could find it mutually beneficial to become so again.'

Ken Stanley got up, looking down at the self-confident American. The high ground seemed a good place to be.

'Tidyman is staring at election defeat. Nobody can blame him for chasing a headline foreign policy deal which might swing enough voters to put him into the White House. It's the kind of idea that might occur to any politician with his back to the wall. But when did this splendid idea come to the Vice-President, *when*?'

The Premier regained his composure. The white-haired American had the decency to look uncomfortable. Ken Stanley went on softly.

'Derek Minton-Briant's murder required resources beyond the reach of any internal group. An American connection was suspected immediately. Now you tell me Tidyman's running the US government, Tidyman's going to win the Presidency despite trailing in the polls. And this man sends you over with a tawdry offer before our PM is decently buried. Derek was a friend and colleague, and I have nothing to discuss with you.'

Vernon Lustbader got up, courteous to the end. He switched off his recorder and extended a hand.

'I'm sorry you feel that way, Prime Minister, though not surprised. Believe me when I say nothing I would have proposed today could impact on the presidential election. Should you reconsider, you know how to reach me. The Vice-President wants to rebuild bridges, hopes new men might come up with new ideas to benefit both our countries. Errol Tidyman is a true visionary, gentlemen.'

Stanley shook the hand, replying more in sorrow than anger.

'Be that as it may, go while the going's good, Vernon.'

Ken Stanley walked from the room. As he went, a dark thought came unbidden. The idea that Vice-President Tidyman might have engineered Derek's death to win a massive electoral prize was convincing. But it was also an *obvious* proposition, now he'd sent his man to make such an overt pitch.

And Ken Stanley always mistrusted the obvious.

Mary-Jo MacInnes slept in. She didn't expect to make progress until official types were back at their desks the next morning. After showering, she dressed in jeans and loose shirt. She phoned Room Service for coffee and Danish, found her purse and put it on the writing table.

Five minutes later, there was a tap at the door. She let in the waiter – a hairless old guy with a face Texas sun had turned into a moonscape of deep lines. She pointed to the table.

'Set it down there.'

He did, pouring coffee from an insulated flask. Mary-Jo handed him two ones. She liked reading people and had him pegged as a single man – divorced or widowed. Not stupid, not bright. Lonely, with the hotel his real home and the staff his only family. Shit, he probably had eight kids in the barrio and hated his menial job.

'I bet you never talk to strange women, right?'

Mary-Jo counted out five twenties, arranging them in a fan on the writing table. The man's eyes followed every move and stayed on the money. But he was cautious.

'Ma'am?'

'You can at least tell me your name.'

She nudged the last bill into position with a bitten fingernail. The waiter wasn't sure where this was leading, but a hundred dollars that wouldn't have to be shared was tempting. He thawed a little.

'I guess there's no harm in that. I'm Walter, and I've worked here in the hotel since the day it opened.'

Translation – I'm not saying anything that might cost me my job. Mary-Jo wasn't deterred. Just as some men have instinctive understanding of the pitch most likely to tumble the sexual defences of women, so Mary-Jo could assess the persona needed to open up an information source. She gave him a little-girl-lost-I-could-be-your-daughter smile.

'Hey, the last thing I want is to get you into trouble. But maybe you can help me solve a problem. So I'm a reporter, but anything we discuss is off the record. No attribution, no comebacks. Believe me, nobody will ever know you said a word.'

His eyes strayed back to the money. He wanted to believe her. She used an urgent we're-both-people-of-the-world tone.

'You can guess what this is about, right?'

The man smoothed non-existent hair and responded reluctantly.

'Would it be Maria, Maria Martinez?'

She switched to her I-buy-you-sell voice.

'That's it, Walter. Did you know her well?'

'Sure, since she came here nine, ten months back we been friends. Nobody guessed she was, well, a wetback. Management squared that with the cops and Immigration. She had papers, a fake security service number. Was gonna marry a film producer when she put together a stake which took her to Hollywood. They're all the same, these young girls, heads fulla dreams. She woulda finished up with six kids in a crummy apartment in East LA same as all the rest. But I liked her.'

'Remember the night she was killed?'

'Days and nights are pretty much the same round here. That was nothing special as I recall, 'cept we was run off our feet 'cause that Pat Stark was in the hotel with his people. Don't remember seeing Maria. But she came on at six, when I finish, so I often didn't run into her unless we met up in the locker room.'

'But you've talked about that night since, with the guys?'

Walter found the carpet merited close attention. He mumbled a reply.

'Hey, I ain't about to dish the dirt on the kid or anyone else. More than my job's worth.'

There *was* something. Mary-Jo didn't press, knowing one more probing question would cause him to clam up.

'Nobody's asking you to get anyone into trouble, Walter. Just tell me who was working with Maria that night.'

He relaxed. The ordeal was coming to an end.

'Candy Paretsky, I guess.'

'She still here?'

'Sure.'

'Still on nights?'

'Comes on at six, same as always.'

Mary-Jo picked up the bills and finalized the deal.

'Okay, Walter, here's what we do. Take this hundred, and if you happen to run into Candy this evening at shift change, mention I'd like a private discussion. After we've talked there's two hundred in it for her and another hundred for you.'

'Hell, I don't know. Maybe I'll see what I can do. None of this goes any further?'

'Nope.'

He snatched the money and ran, almost slamming the

door in his eagerness to get away. Mary-Jo MacInnes contemplated the swinging *DO NOT DISTURB* sign on the inside knob. She had a notion she'd be disturbing some big names before this was over.

As the Nottingham operation wound down, Intelligence Control went quiet. When the switchboard rang through, the Duty Controller was pleased to have something to do.

'An Arthur Wheatley from British Aerospace calling for the Deputy Head. Brigadier Kyle left instructions that he should be put through to him personally. Please advise.'

'He's flying back from Nottingham. I'll take the call.'

There was a click as the connection was made.

'How can we help, Mr Wheatley?'

'Brigadier Kyle?'

'He's not in the building. Can I take a message?'

The reply was irascible.

'I've just spent my Sunday morning at the office, doing research at his request. He said I could reach him at any time. Well, I've come up with important information which may have a direct bearing on the Prime Minister's assassination.'

He was dying to tell someone his secret.

'Your call is logged, sir. I'm sure the Brigadier will get back to you as soon as possible. There's nothing else?'

He waited. Most people were lousy at keeping secrets and couldn't wait to tell someone, anyone. He wasn't wrong.

'I can assure you Kyle will want to talk with me. He wants a missing Bluebird, I've found one. That's all I'm prepared to say.'

The ambitious Intelligence officer reacted fast.

'I can transfer you to Brigadier Kyle's helicopter. Please hold.'

He punched buttons, eager fingers hitting too many keys. He cleared and tried again. This time, the chopper answered immediately.

'Duty Controller for Brigadier Kyle. I have an Arthur Wheatley from British Aerospace. Claims to have a line on the Bluebird aircraft used for the assassination. Will the Brigadier speak to him?'

Kyle's deep voice came in, unmistakable despite radio crackle.

'I heard that on my headset. Put him through.'

No chance of a fumble, there was only one button to hit. His connection was broken. Sixty seconds later, Kyle's voice was back.

'We're rerouting to BA at Weybridge. Inform General Forsyth and have a team waiting to meet me. ETA twenty-nine minutes. Well done.'

The Controller congratulated himself for persevering with the tiresome Wheatley. Kyle was a perfectionist. He might be a hard bastard, but a simple 'well done' did the recipient's prospects no harm at all.

Vernon Lustbader was hardly surprised by his reception, despite Tidyman's assurance that important wheels had been lubricated. Whatever the Vice-President had set up, a deal with the new Prime Minister of Great Britain wasn't it.

The cars swept on to airfield concrete, stopping beside the Gulfstream. Seconds later, as Lustbader climbed aboard, the engines started and the aircraft began to vibrate. Putting his briefcase on the table, he settled into a wide seat, hating a body that dreaded flight.

'Your case should be stowed overhead during take-off. Allow me.'

Lustbader glanced miserably at the cabin attendant as he swung up the polished leather briefcase. A typical example of the breed – tall, good-looking, tanned, totally at ease in a metal box that was about to fling itself from *terra firma* into the thinnest of air. He sat down opposite, smiled and fixed intent grey eyes on Lustbader.

'I see you subscribe to the oft-stated view that if God intended us to fly, he would have given us wings. But the human race has done all sorts of things which might be regarded as contrary to the laws of nature. We must live with the consequences as best we can.'

Pre-flight nerves forgotten, Lustbader shifted his mind into drive. This was no ordinary crew member. He answered the smile with a quiet question.

'You are?'

'Godfrey Cornwell, Home Secretary. I expect you've read all sorts of nasty things about me in newspapers, or digests prepared by your admirable NSA. My people here delayed take-off so we could have a word. Pity to miss the opportunity, as you happen to be passing. I trust your meeting with the PM went well?'

Lustbader was a good judge of people. Even as he warmed to this friendly character, alarm bells rang. The man who faced him was one of those dangerous animals who part old ladies from life savings. He hoped this perception didn't show.

'Does Prime Minister Stanley know you're here?'

The friendliness left the handsome Brit's face and Lustbader knew that he, too, had been rumbled.

'You and Stanley are playing a dangerous game, Mr Special Envoy. Or Tidyman and Stanley are, if you're just the mouthpiece. We won't jump back into bed with America just because you whistle. Tell your man that this thing will blow up in his face if he messes with us.'

He was tough, but Lustbader was no mean operator himself.

'That's it?'

The Home Secretary got up.

'I don't know whether you people were involved in Minton-Briant's murder, or are simply exploiting the situation. Either way, back off. If this gets out of hand, your black master will be sorry. I'd like to say have a nice flight, but there are thunderstorms on your route. I checked. You could be in for a rough ride.'

The tall man departed. Seconds later, the engine note deepened and the Gulfstream started rolling.

General Forsyth had a problem. George had refused to return calls since the previous evening's firefight on the Windsor Road. The Prince Regent had bruised a thumb and his dignity, diving to the floor when the first shot was fired at his bullet-proof Roller. As a result of this trauma, he felt entitled to overlook his loyalty payment from Intelligence.

Unfortunately, George's inflated assessment of his worth was accurate. With conflicting interests in delicate balance, his nominal role as Head of State might take on an importance far beyond that permitted by Derek Minton-Briant. Though using the Prince Regent's signature to give legal gloss, the PM had treated him like an office boy. Now, the decadent aristocrat was perfectly positioned to sell himself to the highest bidder. Forsyth couldn't allow that. He needed George's undivided support should the need arise.

The meeting between American special envoy and Premier had changed Forsyth's attitude. It looked as though the CIA was uninvolved in Minton-Briant's murder, if Mendlebaum was to be believed. Forsyth did believe him. There was no reason to lie to Sheldon, and further confirmation was provided by the enthusiasm with which the late CIA executive had argued for opportunist exploitation of the unexpected assassination.

But that didn't let the Americans off the hook. Forsyth's suspicions of a tie-up between Vice-President Errol Tidyman and PM Ken Stanley had been strengthened. There was no easy alternative to his pact with Stanley, but the Intelligence general was wondering if he'd made a misjudgment, despite Chandler's encouragement. Perhaps his long-time mentor was losing his touch.

Forsyth reluctantly picked up the phone. There *was* a way of forcing the Prince Regent into the Intelligence camp – an option that scarcely bore thinking about. But now there was little choice.

A four-man plain-clothes team was waiting beside the helipad at BA's Weybridge factory. Brigadier Anderson Kyle had seen their car draw up as the chopper landed. The leader came forward to greet him. Kyle took the initiative.

'Lieutenant Dexter, isn't it, or have you made captain? Sorry to drag you out on a Sunday, Phil.'

They'd never met, but Kyle read personnel files and possessed photographic recall. He knew Dexter had recently been promoted, but had no wish to make him feel he'd attracted attention.

'Captain, sir.'

As usual, the ability to address one officer amongst hundreds by name impressed the subject. The youngster's loyalty had already been reinforced. Ever economical, Kyle decided not to mention the wife, Esther, or first-born child. Just as well. He was slipping – the infant's sex and name escaped him.

'Detail two men to return to London in my helicopter. There's a prisoner on board for HQ, Donny Sheldon. Tell them to watch him, this is one tricky character. Lose him and their nuts are in the cracker. When they've handed him over they can ride back in the chopper. I want it here. Then come with me and bring your last man. We need a word with the General Manager.'

'Arthur Wheatley, sir. Took the liberty of dropping by his office as we came in. He's waiting there until you arrive. Pompous chap, but he seemed excited.'

Three minutes later, they arrived at the sprawling plant's admin block. Leaving their spare man at the front desk, Kyle and Dexter took the lift to the top floor of the silent building. Wheatley was ensconced behind a door labelled *VICTOR COPPEL, MANAGING DIRECTOR*.

A scrawny man jumped from behind a large desk as they walked in. He was dressed in a three-piece suit, and his balding head was shiny with sweat. The desktop was bare, apart from two telephones, a leather blotter and onyx pen set. He held out a damp hand.

'Brigadier Kyle? Arthur Wheatley, General Manager. My boss has done a vanishing act, so I'm in charge. Well, he's sick, actually.'

Ignoring the hand, Kyle took the comfortable visitor's chair. Dexter remained standing. Kyle spoke sharply.

'Spit it out.'

Thoughts chased across Wheatley's face – apprehension that his information would be worthless, desire to be somewhere else doing whatever he normally did on Sunday afternoons. His face paled beneath the gleaming pate and the voice became apologetic.

'I hope I was right to contact you, but I wasn't sure I mentioned the Bluebird you people have. I mean, I know you know about it, but I've been through the records and it's the only aircraft unaccounted for in the proper way. Not that I'm suggesting that there's anything improper about the powers that be borrowing a plane from us. But . . .'

'What Bluebird?'

Colour flooded back into Wheatley's face. He was out of jail.

'The new one collected six weeks ago, unregistered off the line. For evaluation. Anti-drug night surveillance, according to the rumours.'

'You said every single aircraft must be registered, without exception.'

'Not this one. My boss talked to the inspector and he cleared the plane for removal without a certificate. I thought that was irregular, but when I asked Coppel for details he told me to shut up. National security. He never listens to anything I say.'

Kyle didn't bother to ask why Wheatley had failed to mention the irregularity before. That would come later.

'Who exactly organized this?'

'Coppel wasn't forthcoming. "Bloody government" was all he said. But he wouldn't break rules. The release order had to be official. After initial notification, the pilot turned up with a docket. Coppel looked up the code and checked back to the authorization number. Normally he'd have his secretary do that. Afterwards he locked the paperwork in the safe. Saw him myself.'

Wheatley gestured at a framed oil of Concorde in flight. Kyle gestured at Dexter. The young officer went to the picture and swung it aside, revealing a recessed grey steel door with central black dial. Kyle turned back to Wheatley.

'Open up. We may as well see this mysterious paperwork.'

Wheatley intertwined thin fingers.

'Coppel's the only one with the combination.'

'Then get on the phone and tell him to come over.'

Kyle's voice became so reasonable that Wheatley's anxiety turned to panic.

'I've been trying to get him all week, including today. He must have gone away to recuperate.'

The Intelligence brigadier stood up, towering over the General Manager.

'Give Coppel's address to Captain Dexter. Phil, get over there and check the place. Wheatley, out of here, but don't go far. Is one of these an outside line?'

Wheatley pointed at the red phone and ran, addressing them over his shoulder.

'Dial nine. I'll get that home address. He lives close by.'

Kyle moved round and sat in the swivel chair behind the elusive MD's desk. In every investigation, you get a break. This, for the world to see, was it.

Beth Highsmith was enjoying a lazy day. Work was a stressful round of air travel, same-again hotels, limos with tinted windows, catwalks, sweltering studios, rapid clothes changes, bitchy colleagues, people whose favourite word was 'darling', temperamental photographers – and men who knew they were God's gift to women in general and herself in particular.

Not that she was complaining. Modelling was what she did. She spent a lot of time on the road, but regarded London as home, returning to her Chelsea studio whenever possible.

She could afford to start thinking about the rest of her life. If she kept working, it was because retirement would pose questions to which there were no easy answers. The irony was not lost on her. Beth valued money because it purchased freedom – but freedom to do what?

There was Bob Forsyth. She couldn't say she loved him, because men had discovered her too early in life. So she built an inner citadel to protect her emotions. But she cared passionately for her lover. The relationship underpinned an otherwise rootless lifestyle. He in turn seemed deeply involved, taking her for the person she was rather than a wall trophy for his masculine den.

Yet she felt the relationship would suffer if she made herself fully available. He would have to consider parting from his wife, to the detriment of a career that meant everything. If he did that for her, he would brood. Worse, what if she forced a decision and he jumped the other way?

The telephone rang. She put down the Zola novel she hadn't been reading. The cover picture of a ragged urchin pushing a coal-laden handcart reminded her that all problems were relative – hers relatively minor. The answerphone cut in, asking the caller to leave a message after the tone. He did.

'Beth, it's me. I want to apologize for being so rude last night. We're under pressure here, but that isn't your problem. Sorry. I also need a big favour. It's important, or I wouldn't ask.'

She picked up the phone, happy to hear his decisive voice. Most people were uneasy when they got a robot. Not him – he treated it like any other subordinate.

'I was just thinking about you, us. So what's this huge favour?'

Silence. She sensed discomfort, had to assist.

'Bob?'

'This sounds awful. For reasons I won't go into, I must get an armlock on our wretched Prince Regent. You know he fancies you. Would you consider inviting him for a meal at your place? He doesn't know about us, but once you've wound him up, I'll hint that I might use my influence to advance his cause – threaten you with official hassle if you don't play footsie with him, that sort of thing.'

He stopped, embarrassed. Beth was pleased he'd asked for help – normally his work was a taboo subject. The George thing was unpleasant, but she was used to handling repulsive men.

'Sure, why not? As long as I'm not expected to sleep with the rat.'

That shocked him, was meant to.

'Christ! I'm not the jealous type, but the thought of you in bed with George makes my flesh crawl. No, I just want you to lead him on a little, get him panting with desire.'

'Shouldn't be difficult for a girl of my undoubted experience. What's the plan?'

'Give him a call, ask him round for supper. His self-esteem is so overdeveloped he won't even wonder why a girl like you would go near him. I'm sure he'll play. Can you make it tomorrow night? Time's short.'

'No problem, assuming he's interested. I've got a session with Greg in the morning but should be through by one, two at the latest. I'll give our Prinnie a call and let you know if he falls for it. But I expect you to thank me for this personally.'

'My pleasure. Can't make tonight, but how about tomorrow, late, to make sure he's safely off the premises?'

'Fine, though I hardly think I'll need rescuing. Where can I reach you?'

'At the office. Use the private line. And Beth, thanks again.'

He gave her George's number and hung up. She put up her knees and hugged her legs, pleased to be helping Bob with his precious work. He never stopped. Unthinkable to expect him to be any other way, because without work he would be another, lesser person.

As she keyed George's code, Beth Highsmith was smiling. She was a past mistress at steering the male ego in directions of her choosing.

While he waited for Beth Highsmith's return call, General Forsyth thought about Tidyman and Stanley. Not that he expected to alter his conclusions – but it was better than brooding about the way he was using a woman he needed more than he cared to admit. But emotion was a luxury. This was a dirty war and Intelligence wouldn't be trampled. The organization was his inheritance, and he intended to enjoy the legacy.

After five minutes, she came through. The mischievous lilt in her voice reassured him – Beth was not the least disturbed by what she had to do. Yet.

'Ratty's out, but I spoke to his man, who'll relay my invitation at the first opportunity. I suggested an intimate dinner at my place tomorrow night, *à deux*. He'll go for it. I know the type. Assumes anything in a skirt becomes orgasmic at the thought of his less-than-perfect body.'

Forsyth kept his reply brief, hoping she wouldn't divine his doubts.

'Be careful. George is a nasty piece of work. If he touches a hair on your head I'll kill him.'

'I can handle it. Which you believe, or you wouldn't have asked. By the time I've given him the full production number he'll want me so much it'll hurt. Should eat out of your hand if you promise to murmur a favourable word in my receptive ear.'

She left him with a giggle. For a moment, he thought about cancelling the arrangement. Perhaps the price was too high, even for the dirtiest of wars. Before he could make up his mind, the other phone went. It was Andy Kyle, sounding pleased with life.

'I know I'm supposed to be there, but I'm at British Aerospace in Weybridge instead. Looks as though that Bluebird came from here. Spirited out using a clearance which must have come right from the top. Can't get details until we open a safe and check the paperwork.'

Forsyth cheered up.

'The plane's important, but don't spend more time there than you have to. If you can delegate, get back here. We need to talk. Sensitive stuff best discussed in person.'

'I'll be there as soon as possible. Your information and my investigation may be pointing in the same direction. Must go.'

Forsyth didn't put down the phone. Instead, he used it to contact the Duty Controller – calling for the surveillance reports on US Vice-Presidential Envoy Vernon Lustbader. It turned out that Intelligence watchers had been running across one another all day as their targets came together.

Lustbader had recently flown out after having face-to-face discussions with both Ken Stanley and – in a surprise development – the ubiquitous Godfrey Cornwell, who had sneaked on to the American's aircraft for a few moments at Northolt.

A rummage squad arrived as he finished his telephone conversation with General Forsyth. Not bad for a Sunday, particularly as the nine-person team included a civilian locksmith. Without saying anything, Kyle pointed. The blue-overalled specialist unpacked tools and went to work on Coppel's safe, lips pursing in a manner that suggested that opening the box would be a major achievement. Kyle detailed the others to set up an incident room in the staff canteen, start on the plant's records and set up communications links.

As they departed, Captain Dexter radioed through. No sign of life at Coppel's house and a scatter of mail seen through the letterbox suggested the occupants had been absent for a while. Kyle told him to break in and search the place.

Wheatley came into the office without knocking, towing a tall man in casual clothes. Now he'd got the taste, there was no subduing the General Manager's desire to help.

He introduced his companion, simultaneously slipping a stiletto between his shoulder blades.

'Eric Strong, our inspector. I took the liberty of phoning him and telling him to come over. Thought you'd want some answers. He's the one who released that Bluebird without certification.'

Kyle preferred to form his own opinion of Strong. Not a bad name – mid-thirties, over-long sandy hair, open face, confident presence. Altogether a more appealing prospect than the shifty Wheatley, whom Kyle dismissed without enthusiasm.

'Go back and help my people dismantle your building. I'm Brigadier Kyle from Intelligence, Eric. You've probably gathered we're looking into the Bluebird removed from this plant by official order about six weeks ago. Can you help? Take off your coat and sit down.'

A moment of confusion followed, as the locksmith knocked off the safe's dial with a cold chisel. Wheatley reluctantly backed out. Strong removed a small pocketbook, before hanging his rumpled jacket over the visitor's chair and sitting down. He opened the book.

'Made contemporaneous notes in my personal log. This had comeback written all over it. A priority signal came through to Coppel on July twenty-two, ordering the release of a new Bluebird. A pilot would call within one week to collect the plane. Drug surveillance was mentioned and the aircraft was to go out unregistered. Typical hush-hush drama.'

Kyle butted in to clarify a point.

'You said typical. This has happened before?'

Strong shook his head impatiently.

'No, I meant typical of the way our faceless masters issue instructions without explanation, expecting them to be carried out without question. No offence.'

Kyle was beginning to like Strong.

'None taken. I know the feeling. This order, can you remember the authorization code?'

'Sorry. I only know it was on the priority list in the Standing Order Book. Execute standing on your head with your feet in a full chamberpot – something like that. Coppel can tell you more. He confirmed the initial instruction, so he must have spoken to someone in authority. He also checked the pilot's paperwork upon arrival.'

'The plane was collected when?'

Strong consulted his log.

'Four days later, Friday July twenty-six, about five in the afternoon when most people had left for the weekend. I watched it go. I was in number-four hangar checking an engine rebuild when Coppel arrived with the pilot in a company jeep. They spent a few minutes going over the Bluebird's controls, then up and away it went.'

'You saw the pilot?'

'Short, fiftyish, good head of dark brown hair. I'd recognize him again.'

The handset on the desk bleeped, interrupting the inspector. Kyle thumbed the receive button. Dexter's voice was taut.

'You'll want to see this. Mulberry Cottage – right out of the main gate, half a mile along Old Chertsey Road on the right. Yew hedge with a topiary pheasant on top.'

'On my way.'

Kyle turned to Strong.

'You almost certainly saw the man and machine responsible for the Prime Minister's assassination. If you go to the staff room you'll find one of my men has an E-fit machine. Try and put together a good likeness of the pilot, then someone will take a statement. Thanks for your help. Please don't mention our conversation to anyone. Especially Wheatley.

As they got up, Kyle looked at the locksmith.

'How long?'

The man essayed a doubtful expression, but only succeeded in looking smug.

'Five minutes. The safe that beats me hasn't been invented.'

'When it's open you can go. Don't look inside. Forget anything you've heard in this room, or you lose your security clearance and the work that goes with it.'

After introducing Strong to the E-fit operator, Kyle sent a man to watch the locksmith. If the safe contained information that identified Minton-Briant's killer, he didn't want hired help discussing the details over a pint.

Lieutenant Dick Schneider owned a white-painted frame-

house on Adams, in the tree-shaded downtown triangle
formed by South Alamo, St Mary's and the San Antonio
River. When he bought the place more than thirty years
before, the neighbourhood had been charming but run-
down. Now, it was merely charming.

Back then, Patrolman Schneider and his new wife were
country kids down to the big city – excited by his appointment to SAPD, glad to be away from the moribund pace
of Hill Country life, ready to enjoy bright lights. After two
months in a one-bedroom walk-up, they saw the house on
Adams.

No matter that paint was peeling, shingles were missing
and several windows lacked glass. A stand of handsome
trees shaded the yard, birds flitted about and there was
room for little Schneiders. They looked at each other before
the realtor showed them around and put in an offer they
could barely afford.

Over time, they fixed the place up. But children never
happened, and now Karen was gone. Schneider felt like a
dry pea in an empty jar. Still, despite offers that would have
returned their investment twentyfold, he stayed put. He
didn't care to dispose of a lifetime's accumulated artifacts,
or abandon all the memories contained within weather-
boarded walls. He occasionally put spare space to good
use, accommodating a young colleague until the rookie
got properly settled.

Most weekends he went back to a simple cabin beside a
clean river on fifty of several thousand family acres near
Fredericksburg which brother Tom and two nephews still
ranched. This weekend was different. There were good reasons for staying in town. Schneider sat in a wicker chair
on the porch, eating a chilled peach from the paper sack
he'd brought back the previous Sunday, a gift from his
sister-in-law.

He was thinking about a pretty Mexican girl who would
never enjoy afternoon sun patterning through leaves, the
texture of fresh peach skin, the sweet taste of life. A comment his father once made said it all. He must have been
eight years old, and wanted to go swimming instead of working the orchard. Pa refused permission. When Schneider
argued, the old man swung him up on to a half-loaded

trailer and made the remark he'd never forgotten: 'There's plenty in the cemetery who'd be only too pleased to trade places with you, son. Finish up your chores then we'll get on down to the creek. Tommy too, if he wants to come. A dollar for the first one to the other side.'

Being two years older, Tom won easily, but Pa gave him a dollar anyway, for coming second. Schneider still had that silver coin tucked away in his bureau.

He flipped the peach stone at a basket on the corner of the porch, missing by a foot. He left it, wiping sticky fingers on his pants. Karen would've killed him for either lapse, but she wasn't around and he missed her like hell. It had been four years, but he still looked up, expecting her to walk around the corner.

He was about to retrieve the stone when an SAPD motorcycle stopped by the gate. It looked like an all-American bike, but was Japanese. He went to meet the patrolman, who handed him an envelope.

'Final forensic report on that vehicle examination, sir.'

'Thanks, Billy. Go get 'em, boy.'

Schneider watched the Honda out of sight before returning to the porch. He suspected the brown package would wreck his Sunday. In the end, he slit the flap with his SOG lock-knife. Japanese, because Japs made the best steel. Everyone knew that.

The tiny bloodstains and hair samples found in the trunk of Pat Stark's campaign Buick had come from the corpse of the woman known as Maria Martinez.

Mulberry Cottage was an ancient dwelling which must have witnessed many domestic dramas since its cruck-frame oak skeleton was erected overnight on common land, thus preventing the authorities from ordering its removal. A small, long-ago victory for have-nots in the timeless struggle with the haves.

The thatch-capped white house hid behind a trim hedge. Late-flowering pink roses climbed the porch on to the roof. As Kyle drove up, Dexter came forward from the front door.

'Upstairs.'

He led on through a beamed living room, furnished

with button-back leather and antique pine. Horse brasses
gleamed from the brick chimney breast and watercolours
decorated white walls. Photographs adorned a sideboard –
a boy and girl at various ages up to their early twenties.
The stairs were behind a narrow door in the corner.

'At the end of the landing, sir.'

Kyle ducked, climbed the dog-leg staircase and walked
along to an open door. Dexter's man stood beside a curtained four-poster bed. An odour of corruption tainted
musty air. The captain came into the room behind him.

'Central heating's been on. Show him, Sergeant.'

The man pulled aside bed hangings, nose wrinkling in
distaste. Kyle walked round and looked down at mortal
remains. The woman was on the far side of the bed, buried
beneath the bedspread, the top of a blue-rinsed head visible. The coverlet did not conceal the man's face. He lay on
his back – bloodless flesh fallen in upon itself, eye sockets
filled with a moving mass of tiny maggots. There was a bullet
wound in the centre of his forehead. Kyle decided against
looking at the woman.

'You haven't touched anything?'

Dexter shook his head. It was impossible to read the
officer's thoughts, but his complexion had paled. Kyle continued briskly.

'I'm dumping the case in your lap. You won't find much.
These bastards are real pros. I'll keep track of the investigation through normal channels, but call me if anything
comes up.'

Slightly disconcerted, Dexter nodded. He recovered quickly,
voicing a firm opinion.

'They were shot in this room, yet there's no sign of forced
entry. Single head shots. Neat and professional, as you say.'

'This *is* Victor Coppel?'

'His works pass is on the dressing table.'

'Bang goes a star witness. Have Wheatley identify the
bodies, which should round off his day nicely. I'll go back
and pick up any papers from the safe, then on to London.'

The investigation was in competent hands, though Kyle
was certain they'd come up empty.

Prime Minister and Cabinet Secretary sat silently, one pondering his complex situation, the other waiting anxiously. Despite the burden of expectation, Ken Stanley was unable to respond.

The meeting with Lustbader had been a mistake. His keen political instincts had been overridden by undue confidence – engendered by new-found authority, stimulated by curiosity concerning Vice-President Tidyman's overture. The risk seemed worthwhile, because he needed to know. Now he felt sure he did, knowledge brought no comfort.

The Prime Minister had begun to appreciate the fragility of his position. Understand the chastening fact that he was a pawn rather than the most powerful piece on the board – liable to sacrifice as a subtle game moved to its cleverly planned climax. Ken Stanley straightened.

'Well, Harry, what did you make of our urbane American friend?'

Higgins had also used the long silence to think.

'The Americans are in this, Prime Minister, or at least Tidyman is. The President's sick, and an active Vice-President has lots of clout, especially when he's a clever so-and-so with a chance of winning the election in November. They must have been behind Derek's murder. Our security people said all along an internal group wasn't responsible for the assassination . . .'

The voice trailed off. Stanley looked at him sharply.

'Do I hear a "but" on the end of that?'

The Cabinet Secretary's normally bland face communicated angst.

'This makes no sense unless Tidyman could count on an outcome which gives his campaign a much-needed boost. I don't understand the pay-off.'

'We've been conned, Harry. By seeing Lustbader I opened an endgame which may well finish with my resignation. Think about it.'

Higgins did. When he worked out what the PM was getting at, his expression became an almost comical study in disbelief.

'You mean . . . ?'

Ken Stanley marvelled at the sheer neatness of the gambit, even as he assessed the negative consequences for himself.

'Someone shot down Minton-Briant and set me up as the
fall guy. Someone who made a deal with Errol Tidyman.
Lustbader came here for one reason and one reason only –
to compromise me. Wouldn't that be a triumph, going down
in history as a five-day PM?'

To his credit, Ken Stanley managed a wry smile.

Andy Kyle reread papers in a cone of brightness from
the downlighter. He had the passenger compartment to
himself. Buffeted by a side wind, the helicopter clattered
on. They were already over the city.

It would be interesting to see how Forsyth reacted when
confronted with evidence that the worst-case scenario was
not only possible, but probable. Documentation from the
safe at Weybridge was explicit. Had BA's Managing Director
still been around there could have been no question of dis-
ciplinary action. Coppel had obeyed instructions carrying
the highest authority. One commandeered a killer Bluebird, the second delivered the aircraft to an assassin. By
order.

The helicopter started to descend. They'd been following
the river. He caught a glimpse of the floodlit Houses of
Parliament through the double skin of his window. Appropriate, somehow – what was all this about, if not the power
to control a country?

Kyle put the documents into his case, to join a black
codebook he had also removed from the safe at the BA
plant. He hoped neither locksmith nor guard had been
foolish enough to examine the ultra-sensitive material.

As the chopper slowed into the final approach to New
Centre Point, Kyle snapped catches shut and rested thick
forearms on the case. The briefest comparison of codebook
and priority codes validating the Bluebird's release indicated where the orders originated.

And that, as events had shown, was terminally dangerous
knowledge.

Mary-Jo MacInnes had set out to do the sights – fighting
her way into the Alamo in Santa Ana's footsteps, just one
of a tourist army. She wondered if Travis and Crockett
would have recognized the place. Mellow limestone walls,

iron-barred windows, distinctive parapet and flag-draped interior looked the part, but she wondered if it reflected the American idea of restoration, which all too often meant remodelled last year the way Hollywood thought it should have looked in the first place.

Her next stop was La Villita, but the cute village with its cobstone streets, old-fashioned lamps and mixture of building styles did nothing to change her mind – besides which half the shops weren't open and the public rest room was disgusting.

Maybe she wasn't one of nature's tourists. In truth, she liked work and people best, in that order, and Sundays were for reading the papers. It took a stroll back to the hotel along River Walk to lift her spirits. The cosmopolitan atmosphere was infectious, and the short journey took the rest of the morning.

After a salad meal at a riverside café, Mary-Jo used her rental to inspect the crime scene. She didn't know the exact location of the Martinez girl's rooming house, but newspaper reports identified the neighbourhood, which she located with the help of a free city map acquired earlier from Alamo Visitor Center. The clerk put a cross in the right place, though puzzled as to why a tourist would want San Pedro Avenue.

In fact, she found the trip fascinating. San Antonio seemed exotic, almost foreign to someone more used to tall East Coast cities. And it came as a surprise to find that the modern downtown area quickly gave way to street after street of run-down wooden houses that would have looked at home in a John Steinbeck movie. On the return trip, she found the police station and Municipal Justice Building, which she would visit next morning.

Then she went back to the hotel and started writing up background, for something to do.

Standing at his window, General Forsyth watched his deputy's Westland swing over Holborn and begin a steady approach to the building, landing lights blazing. Although it hardly seemed to move, the chopper quickly disappeared from view.

Forsyth went to the conference table and picked up the

paper that summarized his conclusions. Turning on the overhead projector, he slipped the sheet underneath and watched words jump onto the wall screen for Kyle's benefit. He forced himself to reread handwritten bullet-points.

- *Tidyman seeks foreign policy boost to electoral chances*
- *Conspires with UK politician bought by promise of power*
- *UK insider exploits position to facilitate assassination*
- *UK conspirator mounts successful government take-over*
- *US pay-off – massive image benefit for Tidyman*
- *UK pay-off – _Power!!!_*

Reading with Kyle's eyes, he sought another scenario that fitted the known data. There were no flaws. However you came at it, his conclusions were entirely reasonable.

Hoping his own safe would prove more secure than the ravished Chubb in Coppel's office, Brigadier Kyle spun the dial on the Weybridge documents. Incriminating evidence of that magnitude was best protected by two inches of hardened steel and a trembler alarm. He left his office and looked around Control.

He saw orderly activity. Just the way he liked things. After telling the Duty Controller he'd be with the Acting Head until further notice, Kyle wandered to the lifts. He didn't hurry. Forsyth might be displeased by the information he brought, but facts were facts.

When the lift decanted him on to the sixtieth floor, his argument was ready. He walked through an empty outer office into the conference room. Forsyth made it easy – looking up from the table and gesturing at the wall. Kyle read his superior's boldly projected mind. When he'd done so, he sat down at the table. Moment of truth.

'Fine as far as it goes, Bob, a fair summary. But I can add a little something as a result of my day's work.'

He reached over and removed Forsyth's offering, his shadow hand appearing briefly before the screen went white. Taking a pen from his pocket, Kyle made swift changes to the script before replacing the paper. Neatly amended text flashed up again – almost the same, but very different.

- *Tidyman seeks foreign policy boost to electoral chances*
- *Conspires with Ken Stanley who's bought by promise of power*
- *Stanley exploits position to facilitate assassination*
- *Stanley mounts successful government takeover*
- *Us pay-off – massive image benefit for Tidyman*
- *UK pay-off – <u>Power for Ken Stanley</u>!!!*

After a moment, Forsyth's troubled gaze wandered to Kyle.
'No mistake, Andy?'
'Evidence to prove it in my safe. Sorry, boss. I've found the Bluebird. Priority codes on the orders which released the plane lead straight to Ken Stanley. The system doesn't let personal authorization codes be fraudulently used. We backed the wrong horse.'
Tactfully, Kyle substituted 'we' for 'you'. Forsyth didn't reply. Instead, he got up and went to the window. Kyle watched the man's stiff back sympathetically.
His investment might be tottering, but facts were facts.

Just as Mary-Jo MacInnes was finishing her background copy, there was a knock at the door. She went over and opened it, revealing a slight young woman with a shock of permed bottle-black curls, carrying a coffee tray. She looked uncertain.
'Room service.'
Mary-Jo glanced along the red-carpeted corridor. Empty. She took the tray from the nervous waitress.
'I hoped you'd be by, Candy. Come on in.'
Once inside, the girl stood by the door, folding arms across her flat chest in a classic gesture of self-protection.
'Wally said you wanted to talk about Maria. Mentioned two hundred bucks, said there wouldn't be no comeback. I booked the coffee to your room, hope that's okay.'
Mary-Jo dropped into an older-sister routine.
'Hey, no sweat. I want to double-check a few things about Maria's last night, honey, that's all. Just local colour. You

won't be quoted by name. Promise. Neither will Walter, and he's told me what he knows. You got time to talk?'

Candy Paretsky advanced two paces.

'Five minutes, else they'll start wonderin' where I got to.'

Mary-Jo took an envelope from her briefcase, sat on the bed and patted the quilt. The girl came closer, but didn't sit down. Mary-Jo handed her the envelope, which she took – turning it in her hands, feeling the wad.

'There's your two hundred, to show I'm on the level. Talk to me.'

When the envelope vanished into a powder-blue skirt pocket, Mary-Jo knew she was in business. Candy Paretsky loosened up. She didn't sit down, but started reciting her tale in the voice of a child who has learned a story by heart, without ever thinking about its real meaning.

'Like I said, there ain't much to tell. Some time after one in the morning Maria took an order for a hot drink. I was joking around with my boyfriend, Randy. Later I put her orders on the computer for billing. One was for that Pat Stark's room – the guy who's running for President. He was staying right here in the hotel.'

Mary-Jo prompted, no trace of irony in her voice.

'No kidding. Go on.'

'Well, about fifteen minutes before we were due off, at two, I go in the rest room and find her there. She's excited, nothing I could put my finger on, but she's humming to herself and says 'Hollywood here I come' with a smile which she tries to hide but comes out anyway. Then she gets serious and says, "Hey, Candy, I'm not feeling so good, how about covering for me." I say sure. It's never busy that time of night and there's only a few minutes to go. She says thanks and goes out.'

The girl hesitated. Mary-Jo said nothing. Candy went on sulkily, as though thinking it unfair she should be asked to remember such painful things, even for two hundred dollars.

'That's the last time I see her alive until they take me down the City Morgue on North Leona to identify her, which is no bundle of laughs. It was kinda scary, I ain't never seen a dead body before. Look, I oughta go, they're pretty strict round here.'

She edged towards the door. Mary-Jo leaned down and grabbed a crumpled sweatshirt from the floor. She tossed it over.

'Say I kept you talking, asked if you could get this cleaned without fading the design. Anything else I should know?'

Candy put her head on one side.

'That reminds me. Just before I go off, Stark phones down and asks if we can get pants and a shirt cleaned by morning. Said drink gotten spilled over them. Funny thing is, he asks if Maria's okay. I say she's fine.'

'Why did he ask after Maria?'

'Wouldn't be the first time a guest asked after a maid, believe me. Maria was real pretty. But she never fooled around with guests or anyone else, far as I know.'

'And was his stuff cleaned?'

'Sure, but I was going off duty so I told my relief. Kid who picked them up told me they were in a laundry bag outside the door, dripping wet like Stark sluiced them under the faucet to get a stain out, or something.'

'Did the cops get all this?'

'Sure, they went over the story three, four times. Look, that's it, lady. I really gotta go.'

Mary-Jo jumped up, sensing that there was no more to be had. She showed her informant out. As a reporter, she liked the possibilities. As a woman, the picture was beginning to suck.

The tiny brick-and-flint lodge cottage at Chequers was witnessing another drama, as was the cracked leather divan used by relief oppos. With both hands cupped tightly over his aching groin, Corporal Terence Seymour was curled up on the couch – his back to switched-off instruments and his face to the whitewashed wall.

Elizabeth Pike was the screw of the decade, the sodding century. All down to chemistry, bloody brilliant chemistry. They'd done it on the lawn not twenty yards from where Minton-Briant copped his. Oh, they'd gone through the ritual of getting to know each other, but there'd never been much doubt where the evening was heading.

Alongside the rose garden they had stopped, turning to face each other. Then they were frantically tearing at clothes, clutching at flesh, rolling across dew-chilled grass. Lizzie finished up on top, breasts crushing into his chest, forearms pinning his shoulders, thrusting as though she were the man.

Afterwards, she stroked his hair and whispered 'That was nice', though both knew it was an understatement. Later, as they walked up to the terrace, they had found an old guy in the shadows, leaning on the stone balustrade. If he'd been there long enough, he must have seen something to make him wish he was forty years younger.

Seymour sniffed hard, trying to clear a persistently running nose. Bastards. He'd dropped Lizzie at her billet, parting with a long kiss. Bastards. They were waiting and watching, concealed in the shrubbery alongside the path.

As the door closed on Lizzie, he'd turned towards his own quarters. Three steps later, a dark shape appeared in front of him. Without warning, a fist smashed into the bridge of his nose. A second later, pain hit him. He'd registered a voice. Dispassionate, conversational.

'Nice shot, Geoff. I'd say that was a direct hit.'

Before he could react, someone had kicked him in the balls. He collapsed on to the rough concrete path and heard himself moaning. The voice came back.

'Right on target. Perhaps that'll cramp lover boy's style, teach him to do his bloody job properly. Come on, lads, let's go. No point in wasting boot leather on this Welsh scumbag.'

A match striking. The smell of cigarette smoke. A matchstick hitting the path. Receding footsteps. Three or four of them. Sergeant Hackett and his mates from the Patriot batteries. Bastards.

When the agony became almost bearable, he'd dragged himself up and staggered to the lodge. Now, after two more hours, the pain had subsided to a dull ache, though he feared his nose was broken. Bastards.

They were working late at the Home Office. A small team of disinformation specialists under the direction of ministerial aide Alec Ambler was assembling data that provided a damning indictment of Prime Minister Ken Stanley. They were in the welcome position of working with some helpful facts. The best lies contain a large measure of verifiable truth.

The light-box was littered with colour slides – Vernon Lustbader leaving the Gulfstream at Northolt, Lustbader entering 10 Downing Street, coming out. There were newspaper file shots of Lustbader and Vice-President Tidyman on the platform at the San Francisco nominating convention – arm in arm as they gave a victory salute, clearly the closest of colleagues. They also had transcripts of the confidential signal exchange between London and Washington.

Ambler listened to the expert who was explaining how to produce an incriminating conversation between Lustbader and Stanley. He'd use a voice synthesizer programmed with archive sound tapes of the PM. The special envoy's voice pattern would be lifted from the tape of Cornwell's brief exchange with him at Northolt.

Godfrey Cornwell might win the day at Special Congress, but it never hurt to be sure.

After making an extended phone call to Head of Covert Operations, General Forsyth decided to leave Intelligence HQ. The Security Minister was back in circulation, and he wanted to talk with the Field Marshal. A phone call to the Chelsea house was answered by his wife. Despite the late hour, Alex greeted him cheerfully. The tetchy invalid had arrived in mid-afternoon and was still awake.

Although he did not anticipate trouble, Forsyth had Armstrong drive him. On the way, they stopped on Beth's street. He looked up at the lighted windows of her top-floor studio. Forsyth wanted to see her, but awareness of her forthcoming encounter with the Prince Regent would spoil everything.

He asked Armstrong to drive on. When they arrived home the bodyguard was first out. Forsyth was amused by the man's diligence. Armstrong paraphrased an old cliché as he hustled his charge into the building.

'Just because I'm paranoid it doesn't mean they're not after you.'

'Doesn't mean they are, either. Put the car away and doss down here. I'll be making an early start.'

There were already three bodyguards in the house, but

one more wouldn't hurt. Forsyth headed for the kitchen –
hoping Chandler wouldn't be difficult, suspecting he would.
Alex greeted him with a smile and presented her cheek.
Without thinking, he gave her a peck, though that routine
had lapsed months ago.

'How's your father, to coin a phrase?'

'Complaining that nobody tells him anything. For "nobody"
read *you*.'

Forsyth smiled at his wife.

'Well, he is the boss.'

Field Marshal David Chandler had explored his room – door,
light switch, window, curtains, wardrobe, chest of drawers,
pictures, bedside table, bed, armchair. He knew the way to
the bathroom and back without stumbling, and thought
he'd mastered the bedside telephone.

Sounds of activity didn't help. Every time a foot fell he
called, summoning a security man who never had any
answers. For the same reason, his daughter's company
was irritating. Alex meant well, but her efforts to cheer
him up only underlined his dependence. Where the hell
was Bob? He'd heard a car, felt sure the boy was in the
house.

Chandler was sitting on the bed. He groped around the
table, knocking an empty glass to the floor before finding the
telephone. He identified the corrugated talk slide, getting a
dial tone. Slowly, he worked out the code for an internal call
to the kitchen and keyed the three-digit sequence. Bob was
probably skulking down there with Alex, talking about him
behind his back.

'At the third stroke, it will be zero-one-forty and . . .'

He threw the female voice across the room. The phone
thudded to the carpet, denying him the satisfaction of
breaking something. Behind their dressings, he felt his
eyes smart – not in self-pity, but rage.

'Temper, temper.'

Chandler swivelled towards the mocking voice.

'Bob! How did you get in here?'

'The door was open. I'll say this once, David. I understand
your frustration. I sympathize. But I won't pity you. That's
not the way forward.'

The field marshal sat up.

'There's work to be done, then?'

'Things have moved fast and we have difficult decisions to make. I need advice and you're going to give it to me. Whether I take it is another matter – depends if I like what you have to say.'

'Thought you'd never ask, you cocky young bugger.'

Chandler was feeling better already.

Two flights in a day were two too many, three would be unlucky. Special Envoy Vernon Lustbader had broken his journey in Ireland, staying overnight at Dromoland Castle before jetting on to Washington. They'd kept his suite free. He put Holst's *Mars, God of War* on the CD player and threw himself on the bed, letting the surging sound assault his senses as he thought about his mission.

The next thing he knew, he was awakened by the bleep-bleep-bleep of his satellite phone, which squatted on the floor beside his bed. Disorientated, he looked at his travel alarm. After four – 11 p.m. in Washington. He'd slept for six hours. He grabbed the handset.

'Lustbader.'

'Vernon.'

Vice-President Tidyman might have been in the next room.

'Hello, Errol.'

Lustbader bought two seconds to get organized as his reply took a four-thousand-mile hike into the stratosphere and back. He tried to shake sleep narcosis from his mind as Tidyman came back at him.

'How was Ken Stanley?'

'Okay.'

'See anyone else?'

'Some kind of note-taker sat in, a fussy little guy called Higgins. Then the Home Secretary caught up at the air-field, warned me off. Otherwise nobody, but I bet plenty saw me.'

'Yeah, I know about Godfrey Cornwell. Bad piece of work, but clever with it. So how did the Stanley meeting go?'

'Practically accused us of masterminding Minton-Briant's killing. Not interested in the goodies, against the idea of better relations between our countries, angry that we should even raise the matter with such unseemly haste. Over and out inside fifteen minutes. I guess it went pretty well.'

'That's my boy. Beginning to put two and two together and come up with Catch Twenty-two. Knew you would. When are you back?'

'No smoke without fire, but you can't start a fire without making smoke? Should be in Washington early tomorrow, your time.'

'I'll pencil you in for around ten. Guess I've got some explaining to do. And Vern, well done. Someone had to take this on, and I can't think of a man who could've handled the job better.'

The link went dead. Lustbader went to the CD, opting for a little light Grieg. The music might help.

Errol Tidyman hadn't just known before it happened. He'd been up to his elbows in the assassination of a British Prime Minister.

DAY FIVE:

Monday 9 September

The milkman had delivered four litres of skimmed and a perfect morning. When General Robert Forsyth opened his front door at seven, the air was mild. Despite tendrils of river mist, the sky was blue. A good day to start making the history Ken Stanley had gone on about so eloquently when they met at Somerset House.

'Inside.'

Armstrong took the milk and shepherded him back into the house. They had the kitchen to themselves. Apart from one special agent on the stairs, the house was sleeping after a late night.

Alex Forsyth had gone to bed at two. The three bodyguards were on eight-hour shifts, with two always off duty, resting or asleep. Chandler and Forsyth had talked until four, when the old man suddenly tired. He'd probably sleep for twelve hours or more, and Forsyth had been happy to grab a few hours himself.

By the time they finished, the situation had been dissected by two keen minds. The old team was working well. But instead of discussing, evaluating and decisively deciding, Chandler seemed more interested in Forsyth's point of view. That was as it should be. The old man enjoyed senior status, but was no longer able to operate at the sharp end.

In fact, he deferred to his deputy's suggestions as never

before. This increased Forsyth's respect. He'd expected to
take over when the time was right, but such plans don't
always come to fruition. Nothing worse than a leader who
wouldn't move over.

Chandler still found difficulty in accepting that Ken
Stanley's prints were all over the murder. But Andy Kyle
didn't make mistakes. They agreed that it was essential
to deal with the situation before Godfrey Cornwell could
address Special Congress – the Home Secretary's ability to
whip up the rank and file was legendary. The mere fact of
Stanley's American connection might be enough.

They'd assumed that, with Intelligence support, Stanley
would be fireproof. But the new PM was starting to look
distinctly flammable. Neither had any intention of being
consumed in the blaze, and agreed their deal with Stanley
might not stand up.

As he took a second cup of breakfast coffee, Forsyth's
mood was buoyant. He had full authority for the course he
wanted to follow. Or at least sufficient authority. No sense
in burdening Chandler with details. The important thing
was settled – the old man stood beside him, would support
him without flinching as events moved to their climax.

Forsyth needed to know no more.

The businessman looked businesslike – grey suit with faint
chalk stripe, tightly rolled umbrella, gleaming black shoes,
pigskin case beneath a well-tailored arm. There was a
photograph of Beth Highsmith in the case.

A tall, attractive woman ran down the front steps of a
stucco-fronted building thirty yards from his vantage point,
hurrying past in the direction of King's Road. It was her.
The man turned and followed. He spoke to the polka-dot
handkerchief in his breast pocket, London accent at odds
with his appearance.

'Subject on the move. Will follow to make sure she doesn't
return.'

He didn't appear to notice the white van which turned
into the street and stopped in front of the house he'd
been watching. In case the bundle of copper piping on the
roof was not enough, it bore a bold red-and-yellow *LEAK
MACHINE* legend. The driver got out, opened the rear doors

and removed a large toolbox. He whistled cheerfully as he mounted the steps, another workman starting his day of dedicated service – plugging leaks, vanquishing worn tap washers, blasting blocked drains.

It was perhaps unusual that he had a front-door key, and amongst more conventional tools his box contained remote fibre optic video equipment. But who was to know he plumbed only in the Nixonian sense?

Captain Phil Dexter was a good investigator, but felt flattered he'd been given the Coppel case. All the younger officers respected Brigadier Kyle and hoped to catch his eye. It was a plum assignment, especially if he managed to get a result.

On the face of it, a successful outcome was unlikely. The killers – there were at least two, because a different 9mm bullet had been found in each corpse – hadn't been seen arriving or leaving. Hadn't broken into the house, made any noise, crapped in the corner. As far as he knew they hadn't stolen anything, or left a fibre of forensic evidence.

His team had dismembered the ancient cottage, finding nothing that threw light on the murders. Still, Phil Dexter had returned alone to the scene of the crime, in case he'd overlooked something. He'd failed to spot anything new, despite going through the whole place twice.

Disappointed, he decided to call in and return to base. He went to the sitting room and reached for the phone. In doing so, he saw an almost imperceptible circle, faintly visible on black plastic that bore traces of white fingerprint dust. A vague memory stirred, and after a moment he remembered.

Once upon a time people used simple little gizmos to record telephone conversations – lick-and-stick sucker mikes with a length of wire and jack plug for the recorder. Maybe brownie points were there for the scoring after all.

As he strolled back from his duty turn at Amersham Station, a probationary police constable noticed that a dusty black BMW saloon by the entrance of the commuters' car park hadn't moved since the previous day. No parking ticket had been purchased and the vehicle was clamped.

Home base was round the corner. Within minutes, detectives were swarming over the car. The boot yielded four M-60 automatic rifles, recently fired, plus two holdalls containing unused ammunition. Others were interviewing station staff. The observant booking clerk who worked Saturday night remembered four strangers catching the 2032 train for Baker Street, though he could only describe the one who purchased tickets.

On-platform video might offer more, and word had already flashed to London. Hopefully, the trail leading to those sought-after Windsor assailants would still be warm. Thames Valley Chief Constable Wendy Millar ordered an all-out effort and the police were cock-a-hoop. The breakthrough owed nothing to their pushy rivals in Intelligence.

Ken Stanley had been slow to see the trap, but belated realization that his neck was at risk galvanized the PM. He intended to avoid the long drop. Unfortunately, allies were thin on the ground. Even Harry Higgins was cool. The Cabinet Secretary concluded their morning review of the day's business swiftly, before ignoring Stanley's attempt to extract an opinion on the developing situation. Ominous. Higgins had radar that made a bat look like an elephant in thick fog.

Stanley's assumption that ratification by Special Congress would be a formality was developing serious fault lines. Support was trickling away to Godfrey Cornwell. If the Home Secretary smeared him with an unpatriotic American connection, the trickle could become a torrent.

Ken Stanley abandoned pessimistic analysis. He called Stoke Mandeville Hospital, but David Chandler had discharged himself into his daughter's care. So, his old buddy was even closer to General Forsyth, the chosen successor who was directing Intelligence firepower. Stanley no longer felt confident about the senior security service's loyalty, either.

If his reading of Lustbader's visit was correct, *someone* was working with the Americans – or rather their rogue Vice-President. And they had to be in a position to exploit the situation their devious activity helped create. But who?

Perversely, the PM found he was enjoying himself. The

cut and thrust of politics was the ultimate stimulant. He buzzed the Cabinet Office and asked Harry Higgins to join him. Time to counter-attack.

She'd been standing inside the entrance for nearly an hour. Mary-Jo MacInnes found no difficulty in rising early when she was on assignment. She had dumped her rental in a three-dollar parking lot and walked one block to the green-panelled glass-and-concrete police station at 214 East Durango, arriving at seven. It hadn't been difficult to pump the chatty clerk on the island desk in the narrow front hallway.

The case officer was Lieutenant Richard Schneider, due in around eight, an old guy built like a bull. There was nowhere to sit, so she stood beside a glass-fronted case containing the badges of forty-one San Antonio police officers who had died in the line of duty, since Assistant City Marshal Federico W. Fieldstrop confronted a notorious gambler and two companions at Market and Alamo on 29 May 1857. It was a rash move – the shoot-out left three dead, including Fieldstrop.

Some of the badges had been damaged in the incidents causing the bearer's demise, and the mason responsible for cutting new names on to the white memorial plaque was two years behind schedule. To avoid attracting attention, she studied neatly typed cards that communicated the circumstances of each death in clipped, police-report language. The majority also bore small monochrome portrait photographs.

Despite professional cynicism, Mary-Jo found the display moving – not just because these casualties of American urban violence had been honoured by their colleagues, nor even because her imagination could weave vivid pictures from the brief descriptions of violent death. But because the faces, each so typical of its era, attracted her.

The then-living police officers who stared at her were dead, most for so long they would by now have died anyway. Each had been extinguished in an instant, surprised – if there was time to think – that a life which meant everything was ending before the owner was ready. But who was ever ready?

A laughing adolescent walked up four steps into the building from a blue-and-white parked out front, cuffed to a cop, waving with his free hand to friends sitting in a side office off the hall while their parents made bail. She felt like shouting that life was what counted – just waking up tomorrow to go on living. But the boy knew better. He was young – why bother about tomorrow? She was fifteen years ahead, and did.

Schneider bustled up the steps. He had an unlit cigar clamped between slightly crooked teeth, wore an open-neck shirt with loose tie which seemed like an afterthought and had untidy white hair. She stepped into his path and flapped her ID.

'Mary-Jo MacInnes, *Washington Post*. I'm down here looking into one of your cases – the Maria Martinez murder. Can we talk?'

He stopped, removed the cigar and looked her up and down. The expression was not unfriendly and his direct appraisal surprised her. The description hadn't prepared her for his sheer presence. Slightly bloodshot brown eyes seemed to look inside her mind. He addressed her politely, voice slow and deep, smoothing the Texas accent which usually offended her Northern ear.

'Most people can talk, Ms MacInnes.'

Did she detect humour? Mary-Jo found herself replying defensively. This was wrong. Reporters attacked, cops got uncomfortable.

'I mean can you give me background on the Martinez case. Please.'

The tough old cop thought about his answer. Mary-Jo didn't know when she'd decided he was tough, but she had. He lectured her patiently, like she was a particularly slow kid.

'Well, it's like this. I made a terrific deal with the taxpayers – I clear up city garbage Monday through Friday and most weekends, they don't expect me to handle public relations. Try the DA's office. Those people love talking to the press. First Assistant DA David Turrow is handling Martinez. He's a hotshot. Find him in the Municipal Justice Building, just up the street on the left. Nice meeting with you.'

He stepped around her and walked. She fired a sour 'What

about the Stark car?' at his retreating back, but he didn't
twitch. The first call of Schneider's garbage-cleaning day
would probably suggest the hotshot DA should get himself
into a meeting. Quick.

Harry Higgins was not a happy Cabinet Secretary. As he
climbed the last flight of stairs, he pretended his concern
was petty – the fact Ken Stanley had summoned him to the
cramped living room of the private apartment at Number
10, rather than meeting in one of the innumerable rooms
designated for official business.

Actually, his unease was based on a growing feeling that
things were getting out of control – his control. He chided
himself for ignoring his favourite maxim, held so dearly that
it was displayed on his desk for all to see – *THINK!*

Well, he hadn't thought very hard at that first Cabinet
meeting, had he? The lapse was understandable, if not
forgivable. They'd all been in shock, and Stanley had played
the situation cleverly. But that was no excuse. Higgins was
starting to fear he'd boarded the wrong bandwagon.

Ken Stanley was waiting at the top of the stairs, exuding
bonhomie. By the time they were settled in the sitting room,
the pragmatist in Higgins had reasserted. All might not
be lost.

'So, Prime Minister, what's to be done?'

Stanley looked at the Cabinet Secretary shrewdly.

'Just found out you only have a month to live, Harry?'

This time, Higgins did think, but he was out of options.

'I've been considering the American connection. I'm sure
Tidyman's involved, and his plan must involve your removal
from office. You go, I go. So yes, I'm depressed. I wasn't
anticipating early retirement.'

The Prime Minister leaned over and patted the Cabinet
Secretary's pinstriped knee. If anyone else had done that,
Higgins would have been outraged. But the gesture was
reassuring. The PM didn't disappoint him.

'Thanks for your honesty. But you may still be on the
right side. With your help and knowledge of the system,
we can head this thing off at the pass, as the Americans
might say. There are two things I intend to do . . .'

As he listened, Higgins cheered up. There was something

about the PM's low, almost hypnotic voice which encouraged confidence, however irrational. Besides, his ideas were
inspired.

Following the Weybridge breakthrough, Brigadier Andy Kyle
hadn't stopped working, apart from brief catnaps. There was
nothing he liked or did better than assembling evidence. The
picture was coming into focus.

The messages ordering the Bluebird's release from British
Aerospace provided a rock-like foundation for the case
against Ken Stanley. A tamper-proof communications system identified the source of official orders transmitted
electronically. In addition, recipients were required to call
a specified number for confirmation before implementing
such orders.

As Deputy Premier, Stanley's name was on the distribution list for Minton-Briant's closely guarded forward
engagement calendar. He was one of the few knowing when
the PM would be vulnerable to air attack. Not conclusive,
but circumstantial confirmation of complicity.

A photograph from the *Surrey Herald* added more. Dated
four months previously, the picture showed Ken Stanley
shaking hands with the late Victor Coppel at BA's Weybridge
plant, on a visit to celebrate an export order. Getting the
Bluebird would be facilitated by personal contact.

And Stanley had met Vice-President Tidyman's mouthpiece, Special Envoy Lustbader. Kyle didn't know what had
been said at Number 10, but the contact looked bad.

Head of Processing had provided a further high-tech
pointer to American complicity. When he accessed the central records computer to provide confirmation that Stanley
sent the Weybridge messages, the supposedly foolproof
system had been penetrated. All back-up data for the day
in question had been corrupted beyond recovery.

The culprit was a selective software virus which could
have been injected into the system through any terminal. The electronic wizard from the top floor had patiently
explained the sophisticated methodology, adding that only
the United States could produce a programme capable of
outwitting in-built firewall.

Besides, the virus had an American sense of humour.

After being found at the end of a chase through several million gigabytes of stored data, it flashed a cheerful
CHARLIE BROWN FOR PRESIDENT on screen and self-
destructed in an explosion of psychedelic colour. Head of
Processing was impressed. Kyle was not.

Still, progress was impressive. He needed more, but the
case was shaping nicely.

For once, the morning was unblurred by late-night drinking. The Prince Regent was a saleable commodity. To take
advantage of market forces, he needed to be in prime shape.
If those power-hungry idiots wanted his support, they could
pay top dollar.

George sipped creamy coffee, lips pursing in distaste.
Without a lacing of spirit, the stuff lacked backbone. He
walked to the drinks cabinet and added brandy. Reckless
to risk withdrawal symptoms at such a historic moment.

And there was Beth Highsmith to think about. He'd been
agreeably surprised by her shameless approach. The bitch
wanted something, but didn't everyone? You-scratch-my-
back-I'll-scratch-yours made the world go round. George
couldn't wait to oblige in the back-scratching department,
but first there was a deal to negotiate.

He looked around the lavish living room. The place was
big enough to house a family, but filled him with dissatis-
faction. The apartment was a gilded cage, the symbol of a life
controlled by others. Well, that was about to be swept away.
A yellow notelet bearing Godfrey Cornwell's number was
stuck to the telephone. Without making an error, George
buttoned the code. Nothing wrong with the old faculties.

'Home Secretary's private office, Ambler speaking.'

George adopted a bullish tone.

'Prince Regent. Is he in?'

The West Country voice took that in its stride.

'We'll call back. You are where?'

'Palace Mews. Make it quick, I'm in no mood to be screwed
about.'

In less than thirty seconds, the phone buzzed. After a
moment, he lifted it, hearing the voice of a man he could
do business with.

'George? Godfrey. What's on your mind?'

'Cut the crap. Stanley's wheels are coming off. All sorts of people are after his job, including you, but my signature is needed on the employment contract. Now, I know it's naughty to tittle-tattle, but my old pal Bob Forsyth has made me a handsome offer to throw in with his team.'

George paused, and was duly rewarded.

'Which is?'

'Five million dollars when Stanley is confirmed as PM. Offshore account. Plus the right to leave this miserable country when it's done. I'm not Head-of-State material, but that doesn't mean I'll shirk my duty, no indeed. The right man will be appointed before I go. Sealed bids by the end of the day.'

The Prince Regent hung up before Cornwell could react. Seller's market, and the ambitious Home Secretary couldn't know he was bluffing. Now, where was Forsyth's number?

Mary-Jo MacInnes liked Texicans. They were so goddam easy-going. She'd slipped a fast colour disk into her tiny Olympus camera, walked right up to the police garage, opened the Judas door and stepped inside. The blue Buick was parked against the opposite wall, licence plate clearly visible. There was only a pair of feet on duty, sticking out from under a Ford pick-up truck.

She aimed at the Buick, extended the zoom and ran through the disk on motordrive, holding the little camera at her side. The precaution was justified. As she finished, the feet turned into a white-overalled Hispanic man pulling himself into view on a wheeled trolley. He stood up, wiped his hands on a rag and called over unsuspiciously.

'Can I help, ma'am?'

She turned on a thousand-volt smile, pushed out her chest and doubted he noticed her slipping the camera into her shoulder bag.

'Schneider around? We were supposed to meet down here. He was going to show me the wheels that came in from California.'

The mechanic threw down the rag and took two steps towards her.

'Who you say you was?'

'I didn't, but shy's not my style. MacInnes of the *Washington*

Post. I spoke to the Loot earlier. Crossed wires. I'll try his office.'

She stepped smartly out of the garage, shut the door and trotted away. The guy didn't have many options. Because he didn't come after her, she assumed he shrugged his shoulders and went back to work. Or was already on the horn to Schneider.

Just for the record, Mary-Jo stopped by the Municipal Justice Building. The obliging woman on the information desk relayed her request for a meeting with Assistant DA David Turrow into a telephone, listened, reported back. Turrow was in conference and would be tied up all day.

Mary-Jo went on her way. If these suckers wanted to play hardball, fine. She walked past Bexar County Courthouse, turned along Villita and found a drugstore on St Mary's which could print out her camera disk while she waited. It was a relief to get into chilled air – street temperature was 90 going on 110, abetted by humidity that would make a hot, wet towel seem dry.

Fully revived, she bought a pack of envelopes, collected disk and prints then walked across to the Gunter Hotel. The pictures clearly showed the Buick's licence plate. She scrawled *One important owner?* on a print and slipped it into an envelope. She added her business card, slapped down the self-stick flap and wrote *DAVID TURROW, PERSONAL* on the front. She added an underscored *URGENT*.

One print went into her Coach bag. The rest she placed in a second envelope which she addressed to Douglas Diehl back at the office. Mary-Jo imagined his expression when he opened the small package, studied the contents and muttered, 'For these we've paid three thousand dollars – thus far?' She'd wire the digital originals later.

Mary-Jo found stamps in her purse and mailed the package from the lobby. Time for Strike Two at the Municipal Justice Building – a special delivery for hotshot Bexar County First Assistant DA David Turrow.

As was often the case with impenetrable investigations, once one brick was prised out, the edifice of deceit crumbled. Brigadier Kyle's phone simply wouldn't stop bringing more information.

The Duty Controller had just talked to Police Central. The men in blue had come good. The car used by the Windsor assailants had been found at the end of the Metropolitan Line, fifteen cross-country miles from the attack scene.

American weapons had been recovered. An empty cigarette packet had provided an old-fashioned set of prints, and two different brands of cigarette butt from the ashtrays would yield saliva traces for genetic matching. An excellent description of one man had been obtained, and enquiries had proceeded along the line to Baker Street. Kyle instructed his Controller to put Intelligence teams into the field.

Before he could start feeling satisfied, Kyle received two more calls. Head of Processing, still chuckling over the cheeky *CHARLIE BROWN* virus, told him that an excellent E-fit description of the Bluebird pilot had been created at Weybridge. A comparison with digitalized headshots from pilot licence records had produced three possibles.

Kyle fired the names at his busy Controller, telling him to locate and check out the trio. Within minutes, the enquiry was superfluous.

The Director of GCHQ, the government's electronic intelligence centre, came through personally. They had intercepted and broken a message from a US air base in Germany. They'd got lucky. Presumably because the information related to a simple transport movement, it had not been encrypted in unbreakable CD-ROM one-time code, but in fallible random-access mode. For the second time that morning, Kyle listened to a complex technical explanation he didn't understand.

But the bottom line was clear. GCHQ's brief intercept related to one James Lyall, who was to be flown from Germany to Washington for a meeting with Vice-President Tidyman later in the day – the only passenger on a special military flight arranged for the purpose.

The Director paused before producing his *pièce de résistance*. He'd tapped into the main Intelligence database. A run through the list of qualified British pilots had produced a James Lyall. Did Kyle suppose?

Kyle did. Lyall was on Head of Processing's three-name

list. He didn't spoil the GCHQ Director's triumph, thanking him and promising to visit Cheltenham soon.

So, they'd identified the pilot. Confirmed the American connection. Established a direct link with the ambitious Tidyman – presidential candidate and a wheeler-dealer who could surely count on unofficial support from all sorts of influential functionaries within the mighty machine that governed and defended the USA.

It certainly looked as though Bob Forsyth had been right about Stanley and Tidyman all along.

The Acting Head of Intelligence received a call from Ken Stanley. The PM chose not to use video. Clearly, Stanley had no desire to show his face. The expressive voice was tuned to earnest wavelength.

'Things are getting sticky, Bob. I'm making defensive moves before Godfrey Cornwell runs riot and thought you'd like the news before it becomes general knowledge. Partner.'

Forsyth responded with asperity.

'You might have talked to me before seeing the American. Not clever. And the Prince Regent is angling for an offer to stay on side. Claims Cornwell's already tried to buy his support for five million dollars. Our scheming Home Secretary must fancy his chances of doing serious damage at Special Congress.'

'That's what I called to tell you. Congress won't be meeting. Cabinet Office is sending out postponement notices. I also took the precaution of taping my conversation with Special Envoy Lustbader. Harry Higgins will confirm authenticity, he sat in. He's sending copies to Cabinet members. The content is innocent, I promise. The visit was no more than an attempt to smear me.'

Unkindly, Forsyth prodded.

'What are the grounds for delaying Congress? Ratification by Special Congress was an integral part of that virtuoso pitch you delivered to Cabinet.'

The PM almost yelped with indignation.

'So it was, Bob, but the position has changed. We're witnessing an attempt by the Americans to increase their influence over this country, orchestrated by Tidyman. Windsor proves they're not through yet. They're hell-bent on wiping out everyone who might stand in their way.'

'Where's the evidence and who are *they*? Cornwell will dismiss your move as blatant self-preservation. Plenty will listen. The activists love him, and you can't ignore the Party.'

'Dammit, Bob, Intelligence is supposed to come up with evidence and catch traitors, I'm just a sodding politician. We have a deal, and it's about time you bloody well delivered.'

Forsyth stayed cool. Stanley's nasal voice rose in pitch.

'I know you're doing your best, but we're out of time. We must hold this together until the full facts emerge. If I go down now the bastards have won. Should postponement of Congress fail to ease the pressure, I'll declare a State of Emergency to give us sweeping powers which can be used against troublemakers.'

The PM's agitation switched to aggression.

'I won't be railroaded, General. Give me an assurance you'll stand with me. If you won't, I'll drag David back. Your resignation will be a formality. For or against, that's the choice.'

Thinking furiously, Forsyth tried to calm the Premier.

'David and I are both on your side. This may be an understandable overreaction. I know you're picking up warning signs, but that doesn't mean everyone's turning on you. Let's meet, talk this through. Four o'clock at Number Ten? That gives me time to make discreet enquiries.'

Stanley wasn't placated.

'Four o'clock, then. But it'd better be good. If I sink, I go down with all guns blazing, and you go with me.'

Godfrey Cornwell's PA was having a bad day. The Home Secretary relied on Alec Ambler's perception, but they were arguing fiercely. The Prince Regent's venal offer had been the catalyst. Cornwell was tempted, but Ambler insisted George was playing both ends against the middle. Besides, they couldn't lay hands on the outrageous fee demanded for his suspect services.

Before they resolved that one, news of the postponement of Special Congress came by messenger, who also brought a tape of Stanley's meeting with the American,

Lustbader. The Home Secretary was furious. Stanley hadn't put a word wrong. And by taping his conversation he'd negated the star item in their disinformation pack – a forged tape purporting to eavesdrop on a Prime Minister talking treason.

The younger man recommended that they should take time to assess the changing situation. Cornwell insisted that forceful action was the only response to the PM's provocation. Ambler stuck to his guns.

'But *what* action, Godfrey? Intelligence will support the PM to the death, even if he's got American connections. The armed forces will remain neutral, though any overt move from us may push them behind Stanley. Parliament will back him, too.'

Alec Ambler's reasoned analysis cooled Cornwell down. When he replied, his voice was sulky.

'We've got the Party, police, even the Prince Regent if we pay his price.'

The Home Secretary's rage subsided. Ambler knew his master's moods. He permitted himself a scolding tone.

'Forget George. His promises are worthless. And we can only rely on the police so far. Chief Constables are loyal, but only because you represent the best chance of protecting their status. Anyway, they have no offensive value. You can hardly order them to arrest Cabinet, MPs and the entire Civil Service, now can you?'

'I suppose not. So we're left with the Party.'

The best political calculator in the land was getting up speed again. If only Godfrey could learn to master his temper. The man was so red-blooded. Ambler returned to his theme.

'The Party? Terrific, if we get to Special Congress and call in our markers. Even Ken Stanley would find it hard to ignore a Congress decision. But he saw that one coming. Cabinet won't reverse the postponement, especially with General Forsyth glowering at them. They're scared shitless. Your stiff new bog brush may look a lot worse than Stanley's flirtation with the Yanks, real or imagined.'

Cornwell's anger flickered back.

'Our most effective power base has been neutralized, so I must watch that old rooster crowing? If he gets away with this Stanley won't stop until he's broken every possible rival. Which actually means me, you useless little bugger.'

Ambler spoke soothingly, keeping his voice calm and slow. But inside he was jubilant.

'I'm not saying that. I won't rest until you're installed in Downing Street. What's more, I know how to get you there. We're far too clever for them, Godfrey.'

The Acting Head of Intelligence had hardly had time to assess Ken Stanley's attacking strategy when Sally Sayers came through.

'Godfrey Cornwell on video, says it's urgent. Yes, no?'

Forsyth decided he could no longer afford to ignore the Home Secretary.

'Yes, Sally, put him through. Then get Andy Kyle up here.'

Cornwell's unlined face jumped on to the screen, smiling pleasantly. He was on a conciliatory mission.

'General, good of you to spare a moment of your valuable time.'

'As guardians of the nation's security we should talk more often. How can Intelligence be of service?'

The Home Secretary leaned towards his camera and spoke confidentially.

'Major developments. Delicate matters best discussed face to face. I think we would be well advised to meet as soon as possible. You won't be disappointed. I want to table a proposition you'll find most interesting. I'm not one for saying sorry, but have to admit I was out of order last Friday, crashing into your china shop and trying to bully you. I misjudged you, Bob, for which I can only apologize.'

It was an olive tree. Forsyth was surprised, must have betrayed the emotion. Godfrey Cornwell pressed home his advantage.

'I believe you're an honest man who cares for his country. Now, our meeting. I'll call on you, of course . . .'

Forsyth had never known a leopard change its spots, but the chameleon had no such difficulty. He shrugged.

'Can't hurt to listen. Close of play this afternoon, here in my office – six o'clock?'

'Perfect!'

As he faded off screen, Cornwell looked very confident. Forsyth tugged his lip. Perhaps the ultra-dangerous Home Secretary had somehow divined the truth.

Schneider and Turrow finally got together after an increasingly terse exchange of phone calls. They had a serious problem – which looked innocent as hell, stood around five-six, weighed in at one-twenty and packed a potentially lethal punch.

Mary-Jo MacInnes of the *Washington Post*.

They settled for the short walk to Farmer's Market. Schneider arrived at La Margarita before the lunch crowd built up, grabbing an outside table against iron railings. He ordered beer and gave the waiter ten bucks for advancing Mexican mariachis, providing they didn't wander off along the terrace. Their enthusiastic crooning should prevent conversation being overheard.

While he waited, Schneider lit a King Edward. One of the reasons he'd chosen the open-air rendezvous was to enjoy a cigar without being treated like a criminal. He blew out smoke, and was so busy watching it eddy under the blue-and-white table umbrella he missed Turrow's arrival.

The First Assistant DA put a cup of coffee beside Schneider's beer. He looked smart as a whip, but strain was evident. The cop leaned his elbows on the wooden table-top and spoke softly. He didn't much care for lawyers, but felt a certain empathy with Turrow.

'You gettin' punished on this?'

'Sure, but that's not what's bothering me.'

Turrow glanced around, half expecting MacInnes to swing down from the trees above them.

'How the hell did she get on to this? I need the media piling in like lung cancer.'

Before continuing, he looked accusingly at the cigar.

'We've got zip. The Stark Buick was used to dump the body, but do I file for an indictment against the next President of the United States and his campaign team on *that*? I might as well get over to the AmTrak depot and lie down on the tracks.'

Schneider picked up his matchbook and studied the cover. He ordered his thoughts, then itemized them.

'We got the car. Stark spent time alone with Martinez in his room. He sent his pants for overnight cleanin'. The girl left before her shift was over. She had more money than she should. The Candidate has zipper problems. So what does this tell us?'

Turrow looked harassed.

'It tells us shit, Dick. We've been through this a hundred times. So maybe Stark made a pass at her. Maybe she grabbed the chance to make him pay in hard cash. Maybe she was promised more money, told someone would bring it over to her place. Maybe some aide decided to go house cleaning, with or without Stark's say-so. But that's ten maybes too many, and grand juries hate maybes. Where's the proof?'

Schneider lit another cigar. When it was burning evenly, he set it down on the Coors ashtray.

'So tell me what you actually think. You talked to the man.'

The Assistant DA seemed to forget his worries. His voice rose a couple of decibels. Schneider was glad of the trio, who were pounding out *The Yellow Rose of Texas* in Spanish, not five feet away.

'Politicians spend their lives being two-faced, but the guy impressed me. Talked openly about what happened and his story covered the tricky points. Even confessed man to man he screwed around, but claimed that's off limits since the campaign got under way. For what it's worth, I believe him.'

Schneider struck like a diamondback.

'But Stark also told you he went to bed after the girl left, spoke to no one till mornin'. So how come his Buick magically turned up at the Martinez place? He's lyin', or somethin' don't add up. But we ain't likely to get anywhere unless we shake the tree.'

Turrow's anxiety returned.

'What are you planning?'

Schneider got up and showed his teeth. He hoped his face wasn't a pretty sight.

'Maybe it's best you don't know, Dave, and that's one maybe you can bet on. This way you get to plead innocent when that boss of yours starts screamin' about abusin' the rights of the privileged classes.'

He let that sink in while he relit the extinct King Edward. Schneider decided he was being too tough. They were on the same side.

'Funny thing is, Dave, I trust you on this one. If the iceman happens to be important, you'll go after him and to hell with the consequences. I respect that. Leave MacInnes to me. Sometimes the best way to deal with a can of worms is to take the lid off, let in a little sunlight. Enjoy your coffee.'

Turrow picked up his cup, inspected the cold contents and put it down again. He smiled brightly at the cop.

'Remind me to contribute handsomely to your retirement collection, Lieutenant.'

Schneider left, slipping another ten to the leader of the band as he went by. His largess was rewarded with an expensive display of gold teeth. Painless dentistry was big business down Old Mehico way, and it sure was more practical than cash in the bank. Until the muggers started carrying pincers.

Brigadier Anderson Kyle's investigation was speeding up. A trace on the Windsor assailants was progressing. With the help of massive police manpower, witnesses who had seen the four men on Saturday night had been found and interviewed.

Ironically, they had been remembered because they looked like security men – large, silent, restless eyes. Even people with clear consciences noted such individuals, watched them safely out of sight.

They'd split up at Baker Street Station. One had taken a Number 6 bus in Marylebone Road, two more had ridden the Circle Line to King's Cross before switching separately to the Northern Line. The last went down to Oxford Circus and transferred to a northbound Victoria Line train. Everything pointed north. With hundreds of men on the job and security tapes from the entire Underground network being studied, they didn't stand a prayer.

Kyle contacted the Special Intelligence Service commander in Hereford, an old acquaintance. He readily agreed to get a team into the air and worry about paperwork later. They would reach London inside ninety minutes. Kyle asked for Roger Nolan. He liked Nolan's performance in Nottingham and preferred working with people he knew. After checking that the captain was on base, the commander approved his request.

Kyle checked his clockwork Omega. The gold hands were flying. Removing the damning Weybridge signals from his safe and gathering up papers, he set off for his appointment with Forsyth on the sixtieth floor.

General Forsyth hated the uncertainty. It was like a horse race, with frantic jockeys putting everything into conjuring a final effort from straining mounts. Somebody had to win, but who? Hopefully, the best investigator in Intelligence was about to produce something that would give him the whip hand.

Forsyth met his deputy at the door, greeted him warmly and motioned the big man to a seat at the conference table.

'You talk, I'll listen.'

Kyle arranged papers on the table-top and scratched wiry hair.

'Where to begin? Okay, let's start with the pilot, James Lyall. Ex-navy flier, Falklands War vet, fifty-two years old, widower. Wife committed suicide ten years ago. Apparently they couldn't have children. The final straw was their local council's refusal to let them adopt two Romanian orphans. Lyall was a pilot with Virgin Atlantic, but after her death he packed in his job. Moved to the sticks and started his own flying business.'

'Where, exactly?'

In spite of his assurance, Forsyth couldn't stop himself butting in. His deputy looked at him curiously.

'Tiny place called Nettlesmere, up in Suffolk, an old World War Two field. Lyall was a jobbing pilot – a bit of air taxi work, crop spraying, aerial surveys. But he did all his own servicing, so he had the workshop facilities to have modified that Bluebird.'

A wave of memories swept over Forsyth, not all of them good.

'Small world. I learned to drive on that airfield, believe it or not. Five miles from where I grew up. Sorry, I didn't mean to interrupt. What else do you know about him?'

'We're still digging, but he's the sort of embittered loner

who might be persuaded to pull a stunt like this. Blamed the authorities for his wife's death if hundreds of angry letters are anything to go by. Of course he could never have targeted Minton-Briant without help. Someone found him and focused the anger. Right now he's sitting in Germany waiting for a flight to America and guess what?'

'Surprise me.'

'A meeting with Vice-President Errol Tidyman. GCHQ got a signal intercept. You were right about the Tidyman connection. Actually, we're mopping up killers left, right and centre. The police got a line on the Windsor gunmen. Four of them. I'll lay odds they also killed Victor Coppel to stop him revealing who released the Bluebird. We should bag them later today. It's brilliant, really.'

Forsyth understood Kyle wasn't praising himself.

'All this mayhem down to one deranged pilot and four hard men with guns? Damn right it's brilliant. Talk about politics by other means. Stanley becomes PM, Tidyman gets a friendly British government and becomes a foreign relations superstar.'

The investigator in Kyle asked an awkward question.

'So why did Tidyman's special envoy charge in, pointing us at Stanley?'

Forsyth had it covered.

'He's circulated a tape of his conversation with Lustbader. Our PM worked himself into a frenzy of indignation and sent the man packing with a flea in his ear. Classic double bluff, well in keeping with the subtlety of the whole operation. The guilty party arouses suspicion, then produces evidence to clear himself. Cabinet won't hear another word against him, you'll see.'

Kyle laid a heavy hand on his pile of papers.

'So evidence against Stanley will be dismissed as a smear. Neat. So where do we go from here?'

Forsyth drummed his fingers on the table, a rapid tattoo that failed to produce an answer. Eventually, he did the best he could.

'I don't know, Andy. I just don't know.'

But of course he did.

Andy Kyle watched the play of emotions on General Robert

Forsyth's face, keeping his own expression neutral. It would be fascinating to see how his superior addressed the dilemma.

Forsyth's drumming fingers slowed, stopped. His eyes roamed restlessly. Kyle went to the drinks cabinet, building a stiff Campari soda. Forsyth accepted the drink, then snapped out of his reverie. He put the glass down and met Kyle's concerned glance.

'You've been around the houses. What would you do in my position?'

Kyle laughed.

'I only work here. I'm not paid to make earth-shattering decisions. I do see we have a problem. Our man's conspired to murder the PM and suckered us into his camp. On the other hand, the beneficiary if we nail Stanley is Godfrey Cornwell, who'd smash Intelligence into little pieces. Nice choice.'

The old Forsyth smiled back. Kyle felt sure he'd made a decision.

'You don't know the half of it. Stanley's suspended Special Congress and intends to introduce a State of Emergency. He rightly assumes his nasty little scheme is unravelling. Meanwhile, Godfrey Cornwell comes on to me and hints that we might kiss and make up.'

Kyle was way ahead, but supplied an appropriately naïve touch.

'We stick with Ken Stanley in the interests of self-preservation, knowing his hands are dirty, or make a deal with Cornwell and pray the devious bastard can be trusted? I love it.'

The Acting Head of Intelligence pounced.

'Wrong. Stanley's damaged goods. Quite apart from his part in the conspiracy, his pre-emptive strike could back-fire. If Cornwell knows a fraction of what we do his Party activists will stop our devious PM dead. And if he doesn't know the truth yet he soon will. We rubbish the police, but they've got clever people.'

'So we go with Cornwell and hope for the best?'

Forsyth shook his head, livid spots of colour showing above prominent cheekbones.

'That would be an even worse misjudgment. We have to

find a third alternative. I have an idea which I want to run past David Chandler. So we keep both of them sweet until we're ready to make our own move. Ken at four, Godfrey at six. Should be a piece of cake.'

Kyle nodded thoughtfully.

'I see.'

Indeed he did.

One phone call confirmed that Mary-Jo MacInnes was who she claimed to be, another located her. There was no answer from her hotel room, but Schneider said it was police business and told the desk to page her. Two minutes later, she came on line.

'MacInnes.'

'Lieutenant Schneider, SAPD. We spoke this mornin'.'

'We sure did. Sorry to keep you. I'm out on the terrace by the river, writing my bit for tomorrow's paper. It won't be much, but even a story of a million words must start with a single paragraph. So, what's cooking?'

Schneider cleared his throat, creating a last second in which to reconsider what he was about to do. Then did it.

'Guess you'd like to talk about a certain vehicle currently in police custody, MacInnes.'

'On the record?'

'Certainly on the record. You people must get it out of your heads that every official you come across is tryin' to conceal sensitive information. Me, I've never been one for conspiracy theories, and I'm damn sure SAPD has nothin' to hide on this one. Let's meet.'

'Where and when?'

'On top of the Tower of the Americas, if you can rustle up two dollars for the elevator. Twenty minutes, observation deck? There won't be much of a view in this haze, but we won't be disturbed. The Tower's across Hemisfair Park from your hotel, by the Federal Buildin'. You can't miss it.'

MacInnes sniffed.

'Sure you can, it's only seven hundred and fifty feet tall. I'll be there, Loot. You'll recognize me by the poison pen tucked behind my ear. Get your story straight, I must file in two hours, whatever.'

Schneider headed out. On the stairway from Homicide in the basement, he ran into Olmos coming the other way. The fat sergeant was working on the Martinez case. He had overflowing file envelopes wedged under his left arm, was carrying a paper cup of iced Coke and eating a hot dog. The lieutenant stopped.

'Did anyone ever mention how disgustin' you are, Sergeant?'

Olmos crammed the dog's tail into his mouth, licked mustard off messy fingers and chewed. After a gargantuan swallow chased down with a generous belt of Coke, he replied.

'Some drunken Rexall ranger I busted when I was a rookie called me an overflowing Mexican cesspit and told me to take a running jump into myself, but disgusting never. Seem to recall he fell over his fancy boots in the holding cell, bust his lip and chipped a front tooth. Bit light on the catsup, but that dog wasn't all bad. I could use another. You gotta minute? I was on the way down to see you.'

'I'm outta here. Catch you when I get back. How about I fetch six jello doughnuts to make sure you're still around?'

Sergeant Olmos looked indignant, slapping the wobbling overhang above a straining leather belt.

'Hey, you trying to make out I'm some kinda pig, or what? This is all muscle, man, solid muscle. I'm one of the fittest guys on the force. Six'll do just fine. King-size. And bring maple syrup. See ya later, if you're holding. If you ain't, don't bother.'

Anyone could be forgiven for assuming that Number 372 was empty behind dirty windows and drawn curtains. Inside, four tough men were feeling the strain. Each knew the security services were efficient, understood that risk increased with every passing hour.

The leader was coping best – stepping in swiftly when an argument over which TV channel to watch ended in a grunting wrestling match, initiating conversation as others started to brood, telling dirty jokes they hadn't heard before.

But even the former SAS major felt relieved when the phone on the kitchen wall finally sounded and he heard the now-familiar *Rule Britannia* – whistled somewhat tune-lessly, but with great verve. After the identification routine was completed, conversation continued for fifteen minutes. When he returned to the front room, the three men were tense with predatory anticipation. He briefed them quickly.

'Gentlemen, we must move fast. Into those Intelligence uniforms, raincoats over the top. Denny and Martin, fetch the Jag and getaway van from the lock-up. Make sure there's nothing in your pockets. We go up west, do the business, back here to pick up travel documents and those fat pass books. You're already soldiers – now for the fortune.'

He paused, allowing the thought of money to do its motivating work.

'It's the last job. Get this done and we're out of this fleapit for good. First stop Zurich, then wherever those hard Swiss francs take us. Me? I fancy Mauritius. The big-game fishing's great and they say the girls are quite something – lovely tits and very obliging.'

After money, sex. In fact, he would be joining his wife and two small daughters in Provence. The powerful combination of stimuli induced an end-of-term atmosphere. Boisterous insults were exchanged and another wrestling match erupted, this time from sheer exuberance. He let tension unwind before standing. They read the signal, immediately going quiet.

'You'll love it, boys, you really will. Our treat for today is the Fairy Queen himself, Godfrey Cornwell. This time we shoot to kill.'

The Prime Minister reminded General Forsyth of an ageing pugilist – accepting mismatches against strong young opponents, coming off the canvas after every knockdown, lurching bravely into another storm of punches, arguing furiously when the ref stepped in to prevent further damage.

This perception was reinforced by Ken Stanley's appearance as he sat at the Cabinet table, hands nursing a tumbler of Scotch. The politician seemed to have shrunk, that which before seemed ageless and wise now looking wizened and uncertain. Perhaps Stanley was about to enter the history he was so fond of discussing.

Forsyth wondered if he knew it yet, or still hoped to retrieve his hopeless position with a last-round knockout. The Acting Head didn't really care. Stanley had become a liability. He spoke gently.

'I gather the suspension of Special Congress hasn't gone down too well with the Party faithful, Ken. To be expected. The delegates will be furious at missing their gravy train to London, and no doubt Cornwell's people are stirring away.'

The PM stared into his glass. When he replied, his voice contained a self-pitying note.

'What else could I do? These scurrilous rumours about me and the Yanks were getting out of hand. Our scheming Home Secretary's behind that. Congress might have blocked my appointment. And now you say the Prince Regent's playing footsie with Cornwell?'

Forsyth found the situation exhilarating.

'Don't worry about George. I've made arrangements to deal with him. All you need to know is that by tomorrow morning he'll do what he's told, however attractive Cornwell's proposition.'

Stanley looked up, hope on his hound-dog face. Forsyth continued, communicating total confidence.

'You're a great politician, but politicians tend to be conspiracy theorists. You got careless, that's all. It was a mistake to meet with that American, and Cornwell can use the fact to make trouble. But nothing we can't handle. With me at your side he can't touch you.'

The Prime Minister seemed satisfied, and Forsyth realized the old maestro's whole performance was aimed at establishing his loyalty. The PM leaned across the table, a glint of triumph in deep-set brown eyes.

'But what about the American connection, which has yet to be explained? Someone set out to smear me.'

'Not necessarily. There was always a possibility the objective was simply destabilization of a regime they hated. We'll soon know. We've sourced the Bluebird and identified the pilot. We also have a good line on the Windsor assailants. We'll get to the bottom of this soon enough, believe me. You can rest easy, Ken.'

General Forsyth, watching Stanley's face attentively,

decided the PM would be receptive to an offer he daren't refuse.

When she walked out of the lift and past the souvenir counter, Mary-Jo MacInnes saw Schneider's broad back. He was using a swivel telescope. She went and stood beside him.

'What do you see, Loot?'

The cop stepped down from the stand. Again, she was aware of questioning eyes. The scrutiny made her feel uncomfortable.

'America. I was watchin' the cheerleaders struttin' their stuff down in the new stadium. A monument to our genius for structural engineerin'.'

Mary-Jo cocked her head.

'The stadium or the girls?'

'Whatever. Let's talk.'

Schneider stooped and picked up a green folder from the floor. He steered her to a bench seat backing on to the central core. Outside, they could hear the excited sound of kids running around the lower gallery, pursued by the voices of anxious parents who expected their offspring to sprout wings and fly over the twelve-foot wire barrier. They had the cool indoor area to themselves.

Mary-Jo removed a recorder from her bag and set it on red imitation leather. She glanced at Schneider, who was staring stolidly at cloudless sky beyond sloping glass walls. He spoke without turning his head.

'You can switch on in a minute. Like I promised, this will be on the record. Better yet, you can quote me by name, providin' you spell it right. Read this.'

He jerked the folder sideways, resuming a study of the blue distance. Mary-Jo scanned the contents. She was looking at a photocopy of the forensic report on the Stark campaign Buick, together with a summary of background data on the case and a morgue photograph of the girl's face. As she started to read, Schneider's voice went on.

'Never had any kids. Wanted them, but things didn't work out. Gets to me when a young life is chopped off. Maybe that's one of the reasons I'm a homicide cop. She was pretty, the Martinez girl, until some animal choked the life out of her. Start the machine.'

She looked up from the final page, hit the button. There were still details to absorb, but she had the general picture. Schneider's voice turned official.

'A Buick automobile owned and operated by the Stark For President Campaign was in San Antonio the night Maria Martinez was murdered, along with the man himself. Forensic tests show Maria's body was transported in the trunk. The girl was an illegal alien using the social security number of the real Maria Martinez, who was badly injured in an auto smash in West Texas last year. She died four months ago. We do not know our victim's true identity . . .'

Mary-Jo came in fast.

'Where was she killed?'

'At her apartment in a roomin' house off San Pedro Avenue. The Buick was seen outside about the time she was killed. We were tipped off by an anonymous caller who claimed to've seen the body thrown in a dumpster from a dark automobile. Licence plate checked with the Stark Buick. Male African-American voice, owner never traced.'

'She worked at Stark's hotel, saw him the night she was killed?'

'Served him a hot drink in his room. Before you ask, we've spoken with Candidate Stark and are satisfied that he had nothing to do with the killin'. Enquiries are continuin'. It's S-C-H-N-E-I-D-E-R, Senior Lieutenant, San Antonio Police Department. Stop the tape.'

Mary-Jo did as she was told. She already knew her man well enough to understand he wasn't through.

The sentiment was motivated by relief, but Ken Stanley felt admiration for his Acting Head of Intelligence. Toughness, ambition, aggression – all predictable in a young tyro. But Stanley liked General Robert Forsyth's mature grasp of political reality. His audacious plan was simple but effective. The PM walked into the Cabinet Room and found Harry Higgins.

'Relax, we're still in business.'

The rotund Cabinet Secretary required more than breezy assurance.

'You got a result with Forsyth, then?'

'Bob's nobody's fool. He put forward ideas you'll appreciate. Feels sure we can see off Cornwell and his Party cronies.'

The Cabinet Secretary's expression sharpened. The older man took perverse satisfaction in pausing, making Higgins declare his interest. Waspishly, he did so.

'So what brilliant ploy will make our problems vanish? Or shouldn't one ask?'

Stanley tired of the game, became businesslike.

'He's seeing Cornwell in an hour, but Bob's sure the wretch has more in mind than a security conference. Now we've deprived our Home Secretary of Special Congress his strategy's lame. I've got the half-crown seat, Intelligence can keep me there. With me so far?'

Higgins was.

'Cornwell hopes to do a deal with Intelligence and put you out in the cold?'

'That's what Bob suspects. The man's suddenly become friendly, which means he's after something.'

'But why should Cornwell think Intelligence would want a pact? He must see they'll do better by sticking with you.'

The cautious Cabinet Secretary was reserving judgment. Stanley replied impatiently.

'An appeal to personal ambition, playing on the likelihood that Cornwell will get to be PM in the end and reward his allies, who knows what he'll say? It doesn't matter. Bob has a plan to rid us of our troublesome priest.'

'Namely?'

'He'll play along and find out what shady deal's on offer, or nudge Cornwell in the right direction if he's slow to declare his duplicity. The whole thing's taped. We announce a State of Emergency at midnight. Forsyth then uses sweeping emergency powers to arrest Cornwell and any key players who stand by him. All perfectly legal and above board.'

Now he had the full picture, Higgins was unhappy.

'Legal, perhaps, but above board? You're empowered to introduce a State of Emergency, though it would be prudent to seek Cabinet approval for such a drastic step. And you're placing an awful lot of trust in General Forsyth.'

The Prime Minister laughed cynically, confident in his

ability to assess and manipulate people. He would always
come through.

'You said yourself Forsyth's better off siding with us.
Anyway, he nailed his true colours to the mast. There's a
price to pay. Wouldn't have trusted him unless there was.
With Cornwell gone, David Chandler gets to be Deputy PM
and General Forsyth becomes Head of Intelligence.'

Higgins looked doubtful.

'And you'll pay?'

Stanley got up and smiled his politician's smile.

'When Cornwell's neutered, we'll see. Start drafting the
paperwork for that State of Emergency.'

As the reporter put folder and recorder into her big leather
bag, Schneider experienced a confusion of emotions. Continuing anger at wanton murder. Renewed determination
to chase down the killer. Nostalgia for his own youth, of
the kind sometimes stimulated by a song that brings back
memories.

In this case, the stimulus was energy radiating from
Mary-Jo MacInnes. Schneider had no desire to trade places,
be young again. She still had a lot of painful living to do;
most of his was done and paid for. After double-checking
his feelings, lest they were motivated by sentimentality,
Schneider decided he did like and trust her.

'That's the official bit. With me as a source and what you
dug out for yourself you got the makin's of a story. Not
big as yet, but interestin'. The lever which might topple a
boulder.'

Scratching her hair, she made a knowing statement without surprise or irritation.

'You're using me.'

Schneider slid a few inches closer along the bench.

'Sure, but what's good for me may be good for you. I'll
level. Off the record, we've had it on Martinez. Looks like
someone in the Stark camp must've been involved, because
of the car. One key held by an aide, no sign the vehicle
was hot-wired. Seen outside Maria's place, proven to have
carried her body. But we ain't goin' to get more without
pressure. You're it.'

Before replying, she nibbled a thumbnail.

'You mean the hyenas who come stampeding along behind me and sink yellow teeth into Stark will supply the leverage. My story will be factual, without innuendo. But they'll gorge themselves and to hell with the truth. This isn't some bent penny-ante politician from the boonies who's about to get caught with his pants down, Loot.'

'If he's got a lot to lose he'll try damn hard to shake out the rotten apple, if there is one. If there ain't, well, he knew he was getting' into a rough game when he stepped forward in the first place.'

'And if I do file and my boss runs with the story?'

'Inside track. Anythin' I get, you get, on the record just as soon as I can, exclusive. Diehl will go for it. I spoke with him earlier, checked you out. Has a pretty good opinion of you. I also recall the *Post*'s politics. Management won't lose sleep over a scoop or two of authentic mud slung at Stark.'

She nodded acceptance of his premise, but looked at him with concern. Probably genuine.

'True enough. But I put your name up in lights, the Republicans have enough heavyweights around here to squash you flatter than a horned toad under a MACK truck.'

'It's not really a toad, it's a lizard. I been dealin' with reptiles since before your mother graduated high school. Old Schneider looks after himself. I got a cabin in the hills, money put by, nobody much to worry about.'

'Then let's do it. I must run. Deadlines wait for no woman.'

Face alive, Mary-Jo MacInnes jumped up. He grabbed her sleeve.

'Got a phone in that bottomless bag? Before you go, I reckon we can rustle up a quote from my good friend Dave in the DA's office.'

Brigadier Anderson Kyle handed the SIS captain a coffee and gestured at the visitor's chair. Nolan looked embarrassed. Kyle realized the seat was piled high with papers.

'Tip that garbage on the floor. Thanks for getting here so fast. How many people have you brought?'

Roger Nolan got settled.

'Thirty-eight. Six five-man squads, two electronic listeners, three women, two comms experts and myself. The Colonel said you'd brief us.'

Kyle studied Nolan, liking the way the SIS man met his appraisal.

'I didn't tell him anything, Roger, and he didn't ask. I wouldn't want to put your colonel in an awkward position, he's an old friend. Did he did say anything else?'

'I'm to place myself under your orders. He did give the impression the work might be sensitive.'

A phone buzzed. Kyle pressed a button. The noise stopped.

'How do you feel about that?'

Nolan reflected, deciding he could speak his mind.

'Following orders, or the sensitive bit? No problem with the orders. The same goes for my team. I'd expect them to climb Nelson's Column and jump off the top if I asked.'

'And sensitivity?'

The question was casual, but Kyle needed to be sure. Nolan appreciated that he was being given a second chance to back off, but SIS didn't retreat.

'I'm here to follow orders, whatever they may be.'

Kyle took a large envelope from the desk.

'Good. I'm not without influence and regard loyalty as a commendable quality. Four men, ex-army, mercenaries. Responsible for all sorts of mayhem. The police have tracked them to a house in North London. Here's the address, pictures. One's a poor video still, possibly the leader. The others have been identified and there are mug shots.'

He handed over the envelope. Nolan studied the contents, looking up when address and faces were memorized. Kyle spoke softly.

'Sort these bastards once and for all. Shoot to kill. They're dangerous and I need your lot in one piece. There may be further assignments. Understood?'

'Perfectly. I don't suppose you could lend me a London *A to Z*?'

The car pulled away from Somerset House behind two police bikes, turning south across Waterloo Bridge. Two more brought up the rear. The circuitous route was a random selection designed to confuse potential assailants.

Godfrey Cornwell relaxed in the sculpted back seat and patted his PA's knee. The Home Secretary was not one for whom expressions of emotion came easily, so the gesture conveyed a great deal.

'Off we go, then. We'll soon know, but you've done well, Alec. Kept your head, as usual. We make a great team. I lost it back there. If you've earned something, it's hard to cope when the cheque bounces. You understand, you're the only one who does.'

The young West Countryman answered sternly, but Cornwell knew he was flattered.

'Don't get carried away, Godfrey. There's no guarantee Forsyth will fall for it. That smug bastard's sitting pretty whatever happens.'

The Rover stopped at traffic lights, tight between outriders who shielded the occupants. Through armoured windows, Godfrey Cornwell noted the security precaution with approval. Pedestrians hurried across in front, studiously ignoring them. Peasants. What did they really know about the system that put food on their tables, allowed them to live their lives in relative comfort? He turned to Ambler, picking up the thread of their conversation.

'Your plan's better than you think. I've met this guy, taken his measure. Oh, he's a good operator, but he's never had to fight for what he's achieved. Chandler's blue-eyed boy all the way, wasn't he?'

The lights changed and the Rover moved off. Alec Ambler had been listening intently, but still didn't see it.

'What are you saying, Godfrey?'

Cornwell revelled in his deep understanding of human weaknesses.

'The General's on an ego trip, Alec. Suddenly, unexpectedly, he finds himself in a position of extraordinary power. His boss is off the scene, government's like a headless chicken, he's in charge of the strongest force in the country. Bob Forsyth likes that, begins to appreciate possibilities, starts thinking he'll sort things out for the good of the nation.'

Alec Ambler followed the argument, thinking aloud in admiration.

'Third World military dictator syndrome? My duty to take

over and sort out this fearful mess, free elections guaranteed within six months, a regime that lasts for years until a stronger man comes along. Perhaps cloaked in conviction, but motivated by personal aggrandizement.'

'Exactly. Forsyth will find my offer of the Premiership irresistible. Even he won't have got that far yet, because without our Party connections it's not possible. But once mooted he'll become convinced he'd make an ideal Prime Minister. Stanley's suspect, probably working with the Yanks. Will Forsyth feel secure with a man like that controlling his destiny? I doubt it.'

Alec Ambler interrupted eagerly.

'He certainly won't want Stanley in Number Ten, Godfrey, or you. But Forsyth may be suspicious at your abrupt about-turn.'

Cornwell grinned wolfishly.

'He's arrogant enough to believe he's holding the best cards. He'll figure I'm settling for the inevitable, accepting that a supporting rôle is better than nothing. And of course he'll also think he can renege on the deal and shove me out when he's consolidated his new position.'

His PA chuckled.

'But he doesn't really have much experience at the top table, does he? Our ambitious General will fail to appreciate that this isn't some tinpot Third World country. Britain can't be run as a dictatorship, the economy and society are too complex. Power must be exercised through the system. Even Minton-Briant understood that.'

Ambler paused, eyes glittering with satisfaction as he savoured the denouement. When he continued, his voice caressed the words.

'Push Forsyth upstairs, separate him from hands-on control of Intelligence, let him think you're no longer a threat and it's only a matter of time before we use the system to knock him down again. He won't have a friend left after pulling a stroke like this, not one.'

Cornwell looked at his young PA in surprise. When Alec had suggested the plan and talked passionately about getting to Number 10, Cornwell assumed he was raising their spirits in an impossible situation. Now, in a rare moment of insight, he saw that Alec Ambler's vision had been greater.

Alec had understood all along that the arrogant Forsyth would blunder into a gossamer web which would enmesh and ultimately destroy him. But he'd prompted subtly and let his master work out the plan's true inventiveness. And take the credit. Full of surprises, was young Alec – one in a million. He felt a rush of affection and patted Ambler's knee again, more vigorously than before.

'I don't know how I'd manage without you, boy child.'

Alec smiled happily. The driver indicated right and the car slowed. Cornwell had lost track of their progress and glanced out of the window. They were at the top of Charing Cross Road, right beside Intelligence Headquarters.

He watched the Rover standing in Charing Cross Road, indicator blinking, waiting to swing on to the forecourt. Cornwell had been instructed to come in the front way. Round One to the bad guys.

They sat in an official look-alike black Jaguar, twenty yards from the jutting main entryway which shared a purpose with the covered carriage porticoes found on so many Georgian mansions. Can't have fat cats wetting fine fur. The day had turned nasty. Drizzle fell and it was getting dark early. So much the better. Above, lights blazed all the way up New Centre Point, until the building vanished into leaden clouds.

They'd been checked by Intelligence patrolmen in the five minutes since they arrived, but genuine uniforms and passes withstood scrutiny. His explanation – protection duty for an important visitor due at any moment – was accepted. The patrol consisted of two sergeants, and he thanked the mind that provided him with a colonel's uniform. Time.

'Right, lads, go. Toddy, ready with the car. Don't be late. Jakes, bikes and bodyguards. Linden, main door. Cornwell's mine.'

He stepped out into the rain and put on his cap. Two motorcycles were turning off New Oxford Street, Cornwell's Rover following, then two more bikes. He marched forward, slipping a finger into the trigger guard of the official-issue Heckler & Koch MP5K that bumped his hip as he walked, supported by its webbing strap. Weapon cocked, pointing forward. Behind, he could hear Jakes and Linden marching in step. Good soldiers.

Car and men arrived simultaneously. Stoop to check occupants. Bodyguard and driver in front, Cornwell and one other in the back. Damn, Cornwell on far side. Click as central locking operates. Get rear door open fast, greet important occupant politely. Step back to give exit room. Touch peaked cap.

'Minister, you're expected.'

The three seconds it took Cornwell's young companion to climb out were critical. Until he did, the target was shielded. For an awful instant, he thought the bodyguard would emerge, open the offside door and let Cornwell out that way. But the bodyguard was slow. Cornwell was following the boy, coming out his side. Perfect.

A shout from the entrance – a damn guard, realizing something wasn't right. Rips of gunfire. Bodyguard going down beyond the car. More shouting. Do it now, now, now. The kid throwing himself in front of Cornwell. Hosing both men back into the car with the force of soft-nosed bullet strikes. Blood spraying. Empty clip.

Turn, assess, reload. Lead bikes both down, guard at entrance down, driver huddled, hands over head. Jag braking hard, sliding on wet tarmac, stopping. Jakes and Linden crouching, also reloading. Third bike on its side, fourth upright blocking their escape, rider behind with handgun up. No time for second bite at Cornwell. Into the Jag after Linden and Jakes, dive through open rear door on to squirming bodies.

Surging acceleration. Door slamming itself, lurching impact, Jag slewing but not stopping, picking up speed again. Bye-bye, bike. Scramble up to see what's happening, fall back as car skids under full power. New Oxford Street. Rapid twists and turns, thrown from side to side. Everyone laughing. Euphoria. Toddy shouting.

'This is your chauffeur speaking. You little pansies can sit up. We're clear. All change in one minute.'

It was nearly over.

Brigadier Andy Kyle and General Robert Forsyth were in conference. Kyle had grabbed the few moments that remained before the Home Secretary arrived to explain the rapid progress of his investigation. But he had barely begun when the door flew open and Sally Sayers ran in. For the first time in Kyle's experience, Forsyth's PA had lost her cool. She stopped, hands making small uncoordinated gestures.

'There's been shooting downstairs, outside the front entrance.'

Forsyth got up fast, staring at his agitated assistant. She repeated the message word for word, hands dropping. Forsyth stood motionless, face paralysed. Kyle looked from one to the other, then asked a calm question.

'What else do you know, Sally?'

She tore her eyes from Forsyth, focused on Kyle. It was almost the usual self-possessed Sally who replied.

'Not much. I just got a call from the front desk saying there'd been shooting on the forecourt. Automatic weapons. No more details. Anything I can do?'

Kyle and Forsyth glanced at one another. Forsyth voiced the suspicion.

'Cornwell?'

'Seems likely. Those trigger-happy bastards are one jump ahead of us again.'

The Acting Head had recovered his composure.

'Get back outside, Sally, see if you can get any more information.'

He watched her out of the room, then turned to Kyle.

'They're actually trying to wipe out the entire command structure.'

Kyle smiled cynically.

'I wouldn't cross Ken Stanley if I were you, it's starting to look like a dangerous occupation.'

'This changes everything. Go downstairs and find out what's happened.'

'On my way, boss.'

The big man followed Sally Sayers.

The changing room was parked in a multistorey off Long Acre. Two minutes after the attack, they dumped the Jag in Endell Street, having scribed an irregular half-circle through streets which brought them back within three hundred yards of New Centre Point. Still protected by Intelligence uniforms, they walked quickly to the car park – going up back stairs past graffiti that spread multicoloured tentacles into every corner.

The panel van was unwatched. A rapid transformation took place – four Intelligence personnel in, four unremarkable civilians in hats and raincoats out. At the bottom of the concrete staircase, they paused. The leader issued ten-pound notes.

'Back to the house. Split up here, use public transport. Go carefully, but be there by twenty hundred hours. Leave the area on foot, they'll probably close nearby stations. I'm going to walk to Euston and take the Northern Line. Don't be late. Travel arrangements have been made and we're on a tight timetable. If I don't make it your tickets, passports and bank books are under my mattress. Good luck.'

He handed Toddy a slip of paper – the former corporal's final contribution to the plan.

'Here's a phone number in case something happens to me and you're in serious trouble, and I do mean serious. Emergency use only, understood? Okay, lads, on your way. Nice and steady.'

A muttered 'Major' and two silent nods later they were gone. The leader turned up his coat collar before following, carrying a briefcase that contained passport, cordless shaver and left-luggage key.

There were blue flashing lights outside the main entrance doors. Before Brigadier Kyle could go out, he was accosted by the Duty Security Officer, a captain. The man wasn't actually twitching, but looked as though it was an effort to restrain himself.

'Four men dressed in Intelligence uniforms were waiting outside in a Jaguar like one of ours. They were checked by an outside patrol, showed identification and claimed to be on protection duty. The one who did the talking was a colonel, and the patrol didn't think to check back with me. They're in custody . . .'

Anxiety showed on the captain's face at this reminder that failure could have painful consequences. When he continued, his voice was subdued and squared shoulders had slipped.

'The Home Secretary arrived with a motorcycle escort. Three men went to the car as though they were meeting him officially. Then the shooting started. It was all over in a matter of seconds. They got away before anyone could move.'

Kyle absorbed information. When he spoke, his voice was brusque.

'Casualties?'

'A guard outside the doors who raised the alarm is dead. Three of the motorcycle escorts were killed, another injured by the Jag during the getaway. The Minister's bodyguard was also killed, so was his PA. It's a slaughterhouse. Cornwell's badly hurt, but alive.'

Kyle regarded the security officer coldly.

'Get back to Control and supervise police reaction.'

He went down the steps into a cool evening, drizzle hitting his face as he left the sheltering canopy and crossed to the ambulance. Godfrey Cornwell was on a wheeled stretcher, wrapped in a blanket. His handsome face was pallid. Two paramedics were about to lift the stretcher, a third was holding up a drip bottle. Kyle stopped beside him. The ambulanceman was used to ghoulish fascination with tragedy and didn't need to be asked.

'This one may survive. Forget the others.'

He followed the stretcher into the ambulance. The rear doors were shut and the vehicle moved off, siren starting as it turned left and spurted down Oxford Street.

Alone again, the leader walked through Covent Garden, avoiding the tourist market. Sirens sounded from every direction. As he went down Bedfordbury, a police car flashed by the far end of Mays Court, heading down St Martin's Lane from Seven Dials. He nearly beat it to the Strand. Coming out of Adelaide Street he saw the car turn through the entrance of Charing Cross Station.

The ex-major crossed the road and slipped down Villiers Street, merging into homebound workers trudging through light rain towards Hungerford Bridge. He liked the narrow iron walkway high above Old Father Thames. A dirty blue train clattered across the railway bridge beside him, lighted interior packed.

Stopping the transport system was out of the question, with half a million commuters still in town. He descended beside the National Arts complex and walked under overhead railway tracks towards Waterloo Station, ignoring ragged figures that sidled from cardboard lairs to beg for tea money.

There were plenty of policemen in evidence when he reached the busy concourse, but they were wandering aimlessly as though unsure what to look for. Four ruthless killers carrying smoking guns, perhaps. He ignored their forlorn perambulation, retrieving a suitcase from the left-luggage lockers without challenge.

His assertion to the men that Cornwell was the last job had not been entirely truthful. Then again, perhaps it had. He looked into the locker and studied four bank books, sitting on top of a black composition suitcase containing a dismantled sniper's rifle. He could take the rifle and catch the Underground to his new safe house in Balham, there to await that final call to arms.

But with a hornet's nest of security activity stirred up, the odds against survival were shortening rapidly. His pension was both safe and rather larger than originally anticipated. Besides, he was fed up with *Rule Britannia*, whistled somewhat tunelessly but with great verve. The clever bastard had got good value for money, so let him see how he liked doing his own dirty work.

Dropping coins into the slot, the retired assassin placed the bank books into his briefcase and shut the locker door. He strolled towards the Gent's at a leisurely pace.

After five minutes in a basement cubicle he was a new man. Long sideburns had been painfully removed with the battery shaver. The itchy toupee had been cut into pieces and flushed away. After running a hand over his prematurely balding head, enjoying air on the smooth scalp, he emerged cautiously.

There was no taxi queue outside the stone entrance arch, with fewer customers than black cabs coming round the raised roadway to drop fares. The first cabbie in line reached out of his window to open the rear door.

'Where to, guv?'

'Victoria Station.'

The leader relaxed on the wide leather seat as the taxi pulled away. The characteristic rumble of its diesel engine was a sound he wouldn't hear for some time, if ever again. Next stop Gatwick Airport, then Nice. He thought briefly about three men making their way back to a house beyond the North Circular. Perhaps they should have paid more attention when the theories of Charles Darwin were explained in school.

Unfair. Poor buggers probably hadn't even heard of natural selection.

The portable printer zipped out hard copy, delivering a single sheet into the waiting hand of Mary-Jo MacInnes. She liked to see her story on paper before filing, but only ten minutes remained before the deadline for Tuesday's edition.

She read the copy, making small corrections. The words were considered, restrained. Even Dealer Diehl wouldn't be able to fault sources or accuse her story of trying to sprint before it could crawl. Despite the small beginning, Mary-Jo felt sure this would run and run.

Returning to her keyboard, she tapped in corrections and made up a file that included her story, digital images of the Buick and summaries of her taped interviews. Diehl would want to be very sure before giving this one the nod.

After switching in the modem, she hooked up to the phone and sent the file away with two minutes to spare. Mary-Jo half expected her Managing Editor to call, but when the phone went it wasn't DD. Instead, she heard her new friend in SAPD, calling from a public phone to judge by the mess of background music and talk. Schneider's voice was ever so slightly slurred.

'Have you filed, MacInnes, or what?'

'My humble offering's down the wire to Washington. Consider your tree shaken, if we make it into print. We're talking felines on hot tin roofs, Loot.'

'Could work out pretty warm at that. Get any reaction from Stark's spin-doctors, or did they clam up?'

'An expansive "no comment" followed by an unspoken

"now hang up so I can go find out what the hell this is all about". I guess we caught them on the hop.'

'Yeah, we had a deal – they give us the car, we keep quiet. But that was before we found what we found. They'll understand. If Stark wins, every promise made in the campaign will be history inside a year, so who are they to complain? Keep on truckin', MacInnes.'

She was about to say 'Look after yourself' when the line went dead. She imagined him walking unsteadily back to order another drink, trying to escape his anger. He wouldn't, because he wasn't that sort of guy.

General Robert Forsyth thought about the dead. Derek Minton-Briant, in a glass-topped coffin at Westminster Abbey, embalmer's skill ensuring his features were rosier in death than life. Would the egocentric old man have liked being the centre of attention to the end, or hated the endless line of morbid spectators who shuffled past?

President Awami and his colleagues, destroyed for taking afternoon tea with the wrong person at the wrong time, threatening a fragile country's very stability. Likewise Chequers domestic staff, leaving no more than scattered cucumber sandwiches and grieving families as their mark on the world.

Policemen kissing wives and children goodbye and going off to another routine day's work, unprepared to encounter oblivion at the hands of Donald Sheldon, killing machine extraordinary. CIA deskman Mendlebaum, shot by his own subordinate.

A deceived industrialist who happened to manufacture aircraft. His wife, who happened to be married to him. Alec Ambler, a clever young man with a rewarding life to live whose last instinct was to protect another. The list seemed endless.

He tried to arrive at a total, failed. All that killing, in pursuit of self-appointed destiny. General Forsyth understood the motivation, all right, and knew the easy rationalization – that they would not have died in vain.

But that brought little comfort.

SIS Captain Roger Nolan was in the attic of Number 372,

stretched uncomfortably on thin joists. Spores from dusty fibreglass insulation had insinuated beneath his dark clothing, irritating skin. He hardly noticed.

By the time Brigadier Kyle's message concerning the attack at New Centre Point had been received, Nolan was sure the safe house was deserted. By going along back gardens and over fences, they had got to the side door of Number 374. After initial suspicion, the occupant was co-operative. The old lady could tell them nothing helpful about the neighbours, but she had settled in her front room behind closed curtains, stroking a grey cat and watching the SIS team's activities with interest.

Sensitive equipment was used to probe the dividing wall, recording a dripping tap and the occasional murmur of a refrigerator. They'd missed the targets. Still, Nolan had deployed his forces with care, in case the killers were foolish enough to return. He'd brought nine people, reasoning that more would get in each others' way.

One electronic listener was inside Number 374, accompanied by a female operative who was minding the owner. Two men were hidden in the overgrown back garden of 372. Two more staked out the street to give warning of an approach from either direction. The last pair were a courting couple in a Ford estate car parked opposite the house. Nolan had taken point, reaching the loft from 374 through a thin partition.

He was observing landing and stairs through a slit beneath the roof hatch, which he'd raised a couple of inches, propping it open with a spare magazine for his MP5SD. The house was dark. He'd undertaken a probe with his pencil torch, which revealed worn carpeting and peeling walls. He wouldn't risk going down to learn more.

His earpiece whispered urgently, causing a hand to tighten on the submachine-gun at his side. One of the lookouts.

'Male pedestrian, northbound, your side of the road.'

The first lookout, not hopeful.

'Subject has walked past the house.'

Half a courting couple peering through a misty car window. The briefest of pauses. Sudden anticipation.

'He's turned. Looks like he's checking the street. Yes, he's going in, going in now.'

As he heard a key turn in the door below, Roger Nolan lowered the hatch. From now on, he would be blind – but not deaf. The earpiece murmured on, supplemented by sounds from below.

'Subject One to kitchen. Kettle on. Coming back. Going upstairs.'

This from electronic ears, listening through the wall.

'Major?'

A real voice, not a yard away, beneath the hatch. Belfast accent. A door opening, the sound of pissing, a toilet flushing.

'Two more male pedestrians, northbound, your side of the road.' The lookout again.

'Going straight in, bold as brass.'

Half a courting couple, getting excited. Footsteps on stairs below, a board creaking.

'All three in hall, talking. Expecting someone else. Subject One identified as Toddy, wants to wait. Subjects Two and Three don't. Toddy to kitchen. Two and Three identified as Jakes and Linden, going upstairs.'

Electronic ears, confirming what he could hear for himself. Muffled footsteps, voices.

'Better bloody be where he said, or I'll kill the bastard.'

'The stuff'll be there, Jakes. We can trust the Major.'

Door opening. Front bedroom. Rustling. The bed? Drawers slamming shut, fabric tearing. Jakes shouting.

'Sod the bleeding tea, Toddy. Get your arse up here, there's nothing.'

Pounding footsteps on stairs. Angry sounds of a room being trashed. Sudden silence. Voices in the bedroom. Low, frightened.

'Two-faced bastard's crossed us, skipped with the lot.'

Jakes. The angry one.

'We don't know that for sure. Let's wait for half an hour.'

Toddy. The strong one.

'Jakes is right. Let's grab the guns and get out fast. To hell with the money. If this place isn't blown it soon will be.'

Linden. The anxious one.

Decision time – for them, for him. One man missing, unlikely to come. Lookouts watching in case. Lovebirds covering the front, two men out the back. Targets in dangerous mood. Possibly armed. As ordered by Kyle, take no chances, though he hardly needed to be told.

Roger Nolan eased up the hatch, propping it with his knife, revealing a weakly lit landing and staircase. A voice from the bedroom, louder now. Toddy. Authoritative, calm.

'Okay, let's split. We'll steal a car, go to ground. Do a post office on benefit day. Then away, out of the bloody country for good. Ireland, maybe. We've still got good contacts over there. Agreed?'

It must have been. Nolan's oblong frame of vision filled with people, turning on to stairs one after another, not looking up. He slid the Heckler & Koch forward, waited for the optimum moment and poured nickel-plated bullets into the stairwell in a juddering burst. They fell – sliding down walls, finishing up as a heap at the foot of the staircase. Nolan peered through eddying powder smoke, but there was no movement.

Eerie quiet was broken by the crashing arrival of back-up through front and side doors.

The Prince Regent only rated two bodyguards. He'd thought briefly of cancelling his assignation with Beth Highsmith on security grounds – along with every other engagement in the foreseeable future – to bring his displeasure to the attention of General Robert Forsyth. George had not forgotten his narrow escape at Windsor.

The humiliating rôle forced upon him by Minton-Briant was a thing of the past. The Forsyths, Stanleys and Cornwells of this world might not like it, but they needed the constitutional credibility he conferred. So by God they'd pay. His chauffeur found Beth's address, sliding the Rolls into a convenient parking bay.

'That's the place, sir. Blue door. Do you wish me to wait here, or return later?'

George got out and looked at the driver.

'Stay here, dickhead. If I wanted you to go I'd bloody well say so. Be here when I get back, even if it's ten o'clock in the morning.'

His driver's lips tightened and the electric window rudely slid up. Luckily for him, George's thoughts were turning to the evening ahead. The bodyguards had parked their Range Rover behind the Roller. He handed one a bottle of chilled champagne, the other a box of Belgian truffle chocolates he particularly liked.

'One of you talk to Miss Highsmith, top floor. Tell her I'm here. Check out the building. Then walk me up and wait for me outside.'

Champagne stayed put, Chocolates headed up the steps. After an exchange with the entryphone, he went in. George pictured Beth Highsmith's perfect face, which he knew from their brief meeting and protracted magazine study. He imagined her body without designer rags.

His own body responded to the mental stimulus. It was all George could do to stop himself hurrying into the house before the place was declared safe. Innate caution prevailed. Silly to get blown away because a few rogue hormones got worked up.

Anyway, anticipation was half the pleasure.

The dream was vivid, consuming. He'd been told that men mostly don't dream in colour, except for fire, that women mostly do. But he was dreaming in colour. Without being able to make things change, become less threatening. The dream would continue to an awful climax and the end would be frightening, catastrophic. But there could be no escape. Was something chasing him – or was it watching and waiting ahead?

He ran soundlessly on fleecy cloud that absorbed his energy. The faster he ran, the slower he went, puffs of white sediment rising at every step. The cloud undulated away as far as he could see. A bell tolled – sonorous, disembodied, echoing in vast spaces beyond comprehension.

A telephone ringing.

Ken Stanley awoke to intense relief. Dreadful images were still in his mind, but he was free. Then, like a switched-off television picture, the dream vanished, leaving no more than an after-image as he picked up the phone.

'Are you there, Prime Minister?'

Unfamiliar room. Sofa. Apricot carpet. Derry watching from his lighted tank. Downing Street. Monday night. State of Emergency. Harry Higgins.

'Harry? I nodded off in my chair.'

'Sorry, but I've had General Forsyth on. There's been another attack, right outside the Intelligence building. Godfrey Cornwell.'

'Dead?'

'Badly injured. The killers were tracked to a house in North London, where they died resisting arrest. Forsyth believes they were the ones who carried out the Windsor attack, and eliminated a witness who could have thrown light on Derek's murder.'

Ken Stanley shook his head to clear the remnants of sleep. The Cabinet Secretary resumed sharply.

'Without Cornwell the pressure's off. There's nobody left to challenge your authority. But if this is a destabilization exercise by the Americans, they're disposing of the old leadership in the hope that a new government might eventually be more sympathetic.'

'I'll be on the hit list?'

'Bound to be. And there's no guarantee that Intelligence has dealt with all the assassins.'

He tried to concentrate. Couldn't.

'Press on with the State of Emergency. I'll feel happier with that in place. Give me fifteen minutes to grab a shower and I'll come down.'

'That would be best.'

Harry Higgins hung up, sounding like a man who thought they still had a problem. The Prime Minister felt bone-weary, ancient, conscious of human mortality. But he climbed out of the armchair, walked over and took a frankfurter from the sandwich box beside the fish tank.

'What do you make of all this, Derry, old friend?'

Ken Stanley dropped the thin sausage. The evil little piranha caught the offering before it hit bottom.

Beth Highsmith was taking her commitment seriously. She'd cut the Tower of London photographic session short, despite Greg Browne's protests, and hurried home via Harrods. Her loyalty to Forsyth's cause didn't extend to cooking, so she purchased scallops in brandy sauce which needed ten minutes in the oven, a mixed cold meat platter with salad and crème brûlée to follow. A simple meal fit for a king.

She watched the man in question from the studio's gabled front window. He was pacing the pavement, shadowed by a short but solid-looking character carrying a bottle of champagne. Beth smiled to herself. The bottle in her fridge was undoubtedly of better quality, because it was the best money could buy.

Confirmation that she was taking the assignment seriously was visible on all sides. In contrast to its habitual chaos, the large studio was tidy and dust-free. The table was set for two on white lace, with bright silverware and crystal glasses. The ensemble came from a Martini commercial. A gushing director had given her the props. Until tonight, the stuff hadn't been out of its box.

Her visitor hurried towards the house, vanishing from sight. She was wearing a white silk blouse, turquoise mini-skirt and black tights. No undergarments. Her thick hair hung loose. Beth knew she looked good.

She opened the door as George arrived. He was panting after climbing steep stairs and perspiration glazed his dissolute face. He was carrying the champagne, plus a box of chocolates. The Prince Regent plodded eagerly into her home, slamming the door behind him. While he got his breath back, he looked around. The calculating gaze finally came to rest on Beth. Voice matched personality – vain and shallow.

'Very nice.'

The remark was not a comment on the decor. He proffered chocolates, hung on to the bottle.

'A little something for the sweetest girl I've seen all week.'

Fighting a wild urge to laugh, Beth took the gift and arranged her face into a shy smile. Communicating the chosen impression was a skill she didn't have to think about.

'That's kind. I didn't think you'd even remember me from our brief meeting, let alone accept a dinner invitation.'

He smirked, setting off rapidly for the sofa, sweeping up two glasses from the table on the way.

'George never forgets a pretty face. Sit.'

After lowering himself on to the sofa, he patted the cushion beside him. She sat, conscious that he was staring at upward movement of an already outrageous hemline. He popped the champagne cork, a feeble 'phut' confirming earlier suspicions. Despite a Krug label, the contents probably originated in Spain. She accepted the fizzing glass graciously, though he leaned rather closer than necessary.

His prominent Adam's apple bobbed as he emptied his own glass, which he promptly refilled. He leaned back and addressed the far wall.

'So, my dear, to what do I owe this unexpected honour? I must say your invitation did come as a surprise.'

He smiled pleasantly, though something in the expression warned her. George might be a worthless wastrel, but he was potentially dangerous. She looked embarrassed, aware he was watching intently.

'You know General Forsyth, don't you? Well, I've been having problems with the authorities. Nothing serious, some questions about overseas earnings and whether I've declared everything for tax purposes. I thought . . .'

Comprehension cascaded over George's face.

'Say no more. I have influence in high places. You want me to put in a word, get you off the hook? No problem. I'll speak with my old school chum Bob tomorrow. You'll hear no more about the matter. I hope you screwed them for millions, greedy bastards.'

'That's kind, George.'

Beth looked suitably grateful, crossed long legs and lay back in her corner of the deep sofa. Now he'd satisfied his curiosity as to motive, she could switch into alluring mode. When would men stop thinking with their testosterone?

The operation in North London had gone well. Three out of four was a result. Although it was inconceivable the leader would show, men had been left to stake out Number 372.

When the team arrived back at New Centre Point, Brigadier Kyle had congratulated Roger Nolan. In return, the SIS officer handed him a slip of paper found on a killer's corpse. It completed his case against Ken Stanley. The telephone number was for the direct private line into the apartment at Number 10, which Stanley had only just occupied. There could be no doubt in anyone's mind that the Acting Premier had been directing four killers hell-bent on wiping out his rivals.

Before updating General Forsyth, Kyle had put the SIS team on stand-by in case they were needed again, then agreed to see the young officer he'd placed in charge of the Coppel case. A sensitive matter, apparently. He ushered Phil Dexter into his office. The captain placed a battery-operated cassette player on Kyle's desk and sat down. His expression was serious. Kyle had an uneasy premonition.

'Well?'

The investigator looked uncomfortable, and replied cautiously.

'Coppel's insurance policy, sir. I found this tape in a sealed container buried in one of the window boxes at Mulberry Cottage. Recorded off his home phone with a lick-and-stick microphone.'

He reached over, moving the machine's volume slide to low and pushing the play button. They heard the agitated voice of the late Victor Coppel as he started in mid-sentence.

'. . . your personal assurance that this highly irregular request to release a new Bluebird aircraft will not have any adverse repercussions for my company or myself.'

'Don't mess me about, Coppel. The paperwork's in order and this is an official Intelligence operation. We need to evaluate that aircraft in conjunction with highly secret surveillance equipment. It's . . .'

Rigid with shock, Kyle somehow reached over and silenced the treacherous voice.

'Nobody else has heard this tape, I hope, or knows of its existence?'

'No, sir, as soon as I played it in the car I knew what to do.'

'You did right to bring this to me.'

Kyle put his elbows on the desktop and looked the young detective in the eye.

'Fine work, though it puts us in a difficult position. Suspicions of complicity in high places are rife, but haven't pointed in that direction. If this blows open now the repercussions for Intelligence hardly bear thinking about, never mind the impact on you and me.'

Captain Dexter inclined his head gravely.

'You can rely on my discretion. I'm sure you'll handle the matter as you think fit.'

'Thanks for the vote of confidence, Phil. You won't regret it. Leave the tape with me, and not a word to anyone.'

Dexter rose from his chair and snapped a salute.

'Sir!'

He about-turned and marched from the office. Kyle looked at the closed door. He had chosen his investigating officer well. The captain would keep quiet until this mess could be cleaned up.

Kyle removed the tape and locked it in his safe. Even the best operators made mistakes, usually over the silliest things. Who could have guessed Coppel would record home phone conversations with an old-fashioned device that beat anti-intercept electronics with sheer simplicity? The tall Intelligence officer returned to his desk and slumped into the chair, feeling profoundly depressed.

His dark mood passed, and with it doubt. By using all the cunning he possessed, he just might be able to bring down General Robert Forsyth before his superior and long-time friend got the slightest hint that the incriminating tape existed.

She had an ulterior motive, wanted to use him. How predictable. Nothing was for nothing. Everyone fighting their corner, trying to use everyone else. Beth Highsmith stretched like a sinuous cat. Almost purred.

'You're very kind to offer your help, George.'

The Prince Regent placed his champagne glass on the floor, reached over and patted her tights, just above the knee.

'Always a pleasure to be of service to a beautiful woman, my dear. I'll bet you haven't got anything else on underneath. Wouldn't do to spoil the lines of that little skirt.'

Her thigh was firm. She put her hand on his, gently moving it on to yellow velvet.

'Shall we have supper? You must be hungry, and I'm sure we'll find a lot to talk about.'

She looked at him with an innocent expression which didn't fool him for a minute. This little tart might be packaged better, but was no different from the rest. A tease, a bloody tease.

George had remained a virgin until he was twenty-three.

Not through want of opportunity, but because his treacherous body refused to obey when the moment came. Every time he remembered those fumbling encounters with naïve young women his flesh shrank, just as it had then. Need to be sure, looking for a meaningful relationship, casual lovemaking not for me, don't want to be the first because you'll only fall in love with me – the pathetic excuses haunted him.

When he reached his twenties, adolescent excuses wore thin. The women were more assertive. Even so they let him down lightly – understanding, sympathetic, kind. He hated them for that, never gave them a second chance to pity his weakness.

One night, after a bash at Tramps, one of them finally went too far. They returned to his place in Islington by cab, drunk enough to wrestle without inhibition on the wide leather seat. For once, his body behaved properly when her inquisitive hands found his manhood.

As soon as the door of his flat closed behind them, they were at each other. Eager, keen, scattering clothes. He almost made it, thrusting wildly but inaccurately against unyielding flesh. Then panic surged through his mind and suddenly he was no longer capable. That's when she made her big mistake. Those inquisitive hands quickly assessed the situation and George braced himself for the familiar 'Never mind, we've probably had too much to drink'.

Instead, she became angry. Taunted him. Said unforgivable things in a shrill voice as she sat up and started to button her blouse. He hit her, wrestled with her on the carpet as she tried to crawl away, hit again. Seconds later, with no recollection of how he got there, he was inside her, experiencing the most incredible sensation. Strength. Power. Shuddering pleasure.

Darling Vanessa wasn't so talkative when he shoved cab money into her hand and showed her the door. That little episode may have cost the old man ten grand, but was worth every penny. It showed him the way.

'George?'

Beth Highsmith was looking at him with an odd expression. Perhaps female antennae had picked up vibrations. He smiled warmly.

'You didn't really ask me up here to exchange sweet nothings over the dinner table, my dear. I think you wanted to use me, take advantage of my valuable contacts to sort out your little spot of financial bother. Am I right or am I right?'

Lieutenant Richard Schneider walked into the basement detectives' room. It was late. He was depressed and slightly drunk. After meeting with MacInnes, he'd gone down to Jim Cullum's Landing on River Walk for hot jazz and one too many cold margaritas.

Okay, it would be a bad break for Stark – but if newspaper coverage helped put cuffs on a killer, the price was worth paying. Also, there was no knowing that Stark's people weren't involved up to their sanitized armpits.

Sergeant Olmos was the darkened room's only occupant, pounding away at his battered IBM with two pudgy fingers, in light cast by a desk lamp with green shade. He looked up eagerly.

'Got the doughnuts?'

Schneider slapped his forehead. The shock reverberated.

'Jeez, Jimmy, I'm sorry. I bet you were really lookin' forward to those sticky jellos with maple syrup.'

The look on the fat sergeant's face was a sight to behold.

'You slimeball, you trick me into doing five hours' unpaid overtime and you're *sorry*?'

He slammed agitated hands on the keyboard. The machine responded with distressed electronic sounds. Olmos groaned.

'What the hell, I was gonna to start dieting anyway. No law says I can't begin right now. I'll make do with this.'

He produced a Snickers bar and started to peel the wrapper. Schneider sat down heavily at the next desk.

'What you got, Jimmy?'

Olmos put down the candy, folded his arms across an expansive chest and looked like the shrewd cop who consistently won the department's annual handgun trophy, to the chagrin of younger officers.

'We found a witness who can ID the driver of that Buick the night Martinez went down. Big crack dealer named Ruiz, Charlie Ruiz. Has a team workin' the brown neighbourhoods in the north-west section and is waiting for a meet across from the Martinez place when he sees this Buick turn in. Shiny clean, two aerials. He figures cop and ducks out of sight behind a tree. Force of habit, not because he's carrying.'

He chewed the candy bar, punishing Schneider. Relented.

'The driver waits until the street's empty then goes in the house. Ruiz thinks he slips the lock. Soon as he's in Ruiz is gone. Claims he got a real good sight of this dude.'

'This big-time dealer volunteered information?'

Olmos grinned.

'Sure. He got careless. Vice takes out his main runner and hopes greed overcomes caution. It does. He handles a drop personally. Nailed with a half-key of angel dust. He's thinkin' about a long vacation at state expense in Huntsville. Wants to trade. Won't finger his own, but his Martinez story checks out. Talked to the man myself. No way could he have put this together. Too much detail that ain't been published.'

'Reliable?'

'Don't use the product, don't smoke, drives a Caddy De Ville when he ain't working, lives on the same block as the Mayor over the west side, has a portfolio of blue-chip stocks an average down-home Texas millionaire would envy and two kids in private school. Plus he's about to become a three-time loser. The guy's a businessman.'

As he reached for the nearest phone, Schneider made a two-fingers-and-thumb pistol with his free hand and shot Olmos.

'You done good. I'll get our bosom buddy David Turrow out of bed.'

Olmos contemplated the Snickers wrapper, his jowly face collapsing into gloom.

'Tell me you was kidding about them frigging doughnuts, Dick.'

After the Prince Regent had gone, tiny fibre optic eyes observed Beth Highsmith's first painful movements, relaying them to twin video machines in the back of a Telecom van parked in the street below. As a member of the Intelligence Covert Operations team, the watcher was used to dark dimensions of the human psyche. Sergeant Egleton used his digital cellphone to call base.

When they heard General Forsyth was expecting his call, Control put him on hold. While he waited, Egleton tried to look anywhere but at her, but kept returning to the colour monitor. The girl was up now. She discarded remnants of clothing, letting torn garments fall in a ragged pile where she stood. Moving slowly, she headed for the bathroom.

The Sergeant switched shots, watching her take a white silk robe from behind the bathroom door and put it on. Livid bruises were forming on breasts and buttocks. He was glad when her body was covered, as though that somehow made his observation less obscene.

Beth Highsmith rested against the basin counter and stared into the big mirror for a long time. The ordeal he had witnessed would have shattered anyone. But to a woman who lived by her physical attributes, the sight of an awkwardly broken nose and bottom lip split right through must have been soul destroying.

The Acting Head came onto the phone, his calm voice providing an ideal excuse to turn away from the screen.

'Report, Sergeant.'

'Required material obtained. Status of female subject damaged but repairable. Male subject has left the scene.'

'Be advised that a medical unit is on the way. Break off surveillance and bring the tapes to me personally.'

As Egleton put down his phone, the woman reached for a tissue. Ignoring blood which oozed from her ruined lip, she started crying softly, dabbing ineffectually at tears which streaked her cheeks. It was the only sound Beth Highsmith had uttered since the first blow was struck.

DAY SIX:

Tuesday 10 September

The old day had merged with the new as Melvin Egleton arrived in the outer office. Forsyth was there to meet him. The stocky sergeant from Covert Operations was wearing British Telecom overalls with an Intelligence badge clipped on to the top pocket.

'Original and back-up, no other copies made. Pretty lady, wasn't she? And I do mean was.'

He thrust out two boxed videotapes with ill-concealed distaste. The remark came close to insubordination, but Forsyth couldn't pull him up. He took the tapes.

'Thank you, Sergeant. Go home. And keep this to yourself.'

Egleton stiffened. Forsyth had insulted already-stressed professionalism.

'Glad you mentioned that, sir. I was going to give the papers a blow-by-blow account and discuss rape technique with the wife and kids over the cornflakes.'

The sergeant turned and marched. Forsyth sighed. Acting Head of Intelligence, one of the most powerful people in the country, put in his place by an enlisted man who could distinguish right from wrong.

He went through to the main room, broke a seal bearing Egleton's signature and pushed the tape into his player. The anguish was almost unbearable. Why, dammit, why? Because he had to be certain, cover every angle, get that nasty little pervert under control.

Forsyth pressed play and fast forward simultaneously. The drama unfolded at high speed, which gave the performance an air of unreality. Even so, he switched off when the violence began, blinking hard. He spoke aloud, though there was no one to hear.

'Beth, I'm so sorry.'

He considered an insidious thought that slithered venomously into his mind. This was hard enough when a greater need was being served. But suppose he sacrificed Beth because she was with that photographer when he wanted her himself? He rejected the idea, but it didn't go away. After locking the tapes in a cupboard, he went through to his study bedroom and sat stiffly on the bed.

For once, Joseph Mallord William Turner was unable to help – *Rain, Steam and Speed* merged into an amorphous mass of colour that brought no relief. Eventually he went back outside, to his big window, gazing down on the city from a God-like height. The rain had blown away. London's lights were bright, the night clear.

The thing was done, could not be undone. Forsyth straightened his uniform jacket, took a steadying breath and started for the door.

When General Forsyth bustled in, the portable tape player was still sitting on Andy Kyle's desk. The Acting Head didn't usually visit without notice. Startled, Kyle looked up from his keyboard. Could Forsyth know what had been found, somehow sense a threat to his ambitious plans? He gestured at the screen, tried to sound cheerful.

'I'm drafting a report on the latest shenanigans. Would've been on your desk first thing in the morning, but I can see why you couldn't wait. Let me clear that chair.'

He went round and removed box files that had found their way on to the seat since it was used by Captain Dexter. Kyle wished the investigator hadn't been quite so clever. Some things were best left buried deep, and Coppel's tape was one of them. Still, he had to live with Forsyth, and normality was the best form of defence.

'Want to hear the gruesome details, *mon général*?'

As he returned to his own side of the desk, Kyle casually picked up the tape machine and slipped it into a drawer.

Forsyth didn't notice. He seemed depressed – slumping into the swivel chair and turning listlessly from side to side, eyes unfocused, unaware of an irritating squeak from the spindle.

'Something bothering you?'

In a performance that was becoming increasingly familiar, Forsyth switched on his concentration. As always, the contrast was striking. The squeaking stopped, Forsyth sat up. Kyle was facing an angry man.

'I did something bad, Andy. I had my reasons, but it's still hard. Golden rule – never start something you can't finish. So let's finish this for good. Where are we?'

'SIS terminated three of Cornwell's killers. Identified as British, ex-army guns for hire. Between them they've fought in most of the world's trouble spots. No sign of the fourth man, the leader. We don't know who he is, but it's only a matter of time. That should end the attacks. I don't think there's another team.'

Kyle picked up the slip of paper recovered in North London, looked at Forsyth and decided to tell him. Even though he was putting an innocent man's head on the block.

'Stanley's bang to rights. His phone number was found on one of the dead killers, the direct line in his apartment at Number Ten. We were too slow. Cornwell's not dead, but might as well be. He's got a collapsed left lung and one arm practically cut off. With him gone there's no opposition left.'

Forsyth stood up.

'We'll see about that. Get a squad round to Palace Mews and drag George out of bed. I want him arrested and brought here. Put him in the smallest cell we've got and make sure he doesn't talk to anyone. Make the little sod sweat. The charge is aggravated rape. Beth Highsmith.'

So that was it. No wonder Forsyth was in a state. His lust for power was getting out of control, but Kyle was careful to conceal his thoughts as he reached for the phone.

'Been up to his old tricks again, has he?'

'He has. But this time he'll suffer the consequences. I'll see to that personally. Phone me at home when you've nailed the little prick to the wall. By the time I'm finished he'll wish he was dead.'

Andy Kyle watched the Acting Head's retreating back. They were friends. But some things were more important than friendship.

The government clinic was in Lisson Grove, behind Marylebone Station. Apart from soothing the slightest ache of the élite, the small hospital was equipped to handle major surgical procedures. State-of-the-art technology was everywhere, and with a staff–patient ratio of two to one the clinic housed some of the best-cared-for sufferers in the world.

The night sister was unimpressed by Forsyth's status and refused to discuss Beth Highsmith, instead calling the duty doctor. He was adamant that Forsyth couldn't visit the patient, but described her injuries – a badly broken nose, deeply lacerated lip, assorted scratches, bruises and abrasions. The white-coated medical man paused, looking shrewdly at the agitated Intelligence officer.

'You're a sort of policeman, aren't you? Perhaps she's blaming you for failing to protect her. Irrational, but useful. In a case like this the worst possible thing is for the woman to blame herself. If she's transferring guilt that's healthy, means she'll eventually come to terms with it. You must give her time, perhaps a long time.'

It was an effort to nod. Forsyth felt bile rising, swallowed hard.

'Thank you for your frankness. And the Home Secretary?'

The doctor relaxed his stern expression.

'No psychological problems there. Hit by three bullets, one through the left lung, two in the arm. Surgery went well. Nine or ten weeks on his back and he'll be good as new, barring permanent stiffness of the left arm. Incidentally, do you know anyone called Alec? He kept asking for him. Might be nice if we could get this chap to the bedside. Always helps to see a familiar face when you wake up.'

The Intelligence general looked blankly at the doctor.

Bagley would never work again. Not only had his manservant admitted those clodhopping Intelligence cretins without a murmur of protest, but he'd also bagged up the discarded clothing they asked for, then held out an overcoat as George was taken out. A smirk had besmirched his normally impassive countenance.

Now the Prince Regent was regretting the angry gesture with which he'd pushed the warm coat away. One thing was certain. Within minutes of his release from this pisshole, Bagley's bollocks would be mincemeat.

George had been ingested into the bowels of New Centre Point. His pitch-dark cell was unheated. Shivering uncontrollably, he huddled on the basic bed, arms wrapped around the knees of silk pyjamas.

Everything would get sorted, but how soon? Her word against his. No harm meant, no harm done. Let them prove otherwise, especially as they needed him to play their silly political games. Forsyth was reminding him who called the shots, just because he murmured in Godfrey Cornwell's ear. No harm meant or done there, either.

This was all so unfair. Hours had passed. It must be morning, but there was no sign of breakfast, hot coffee. Sod that, he'd settle for lukewarm. Getting to his feet, the Prince Regent groped to the door, slapping smooth metal and shouting obscenities.

The overhead light came on, searingly bright after prolonged darkness. He closed his eyes, hearing the door's spyhole slide open, click shut. As he reopened them, the light went out. George dropped to his knees, pounding the floor with clenched fists.

On the fifth morning after Minton-Briant's assassination, General Robert Forsyth woke on the settee at his home, fully clothed under a red wool blanket. Curtains were closed. The drawing room was lit by a single table lamp and his chauffeur-bodyguard stood silently beside him. Armstrong was holding a steaming mug.

Forsyth threw off the blanket and sat up. He massaged an arm that was still asleep, circulation returning painfully. His watch said just after six. He felt rested, revived – flexing his hand and taking the mug from his driver.

'I suppose you've been guarding me like a Rottweiler. Hope I didn't say anything indiscreet in my sleep.'

'Wouldn't know. You fell on that sofa, told me to wake you at six and went out like a light. I scrounged the blanket and left you to it. Grabbed a bed and got in a couple of hours myself. Brigadier Kyle called. The prick's nailed to the wall. Said you'd understand.'

Forsyth's good mood vanished.

'Is the Field Marshal awake?'

'Your wife went up with a tray. He slept all day yesterday, had supper then went back to sleep.'

'He needed a decent rest. I'll shower and change, then have a chat with him. Ask Brigadier Kyle to fix a breakfast meeting with the PM at Number Ten, eight o'clock would be ideal. And tell him to leave the prick dangling till I get in.'

Armstrong nodded, took the empty mug and left. Forsyth followed him out. On the way upstairs, he saw Chandler. The Field Marshal's door was open, and Alex was with him. The old man sat with a tray on his lap, trying to eat breakfast – bacon, sausage, tomatoes, fried bread. The food had been cut up, but it was still a struggle. Chandler was right-handed, but only had the use of his left arm. He was stabbing at the plate, trying to impale something. As Forsyth watched, his wife reached over and guided the fork to an elusive segment of sausage.

With an impatient gesture, her father lifted the forkful to his mouth. He made it, though stains on the white napkin under his chin suggested there had been plenty of near misses. Alex became aware of her husband's presence. He put a finger to his lips and tiptoed away. Before he'd gone two paces, the Field Marshal bellowed angrily.

'Bob, is that you skulking out there?'

Forsyth addressed his father-in-law sternly.

'Nothing wrong with your ears, then. I'll be with you in ten minutes, so finish your breakfast. If you can.'

David Chandler moved his strapped right arm. At least he could still wiggle fingers. His back and buttocks itched unmercifully where dozens of small wounds were healing. Stitches out in two days. His damaged eyes throbbed. But he'd slept well, and felt strength returning.

Breakfast had been a disaster, and now Alex was wiping his face with a damp flannel. He could smell soap, his daughter's delicate perfume, toothpaste on her breath. Gentle scrubbing stopped.

'Sorry, Dad, this must be awful. At least you're alive. Time for your painkillers. I'll put them in your hand.'

He transferred the slippery capsules to his mouth and felt them crawl down. Before he could ask for water, there was a cheerful distraction.

'What's the verdict, Nurse Forsyth – can the old reprobate still think, or is his mind shot to hell as well?'

Bob, back at last. No sympathy there, thank God. The last thing he needed was people fussing. Alex laughed.

'He's a lousy patient, but definitely *compos mentis*. I'll leave you to talk.'

The door closed. Chandler was glad his daughter sounded so relaxed. He'd begun to think there was something wrong with the marriage, but the light-hearted interchange undermined that theory. He turned towards the bedside chair and Bob's breathing.

'Talk.'

'I'm seeing Ken Stanley in an hour. Things have moved fast since we last spoke. You won't like what I have to say.'

Exasperatingly, Forsyth stopped. Chandler thumped his good arm on the eiderdown.

'Stop pussyfooting about. Tell me what you came to say or sod off and sort the mess yourself.'

'Sorry. Two major developments. The hit squad had a crack at Godfrey Cornwell last night. He isn't dead, but won't be around for a while. We got the boys who did it a couple of hours later, and there's proof Ken Stanley was their inside contact.'

This time, the pause owed nothing to diffidence. Bob was giving him time to absorb the information. True, Ken had fallen out with Minton-Briant – but it was no more than irritation at slipping standards. Hardly grounds for conspiring to murder him.

'No, Bob. As I said before, this isn't Ken's style.'

Forsyth's voice made the case for the prosecution.

'He was one of the few with access to Minton-Briant's itinerary, to direct the attack. The authorization codes which released the aircraft were his. He met Vice-Presidential Envoy Lustbader. His new direct line telephone number in Downing Street was found on one of the killers.'

In the silence that followed, Chandler reflected. The effort
to concentrate had made his head ache.

'You haven't said anything that would establish Ken's
culpability in a court of law.'

Forsyth countered.

'Apart from Minton-Briant's murder, leading figures have
been attacked by professional killers. You, me, Cornwell,
forces chiefs, even the Prince Regent.'

'Leaving nobody in a position to ask awkward questions
or challenge Ken's authority?'

'Exactly.'

'And you want to stop him?'

'I do, yes. He needs us now, but what happens when
he's firmly in power? Will Tidyman be satisfied with anything less than a return to the free-market chaos we had
before?'

Chandler's earlier sense of impotence and despair rolled
back. It was over. For Derek Minton-Briant. For Ken Stanley.
For him. A young lion was claiming the pride from a tooth-
less predecessor. He'd always known Bob would take over
one day. The day had come.

'So you want the old man's blessing to move against
Stanley, an assurance I won't undermine your authority
within Intelligence?'

Forsyth surprised him.

'You are feeling sorry for yourself. Don't undervalue your
experience, the respect you enjoy. I came to ask if you're
fit enough to attend a Cabinet meeting later today, to seek
nomination as Deputy Premier. We might not stop Stanley,
but we can slow him down.'

The Cabinet Secretary stood aside to let the Intelligence officer enter. Forsyth saw a large room – comfortably furnished,
white fireplace, Regency-striped pink and green wallpaper,
two windows, yellow curtains held back by plaited cord,
watercolours of nautical scenes. He'd been to Number 10
many times, but never this early and never here.

The Prime Minister was on his feet, but a red dispatch
box lay open on one of two facing sofas, surrounded by
papers. Ken Stanley stepped forward – pen in one hand, the
other outstretched in greeting. Higgins settled himself on

an upright chair as the principals exchanged a perfunctory handshake. Stanley indicated the spare sofa.

'Harry will take notes. Did he tell you on the way up? A State of Emergency comes into effect at midnight, Cabinet meets at two this afternoon. Now, you've got some explaining to do. I know that attempt on the Home Secretary's life may have made mine easier, but I don't like this sort of thing.'

'Who does? The shooting took place on my own doorstep, which is embarrassing. Still, Cornwell will survive, and the three perpetrators were killed by SIS last night in North London.'

'Does that leave any at large?'

'The leader. He probably guessed we were on to their safe house and got out. But this destructive campaign is over. It was orchestrated by the Americans and carried out by the pilot, plus a four-man hit team.'

'So what precisely has this conspiracy achieved?'

Stanley must know that Intelligence had implicated him. Perhaps he was being put to the test. Forsyth answered pleasantly.

'Who knows where it would have ended if we hadn't caught up with the killers? I think Tidyman set out to throw this country into political chaos. What matters now is continuity, to rob the Americans of that prize. Which is why I requested this meeting.'

Since hearing from Zak Sohmer about the call from Mary-Jo MacInnes, Ella Stark had been preparing for bad news. Sohmer was the campaign's PR chief, who thus far hadn't put a toe wrong. Now he'd gone in up to the knees. The graduate student who brought the papers to her breakfast table opened the *Washington Post* at an inside page and laid the newspaper down. Before he could retreat, Ella issued a curt instruction.

'Send Zak in here.'

The aide backed out, delivering an ominous remark from the door.

'There are reporters downstairs. Not just the usual faces, new ones. TV crews, too. It's worse than Superbowl. We'll stall until you've talked this through with Zak.'

Ella Stark had never subscribed to the view that all publicity was good publicity. As nitroglycerine went, the story was mild. But the content was deadly. After the first rapid skim, she settled down to read the report word for word.

STARK CAMPAIGN CAR IN MURDER MYSTERY

From *Post* reporter Mary-Jo MacInnes

San Antonio Police Department detectives investigating the murder of a young Hispanic woman in the city on the night of August 20 last have established a firm link with a Buick automobile owned and operated by the Stark For President Campaign. The unidentified victim – beaten and strangled to death by unknown assailants – had assumed the identity of Mexican alien Maria Martinez, who was badly injured in an auto accident in West Texas before returning to Mexico, where she died earlier this year.

Presidential candidate Patrick Stark was on the campaign trail in San Antonio at the time of the murder, and the victim is known to have been a room service waitress at the luxury hotel where the Stark entourage was staying.

SAPD investigating officer Lieutenant Richard Schneider states that Stark was one of the last people to see the woman alive, and revealed to this reporter forensic evidence which confirms that her corpse was transported in the trunk of a blue Buick automobile used regularly by Stark staffers, though not by the Candidate himself.

Lieutenant Schneider further indicated that Patrick Stark and members of his travelling campaign team have been interviewed in connection with the case, and stated they offered full co-operation, including voluntary return of the vehicle from California to Texas for forensic examination.

Bexar County First Assistant District Attorney David Turrow went on record with this brief statement: 'Substantive progress is being made in the

Martinez investigation, but I am not yet ready to take the case before a Grand Jury. I must stress absolutely that no individual associated with the Stark campaign is in any way a suspect in this matter at this time.'

A spokesperson for Candidate Stark refused to comment on what he described as 'unsubstantiated rumour'.

As she finished reading, Zak Sohmer came in. He was a high-achieving thirty-five-year-old from Madison Avenue, but could kiss his new political career goodbye. Ella looked up from the newspaper.

'That "unsubstantiated rumour" quote of yours looks pretty dumb at the bottom of this ticking time bomb, wouldn't you say?'

He was flustered.

'She caught me on the hop. How was I to know she'd found other sources? Those people down in San Antonio were supposed to keep quiet. I wasn't about to hand anything to MacInnes on a plate.'

'She was against her deadline, so handing it to her is exactly what you did. They might not have published without some sort of quote from us. You should have promised to get back with a proper response, bought us an extra day. Now . . .'

She shrugged. There was no need to elaborate. Sohmer knew what was about to happen.

'Sorry, Ella, I really am.'

Her voice became colder than Alaskan wind.

'Sorry doesn't win votes, Zak, it loses them. I'd fire you now, but that would only make things worse. Get your ass downstairs and set up a press conference. I'll tell Pat. He won't like this any better than me.'

The disbarred spin-doctor scurried off. Her mind already attacking the problem, Ella Stark got up from the table and walked towards the connecting door to her husband's suite.

Try as he might, Ken Stanley couldn't raise much sympathy for the Home Secretary. The bastard was trying to grab the top job, would have been delighted if Stanley had been on the receiving end.

'I talked with Field Marshal Chandler at breakfast. He's making a rapid recovery, though it will take a while for him to acclimatize to his blindness. He made some interesting suggestions.'

General Forsyth was making his pitch.

'That's welcome news, Bob. We need all the wise heads we can find. Harry tells me the Party's up in arms about postponement of Special Congress, and what happened to Cornwell won't improve their mood. If David has helpful ideas, so much the better.'

He stopped, unsure which line to take. Forsyth spoke coldly.

'I'm sure you'll find his input valuable, Prime Minister. Last night's attack confirms one thing. Whatever ambitions he was pursuing, the Home Secretary wasn't part of the plot. We must therefore assume that the object of this violent exercise was destabilization of the British government. The country's like a pressure cooker with the safety valve screwed down.'

The self-assured Intelligence officer paused, wondering if the moment to say whatever he'd come to say had arrived. Self-important sod. Stanley prompted.

'We're obviously curious about what you think, General, but unless you're prepared to share your thoughts we won't get very far.'

Forsyth nodded, launching a prepared speech.

'Very well. Field Marshal Chandler believes it's necessary to act decisively to maintain stability. Since the late PM came to power the emphasis has been on public order, disciplined social behaviour.'

He stood up and wandered – looking over Higgins' shoulder at the Cabinet Secretary's notes, studying paintings. Stanley watched, fascinated. Forsyth stood with his back to the fireplace and resumed angrily.

'Remember how it was? Communities turned into no-go areas by a drug culture feeding on greed and despair. Boy racers in stolen hot hatches mowing people down. Women in fear of rape or murder in broad daylight. Pensioners battered in their own homes for a few pence. Children abducted and molested if they strayed for a minute. Filth beamed into living rooms from the sky, smutty newspapers destroying lives, caring services crippled by accountants with calculators.'

Forsyth marched back to the sofa and sat down.

'You, Minton-Briant, Chandler – you swept that away. I admire that. But some people have short memories. They chafe against the discipline which made your reforms possible. Give these agitators their head and inside a decade this country won't be fit to live in. Don't you see? Unless we get a grip now, everything that matters will be put at risk.'

Stanley was beginning to understand.

'Slow down, Bob. You're not saying anything I haven't thought a thousand times. If Derek lost sight of our principles towards the end, I never did. I want to carry on our work.'

'Do you?'

Forsyth snapped out the question. So that was it. He feared liberalization would weaken the pervasive power of Intelligence. The Prime Minister sighed.

'Forget the sermon. Just tell us what David has in mind.'

Forsyth studied him closely, eyes unwavering. Apparently satisfied, he started down his shopping list.

'The Field Marshal has wanted to merge both security services under unified command for some time. Minton-Briant blocked the proposal, but this arrangement must now be implemented. Police and Intelligence should be combined under David Chandler's Security Ministry. In view of the importance of this new role, the incumbent should also be appointed Deputy Premier, preferably at today's Cabinet meeting.'

The demand was breathtaking. Stanley stared at Forsyth.

'That's the price of Intelligence support?'

'It is.'

General Forsyth folded his arms expectantly.

The politician was like a butterfly in the killing bottle, fluttering frantically as the lepidopterist watches. Stanley's mournful brown eyes flicked to Forsyth, strayed towards Higgins, returned to his tormentor. He certainly couldn't expect help from the Cabinet Secretary, never one to volunteer for a hazardous mission.

Stanley managed to make his tone reasonable.

'Chief Constables will never accept such an arrangement. They'll insist on retaining their autonomy, at least until they're able to discuss the proposal with Cornwell. We can't afford a police force working at half-speed if we need them to maintain order.'

Forsyth allowed himself a small moment of self-congratulation, for predicting the PM's move and being ready.

'They're pragmatists. Godfrey Cornwell is in no position to offer them anything. Besides, we're proposing a genuine partnership. This won't be an Intelligence takeover. Chief Constables will assume control of local Intelligence units and become senior exeuctives in the merged organization, with real clout in decision-taking and policy-making. They can be persuaded. And you'll do the persuading.'

Stanley wasn't ready to roll over. Having failed with reason, he applied a touch of the old asperity.

'I can't have Intelligence dictating policy to the British government, that's not how things work.'

The authority was no longer there. Forsyth shrugged.

'No good shooting the messenger. I'm here to convey David's views, nothing more. We all respect his judgment.'

Masterly. Even the ultra-cautious Cabinet Secretary was moved to intervene.

'Wouldn't it make more sense to let the dust settle before taking on a complex restructuring? There's no reason to suppose the police won't do their duty through this difficult period.'

Higgins might be trying to assist his master, but Forsyth suspected he'd seen what was coming – which was more than could be said for the PM. Well, see how the old fool liked the coup de grâce. Forsyth addressed the Cabinet Secretary, ignoring Stanley.

'Godfrey Cornwell has spent the last day and a half persuading Chief Constables and key Party activists that Ken was involved in the conspiracy to murder Minton-Briant. Ridiculous, but damaging. The meeting with Vice-President Tidyman's man was a mistake, and your tape of the conversation has done little to remedy it. It's no-smoke-without-fire syndrome. There's only been one obvious beneficiary, especially now their precious Home Secretary's been hit.'

'That's outrageous. The whole thing was a deliberate smear.'

Ken Stanley was on his feet, looking as though he wanted to strike out physically. Forsyth sensed victory.

'Of course, but that doesn't alter the facts. David's offering to dilute the influence of Intelligence, share power with police chiefs, buy their loyalty with the sort of concession they've been after for years. If you want to come through this and out the other side as PM, you should consider that offer very seriously.'

Stanley's rage crumpled. He sat down and turned to Higgins.

'Harry?'

It was almost possible to feel sorry for the soon-to-be-deposed Prime Minister.

Air Force 2 had taken off from Shannon before dawn, fleeing a spectacular sunrise. The cabin crew left the Vice-Presidential Special Envoy alone with his thoughts.

Vernon Lustbader had never considered that life contained absolutes. A coin has two sides, and an edge upon which it can roll for miles. But lines had to be drawn which decent people wouldn't cross, and his step-back point was close.

He knew when he joined Tidyman that he was getting into a bare-knuckle fight. Politicians were expected to deliver the impossible and solve the insoluble. And were meant to be honest. Yet any fool unwise enough to stand up and tell things the way they were would be savaged and destroyed by the very people who put honesty as the quality most valued in their leaders.

So Lustbader could live with image-making and manipulation, because at the end of the day Errol Tidyman would use office more constructively than anyone else. They'd spent hundreds of hours talking over the years, as lawyer turned tycoon turned politician, and the college professor trusted and admired the man. But this was something else.

Vernon Lustbader was starting to ask if he knew Errol Tidyman at all, and when the answers threaten things you believe in, some questions are best dumped on the back burner for as long as you can bear to leave them simmering.

By the time a sign instructed him to fasten his seat belt and quit smoking, he'd resolved nothing. The captain's calm Mid-Western voice told him they were on final approach to Andrews, and would be down in five minutes. Lustbader hated landings. As the 747 began its run-in, he cinched up the seat belt and prepared to meet his doom.

The front of Intelligence Headquarters would never be the same again. As his car turned on to the forecourt, General Robert Forsyth noted construction activity with interest.

A temporary barrier at the vehicle entrance was being replaced by twin guardhouses joined by an electronically operated gate. A concrete curtain wall was going up behind, preventing a ram-raid. Sparks flew as a welding team erected an arched frame in front of the main doors. Armoured glass would be hung, allowing vehicular visitors to enter the building safely, protected from a distant sniper's bullet.

It was an impressive exercise in stable-door-closing. Pity about the horse. But it would never do to be seen to do nothing. After instructing Armstrong to keep the car on stand-by, Forsyth ran into the building and headed for Control.

Andy Kyle must have been getting used to unannounced visits. On the last occasion he'd looked almost startled. This time he merely glanced up and continued discussing the search for the missing fourth man with his Duty Controller. Forsyth stood by the door and listened. They had finally identified the leader from video images captured by security cameras outside New Centre Point, cross-referenced to footage from London Underground platforms.

No wonder the task had taken time. Major Anton Carney, formerly of the Special Air Service, was dead – reported 'missing, believed killed' in Bosnia years ago, before SAS became SIS. The major had been working under cover, sabotaging Serbian heavy guns that threatened aid convoys into Sarajevo. It was assumed he'd been caught by Serb fighters who forgot to sign the Geneva Convention.

The Duty Controller departed. Forsyth sat in the vacated chair and addressed his deputy.

'Men like that don't wait for a tap on the shoulder.'

'The pilot's headed Stateside. Three of the hit squad are dead, along with the only witness who could directly link Ken Stanley to the conspiracy. Of course Carney's gone.'

Forsyth's deputy looked haggard. He'd probably worked through the night, but that wasn't the whole story. Knowing the man, he surmised Kyle was deeply disturbed by the prospect of the PM escaping unpunished, as realpolitik trampled his innate sense of justice. Perhaps it was time to offer encouragement.

'I want a file containing every scrap of evidence against Stanley, Andy, physical or circumstantial, as though you were preparing a case for trial. By tonight. The idea of Stanley getting away with it sticks in my throat too. Now, how's our nailed-to-the-wall prick bearing up?'

Looking no happier, Kyle shrugged his wide shoulders.

'Sagging. He's been in the dark for hours.'

Forsyth stood up.

'Time to pay him a visit. Then I'll get Department Heads together to brief them on some interesting organizational developments.'

With an expression that could only be described as predatory, Forsyth turned and left the cluttered office.

As the door closed behind his superior, Brigadier Kyle shook his head in disbelief. The arrogance of these power players was amazing. He hoped his attitude hadn't been too obvious. Forsyth was perceptive, but the Acting Head was absorbed with his grand strategy.

George's brutal rape of Beth Highsmith hadn't even been mentioned, though discreet enquiries suggested Forsyth not only set up the assignation but recorded the result on video. It had been an ugly exercise aimed at gaining control over the Prince Regent. Intelligence files contained details of seven similar assaults committed by George over the years, all hushed up in the public interest. Forsyth could have had no illusions.

What about fall guy Stanley? Doubtless blackmailed by veiled threats into supporting a move on the police, now Cornwell had become a casualty. It would be dressed in respectable clothes, but the naked fact would be simple.

Chief Constables would be tricked, cajoled or coerced into a position of subservience to Intelligence.

Even David Chandler – a man Andy Kyle respected – was vulnerable. Disorientated by disfigurement, disturbed by abrupt removal from the centre of events, desperate to retain or regain his influence . . . he'd be easy meat for Forsyth, who was turning out to be the greediest of all.

Andy Kyle locked the door, opened his safe and patted the thick file that condemned the Prime Minister as a traitor. Kyle didn't need time to finish Forsyth's dirty job. It was done.

The file contained an audio cassette recovered from Alec Ambler's briefcase after the previous evening's attack, recording a conversation between Ken Stanley and Vice-Presidential Special Envoy Lustbader. Who could listen without being convinced the PM had been part of a murderous conspiracy with the Americans? Together with supporting evidence gathered by Kyle, the result was a case capable of withstanding the most sceptical examination.

But Ambler's tape was a fake, as was the whole fistful of incriminating evidence. Kyle removed another cassette from the safe – the one from Mulberry Cottage which told the truth. Dexter had taken his young family to a remote cottage without a phone on the Erme estuary in South Devon, at the end of a steep unmade track three miles from the nearest village. The captain wouldn't be talking about his discovery.

Returning to his desk, Kyle laced big hands behind his head and leaned back in his swivel chair. Bob Forsyth would be making a serious mistake if he assumed the game was over.

He was dozing fitfully, curled on the hard bunk, hands between thighs in an attempt to find warmth. When the downlighter came on, George blinked rapidly. They had used it to torment him, snatching away precious illumination and hurling him back into darkness the instant he began to hope. But the ceiling lamp burned on behind flush-mounted glass. He sat up, dropped slippered feet to the floor and wiggled icy toes to restore circulation.

The tiny cell was a perfect cube, with every dimension just

under nine feet. Ceiling, windowless walls and door were painted in glossy green that could be scrubbed to remove splattered puke or graffiti. The floor was concrete, covered in grey sealant. Toilet – stainless steel. Bunk – tubular iron bolted to the floor. Not even a spider's web to disturb clinical functionality.

The Prince Regent forced himself to be calm, put the awful night behind. However justifiable, fear or anger wouldn't help. They needed him, wanted something only he could provide. Their bullying tactics would be counter-productive. When the time came, he would drive a harder bargain.

Bitter thoughts were interrupted by an electronic click from the door. The effort to pump himself up was instantly punctured. His old school chum Robert Forsyth walked into the cell, looking down with an expression of cold contempt. He tossed a sweater on to the bunk.

'You've been a bad lad. Beth Highsmith's in hospital, worn and torn. Some things can be overlooked, but the rape of a prominent citizen isn't one of them.'

George wanted to resist the sweater, couldn't. He stood up, fought his way into the thick garment and began the case for the defence.

'The bitch owes millions in tax, Bob, wanted me to get her off the hook. She was prepared to be nice if I helped, practically threw herself at me. So maybe things got out of hand, but no way was she unwilling.'

George stared defiantly at his tormentor. Without warning, Forsyth swung an open hand. George was too numbed to react. The impact knocked him off balance. He sat down abruptly. Forsyth's stare bored into his watering eyes.

'Bad luck, George. Beth Highsmith has paid every penny due in tax on overseas earnings. And don't bother with that pathetic consenting adults routine. I have a videotape of the whole sordid encounter. If necessary, I'll use it to ruin you. I can promise you a life sentence in one of our less salubrious penal establishments.'

Comprehension surged bitterly into George's head.

'You set me up!'

Forsyth smiled unpleasantly.

'If I'd been able to trust you it might not have been necessary, but you've been treating this too lightly. Your

signature may be important before this business is over
and I must be certain it's on my bit of paper. Now, let's get
you into better quarters, shall we?'

The uniformed Intelligence general patted his victim on
the shoulder and turned to leave. Obediently, George stood
up. Sod the money. Another hour and he would have been
barking mad.

He was too slow. The door slammed behind Forsyth. A
second later, the light went out.

The minute Patrick Stark walked into the hotel's largest
function room, one pace behind Zak Sohmer and one step
ahead of his wife, he knew they were in deep trouble.

His press conferences were usually relaxed affairs, with
predictable questions attracting slick replies. He addressed
reporters by name. That scored points, because the Next
President had acquainted himself with humble hacks who
represented all those good folk with TV sets in Pitchfork,
Wyoming. Or wherever.

The trick wasn't hard – the media pack flew on his plane,
stayed at his hotel, showed at his meetings and attended
his press conferences. Usually, he played them like a Strad,
producing a tune sweet to his ear when he caught the
newscasts. Everyone loved a winner, and he was in front
by a mile.

Today was different. As he saw unfamiliar faces and
braved shouted questions, Pat Stark thought of the contrast
between swimming in warm tropical waters with pretty
coloured fish playing around the reef below – and the same
setting when there's blood in the water and sharks are in a
feeding frenzy.

When they made the rostrum, he held out a chair for
Ella. She sat, staring down at the noisy pack with a relaxed
expression. A real pro. He remembered that same friendly
face up in the suite, not fifteen minutes before, thin-lipped
with fury as she verbally lashed Zak Sohmer.

To be fair, it wasn't Zak's fault – he might have delayed the
inevitable, but hadn't created the situation that faced them.
Stark sat beside his wife, fear squeezed out by adrenalin.
This was what he did, and by God he did it well. Zak Sohmer
stood at the lectern, eventually winning the first point. They

went quiet, turning from sharks into hunting lions. Zak spoke firmly.

'There will be a statement, then we take questions one at a time. You people start shouting again that's it, finished, end of conference. Do I make myself clear?'

There was silence – the calm before the storm. At least Zak had them under temporary control, and he introduced his leader with the familiar flourish.

'The Next President of the United States!'

Stark stood beside the lectern. Collective anticipation was frightening. He spread his hands and smiled easily.

'Sorry, people, I forgot my notes. If I screw up my lines, you be sure and tell me.'

They stirred. One or two even laughed, before remembering this was no ordinary press conference. Stark moved on quickly.

'We all know why you're here this morning, and it isn't to check on the progress of the campaign. I guess I better start by congratulating Carl. Seems the *Post* has come up with a little story the rest of you missed. But I have to say that's not our fault. You only had to ask and we would've laid out the facts, though they don't add up to much . . .'

He gauged their reaction and let those recording his words in shorthand catch up. The jury was out.

'We've been helping the DA down in San Antonio, just like any concerned citizens with useful information and nothing to hide. A room service waitress at the hotel where we stayed was murdered at her home on our last night in the city. The victim was using the name Maria Martinez and is thought to have been an unknown illegal alien from Mexico. I shall refer to her as Maria Martinez to avoid confusion.'

He was interrupted by a shout of 'What about your Buick?' The offender was the *National Enquirer*'s politician-basher. Stark didn't dignify the intrusion with a reply.

'Martinez handled room service for our floor. I met her twice. She brought hot drinks to my room on both occasions and we exchanged casual words. When the Bexar County District Attorney's office contacted me in the normal course of the investigation, I was able to establish these simple facts to their complete satisfaction.'

In the catch-up pause, he composed his thoughts. The next bit was tricky.

'Subsequently, the possibility arose that a Buick automobile used by my team had been unlawfully removed from the hotel garage and used in connection with the crime. We arranged for the vehicle to be returned to Texas for examination, though we had no statutory duty to do so. Furthermore, we conducted a rigorous enquiry which established that none of our people went near that Buick on the night in question. The *Post* report was the first intimation we received that linkage with the Martinez killing had been established.'

Too many words. They were getting restless. Last chance.

'I know this is something you guys must chase down. Maybe the campaign was getting stale. But the facts are as stated. We're keen as you to get to the bottom of this so we can get on with the serious business of winning an election. I'll take questions, but please be brief. We try to help you people, but this conference was unscheduled and I have a prior engagement.'

They may have taken Zak's warning on board earlier, but that didn't stop sixty arms going up and voices bellowing for precedence. Peering into Klieg lights, Stark pointed at the *Washington Post* and shouted over the din.

'Seems only fair you should get first crack, Carl.'

Carl DiMona stood up – a slight, dark-haired man with a mild expression. Stark had to strain to hear the question, then wished he hadn't bothered. The little SOB had obviously been briefed by his interfering colleague back in San Antonio.

'Is it true that you were one of the last people to see the victim alive, and spent time alone with her in your hotel room after midnight, only hours before the killing?'

The ordeal had begun.

The Prime Minister telephoned Alexandra Forsyth and she put her father on the line. Chandler sounded cheerful.

'Ken, you old bugger. Bob tells me you've stamped your authority on a difficult situation. Good man. The Americans have done us a favour by trimming Cornwell's wick, though I'm glad he survived.'

Stanley was irritated.

'You're a pain in the arse, David, sending Bob Forsyth in punching like a heavyweight on speed. I assume he was following orders, but your boy's getting ideas above his station.'

Chandler's voice became less friendly.

'Don't rubbish Bob, or ignore what he's saying. Remember what we agreed on Saturday? Equal partners was the phrase used. He was reminding you of your obligation, suggesting an arrangement which should work to mutual advantage. Stability, that's what everyone wants, the sooner the better.'

Ken Stanley relaxed. His old friend's admonition brought relief. So Forsyth was acting on David's instructions rather than pursuing some agenda of his own.

'Put this call down to unfounded anxieties. It'll be great to have you back, get the old double act working again.'

'Let's hope so. How are you getting on with those Chief Constables? Bloody old women, but we need their co-operation.'

Privately, Ken Stanley hoped the police chiefs would retain a degree of influence. He wasn't convinced an all-powerful Intelligence organization was in anyone's best interest, especially his. He revealed none of this concern.

'Harry Higgins has spoken to each of them, explaining the proposed arrangement. The Cornwell business threw them. No chance to get heads together and agree policy, so I think they'll bite, particularly as there's a juicy concession they can fasten on to save face.'

Chandler sensed misgiving.

'Don't worry, Ken, we don't mean to neuter the police, whatever you may think. I don't care for them, but we won't get anywhere if they're humiliated, resentful and angry. They'll come out well. All we want is a workable arrangement. Use your legendary powers of persuasion.'

The man who would be Deputy Premier paused, then continued.

'I've decided to rise from the grave, so I'll see you at the Cabinet meeting this afternoon. With any luck there'll be nothing more than a rubber-stamping exercise for our bold fellow-politicans to bend their agile minds round. Those time-servers are even more committed to maintaining the status quo than you or I.'

The line went dead. As he put down the phone, Stanley wondered whatever happened to friendship and trust.

There would be no escape from Intelligence Headquarters. But freedom no longer bothered the nondescript American. The week had provided a shattering climax to years spent on the edge – suppressing emotion, using people ruthlessly, ending life for no better reason than its obstruction of something he had to do.

Donny Sheldon lay on the hard bed, thinking about growing up in the Mid-West with its huge skies, harsh winters and hot summers. An unchanging flat landscape broken by grain silos, totems to the gods of fertile soil and cheap food. Slender, wholesome girls who turned into large women straining the seams of Sunday clothes bought at Merle Hay Mall. Their menfolk, John Deere baseball caps shading sun-seamed faces.

Slow-moving, friendly people doing and thinking the same things as their parents. Time in suspension. For him, then, a passionate desire to be something different, somewhere else.

There had been a spreading walnut tree in the back yard of the family home on North Waterburt Street. You start off green, with soft shell and moist kernel – one of thousands growing together on a great tree. Still wet, you fall to the ground. Time passes. The shell hardens and the inside dries, eventually decaying to an acrid husk. Some life.

Was it only a few days since he'd seriously considered suicide, to protect useless knowledge? As they had again and again, painful images returned to torment him. Mendlebaum's shocked face when the windows went. A gun going off. The man's head jerking as he died.

Sheldon was in crisis. Not because he'd been caught. Not because Langley would disown him. Not because imprisonment and emptiness stretched ahead. But because a patriot was dead. He, who increasingly felt commitment to nothing, was alive.

Once, there was satisfaction in secret work. In using exciting skills to outwit the cleverest minds the opposition could deploy. Revelling in knowledge that none but the chosen few were allowed to have. Taking pride in dirty jobs that protected freedoms people in their trailer parks or expensive condos took as a God-given right.

In his never-ending war, victory was never an option. He felt the futility of it all. Anger at a system that used and abused. Shame at the loss of pride which had sustained him for so long. Donald Sheldon wanted to come through this and see if anything lay on the other side.

But the effort was painful, and he was desperately tired.

Serious rivalry divided Intelligence and Chief Constables. The late Prime Minister had encouraged this antipathy on the divide-and-rule principle. But now old certainties were being re-examined.

General Robert Forsyth was investing his morning in the Chiefs, speaking to each one in turn. He was trying to communicate a positive message. Whatever divided them, police and Intelligence had a common interest.

The American-inspired attempt to destabilize Britain threatened them all. Not only because they shared a desire for orderly society, but also because the privileged status of the nation's guardians was at risk. Nobody wanted that, and seven Chiefs had so far heard him out.

He made much of the fact that Godfrey Cornwell had been on the way to visit him when shamefully attacked. Because they would be unable to check with the hospitalized Home Secretary, Forsyth exaggerated progress, claiming that agreement had practically been reached on a marriage of the two security services.

They may have listened courteously, but the powerful policemen would talk amongst themselves. This didn't bother Forsyth. His curve ball had them swishing at air. The plan to unify command under David Chandler would be discussed and approved by Cabinet before they could organize coherent resistance. And he'd offered attractive rewards – maintenance of their senior status and control of local Intelligence units whose independent presence they had long resented.

Besides, without Godfrey Cornwell to protect his interests by defending theirs, the Chiefs had lost their clout.

Before making the next call, Forsyth recalled a television wildlife film featuring confrontation between fox and pheasant one snowy winter dawn. The gaudy bird was roosting in the lower branches of a hawthorn tree. Reynard appeared, stopped dead. Recognition was mutual. The pheasant's beady black and orange eye fastened on to danger, but that bird knew he was safe. Slowly at first, then faster and faster, the fox began running round the tree.

Slowly at first, then faster and faster, the bird's head swivelled as it attempted to keep the enemy in sight, remain alert to any deadly trick. Suddenly, with a thrashing of uncoordinated wings, the dizzied pheasant fell to the ground. Five seconds later the bird was dead, predator and prey were gone.

The Chiefs were the pheasant, Forsyth the fox.

Louise Tidyman showed him to the Georgetown library, after explaining that Errol had been detained by an over-running tête-à-tête with the Senate Majority Leader on the Hill. She offered the *Washington Post* and a drink by way of recompense.

It was early for alcohol, but what the hell – Lustbader's body was still on European time. He asked for a glass and pitcher of water, then poured a stiff Jameson's from the litre bottle purchased at Shannon. The smoky liquor did a slow burn down to his empty stomach. After he read the short article by Mary-Jo MacInnes, a reporter he knew and liked, he had another drink. Pieces started meshing.

When Errol breezed in fifteen minutes later, flashing his easy grin, the Jameson bottle was a quarter empty and Lustbader was feeling light-headed. The alcohol hadn't clouded his mind – merely loosened his inhibitions. The Veep sounded cheerful.

'The wanderer's return. So, how was London?'

The Vice-President helped himself to Irish, murdering it with ice from a bucket fashioned like a uniformed Negro page-boy on an antebellum Southern plantation. Who said Tidyman didn't have a sense of humour? He fell into an armchair and sniffed the drink. Lustbader pointed at the newspaper on the coffee table that separated them.

'I see your rival is about to become the focus of intense media attention.'

Errol Tidyman looked sad.

'Yeah, none of it good. Bad break. They could crucify him, which shouldn't do us any harm. Polls should make interesting reading by the weekend. Not that I'd want to win this way.'

'No point in asking if the Tidyman arm reached out and spiked Stark's tyres? As for London, it was a waste of time, like I said on the phone. Except it wasn't, was it?'

The Vice-President poured them both another drink before looking up. His expression was almost cruel.

'Nope. You did great. Couldn't tell you what was goin' down before you left, because I wanted you to play it straight, act with conviction. Let's just say I had advance intelligence of a move against Minton-Briant. No involvement, no idea they were actually planning to kill the man, but knowledge. Your job was to take out Ken Stanley by rather more peaceful means.'

Lustbader added water to his whiskey and swirled the mixture.

'These long-term contacts of yours, they'll move against Stanley now I've tarred him with an American brush?'

'Sure. The Brits have had enough ideological garbage rammed down their throats. Some of them want to renew old friendships, see that little country of theirs back on its feet. The Special Relationship is ready for revival. Lots of points in that for the new President. Ken Stanley is a price worth paying. He's history.'

The Vice-President sat back, pleased with his performance. Lustbader caught and held his eyes, asking the question for which he hadn't been able to find a satisfactory answer.

'None of this means a thing unless you win the election, Errol. How come you were always so sure you'd come through?'

'I wasn't sure then and I'm not now. But you didn't ought to run unless you believe you can win. And win we surely can, specially now Stark's headed for trouble.'

The Vice-President paused, his face softening.

'Don't forget why we're in this, Vernon. Election shit's

something we have to go through to get where we want to be. If we win we get to do things we both believe in. Don't go flaky on me, I need that sharp brain of yours more than ever. Borrow the guest bedroom and get some sleep. We can talk some more when you're ready.'

Lustbader set himself to argue, demand explanations for flapping loose ends. But his mind saw a bed and his body betrayed him. He found himself nodding.

'Okay, Errol, you win. As usual.'

The combined assault by General Forsyth and the Prime Minister had left them reeling. But Chief Constables didn't lose their wits, or nerve. After a flurry of conference calls, they delegated the task of making the best possible deal to their superior trade union, the Association of Chief Police Officers.

ACPO was used to dealing with government, and went right to the top. To the General Secretary's surprise, the PM not only agreed to listen to his worries, but seemed sympathetic. Ken Stanley liked the idea of senior policemen retaining high status and significant powers, to counterbalance the inexorable rise of Intelligence.

Inside ten minutes, the agile mind of Harry Higgins had devised a neat solution. The Chiefs would be invited to send one of their number to the forthcoming Cabinet meeting in an *ex officio* capacity – without a vote, but empowered to join the discussion. Furthermore, that individual would retain a Cabinet seat until the Home Secretary recovered from his injuries and returned to work.

The ACPO General Secretary's satisfaction at this turn of events was tempered by a practical problem. It wouldn't be easy to get the membership to agree on a suitable representative. Each Chief would think there was one ideal candidate, and it wouldn't be anyone else. But the former Assistant Chief Constable was used to dealing with the superegos of his employers.

He was confident of finding an acceptable compromise choice, if only because more than half the Chiefs wouldn't be able to reach London in time for the looming Cabinet meeting.

Intelligence was not informed of the new development.

General Forsyth might think he was calling the shots, but no man was bigger than the system. Harry Higgins was using his knowledge of the way things worked to fight back.

She'd caught the dawn flight to El Paso and paid a quarter to walk over the one-way Stanton Bridge into Ciudad Juárez, doing her bit towards that month's three million border crossings between the two cities. Mary-Jo MacInnes wanted to find the true identity of Maria Martinez.

With the help of an American-speaking taxi driver named Victor, who put himself at her disposal for the morning in return for fifty okay lady if you wanna argue make it forty dollars, she set about the task with enthusiasm, which quickly waned as the reality of investigative journalism south of the border became apparent.

Their first call was police headquarters, looking for the Martinez family's address. The middle-aged officer they got to see after an hour looked like a generalissimo and had trouble understanding what she wanted, even with the voluble assistance of Victor – until she suggested 'One hundred dollars for the Police Benevolent Fund?' Whatever went over in translation did the trick.

After being examined from all angles, the C-note vanished into an old cigar box on the wooden desk. Suddenly, the order of the day was '*Sí, sí comprendo*', backed by nods and smiles all round.

Moments later, Victor explained that Capitano Pulido had spoken with the Martinez parents at the request of the American authorities. These peasants admitted nothing. But experience suggested that funeral expenses of their beloved daughter Maria would have been obtained by selling her precious Yanqui green card, which sadly was of no further use to her. Bad men dealt with these matters, men so far untraced despite tireless effort. End of story.

They drove to the address provided by the captain, an adobe house high on a hillside covered by shacks built from anything that came to hand. Mary-Jo watched as Victor banged on the weathered door. A thin yellow dog lying on the dusty sidewalk opened an eye before returning to siesta. The door opened and Victor conducted a lively exchange with an old woman dressed in black, whose sunken eyes kept straying past his animated gestures to the cab. After a while, he beckoned.

Inside, the two-room house was dark and cool. There was a smell of pungent cooking. A baby slept in a simple crib on the packed dirt floor. The only ornaments were a raffia crucifix on the wall and Sony ghetto-blaster on the packing-case table. The old woman returned to a rocker beside the child and moved the white blouse she had been embroidering. Mary-Jo marvelled at the quality of the workmanship.

Victor made the introductions. This was Consuela Martinez, mother of Maria's father. She would be happy to help in any way she could. Mary-Jo didn't understand what was said about her, but it sounded impressive. The old woman bobbed her head and waved them to plastic-covered bar stools with cut-off legs. Mary-Jo rummaged in her shoulder bag and found the morgue photograph Schneider had given her.

The driver passed the picture to Consuela, who took it in gnarled hands and looked closely. They exchanged a volley of Spanish. After a moment, tears started in the sunken dark eyes, running unchecked down wrinkled brown cheeks. Then Consuela Martinez dropped the photograph into her lap, threw back her head and let out a keening wail. Victor knelt beside the old woman and tried to calm her with rapid words. The baby woke up and started yelling.

Instinctively, Mary-Jo went over and lifted the howling child, offering the tiny white-swaddled body with its angry face to the old woman. Victor looked up gratefully. Consuela's grief subsided into spasmodic sobs. She accepted the baby and clasped the small bundle to her chest, rocking back and forth until both fell silent.

At the table, Victor filled her in. The girl in the picture was Linda Martinez, granddaughter to Consuela, cousin to Maria. The police had not spoken at all with the family. Only now had Consuela learned of Linda's death, and the cruel manner of it. True, they had given Maria's papers to Linda, whose older brother was already in the United States. Victor closed with an observation of his own.

'Tough break, losing two inside a year. The boy was caught, sent back to Mexico. This ain't a happy family.'

They talked some more with the old lady, who was now calm but uncommunicative, wanting to be alone with grief. But she answered Victor's questions briefly, falling silent as he translated the answer and relayed Mary-Jo's next question.

It was a painful way of learning a little about Linda – a good girl just twenty-one years old who worked hard to study English, because she had thought of nothing but America since she understood how different life could be beyond the concrete banks of the Rio Grande. A girl not interested in boys who wished to give her babies and chain her to a house like this.

This girl was making her dream come true, and after Maria she was the family's pride and joy. Then the tears started again. Mary-Jo swivelled her eyes to the door, and Victor nodded. She tucked fifty dollars under the corner of the Sony. As they left, the old woman was hugging the baby fiercely, crooning words that were part lullaby, part lament. Mary-Jo doubted she even noticed them leave.

Back at the top of Juárez Avenue, she thanked Victor for his help, counting out his forty dollars and adding a generous tip. He shook her hand through the cab's open window.

With the exception of one weekend fling in Tijuana with a two-orgasms-a-night fellow-student, she hadn't visited Mexico before. This teeming, dirty working city was very different from the resort, and she found the place unsettling. As a northerner, she didn't even have a smattering of Spanish, and hated feeling powerless.

The price of walking back across the northbound Santa Fe bridge into the States was double – the best fifty cents Mary-Jo had spent all year. She had to stand in line before clearing the gloomy immigration hall and stepping into all-American sunshine, but it was worth the wait.

Bob Forsyth had loaned his driver, Armstrong. The journey from Chelsea to Downing Street was a voyage of discovery. Field Marshal Chandler was feeling well enough – superficial cuts and bruises no longer caused much discomfort, whilst the pain from his lacerated arm and ruined eyes was blunted by medication.

It was harder to cope with blindness. As a soldier who'd seen active service, he'd witnessed violent death and cruel maiming. He had long ago accepted that his own flesh was as vulnerable as the next person's.

But the everyday reality of living in darkness was something else. Easy enough in the hospital, confined to bed. Frustrating when he went to stay with Alex and discovered how many obstacles a bedroom could contain. Frightening when making his first foray into the outside world, though the chauffeur was a reassuring presence at his right elbow.

He'd dressed in his Field Marshal's uniform with a little help from his daughter, then Armstrong had guided him out to the waiting car. He'd nearly fallen three times and banged his head getting in. Visually orientated guidance systems need time to readjust.

On the drive to Downing Street he tried a childhood game. When travelling on the London Underground he would close his eyes and count off stops, looking after five minutes to see if the train was arriving at the expected station. But despite valiant attempts to connect the car's movements to particular locations on the familiar journey, he was constantly forced to ask where they were.

After helping him up two shallow steps and through the front door of Number 10, Armstrong passed him on like a relay baton. His new guardian was Harry Higgins, the Cabinet Secretary.

'David, great to have you back. The meeting won't be starting for an hour, but I suggest we go along and get you settled in the Cabinet Room before the others arrive. Here, let me take your arm.'

'Good to be back, Harry. What's happening?'

He hated the hand that gripped his forearm, but forced himself to accept well-intentioned help.

'We've talked to the Chief Constables, and your man Forsyth's been doing the same. I don't expect problems with the merger. What choice do they have? Turn left, that's it. Now round the table. There, you're at your usual place. Can you manage?'

He took satisfaction from the small victory over a chair. Higgins excused himself.

'I must be off, unless you need anything. A cold drink? Ken and I have a few things to go over before the meeting.'

'I'll be fine.'

'If you're sure.'

The door closed. He sat quietly, running his palms over the polished table. It wasn't imagination – his sense of touch was becoming more acute. Perhaps the necessity of living in his head would sharpen mental faculties, too.

Competition amongst the Chief Constables was keen, and most were unwilling to accept a strong colleague to represent their interests in Cabinet. But for each the price of frustrating rivals' ambitions was accepting that they couldn't be chosen either. In the end, the choice was surprisingly uncontroversial.

Wendy Millar was one of only two female Chiefs, the more self-effacing of the distaff pair. Millar's area was Thames Valley, but she was not being rewarded for her force's leading role in tracking the Windsor gunmen. Her elevation depended on other factors.

Favourable geographical location – just thirty minutes from the Cabinet meeting by helicopter – was an accident beyond her control. But the credit for a general perception amongst fellow Chiefs that Wendy Millar threatened no one was entirely hers. They simply opted for the person least likely to be motivated by personal ambition and most likely to defend their collective interests.

A plain but well-groomed woman in her mid-forties, Wendy Millar had a self-deprecating style that encouraged male colleagues to remind themselves they were not prejudiced against the weaker sex. She was an intelligent manager who knew how to delegate, and wore success lightly – neither feeling the need to be twice as tough as the men, nor losing sleep over the possibility that she might be a token female.

After her long day's work, Wendy Millar shut the office door and went home to a house husband and three teenage children. But they wouldn't see her for supper on this particular Tuesday. The ACPO General Secretary had counted votes, congratulated the members' choice and informed the also-rans that Chief Constable Millar would be honoured to serve as their *ex officio* representative in Cabinet.

Candy Paretsky came off at four. Tomorrow was her twenty-third birthday. She was celebrating early – meeting her boyfriend at seven for a meal at Dick's Last Resort on Navarro. Randy also worked at the hotel, as a short-order cook, but couldn't get away early. She'd changed into her best dress before leaving work, but was dissatisfied with her appearance – wandering through Rivercenter, pausing to peer into stores that were enticing caverns of desire.

Occasionally, she was drawn into a beckoning doorway by the offer of twofers, but couldn't afford to buy. She was pretty, and it made her mad that nice things were beyond her grasp. The mall was busy, with people spending as though they had nothing better to do. Life was unfair.

Candy didn't see the couple following close behind. They moved in at Foley's, catching her as she paused in Fragrances to dab scent on to one wrist then, surreptitiously, the other. The woman made the first approach.

'That smell good? Buy Candy the bottle, Gene.'

Startled, she took a step back from the display. Her first thought was that these people were store detectives, who thought she'd slipped something into her skirt pocket. They looked like store detectives – the woman young, smart and tough, the man middle-aged with thick arms and a gut that thrust against his white shirt.

He produced a billfold from his hip pocket, counted off seven tens and handed the money to a sales assistant.

'She'll take one of those, gift-wrapped.'

When the small package was ready, he presented it to her.

'Down payment for services to be rendered, Candy.'

The woman chimed in from the other side, forcing her to turn her head like a spectator at a tennis match.

'How does a thousand dollars sound?'

'We're talking cash money for one, two days' work. Hell, you could call in sick and be back at work Thursday.'

The male voice was used to getting what it wanted. Candy found she was being walked along the carpet road to the nearest exit. She stopped, looking again from one to the other.

'What is this? Are you guys crazy? I don't even know you. I mean, thanks for the scent, but . . .'

The woman smiled mechanically, stepped around in front and spoke crisply.

'I'm Frances Clifford, this is my partner Gene Zarubica. Maybe you've heard of us? We're writers on the *National Enquirer*. No big deal, we only get read by ten zillion people. We figure you may have something interesting to tell us.'

Gene tightened his grip on her elbow.

'Like the sort of stuff that keeps people glued to the page and sells copies, Candy. Let's go where we can talk. We have a car in the parking garage.'

Candy did know the names but played it cool, pulling her arm free.

'The woman from the *Washington Post* said this could be worth two, three thousand.'

Gene chuckled warmly into her ear.

'Oh, I doubt that, my dear. Those heavyweights are cheap-skates. But we can cut the deal that delights, if you tell us what we want to hear.'

Candy Paretsky imagined his heavy body on top of hers. The thought filled her with disgust, but also sent a shiver down her spine.

'I guess it wouldn't do no harm to talk.'

Word arrived from ACPO that the Chief Constables had selected Wendy Millar to speak for them at Cabinet. She would be arriving at Number 10 shortly. Harry Higgins was surprised – he'd expected one of the pushier types. So much the better. Millar was clever but not arrogant, easy to do business with.

The PM accepted the news without comment, asked Higgins to convene the meeting and disappeared into the Cabinet Room. Quite a contrast to last time, when Stanley kept everyone waiting. He wanted Chandler and Forsyth to confirm that his back was covered. The two Intelligence officers had been in there for fifteen minutes, and hadn't been discussing the weather. Higgins popped his head into the anteroom.

'We're ready. The PM's gone in and Field Marshal Chandler's there too. Go easy on him. Getting to the meeting has been a brave effort.'

That caused a frisson of interest. Cabinet members rose *en masse* and followed him. A crowd formed round David Chandler. Everyone wanted to slap his shoulder and welcome him back. Dark glasses failed to mask disfiguring injuries – the face was pallid, pocked with healing scar tissue. He responded well – enduring jostling and finding friendly words for each person who greeted him.

Ken Stanley sat hunched in his chair on the edge of the crowd. One or two Cabinet members glanced at him, and Higgins saw awareness growing that circumstances had changed. The assured politician who triumphed only five days ago had gone, replaced by a loner who communicated siege mentality.

The Cabinet Secretary shepherded people to their places. With Chandler once more occupying his regular seat, General Forsyth marched to Godfrey Cornwell's chair and sat down.

Higgins said nothing. If Forsyth wanted Cabinet members to see that his status was on the up, why not? It was. Besides, the Chiefs' representative wouldn't know that their prestigious location had been pirated. The Prince Regent had sent apologies and Wendy Millar would have to live with his remote spot at the foot of the table.

Everyone settled – pouring glasses of water, covertly studying the main protagonists, hanging jackets over chair backs. Now the crush had subsided, Ken Stanley was whispering urgently to Chandler.

Higgins had instructed his assistant to bring Wendy Millar along the minute she arrived. Alan Forbes and the Chief – resplendent in her dark blue dress uniform – appeared in the doorway. The Cabinet Secretary got up and introduced her, noting that Forsyth's lips tightened.

'In view of Godfrey Cornwell's indisposition, the Prime Minister asked the Chief Constables to be represented. They have chosen Mrs Millar to speak for them. Those of you who don't know Wendy personally will get the chance to meet her later, and I'm sure she'll make a useful contribution to today's agenda.'

The female Chief seemed unflustered by the piercing scrutiny of the nation's most powerful politicians. Her stance was relaxed and she nodded easily in response to the introduction. Higgins found himself thinking that this was the sort of woman one would like as a friend. He considered taking her arm, but confined himself to a whispered comment.

'Well done indeed, my dear. Your colleagues are to be commended on an excellent if surprising choice.'

Harry Higgins belatedly realized his aside was patronizing. She took no offence, her reply making him like her all the more.

'Thanks. Which god-forsaken spot is reserved for the bloody idiot who arrives last?'

As he showed the Thames Valley Chief to her distant seat, Higgins reminded himself that Millar had a track record that suggested she shouldn't be dismissed lightly.

Displeased by the appointment of a Chief Constable to Cabinet, General Forsyth watched Millar settle and Higgins return to his seat, before asking him for a security briefing. These self-serving people had to understand that things were changing. But he didn't want to antagonize them, speaking in the neutral tone of an expert.

'The pilot of the Chequers plane has been identified. He's British, but is currently at an American air base in Germany. They're flying him back to the States for a meeting with Vice-President Tidyman, which tells its own story. Three men responsible for the other attacks were killed by an SIS unit in North London last night. Also British, but seasoned mercenaries. The terror campaign is over.'

He assessed the reaction. Stanley, Chandler and Higgins already knew, but the others were delighted. With the threat of violence lifted, Cabinet members anticipated a return to the privileged politics they knew and loved. They might be in for a surprise. He cleared his throat and continued.

'We've frustrated an American attempt to destabilize Britain, which came dangerously close to succeeding. This was initiated by Errol Tidyman rather than the US government, and the whole operation was based on clever evaluation of one fundamental weakness in our set-up.'

Forsyth wondered when the uninitiated would discern where these innocuous preliminaries were leading. To his surprise, Wendy Millar came in, jumping to the point he was working towards. Her pleasant contralto voice commanded attention.

'We were vulnerable because the late PM had established complete control? Senior politicians owed their positions to him and he deliberately played off one security service against the other. Remove the head and the body spasms.'

She stopped, allowing them to slap her into line. Forsyth wasn't alone in being startled. Everyone looked at the Thames Valley Chief as though seeing her for the first time. Even Chandler turned his dark glasses in her direction. When nobody said anything, Wendy Millar went on.

'Killing Minton-Briant created confusion and uncertainty. Throw in controlled violence targeting senior people, which causes the rest to look suspiciously over their shoulders at colleagues, and the job's done. Except they've failed.'

Who was this outsider, speaking like a veteran and saying things that came perilously close to the knuckle? She was unabashed. Far from being intimidated by an atmosphere that was suddenly taut, she continued in the same even voice.

'I'm sorry if this is the wrong moment, but as we've started with security matters and I'm here to represent my fellow Chief Constables, it seems sensible to get our position on the record before you move to the formal agenda.'

Higgins looked at Ken Stanley, who shrugged. Thus led, nobody seemed inclined to argue. They were intrigued by this woman's bravura performance. As Wendy Millar went on, the tactician in Forsyth admired the way she was building a strong position from nothing.

'The Home Secretary looked after our interests here in Cabinet. But he's gone and we Chiefs won't let operational efficiency suffer. The police are interested in efficient law and order. There's no question of joining the sort of power struggle the Americans were hoping for. We're in favour of anything that enhances this country's security and offer full support for the process of restoring stability. That's all I have to say. Thank you for listening so patiently.'

Wendy Millar sat back, catching Forsyth's eye. She'd

been smart. By accepting the inevitability of the security merger rather than fighting it, she had avoided loss of face amongst the people who mattered. He addressed Cabinet members who had no idea what was going on. He nodded.

'I'm sure we appreciate that constructive contribution. Proposals for streamlining security activities have been formulated. Make no mistake, we all have a duty to ensure that normality is restored. I will now ask the Prime Minister to tell you what must be done.'

Forsyth glanced across at Millar, but she was examining her lap. Clever – light blue touch-paper and stand clear. He might be able to work with an operator like that.

As Ken Stanley started to speak, Forsyth looked around. Cabinet members knew the rules. Providing they didn't make trouble, they'd get their slice of cake.

The Prime Minister didn't care for the script, but would deliver it anyway. He hardly listened to Wendy Millar and Bob Forsyth, allowing his mind to wander back over the traumatic days since Derek Minton-Briant's powerful personality had been extinguished.

Initial certainty that his time had come, awareness of what needed to be done, a sense of destiny, confidence he could impose his will on Cabinet and Party, easy assumption of the PM's mantle – all had come and gone. That which seemed infinitely desirable less than a week ago had become a burden.

He always assumed one merely needed the opportunity, but there was more to it than that. Easy enough to understudy the lead, quite another thing to face glaring spotlights and deliver. General Forsyth came to the end of his preamble and looked at him expectantly. Ken Stanley felt angry. Why couldn't they leave him alone? He concealed the emotion.

'Chief Constable Millar, General Forsyth, thank you for setting the scene. In view of recent upheavals, I feel the time has come to unify the command structure of police and Intelligence. In future, both services will report to the Security Minister, David Chandler.'

The Prime Minister knew his presentation was uninspired

but trudged on, briefly communicating the message without frills or any attempt to sell the package.

'I also propose that David should be appointed Deputy PM to clarify the succession. A State of Emergency will be declared from midnight and remain in force until the situation has returned to normal.'

He stopped. From his right, Harry Higgins came in.

'Thank you, Prime Minister. I suggest we take individual comments before voting on the motion. As the continuing stability of our country lies at the heart of these proposals, perhaps we might ask the Security Minister to begin.'

Ken Stanley looked at Chandler. His head was turning, though he could see nothing. Perhaps he was building a mental picture. When he spoke, it was with the conviction of a dedicated professional.

'This has been an ordeal. But we must learn from our mistakes. Recent atrocities illustrate how vulnerable we have become. It's unacceptable for the properly constituted government of a sophisticated industrial nation to be threatened by the murder of our Prime Minister and a well-planned terror campaign.'

Again, Chandler's opaque gaze wandered. Various Cabinet members stirred uncomfortably. After a moment, the Security Minister continued, his voice containing no hint of disapproval.

'No one in this room can be blamed. Without belittling Derek's achievements, he concentrated power in his own hands. He encouraged rivalries which strengthened his own position. We're left to put the pieces together. The economy isn't going well and public discontent's building. We must contain that pressure, so I commend Ken's constructive proposal and commit my energies to its successful implementation.'

He looked tired and frail. Ken Stanley admired the strength of character that had carried Chandler through. He placed a hand on his old friend's shoulder.

'Well said, David.'

Perhaps things would work out, after all.

Human predictability amused Wendy Millar. Time after time she waited for an aberrant response, willing people to kick over the traces and do something original. They rarely did.

The Thames Valley Chief was unsurprised by the way in which the Cabinet meeting developed. Her call to the epicentre of power had been daunting. She expected the nation's leaders to be on a superior plane, operating with acumen and awareness. Not so.

As soon as she entered the Cabinet Room, Wendy Millar felt there was nothing to fear. She knew Cabinet members by sight and had met several, but got no sense of dynamism or purpose. There were exceptions. One was the Intelligence general, Forsyth, who radiated self-confidence. His boss was a remote but strong presence behind dark glasses.

It had only taken a moment to pick up vibrations from the others. They were afraid – afraid they didn't understand what was happening, afraid they'd hate it when they did, afraid seductive privileges and status might be snatched away. Even the PM was lost in a world of his own.

When General Forsyth began the discussion, her diagnosis had been confirmed. In that instant, Wendy Millar made a snap decision. Forsyth was the coming man, and she would step into line behind him. She certainly preferred the idea of working with Forsyth to becoming the opposition.

She had seized an early opportunity to make this clear to anyone who was listening. Most Cabinet members weren't, reacting to her forthright statement with expressions ranging from surprise at her nerve to irritation that a newcomer – female at that – should be so pushy. Forsyth let her see that he not only heard, but understood. She doubted anyone else noticed the exchange, but did anyone else much matter?

Satisfied, Wendy Millar returned to the anonymous persona they expected and enjoyed her afternoon out. Stanley's opening contribution had been weak. Far from taking the lead, the PM sounded depressed – like an actor reading for a part he didn't want, without emotion or passion.

Field Marshal Chandler's follow-up was better. The plucky old boy had suffered a rough ride, yet was back in the saddle only days after a crashing fall. She liked the image – her teenage daughters were horse-mad.

Thereafter, a series of lightweight contributions had her

wanting to scream. The motivation of Cabinet members was transparent. They spewed out lots of words – diatribes on the need to clamp down on social unrest, supportive comments on the imminent State of Emergency, demands for repeated details of the American plot, ideas for revitalizing the economy – but the underlying theme was self-justification. They were going on record as worthwhile contributors.

Wendy Millar watched, listened and learned. For all her awareness, these powerful people were outside her experience. It would be wrong to assume their motivation was entirely selfish. They probably couldn't themselves unravel the tangled skein that bound political philosophy and the advantages enjoyed by its standard-bearers. Interestingly, with the well-maintained exception of the Arts Minister, they were all men.

When Cabinet members finally dried, Harry Higgins suggested a vote. There was no dissent. A temporary State of Emergency was endorsed. The proposed security merger was unanimously approved. The Security Ministry's new empire was validated by David Chandler's appointment as Deputy Premier. For Chandler, read Forsyth – though she doubted that more than two or three of the nation's leaders had seen it.

The meeting started to break up, a congratulatory group forming around the PM and Chandler, his new number two. A few Cabinet members left immediately, no doubt to brief civil servants. General Forsyth was the only one who approached her, taking the next chair.

'Nice start, Wendy. Shall we meet up, say tomorrow morning, first thing? I'm sure we'll find plenty to discuss.'

His expression was bland, but strong chemistry was at work. Wendy Millar shook his hand firmly. Chemistry cut two ways. If he thought her judgment would be clouded by the fact he was an attractive man, he was out of his tiny male skull.

'I'll stay in town and wait for your call. Try the Savoy.'

After holding on for a few seconds, she released his hand. Unnoticed by anyone but Forsyth and Higgins, who gave her a farewell wave, Wendy Millar drifted away from the disintegrating meeting.

No doubt her fellow Chiefs would be eagerly waiting for their self-effacing, trusty representative to report back.

Although Mary-Jo MacInnes had made progress, it hadn't been a good day. The Mexican trip had rattled professional detachment.

When she got back to the hotel in late afternoon, Mary-Jo was tired, looking forward to a shower before honing the story she'd started on the plane back from El Paso. She collected an e-mail from colleague Carl DiMona, detailing a torrid Stark press conference, together with messages to call Managing Editor Douglas Diehl and Lieutenant Schneider of SAPD.

She got as far as the bathrobe before a work ethic inherited from Scottish-American parents rolled over her. With no more than a resentful thought about hot water, she sat on the bed and excavated her mobile from the Coach bag. Dick Schneider was still at his desk.

'MacInnes? Thought I'd lost you.'

'Yeah, well, I took a vacation in Mexico. Juárez. Terrific place. Ever been down there?'

'A few years back, extradition case. Can't say I saw much of the city. You come up with anythin' I want to know?'

Schneider didn't sound hopeful. Mary-Jo decided to wake him up.

'You recall a Captain Pulido, by any chance?'

'Ain't he the Mexican cop who talked to the Martinez family for us? Didn't come up with much, but my man Olmos said he was helpful enough.'

'Sure he was. Never got off his butt, never spoke to anyone. Your corpse wasn't so hard to identify. Catch tomorrow's *Post* and find out who she was.'

'Son of a bitch!'

For the first time since she had met him, the Loot sounded surprised. She took pity on him.

'Linda Martinez, Maria's first cousin. I have an address and personal details. They just handed on the green card to the next in line. Knew nothing about the kid's murder.'

'I owe you. Speakin' of which, we got a description of the presumed killer. He no way resembles anyone on Stark's team. And we traced a maid who worked at the hotel till she

got a job up at Houston. Says someone was asking about
Martinez back in July. Showed an Immigration ID, wanted
to know everythin'. Told the witness to keep quiet, which
she did. Guess what this guy the Immigration Service never
heard of looks like?'

Mary-Jo wished she'd taken that shower.

'Your new suspect? Shit. What got me started was an
unsigned letter that pointed right at this story. Didn't
strike me as strange, because we get that sort of thing all
the time. Now I'm remembering that anonymous informant
who noted down a licence plate at four in the morning, but
declined to give a name. Goddammit.'

'Maybe we should start lookin' for someone with a grudge
against Stark. Got time to file a new story for tomorrow?'

'Saying what?'

'We never released the Martinez autopsy findings, but the
girl was a virgin, pure as desert sand. Any help?'

Mary-Jo was thinking fast, angry that someone had tried
to use her.

'The Yellow Press won't pass on a meal like this. Those
guys are fighting a dirty circulation war and will use any
ammo they can get. The story still runs if Stark only made
a pass at her, or did no more than he said, come to that.'

After a short pause, Schneider made a suggestion.

'Here's what we do. Turrow's sent for me and I'm going on
over there. He'll be mad, but I'll prime him to give you a real
good quote. Then I'll drop by your hotel with that autopsy
report and we can try and work something out.'

'See you later, Loot. Clear the line, I got work to do.'

She punched her managing editor's direct number, almost
hoping it would be busy.

'Diehl.'

'DD, it's Mary-Jo.'

'Great story. Got 'em all chasing our tail. More of the same
on the way, I trust. You only have three short hours to make
an old man happy.'

Mary-Jo took a deep breath.

'I'd love to say hold the front page, but we may have a
small problem.'

Against expectation, the Cabinet Meeting improved the

Prime Minister's mood. There was important work to be done, the others were supportive and nobody had questioned his right to the Premiership. But the merged security force would be formidable when teething troubles were resolved.

Forsyth and Millar had been talking quietly at the foot of the table, body language suggesting they got on well. But even as he watched, the woman got up and left the room without a backward glance. Perhaps he was imagining a threat where none existed. David Chandler was right. They all needed to work together.

Once key Cabinet committees were reconstituted – their composition remaining exclusively in the PM's gift – his influence on decision-making would be enormous. Ken Stanley relaxed. The whole business had been unpleasant, but he'd come through.

The crush thinned as tenacious well-wishers drifted away. Relieved of the need to put on a brave façade, Chandler looked exhausted. Ken Stanley felt ashamed. He'd hardly spared a thought for David. The meeting must have been a nightmare – yet he needed the Field Marshal to be supportive, strong.

Chandler's head turned, searching for something. Forsyth hadn't moved since Millar left, but was up in an instant.

'Ready for the off, David?'

For the first time since the meeting began, Chandler relaxed.

'More than ready, Bob, I'm shattered.'

The Field Marshal stood up, almost overbalancing. Forsyth's hand slipped around the old man's shoulder. Chandler swore. Forsyth raised his eyes and dropped his arm.

'You can't adjust overnight and in the meantime you need help. No shame in that. Come on.'

Chandler allowed himself to be steered towards the door, still complaining. Despite the grumbling tone, there was no mistaking his affection for the younger man. When they'd gone, Stanley glanced at Harry Higgins. The Cabinet Secretary's comment was thoughtful.

'David will depend heavily on Forsyth, which puts our ambitious young general in a position of undue influence.'

Ken Stanley nodded morosely.

'We're too old for this game, at least I am. I'll go upstairs and rest for a bit.'

Higgins gathered papers and went through the Greek Doors. The Prime Minister walked slowly out of the Cabinet Room, last to leave. Quite some day – but he was still standing. He paused to watch Forsyth and Chandler leaving through the famous front door, chattering away. He envied the Field Marshal.

The idea of a young, energetic heir apparent standing loyally beside you was decidedly appealing.

Dick Schneider shuffled towards his appointment, the years dragging at his feet. The lieutenant hated signs of ageing – the need for reading glasses, slipping scores in the annual handgun refresher, an aching hip when the atmosphere was damp, a leak taking for ever. But until today his mind never felt old, because he was good at what he did, and what he did was worth doing.

He pushed open Turrow's door. The lawyer looked up from his desk. The expression on his thin, intense face was hard to read, but wasn't the justifiable anger Schneider expected. He sat down. The First Assistant DA abandoned his paperwork, studying him as though he were a suspect about to confess to some terrible crime. Schneider said the first thing that came into his head.

'I'm goin' to see MacInnes, the *Post* reporter. She'll set the record straight.'

As he uttered the words, he knew they were meaningless. Turrow folded his arms.

'I remember reading a story in first grade about some Dutch kid who spotted a leak in this dike, stuck his fist in until help arrived and saved the goddam country from disappearing under the ocean. He was a hero, but you know what?'

Turrow leaned forward, giving an idea how sharp his legal eagle talons could be in court. Schneider answered wearily.

'What?'

'He wasn't dumb enough to pull his fist out, decide he'd made a mistake and try to put it back again. Congressman

Warren crashed my party to give me a similar message. MacInnes can write what she likes in the *Post*. But the damage will be done by papers which aren't fit to hang in the privy. Imagine what Billy Ray Brandon is going to do to me when Ella Stark is through barbecuing his ass. That woman spits fire on a good day.'

The Assistant DA hadn't gone far enough, as Schneider pointed out.

'Plus our sainted DA needs all the help he can get from the GOP if his ambition to occupy the Governor's mansion up in Austin is to advance by one inch. Boy, will he be sore, especially as he's been warnin' you off from day one. Sorry, I was wrong, simple as that. But whoever planned this fitted everythin' together like a sewing machine. We can close the Martinez file right now, because we ain't never goin' to get near that killer.'

They fell silent, all talked out. Eventually, Turrow stood up. He loosened his silk necktie, grabbed a white linen jacket from the chair back, hooked a finger into the collar and slung the coat over his shoulder.

'You're probably right. We've been worked over good by experts. Always hurts bright guys like us to be reminded someone out there's three times as clever. What the hell, we tried. I'm going home. Last time I looked I had a wife, maybe some kids, money in the bank, the rest of my life to live. Go see MacInnes, give her a quote from me. Anything you think might help.'

The lieutenant rose to follow Turrow, then stumbled into a bulky black briefcase.

'Hey, you forgot your case.'

Turrow paused at the door and smiled in a self-mocking way that got through to Schneider.

'The damn thing can stay here for the night.'

Schneider joined the First Assistant DA in the doorway. Physical contact didn't come easy, but he placed a light hand on Turrow's arm.

'For a lawyer, you ain't all bad. I'll walk you to your car, case Billy Ray's hidin' somewhere with a forty-four magnum. Consider yourself under police protection.'

Donald Sheldon was sleeping when they came – three green-uniformed Intelligence sergeants and a tough-looking officer with a nose broken in some long-forgotten brawl and set by a cross-eyed paramedic. The officer kicked the metal bed frame.

'Shake a leg, sunshine. You're in for a nice change of scene, you lucky terrorist. Nothing but the best for the CIA.'

As Sheldon sat up one of the sergeants stepped forward with handcuffs and a leg chain. The American held out his hands and the plastic cuffs were snapped in place. The sergeant knelt and fastened the leg chain, locking a bracelet above each ankle. Dark thoughts flashed through his mind. Perhaps this was the end, an anonymous disappearance that avoided serious embarrassment all round. Not that he cared.

'Where are you taking me?'

The officer grinned, showing a chipped incisor, and jerked a thumb towards the cell door.

'You'll see. But it's an improvement on this place. You must have friends in high places. Orders right from the top.'

He turned and led off. The procession moved along to the lifts. The leg chain rattled as Sheldon walked, but scarcely slowed him down. A digital display charted the progress of a rapidly descending lift, which stopped on their floor. Doors slid open on an empty car and a disembodied female voice chanted 'This is a down lift.' When they were safely inside, she switched to 'Stand clear of the doors, please.'

A key slipped into the control panel ensured they made the basement without stopping. Their car was waiting – a green Discovery. He followed one of the silent sergeants into the back, stumbling as he negotiated the awkward entry. Another scrambled in beside him, leaving a third to drive. The officer took the front passenger seat.

They drove up a ramp, paused for the security barrier and proceeded into the night. Sheldon looked around. The streets were well peopled, though few seemed inclined to linger in front of enticing shop windows.

Their route crossed familiar territory – Oxford Street, Marble Arch, up Edgware Road. After passing the red pile of Maida Vale Hospital the driver blinked right, accelerated up a short hill and turned left. Sheldon knew Hamilton Terrace well. It was one of the most attractive residential streets in London.

The Discovery stopped in front of a tall white mansion with a glass-roofed walkway stepping up to the main entrance. They were expected. The front door swung open as the small group came slowly up the steps. A white-coated man stood in a large entrance hall. When his visitors were inside, he issued an order before addressing Sheldon in a chatty tone.

'Remove the restraints. Welcome to Kinnock House, Donny. I'm Dr Whittier. You're here for what you Americans refer to as R and R. This is a secure facility, though you'll find it more agreeable than your last quarters. Thank you, I'll take him from here.'

The doctor stood beside Sheldon as the Intelligence unit departed without a word. He shut the front door and engaged an electronic combination lock, then indicated the stairs.

'I'll show you your room. We have every comfort, loose women excepted, but don't try and leave. We have sophisticated security arrangements and I'd hate you to make a fool of yourself. Besides, someone's coming to talk to you tomorrow, so you may want to satisfy innate curiosity before trying your famous vanishing act.'

He gave his guest a conspiratorial wink. Sheldon followed him up a wide staircase. He *was* intrigued. Events had taken an unexpected turn, and a small surge of excitement tingled through burned-out professional circuits.

The new Deputy Premier was suffering from premature reintroduction to power politics, dozing during the short car journey to New Centre Point. Chandler nearly collapsed in the lift, but insisted he would last out. In an ideal world he would still be in hospital, but the world hadn't been ideal since Adam went scrumping.

Forsyth settled the invalid in a chair with a glass of port, then sent for Andy Kyle. He was out and about in the building, but would be paged. After refilling Chandler's empty glass, Forsyth went to Sally Sayers' deserted work station in the outer office. Some things were best kept from the boss, especially when the supremo in question was a father-in-law who doted on his only daughter.

He phoned the clinic and asked to be put through to Beth Highsmith, annoyed with himself for leaving the call so late. While he waited, he tried to rationalize the lapse – it had been a frantic day, perhaps the most significant of his life. But that didn't justify the omission. The switchboard refused to connect him. Miss Highsmith's operation had been a success, but she wasn't taking calls. Forsyth was still contemplating the insubordinate telephone when his deputy hurried in. The big man frowned down at him.

'I was sitting on the kazi reading my horoscope when my bleeper went. Scared the shit out of me. First chance I've had to relax all day and it was just getting exciting. Apparently I'm going to meet a tall dark stranger who will transform my life.'

Forsyth forced himself to respond.

'Chandler's in there looking like death. Cabinet made him Deputy PM. He did bloody well at the meeting but he'll need time to get into shape. Let's go in and I'll bring you up to date. We have a decision to make. Our respected PM's future hangs in the balance.'

Feeling more cheerful, Forsyth stood up and headed for his destiny.

Brigadier Anderson Kyle admired the skill with which Forsyth nudged Chandler in the desired direction. Kyle knew where the discussion was leading, but the Field Marshal had not yet appreciated the full ramifications of his deputy's grand design.

Even so, David Chandler contributed incisive insights as Forsyth explained the new security arrangements to Kyle – who had managed to listen attentively, noting the barely disguised pleasure with which his superiors listed the changes. The dynamic duo had pulled it off – or Forsyth had.

Kyle was under no illusion. Whatever Chandler might think, he would never be more than a figurehead – accorded deferential status, consulted about policy, respected for wisdom and experience. But politically impotent. Power was passing to a hungrier generation. Bob Forsyth had grabbed his chance by the throat, and wasn't about to release the stranglehold.

Chandler's eclipse was confirmed when he sought reassurance. Would Intelligence accept the merger, even though ground had been given to the police? Were morale and discipline in good shape? Could officers and other ranks be relied upon to obey orders, however dramatic? They weren't the sort of questions asked by a commander on top of his job.

Forsyth adroitly terminated the question-and-answer session with a final query of his own, delivered casually – but no less explosive for that.

'So, what do we propose to do about our double-dealing Prime Minister, David?'

Chandler's face tensed. He adjusted his dark glasses. Troubled thoughts would not have been soothed if he'd been able to see the questioner's expression. Forsyth was smiling sardonically, amused by the old man's dilemma. Eventually, Chandler stalled.

'No chance you got this American connection wrong?'

Forsyth's smile widened. He raised his eyebrows, wickedly mocking Chandler's indecision.

'Andy?'

Kyle's turn had come. He spoke slowly and clearly. It was vital to convince both men that he believed what he was saying.

'None. I gather Bob ran through the evidence with you earlier, sir. Nothing's changed. The case against Stanley is unanswerable.'

Sensing Chandler wanted to protest, Forsyth came in persuasively.

'Look, David. Stanley's got the top job – something he'd never have achieved while Minton-Briant was around. Derek would have hung in there till he dropped, by which time Godfrey Cornwell would have been ready to take over. Perhaps Ken wanted a taste of glory.'

The Field Marshal got angry.

'No. He's a man of principle, a reformer. Ken was happy working behind the scenes, seeing his ideas put into practice. Derek implemented almost all his strategies. The three of us worked well together. Why should he become involved in a murderous scheme like this?'

Like a hunter, Forsyth had stalked the old man. Now, he struck.

'That rose-tinted version isn't quite accurate, is it? As the economy started failing, Stanley had doubts about Minton-Briant, his ability to cope. Even you were becoming restive. Ken could see everything he'd worked for collapsing. Popular discontent threatening a life's work.'

Cunningly, Forsyth paused, knowing his reading of the PM's character was too accurate for Chandler to challenge. He tried, without conviction.

'Yes, but . . .'

'But nothing. Ken would fight for his dream. This deal with Tidyman removed an immovable Minton-Briant before he could perpetrate the worst excesses of senile megalomania. It started the process of mending fences with the Yanks, vital if the economy's to be rebuilt. And put him in charge, able to further those cherished objectives of his.'

Kyle could see Chandler weakening, putting hands to his head as though the weight of argument was too heavy. Forsyth continued silkily.

'Wouldn't rapprochement with the USA serve him well? Don't forget, the split was manufactured by Minton-Briant to provide an external focus for discontent. Things went from bad to impossible in ten seconds flat when we used our Security Council veto to screw their domination of the UN. Tidyman would pay handsomely to reverse that, and US dollars would certainly improve the economic outlook here. With me so far?'

Chandler's reply was almost inaudible.

'I suppose so.'

'I think Ken did what he did for the best of reasons. He's that sort of man. But can the ends be allowed to justify such drastic means, however well intentioned? Is assassination an acceptable method of resolving political differences in a civilized society?'

Forsyth made it sound as though they were facing an agonizing moral dilemma. If the situation hadn't been so grave, Kyle would have laughed. As far as he could tell, Field Marshal Chandler was giving the question serious consideration. He needn't have bothered. Kyle knew what was coming, and it had nothing to with political morality.

Forsyth was about to make a naked bid for power.

A sharp double rap caused Mary-Jo MacInnes to save her almost-rewritten story and shut down the Powerbook. She checked her robe, then went to the door. A cop who'd had a tough day stood outside. He produced a folder from under his jacket and held it out like a peace offering.

'Autopsy report.'

In spite of the bad news, she was pleased to see him.

'You better come in. I have a few minutes before I must file. So, we get to share sucker of the month award.'

The lieutenant followed her in, closing the door behind him. He took off his check jacket, threw it on the floor and sat back on the bed, spreading thick arms to support himself. Mary-Jo put the folder on the table and turned her chair. She sat down and leaned forward.

'How do you read this one, Loot?'

The top of her robe parted, and Schneider inspected the tantalizing revelation. The cop sniffed.

'Boy, there's a sight for sore eyes, but I have to tell you I got a headache. Mind if I smoke? Always seems to help when I'm hell-bent on givin' the brain cell a work-out.'

He produced a cigar from his vest pocket, stripping wrapper and band. After flicking debris in the general direction of the waste bin without getting close, he reached down and rummaged through his jacket.

When he came up empty Mary-Jo lifted a throwaway lighter from her pack of Pall Mall and tossed it over. When the cigar was stoked up, Schneider started pacing the room.

'Stark's got a reputation as a stud, right? I figure this was a set-up that went wrong, except they got lucky. Old tomato-head here saw to that. Martinez was bribed or blackmailed into settin' up that after-hours scene in the hope Stark would grab the opportunity to burn off sexual energy.'

Mary-Jo touched the folder.

'But the virgin corpse says he didn't.'

'The Candidate's mindful of the dangers, she's not his type or he's too decent to take advantage. Whatever, nothin' worse than a mild pass happens, probably not even that.

Makes no odds. Maybe the kid lies about screwin' Stark
to the puppet-master, but she's dead anyway. A murdered
girl fresh from Stark's bedroom is dynamite even without
a semen match.'

Schneider returned to the bed, slumped down and made
smoke. Mary-Jo didn't interrupt again. After a minute, he
continued slowly – the gravelly Texan voice full of self-
contempt.

'We get the tip, you get the tip, and I snatch the bait like a
trout five minutes out of the stockin' tank. Jesus H. Christ,
I've only been on the job for thirty years. Sure, the scam was
clever, but I guess I wanted Stark to be responsible. All my
life I hated the way people with power and influence put in
the fix. I meant to nail someone for killin' that little girl and
charged after the first scent I got. Some smart cop, huh?'

Mary-Jo glanced at her travel alarm. This was good stuff,
but Dealer Diehl would be expecting her story and there
was repair work to be done before she could send it to
Washington.

'Who did this?'

He shrugged.

'Could be anyone. Stark's tough on organized crime. The
dons are not above a bit of revenge or insurance for a
quieter future. Remember Kennedy? Then again Honest
Pat's offerin' a major anti-drug programme with big new
resources. I can think of a few South American exporters
who ain't exactly celebratin' that prospect.'

She suggested another possibility.

'How about defence interests? Stark's promised to cut the
budget deficit much further than Tidyman and more than
a few contractors are way overstretched already.'

'Them too. Whatever, the thing was a long time in the
plannin'. They must've targeted him months ago. If it hadn't
been Martinez in San Antonio it would've been another poor
kid and another dumb cop in another city. Can you do
anythin'? Turrow's told me to give you any quote which
will help. Hell, make up your own and clear it with me.'

Mary-Jo thought for a bit, reluctantly admiring the devious minds that had fooled them both.

'I'll do my best, which doesn't add up to spit. My story
this morning was true, if misleading. I can try and set the

record straight, but the news has broken. Everything you said is hypothesis. Sure, I believe you, but where's your evidence? Martinez was in Stark's room after midnight, she was battered to death within hours, his campaign car was used to move the body. This'll spread like a Californian bushfire in a high wind.'

Schneider crushed out his cigar and stood up.

'Think I don't know that? Me, I can keep tryin'. If anythin' comes up I'll let you know, but don't hold your breath.'

Mary-Jo shared his impotent anger. She felt a need to comfort him, and once her mind was made up she wasn't shy.

'You want to stay the night, Loot? No big deal, but I'll be finished in thirty minutes then we can cry on each other's shoulders till dawn. Sound good?'

He looked her up and down.

'Sounds terrific, MacInnes. Thanks for tryin'. You made an old man's day. You're one heck of a woman and I'm never goin' to forgive myself for takin' a raincheck, but I'd like us to be friends. You hear what I'm sayin'?'

He placed a large hand on each of her shoulders, leaned down and gently kissed her cheek. As his lips brushed her skin, she felt his warmth and smelt rich tobacco. Lieutenant Schneider picked up his crumpled jacket and went, holding an arm out sideways and waggling fingers in farewell.

Mary-Jo returned to her chair and booted up the Powerbook, but her mind wasn't on the impossible-to-write story.

DAY SEVEN:

Wednesday 11 September

The sense of involvement that briefly lifted David Chandler was a memory. He woke with a deep feeling of unease, and everything flooded back – the Cabinet meeting, Bob's condemnation of Ken Stanley, physical collapse. God, he'd degenerated into a pathetic creature. And to think he'd eagerly anticipated a leading rôle in the reconstruction.

Chandler lay still. Try as he might, he couldn't summon the energy to challenge his deputy's dangerous interference with the due process of government. Eventually, he reached for the handbell that would summon assistance. Better to talk with Bob than be left in a vacuum of uncertainty. Before he could locate the bell, his daughter spoke.

'Anything you want, Dad?'

Alex must have sat with him, bless her. Covers were rearranged and he felt the back of a cool hand on his forehead, testing temperature.

'Go back to sleep. I should never have let you go out yesterday and Bob should have known better than to drag you back to work.'

He found her hand, covering it with his own.

'Not his fault, my dear. Bob needs my support. Look, I'll feel easier when I've had a chat with him. We've got things to sort out, then I'll sleep. Promise. What's the time?'

'Five in the morning, and you look bloody awful.'

Her voice seethed with filial indignation. He tried again,

resisting the temptation to raise his voice – hating his reliance on others, but accepting it as a new fact of life.

'Alex, I *feel* bloody awful, but I have responsibilities and can't ignore them, even if my contribution isn't worth much. But until I've tried I can't relax, let alone sleep. Give me ten minutes with Bob, that's all I ask. Is he here?'

'He went downstairs a while back. You're not the only one who can't sleep. All right, I'll fetch him, but only because you'll never settle until whatever's bothering you is off your chest. Ten minutes, and after that you start behaving like a proper patient. Agreed?'

'Agreed. And Alex, you know I'm always saying you remind me of your mother? You don't, really. You remind me of you.'

Chandler squeezed his daughter's hand.

Eating a bacon sandwich, General Robert Forsyth sat at the kitchen table, drafting the speech he would deliver to the nation later in the day. As he chewed, he wondered when Chandler would surface.

The previous evening's meeting at Intelligence HQ had ended indecisively. The Field Marshal finally cracked – refusing to hear another word about the PM's alleged treachery or discuss possible responses. Forsyth had steered a catatonic Chandler downstairs and Armstrong drove them back to the Chelsea house.

Alex was waiting, horrified when she saw her father. He certainly looked ill. His waxy skin had taken on a terrible pallor and he found difficulty in walking. After berating Forsyth for putting him through such a stressful experience, Alex enlisted Armstrong's assistance to get Chandler upstairs.

Half an hour later she was back. A few well-chosen verbal salvos suggested their recent truce was over. Forsyth didn't fire back. She'd never understand that some things took precedence over the interests of any individual, however important or well loved. His silence infuriated her. She stormed out of the living room and went back up to sit with her father, who was mercifully asleep.

Forsyth had gone up to the master bedroom and showered, washing his hair vigorously and scrubbing himself with an abrasive loofah till the skin tingled. He needed action, but there was nothing he could do for the moment. Win or lose, events would take their course.

He'd towelled off, put on sweatshirt and slacks and fallen on the bed. He wanted to make peace with Alex, but his wife didn't appear. She presumably intended to stay at Chandler's side. He dozed intermittently, always starting awake after a few moments, mind worrying some tricky aspect of his scheme.

Eventually he got up, fetching pen and pad on the way to the kitchen, where he had found one of the bodyguards drinking tea and reading a thriller. Forsyth sent the man off to do sentry duty elsewhere, made a thick bacon sandwich and settled at the table.

Committing the message that would save a nation to paper wasn't easy. The first sentence had thrice been composed, thrice crossed out. Forsyth finished the sandwich and washed his hands. Anything to put off the wrestling match with elusive words. Decisive action was justified, but he needed a convincing explanation for those who might assess his motivation with cynicism. If firm leadership meant accusations of self-aggrandizement, too bad.

Alex came into the kitchen, leaning against the door frame with arms folded. Her posture suggested that he was neither forgiven nor his abuse of Chandler forgotten.

'The silly sod's awake, won't sleep until he's talked to you. You can have ten minutes. After that I settle him down without fail, whatever either of you say. Understood?'

Forsyth abandoned introversion with relief.

The door opened, closed. Chandler felt the double bed sag as someone sat down, heard relaxed breathing. Forsyth's voice spoke with a hint of amusement that might be interpreted as condescension.

'Here we are again, just like old times.'

Chandler disciplined his anger. In the few moments since Alex left, he had forced himself to face reality.

'Ever wondered what it's like to be blinded, Bob? Don't think I really know, not yet. You wake up, open your eyes before you remember, then nothing. You're helpless without someone to fetch and carry, cut up your food, sit you on the lavatory, make sure you don't fall down stairs or walk into walls. I can't answer the phone without help, much less discharge my duties. But you've worked that out, haven't you?'

'Yes, David, I have.'

An assured reply – or was it arrogant? Chandler continued gently.

'You're deprived of stimuli sighted people take for granted. No movement, faces or words to read, colours to see . . . nothing. Then the mind starts to compensate. We're resilient. I'll learn to cope physically, and have already discovered that you think more intensely. I can't explain, but somehow your mind sees things better without external distractions.'

'And what do you see now?'

Forsyth sounded interested. Chandler shook his head sadly.

'I see an old man training up a successor who learned his lessons well. Perhaps too well. You intend to depose Ken Stanley, don't you? I'm still not convinced he betrayed us. Even if he did, there's a strong argument for leaving him in place. The method may have been wrong, but you may be sure his motives were honourable. Minton-Briant *was* going soft. The country's on a knife-edge. We need continuity, time to rebuild. The whole fabric of society could collapse into anarchy if you pursue this reckless course, Bob.'

Forsyth moved on the bed. Leaning towards him? The voice was certainly louder, almost hectoring.

'That's why I must take decisive action. If you taught me anything it's to loathe and despise weakness, indiscipline. Intelligence is the strong arm of government, charged with maintaining order and stability. Don't get me wrong. I'm not in this for myself. You'll have a full part to play. When Stanley's discredited, you automatically become PM. Trust me on this one, David, that's all I ask.'

'Ask, or tell?'

Silence as Forsyth considered his answer, then a decision to speak plainly.

'I'm afraid it's tell. Stanley's finished, providing I get the support of police chiefs. I'm seeing Wendy Millar for breakfast, but there are times when security professionals stick together and this is one of them. We're fed up with being used as opposing pieces in some political game. We all share a belief in law and order.'

Chandler hadn't got the strength to dispute twisted logic.

'Do I have a say in this?'

The weight was lifted from the bed. No hesitation this time.

'Look how much yesterday took out of you. Today's going to be far worse, believe me. You and Ken Stanley go back a long way, so you're not the best person to make rational decisions about his status. I'm afraid you must remain incommunicado. You need complete rest. No phone calls, no visitors. Now, get some sleep. Our ten minutes is up. Besides, I have to get into the office before my meeting with Millar.'

Once more the door opened, closed. Chandler pulled up the blankets. If only he could believe Bob was doing this for the right reasons. But he couldn't.

Brigadier Andy Kyle waited for Forsyth's summons. He knew his superior had arrived to make an early start and presumed a course of action had been agreed with Field Marshal Chandler. Kyle had decisions of his own to make, but needed to know which way Forsyth would jump.

If he'd read the signs, the Acting Head of Intelligence was preparing to strike at Ken Stanley. Most people were incapable of satisfaction with their lot. Poor men aspired to comfort, comfortable men wanted to be rich, rich men lusted for more. Stanley stood in Forsyth's way, so the Prime Minister would have to go.

Forsyth had probably secured Chandler's agreement, railing at Ken Stanley's duplicity and adopting a potent mixture of high moral tone and scaremongering to railroad the confused old man. Forsyth would have played on Chandler's fear of being pushed aside, claimed personal ambition played no part in his dramatic proposal, insisted Chandler should take the Premiership, emphasized his own loyalty, offered Chandler the choice between firm government and chaos.

He went out into Control. Since the SIS team had taken

out the hit squad a semblance of normality had returned. The night staff weren't busy in the last hour of their shift. Kyle returned to the office, looked at the safe and thought briefly about that revealing tape.

He was worried about timing. There was no margin of error and the smallest mistake would be catastrophic. Forsyth wouldn't give him a second chance. He reflected on friendship, camaraderie, respect, trust. All had made a rewarding contribution to his relationship with Bob over the years and meant a great deal to both of them. Without Forsyth's support, he would still be a training officer.

But these things were not enough. When he thought about Forsyth now, he felt sorry his old friend had behaved so predictably. People were always tempted when they saw an opportunity. The phone went and his Duty Controller came on.

'General Forsyth on the line. Will you take the call?'

Even when you reached the exalted heights of Intelligence brigadier, refusing calls from the Acting Head wasn't an option.

'Put him through.'

Forsyth's confident voice boomed from the speaker.

'Andy, do me a favour. I've been trying to get Ken Stanley over here later this morning to discuss the new State of Emergency, but he won't play. Harry Higgins offered a noon date at Number Ten instead. Are those SIS boys of yours still around?'

'On stand-by in the building.'

'Put them in a state of instant readiness. I've got a breakfast meeting with Wendy Millar, the Thames Valley Chief. I'll be back within the hour, then we can get together for a full briefing. Chandler's far from happy about this Stanley business.'

He broke the connection. After a moment, Kyle retrieved the Duty Controller.

'Get me Captain Nolan. Not on the phone, in person. My office.'

The die was being cast.

The corner table in the Savoy's stylish dining room had a single red tulip as the centrepiece. As he approached,

Wendy Millar was sipping from a dainty cup and the only evidence of food was a plate bearing flakes of croissant. General Forsyth realized she had made herself seem dowdy at the Cabinet meeting. Now, the finely boned face looked more attractive. She wore subtle make-up and her hair was done differently. He pulled out a chair.

'Tea?'

'Why not? I don't drink the stuff, but there are exceptions to every rule.'

Wendy Millar smiled as she poured.

'I could tell you not to make an exception of that one. But my London adventure will use up this month's expense allowance and I'd hate to see a single drop of taxpayers' money wasted.'

He grimaced and put the cup down.

'God, that's well stewed. Sod the taxpayers, they'll never know.'

Forsyth sensed they would get along well. He checked they couldn't be overheard and opened elliptically.

'I think you're more ambitious than your colleagues realize. Oh, they know you're bright. But they think that because you're a woman merely achieving high office is sufficient reward.'

The Thames Valley Chief stooped to get a cigarette from the leather shoulder bag beside her chair. He lit it with a silver Dunhill lighter he always carried. After a couple of token puffs, she showed some low cards.

'It might be disappointing for a girl to think she'd spend the rest of her working life in downtown Reading. But you'd be right to assume that men tend to underestimate women. My turn. What might a tough security professional who knew his way around the corridors of power do if he felt the men at the top were performing less than adequately?'

Forsyth appreciated her clever riposte, and made up his mind.

'This is strictly confidential, but Ken Stanley was involved in Minton-Briant's murder, with help from the Americans. My boss isn't happy. Chandler and Minton-Briant went back a long way. Our new PM was part of the triumvirate, which makes his betrayal even more unforgivable.'

Wendy Millar blew a perfect smoke ring. Forsyth hurried on – his voice urgent.

'Chandler can sort out Stanley. But only if he's sure the move will be supported, and I don't mean by the bloody politicians. Now, I could talk to Frank Fleming as the senior Chief. On the other hand, I see problems there. Frank would drag his feet. If we go against Stanley we must move fast, before he gets the chance to consolidate his position.'

He'd said enough – if his judgment of the self-possessed woman across the table was inaccurate, too much. Forsyth watched as Wendy Millar stubbed out the cigarette in her saucer and looked up.

'Field Marshal Chandler wants to be sure there would be no objection from my colleagues?'

Forsyth relaxed.

'How do you suppose such an objective might be achieved?'

She produced another cigarette. This time, she cupped his hands to keep the Dunhill's flame steady, meeting his eyes.

'I think Frank could be persuaded to co-operate. Assuming all those fine words about a joint security set-up were kosher, he might be impressed by an offer of that Cabinet seat.'

After thinking for a moment, she continued.

'You really do intend to honour the arrangement with us, don't you? That's your vision – decisive government and firm social control backed by a unified security service. Though I doubt this altruistic attitude is unqualified by a feeling that you should contribute significantly to the ongoing crusade.'

Forsyth was startled, unaware he'd revealed so much of himself. Wendy Millar reached over and placed a small hand on his.

'Now you're wondering what to promise me if I agree to work the magic on Frank Fleming. I never threaten anyone, least of all men. But I'm not ashamed of using what are disparagingly called feminine wiles. Those include patience and willingness to trust one's intuition. Mine tells me you're someone who pays his debts. Frank's fifty-nine, Bob, nearing retirement. Why don't I arrange to see him at New Scotland Yard as soon as possible?'

'What about the others? No good sorting out Fleming if they don't buy.'

She brushed aside his concern.

'Normal jealousies aside, Frank's highly respected. He would have represented us at the Cabinet meeting yesterday, but was flying back from a conference in Berlin. If he's happy, they're all happy, especially as our influence will increase.'

'Good. But you don't need to bury your light under a bushel. I intend to put together a small security committee. Unofficial, but we may assume its recommendations will carry considerable weight. The three forces chiefs will be invited, and I'm also asking two Chief Constables. Perhaps you'd like to come along and hold Frank's hand?'

Wendy Millar smiled with infectious humour.

'What a stimulating thought. How much can I tell him?'

Forsyth got up.

'Ask him to stand by for our first committee meeting later this morning. Beyond that it's up to you. You don't have a monopoly on intuition. I was watching you in action at Cabinet and felt then we'd make a great team. Not that I'm in the habit of propositioning strange women, you understand.'

She joined him, unselfconsciously smoothing down her charcoal skirt and touching immaculate brown hair.

'Nothing strange about me, just your average wife and mum trying to scrape a decent crust. Where can I reach you when Frank's talked himself into this?'

'Headquarters.'

'Fine. Let's make love, then go to war.'

She stretched up and kissed his cheek. He was aware of the brief pressure of a soft breast on his right bicep. Forsyth didn't misunderstand. The chemistry between them wasn't sexual, but something altogether more powerful.

He slipped his arm through hers. Side by side, they walked out of the restaurant, looking for all the world like a married couple.

Captain Roger Nolan of the SIS had repeated that his team would carry out Brigadier Kyle's orders – however sensitive the mission. After dismissing him, Kyle told the

Duty Controller to hold the fort and took the fast lift to the basement car park. With luck he could be there and back before Forsyth returned from fettling the Trojan Horse that would destroy the Chief Constables' defences. He signed out a Vauxhall estate car from the pool, refusing a driver.

As he turned into the street where Forsyth lived, Kyle saw a ministerial Jaguar parked outside the house, with a chauffeur loading suitcases into the boot. He parked untidily behind the Jag, ran up the front steps and through the open front door.

Two large bodyguards blocked further progress. He topped them by half a head, but they represented a solid obstacle. Behind them, Alex Forsyth was helping her father down the stairs. Chandler's patrician features were drawn. Kyle returned his attention to the guards. Sidelong glances failed to produce a spokesman. One began, rather unwillingly, his voice low.

'Orders, sir.'

He dried. The other finished in a rush.

'Nobody to see the Field Marshal, no callers, no phone calls in or out. Orders direct from General Forsyth.'

Chandler's voice cut into the confrontation from the bottom of the staircase. In contrast to his frail appearance, the tone was firm.

'Who's that?'

'It's Kyle, sir. I'd like a word.'

'Andy, Andy Kyle. Is it really you? Come on, Alex, get me off these stairs and into the sitting room so I can have a quick word with the man. If I'm slinking off to Hampshire, at least I can take the latest news with me.'

The guards parted. Kyle stepped between them. Alexandra Forsyth nodded. He fell in on Chandler's left and between them they guided the old man across the hall, through an open door and settled him on to a long sofa. He felt around to get his bearings and managed a passable imitation of humour.

'See no evil, hear no evil. I've decided to retreat from the fray and let the serious players fight it out among themselves. So how's tricks at the factory?'

Kyle glanced at Alex, who took the hint.

'I'll leave you alone.'

He closed the door behind her, went back and sat in the

armchair opposite Chandler. After a moment's deliberation, Kyle answered.

'Not good, sir. I'd like to say I happened to be passing, but that isn't true. I need to know if you're aware of what's likely to happen today.'

Chandler cocked his head, expression intent.

'Bob's going after Ken Stanley, isn't he? We talked this morning. I can't believe Ken conspired with the Yanks. Even if he did it's not right to bring him down. Said as much. But Bob's determined. Oh, he's promised me the earth, or that part of it currently occupied by Ken. But if he won't listen to me now there's not much hope he will afterwards. Trouble is I'm useless in this condition, which is why I'm off to the country for a few days. Intelligence is behind him, I suppose?'

Kyle answered honestly.

'In your continued absence, I'd have to say yes. He's kept Department Heads fully informed, and they'll give him their loyalty.'

'As it should be. What about Chief Constables?'

'Not sure, but they benefit from the security reorganization. Bob's having breakfast with Wendy Millar now, so he's trying to secure that flank. But you were right about Ken Stanley. He wasn't involved with the Yanks, Minton-Briant's murder, any of it.'

The Field Marshal was startled.

'What?'

'Stanley's in the clear. I know that now, but was taken in at first. The evidence against him was fabricated. No wonder we kept stumbling across American connections that pointed to Stanley. The Yanks *wanted* to discredit him, and divert attention from the real inside man at the same time. Even the Windsor attack was a blind. We were never at risk. Rifles against toughened vehicles? Very clever.'

Chandler nodded to himself, as though confirming suspicion he hadn't wanted to entertain.

'Bob?'

Kyle replied with regret.

'Looks that way. I'm sorry, because we've been friends for a long time. Angry, too. He's used us all and will get away with it.'

'Can't you warn Ken?'

'What good would it do? Bob has tremendous power under the State of Emergency. If he stitches up the Chiefs, Stanley's isolated. I've taken a big risk even coming here, but I must know where you stand. It's just possible I may come up with something.'

Chandler slumped back on the sofa.

'I'd go back with you to try and get things sorted, but the last thing the country needs is Intelligence thrown into turmoil. Besides, I'm in bad shape. I couldn't handle it. Still, I'm on your side. I like Bob too, but he's over the top on this one.'

Kyle got up.

'I must go. If Bob misses me and finds out where I've been, I won't be in a position to do anything at all. I'll try and keep you informed.'

The Field Marshal remained silent, dark glasses turning helplessly. Kyle left. The security men were in the hall. He addressed them briskly.

'I suggest you keep my visit to yourselves. If you have any doubts, check with the Field Marshal before saying anything.'

Andy Kyle let himself out of Forsyth's house.

Candidate Stark had kept his emotions on the leash for so long he almost believed his reputation as one of the coolest operators on the Hill. But sometimes the lid blew. Boom. After he finished the morning papers, it had blown.

They were full of garbage, and the growing stink wasn't masked by the *Washington Post*, which stated that San Antonio police had eliminated any Stark connection from the Martinez investigation. The story stated that the girl was a virgin and speculated about a smear by one of many powerful groups he'd alienated. Talk about howling over spilled milk.

The fact remained he had been alone with her in his hotel room for fifteen minutes on the wrong side of midnight. And his campaign car had been used to move the body. Now open season had been declared, some hack would come up with a one-night stand from his past who would revel in revealing all. Then another. When shit flew, something always stuck.

His wife watched impassively. Ella had been right all along – this whole business throbbed with bad vibrations. After he'd gotten into screaming mode with press chief Zak Sohmer, she'd stepped in.

Ella banished everyone before he could damage morale, then sat down and read the papers thoroughly. While she did so, The Candidate numbly watched the mute TV set. He didn't need the sound to know they'd jumped the band-wagon, as the director cut from a gabbing reporter to a clip of Pat Stark in oratorical action.

He remembered that speech. The keynote theme was a return to family values that made America great, the pressing need to roll back the tide of moral degradation threatening the nation. The Daughters of the American Revolution had loved every word, but now . . .

Ella's silence was offensive. If he couldn't rely on her, who was left? He got up and went to the window, staring down at traffic on Sunset, making smog as though it were just another goddam day. Violently, he punched thick glass. The impact hurt his fist, but pain didn't make him feel any better. He shook his hand. Behind him, Ella spoke. Her voice was quiet, expressionless.

'You pathetic child. We were that close to the White House.'

Surprised, he turned. Her thumb and forefinger were an inch apart. Stark was shocked by the bitterness on her face.

'I'm not blaming you for this mess, Pat. It's a set-up, but no less effective for that. These coyotes are going to tear you apart, piece by piece. Time they're through, your presiden-tial ambitions may be nothing more than a memory.'

'Ella . . .'

She ignored the interruption.

'We all know you've had zipper problems, so who'll believe you now? I spent twenty years of my life getting you this far. Twenty years building you up, pushing you, helping you, covering your back, stroking your ego, burying my own. For what?'

Stark experienced a revelation. He'd been wrong to drop comfortably into the assumption that he and Ella had a mature partnership, an unspoken agreement based on a shared objective and mutual respect. Totally wrong.

She didn't even like him any more. There was certainly no respect. He looked at her in amazement, preparing to get angry, batter her with harsh words, assert his authority. What came out was a question in a small, uncertain voice he hardly recognized as his own.

'What are we going to do?'

She made no attempt to hide contempt.

'We fight like hell, same as always. Hit them with everything. There's a chance the pack won't come up with anything undeniable in time to hurt us. We hold a solid lead over Tidyman and he's black. Have a cigarette, two if you need them. Take a shower, get your head back together. There's work to be done.'

The Next President of the United States felt confidence flow back, warming him like a Jack Daniels. He was a politician, dammit, the best. Too clever and experienced to be beaten down by a little hysterical media coverage. Ready and waiting to fulfil his destiny.

'You're right, Ella. They won't come up with anything but old gossip. We're still on track.'

Pat Stark reached for a Marlboro.

Joe 'Goebbels' Granger ushered General Robert Forsyth from his state-of-the-art video studio. The small but efficient propagandist was hopping from foot to foot, creating an unconsciously comic effect as he crabbed along beside the taller man.

'Excellent performance, sir. So many people simply go to pieces in front of a camera, but you're a natural. This is a great day for Intelligence. I'll edit the video and sound tapes myself to ensure complete security and send proof copies up. Once you've approved the material I'll run duplicates off, ready for distribution when you give the nod. Until then, mum's the word.'

Forsyth stopped, replying cheerfully.

'Timing's everything on this one. You've done well, Colonel.'

He left Granger hopping on the spot and walked to the lifts. He was pleased with the performance himself. After that early-morning angst when ideas wouldn't translate into a script, he'd simply sat in front of the camera and talked. Words flowed – dignified, sober, statesmanlike words that explained to the nation what must be done in the interests of justice and stability for all. Perhaps he'd make a politician yet – a prospect he found surprisingly appealing, considering the contempt in which he'd always held the species.

Forsyth rode down to the detention floor and went to the guardroom. He was faced with a bank of forty colour monitors. The duty lieutenant pointed out the Prince Regent's cell. George was lying on the bed, staring at the ceiling. Forsyth pressed the screen's talk button.

'Good morning, camper. Rise and shine.'

George sat up, looking around wildly for the source of the mocking voice. Forsyth hated the pathetic creature, but it had a part to play. The reckoning would come later.

'You're going home. Freshen up, put on some decent clothes. There will be a Cabinet meeting this afternoon and I want you there, on your very best behaviour.'

Forsyth released the button, watching George's moving lips and agitated gestures. He turned to the lieutenant.

'Organize a car to take him home. Send two men. They're not to let him out of their sight until they've delivered him to Downing Street. I'll give you details later. Which is the internal phone?'

The young officer picked up a telephone and handed it to Forsyth.

'Who do you want, sir?'

'Brigadier Kyle.'

Numbers were punched. Kyle answered immediately.

'Can you get up to my office straight away? I'll be there shortly. You'll find a bottle of good hock in the fridge. Get it open. I feel like celebrating. By the way, how are those SIS types of yours?'

'Rarin' to go.'

Never one to waste words, Kyle hung up. As Forsyth was leaving, his bleeper went. He returned to the guardroom and retrieved the phone. The switchboard had Chief Constable Millar calling from New Scotland Yard. A click, then Millar's assured voice.

'Bob? Wendy Millar.'

'Hold on.'

Forsyth addressed the lieutenant.

'Give me a minute. Go and make those arrangements.'

He watched the man out and returned to the Thames Valley Chief.

'How did it go?'

'Frank was good as gold. The prospect of mixing with the great and good at Cabinet level rather appealed, though of course such stratospheric elevation is no more than his due. He's selling the deal to the other Chiefs even as we speak.'

'Excellent. See you both at the security committee. And Wendy, you're right. I pay my debts.'

Forsyth hadn't returned, but Sally Sayers sent him into the office to wait. Brigadier Kyle went to the window and studied toy cabs and buses far below. He remembered the wine. He didn't feel like drinking, but fetched the slim green bottle from the refrigerator.

There were glasses on the sideboard, but no corkscrew. Kyle went to the cupboard under the TV and video where bits and pieces were kept. Locked. He clicked his tongue in irritation. That cupboard was always open. He looked in the small drawer above the cupboard door. The key had been dropped amongst a litter of pens and pencils. Security gurus could be as careless as everyone else.

Kyle opened the door and studied the contents. Assuming Forsyth wasn't worried about his corkscrew, which nestled to one side, it had to be the boxed video bearing a broken security sticker. He turned on the TV set and slipped the tape into the machine.

Colour pictures jumped on to the big screen. Kyle immediately identified Beth Highsmith at what he presumed to be her apartment, saw the Prince Regent's arrival. He watched with growing repugnance. Concentration was so complete that he jumped when the intercom buzzed. Sally Sayers came through, chirpy as ever.

'The boss just called in, he's on his way up from Detention and wanted to check that you're present and correct. Are you? I've sometimes had my doubts.'

'All here except my heart, Sal. You stole that years ago.'

Kyle quickly rewound the tape, replaced it in the box and locked the cupboard. When Forsyth bustled in, he was back at the window.

'I can understand why you love this view, Bob, I could stand here for hours watching the world go by. I got the wine out, but couldn't find a corkscrew. Short of knocking the neck off the bottle I was stymied.'

Kyle smiled blandly. Forsyth went to the cupboard, tried it, remembered. He found the key, opened the door and handed over the corkscrew with a wink.

'Can't be too careful, Andy, lots of dubious types about.'

'You're right there.'

The retort slipped out. Despite Forsyth's mood of preoccupied excitement, he threw a sharp glance at his deputy. Kyle would have to be careful. The man was clever, intuitive, dangerous. To defuse the awkward moment he pulled the cork, poured two glasses and carried them to the table.

'What are we drinking to at this ungodly hour?'

General Forsyth raised his glass, any suspicions apparently forgotten.

'Let's toast soon-to-be-absent friends. I've been talking to Wendy Millar and the Chiefs are with us. The policemen at Number Ten will be briefed to do nothing if we come calling and invite the PM for a chat about the demise of his predecessor. Intelligence really does have extraordinary powers under the State of Emergency Ken Stanley was kind enough to declare.'

He grinned wickedly and sipped his wine. Kyle followed suit, drinking deeply. Either it was over-chilled or he swallowed too fast, because he didn't even taste the expensive hock.

'Delicious. So you're moving against him?'

Forsyth nodded.

'Nobody gets away with behaviour like that while I'm in charge of Intelligence, and the pieces have fallen into place. Chandler's agreed to take over from Stanley. Wendy Millar has delivered the Chiefs. The Prince Regent will offer full support and I'm sure our gallant armed forces will fall in, too. They love firm leadership. Once all that's in place I don't see the Party coming on to the streets with banners and petrol bombs, do you?'

He stopped, taking indecent satisfaction from treating the matter as though one deposed Prime Ministers and manipulated governments every day of the week. Forsyth became expansive, refilling the empty glasses.

'Let's drink to success, my friend. Then you can round up your shock troops and we'll pay Ken Stanley a visit. I can't wait to see his face when he realizes what's happening.'

Ignoring the drink, Kyle stood up, as casually as he could manage.

'I'd better talk to the SIS boys, then.'

Something alerted Forsyth, who looked at him sharply.

'You'll do well out of this. You are with me, aren't you?'

Andy Kyle met Forsyth's hard stare.

'Of course.'

Sometimes, Errol Tidyman wondered if the game was worth a candle. The hassle could be relentless, and the need to make your life public property was the worst part. It hadn't been too bad back when he first became Vice-President. Despite fine words about team play during the campaign, nobody was fooled – least of all the media. He was a politically correct sideshow.

Tidyman remembered statistics compiled by his research unit. In three months following the second-term inauguration, the President received 359 mentions on television network news, the First Partner secured 394, the Presidential Teenager 103. He got 71. Only the White House cat with 43 did worse. The ratio was similar in newspapers and magazines.

Things were different now. He straightened his blue-and-red polka-dot silk tie and looked at Louise. Thank God for Lulu – always cheerful, optimism never wavering. A rock. She gave him a little push.

'Go get 'em, boy.'

He walked on to the carpeted podium and strode to the lectern. Errol Tidyman looked past the autocue, straight into the lights and lenses that were the eyes of the American people.

'I am making this unscheduled press announcement because I wish to make a statement on a matter of grave concern to us all, which goes to the very heart of the democratic process that has made America the greatest country on earth . . .'

He allowed his glance to range sternly over the assembled company.

'The Tidyman for President Campaign has noted with concern speculation concerning Patrick Stark in this morning's papers. Despite our political differences he is an honourable man entirely fitted to hold the nation's highest office. Personal attacks on the private lives of individuals make no contribution to political debate, and we disassociate ourselves from this circulation-building nonsense. Neither I nor anyone who speaks for me will comment on these unfounded allegations. This election must be decided on the issues that are vital to the future of the American people in the twenty-first century. I have no desire for victory based on anything else. That's all.'

Errol Tidyman stepped away from the lectern and a wave of questions hit him. He paused – knowing they expected him to throw out soundbites that would turn Stark's discomfort to his advantage. He'd give them a soundbite, all right. He turned, faced them down, waited until the room went quiet.

'You guys listen but you don't hear. I repeat, there will be no comment on these cheap allegations against Patrick Stark, now or in the future. Believe it.'

They didn't. The Vice-President left the podium to a chorus of protest and rejoined his half-sister.

'How did big bro do out there, Lulu?'

She took his arm.

'Very dignified, very moral. Everyone just loves a man of principle, but despite your best efforts I'm afraid Pat Stark's going to get a lot of negative coverage in the next few days. The more you refuse to speak out, the more interested they'll get. I bet you never even thought about that.'

The Next President of the United States smiled.

Steel gates that prevented unauthorized access to Downing Street were manned by Intelligence personnel. Word had gone down the line. There wouldn't normally be a senior officer supervising traffic, but a uniformed major was on duty.

He must have seen the five-car convoy coming from the direction of Trafalgar Square. As they stopped for a northbound bus before turning right, General Forsyth saw the gates swing back. As they drove by, the major snapped a salute. Although he wouldn't normally have bothered, Forsyth touched the peak of his cap in acknowledgment. It was that sort of occasion.

Brigadier Kyle was with him in the first vehicle, driven by Armstrong. The others contained Captain Roger Nolan with sixteen hand-picked SIS men – the *crème de la crème*. Kyle had been silent on the brief journey from New Centre Point, perhaps overawed by what they were about to do.

Forsyth understood the feeling. He told himself there was time to back off, change his mind, send the SIS boys back to Hereford. But he never considered these craven options seriously – they were idle thoughts to fill crawling seconds.

Their car stopped outside Number 10 and Forsyth was gratified to see the police constable at the top of the steps reach over without hesitation and bang the door knocker. Wendy Millar had done her stuff. The woman was pure gold.

Followed by Kyle, he jumped out. The door opened. Alan Forbes stood inside. The Cabinet Secretary's assistant hadn't been told what was happening but wouldn't make trouble – he was their inside man. Kyle stopped in the doorway, in case the constable tried to shut the door on his SIS men. Forbes noticed, looking at them with the first glimmer of understanding.

'Harry Higgins sent me along to meet you, General. I believe you have a meeting scheduled with the PM, although there was no mention of the fact you'd be accompanied. Should be quite a party. Between you and me, Ken Stanley has already started. He's sharing the Cabinet Room with a bottle of Scotch.'

In the time it took Forbes to greet them, Nolan's men had run into the entrance hall, rubber soles padding over black-and-white tiles as they spread out around the walls. Mottled camouflage coveralls did nothing to help them blend into the Regency decor. Each man carried a machine-pistol, and darting eyes gave them a dangerous air. Kyle made a small gesture and the constable closed the door. Alan Forbes continued formally as though nothing unusual was happening.

'If you care to come with me, gentlemen, I'll take you to the Prime Minister.'

He led off. Forsyth fell in, outwardly calm. But his mouth was dry and he could feel sweat beneath his arms. A moment to remember for the rest of his life. Kyle was immediately behind, followed by Nolan and six men. The rest watched the foyer.

When they reached the Cabinet Room, Alan Forbes stopped, glanced at Forsyth apologetically and rapped with raised knuckles.

'Come.'

The Prime Minister's voice was slightly slurred. Forbes opened the door. Forsyth stepped into the big room. Ken Stanley was sitting in the prime ministerial chair. An unopened red leather dispatch box occupied the centre of the long table. Beside the box was a silver tray bearing a bottle of Johnny Walker Black Label, jug of water and chunky tumbler.

Pale amber liquid caught and refracted light as Stanley lifted the tumbler, drinking with studied deliberation. He put the empty glass down and turned to face them.

'Hello, General. I'm slightly drunk. Just as well. So you're not here to discuss the security merger, after all. I'm disappointed, Bob, though not surprised. After four decades in politics I can't pretend people ever surprise me. David Chandler knows what you're doing, of course? Poor old sod. He's a victim too, isn't he, in his way?'

Stanley reached over and poured another Scotch, not bothering to top up with water. He stared into the glass, as though seeing some elemental truth. Forsyth had to admire the dignity with which Stanley had assessed and accepted the inevitable. But business was business, and there was no going back. He spoke harshly, anger overwhelming residual doubts.

'Kenneth Stanley, it is alleged that on or before September fifth you did conspire with a foreign power, namely the United States of America, to bring about the murder of Derek Minton-Briant. You will be taken from here and charged with high treason under the Emergency Powers Act, and in due course be brought to trial. Take him, Captain.'

Ken Stanley looked up as Roger Nolan and one of his men marched round and stood behind his chair. Forsyth frowned, unwilling to accept the evidence of his own eyes. Surely that wasn't contempt on the old fool's face – or worse still pity? Stanley spoke, his voice ironical.

'One of only two offences for which the law still allows the death penalty. I'm sorry you didn't manage to apprehend me in the act of setting fire to one of the government's few remaining naval dockyards, to be doubly sure.'

Before Forsyth could reply the Greek Doors opened and Harry Higgins came in. He tried to control his initial reaction, but looked horrified. Forsyth looked at him sternly.

'Don't say anything until you're in possession of the facts, which I'll give you as soon as the PM's safely away.'

He turned to Kyle.

'Take him to Headquarters. Secure detention suite, not a cell. No interrogation until I get there. Then come back here for the security committee meeting.'

Kyle nodded to Nolan, who put a hand on the Prime Minister's shoulder. Ken Stanley stood up, took a last look around the room and spoke softly to himself and anyone who cared to listen.

'There's still so much to achieve. So much.'

He walked past without looking at Forsyth, an erect but insubstantial presence between the two SIS men. Brigadier Kyle turned and followed them out. Forsyth's attention turned to Harry Higgins. He sternly addressed the transfixed Cabinet Secretary.

'This isn't the end of the world. There's a great deal to discuss, arrangements to be made. I don't believe you had knowledge of Ken's treasonable activities, and see no reason why you shouldn't carry on. Indeed, I'll find your input indispensable.'

Forsyth took a deep breath, exhaled and flexed his fingers. Everything had gone like a dream.

The Prime Minister hadn't said a word, but meekly accompanied Brigadier Kyle to the door of Number 10, walking amongst a protective crowd of SIS men. Kyle briefed Captain Nolan.

'He can travel in the Jaguar with me. I'll look after him. Two of your men follow in another car, the rest including yourself stay here in case General Forsyth needs you, though I don't suppose there will be any trouble now.'

Nolan turned away to issue orders. Kyle led Ken Stanley out to the car, followed by two SIS men who peeled off to their own vehicle. Armstrong opened the rear door. Stanley ducked inside without protest. Kyle spoke briefly to the driver.

'Headquarters, then we're coming back here. Put the partition up.'

Kyle climbed in beside Stanley. As the Jaguar pulled away a glass screen slid up. Ken Stanley may have been drunk, but he noticed the move and looked questioningly at Kyle.

'Are you Forsyth's creature too, Brigadier Kyle? I wonder. We've only met on a couple of occasions, never really talked, but I formed the view that you're your own man.'

Kyle permitted himself an enigmatic smile. Stanley continued, delivering a monologue that Kyle could choose to ignore, or not.

'These allegations are nonsense. Oh, there will be evidence, witnesses prepared to perjure themselves. But there are always people willing to sell their souls for forty pieces of silver. I wasn't clever enough, or ran out of friends. David Chandler was my best hope, but he's under Forsyth's thumb. I suppose he's pencilled in for my job, for all the good it'll do him, though I can't imagine he believes I was in this with the Americans.'

The car swung around Trafalgar Square past the National Gallery. Looking straight ahead, Kyle replied. It wouldn't do any harm to tell him, not now.

'No, Prime Minister, he doesn't believe that. We spoke earlier, in confidence. I was able to tell him the evidence against you was fabricated. But as you point out, the Field Marshal is powerless to act. General Forsyth has done a deal with the police and will shortly be bringing forces chiefs into line. Chandler's blind and physically weak. Perhaps he hopes to exert some influence later.'

Stanley snorted.

'Some hope! Incredible, really. Here we are in a country

with fifty-five million people, strong institutions, a sophisticated bureaucracy – and the whole thing can be destroyed by a military-style coup.'

'With respect, Prime Minister, that's the proverbial pot calling a kettle black. It wasn't Bob Forsyth who created the conditions where that could happen. It was you and Minton-Briant, the Chandlers of this world. Perhaps you did so with good intentions, maybe what you achieved was worthwhile. But once you've established a situation where power is concentrated in the hands of a few, it's only a matter of time before someone like General Forsyth comes along.'

The PM went quiet, head sinking forward as he considered Kyle's argument, all the way along the Strand and into Kingsway. When he spoke, he sounded resigned.

'Nothing you can do?'

Kyle shrugged broad shoulders.

'What chance have I got, even if I wanted to try? Besides, there's no way back for you. Forsyth's going on television later to impeach you publicly. Once that's happened you can never be rehabilitated. But I don't suppose your punishment will be severe. A few years in comfortable confinement, then quiet retirement.'

The Jaguar rolled into the basement of New Centre Point. Armstrong had radioed ahead. A senior Intelligence officer and six privates were waiting. Kyle buttoned down his window.

'Take the PM to one of the secure accommodation suites. No communication with anyone until you hear from General Forsyth.'

As the men walked round to Stanley's door, the Prime Minister turned to Kyle. He was recovering his self-assurance.

'Thank you, Brigadier. It can be valuable to get another perspective. Perhaps you're right, and we did lose sight of something important.'

Kyle had been economical with the truth when talking to the Prime Minister, though he shouldn't really have talked to him at all. But he felt sorry for Stanley. The man was both sincere and innocent of the crime of which he stood accused. He believed in his vision of a just society, pursued for so many years.

Sadly, when the opportunity to do things his way finally arrived, he couldn't understand the forces ranged against him, let alone cope with them.

The tête-à-tête at one end of the lozenge-shaped table in the Cabinet Room was going well. Harry Higgins had proved subdued but co-operative. Forsyth was careful to insist he wouldn't be tainted by Stanley's misfortune – diffidently, to ensure that the Cabinet Secretary would do somersaults on the high wire to prove his loyalty.

Higgins made nominal noises of protest when the case against Ken Stanley was explained, but hadn't persevered when he heard the facts. In truth, Forsyth didn't care about the fussy little man's opinion. He was more interested in enlisting his help.

There was no denying that Higgins was a master manipulator of the system. He'd been running the bureaucracy for years – nudging here, pushing there, dropping words in appropriate ears, making sure Minton-Briant's grand designs were actually built. He listened carefully when Forsyth mooted David Chandler's elevation, positively glowing when his opinion was sought.

'Constitutionally sound, beyond question. The PM's arrest and detention without trial are legal under the State of Emergency. In those circumstances the Deputy PM is an automatic successor. You thought this through carefully, didn't you? Quite right, knowing what you knew about Ken Stanley. But the appointment must be ratified by Cabinet.'

'Any problem?'

'Members should be contacted before this afternoon's meeting and be individually primed. It wouldn't do for them to find out about Stanley through unofficial channels, and you know how fast rumours spread. What they want is stability, maintenance of their own positions. Promise them that and you shouldn't have any difficulty.'

He neatly sought to stress how valuable his skill and knowledge could be to Intelligence – experts in matters of security and *de facto* masters of the country, but unfamiliar with the idiosyncrasies of the government machine.

'Could you handle that, Harry, set them straight before the meeting?'

Higgins nearly tore off the friendly hand.

'Absolutely! They'll see things your way once I've explained the situation. I'll also brief senior civil servants in the various departments to be sure they understand what's wanted. That's most important. But the Joint Chiefs may be put out. You know what an overinflated opinion the military has of their own status.'

Forsyth couldn't resist a touch of smugness – which also served to remind Higgins he wasn't dealing with a political novice.

'I want you to invite all three of them to sit in on the Cabinet meeting. They'll accept their piece of the action. And don't worry about the Prince Regent, he and I have an understanding. Incidentally, we're proposing that Frank Fleming should be the Cabinet's police rep.'

Higgins' antennae were receiving loud and clear.

'Splendid. As the police hierarchy is party to this arrangement, I can tell Cabinet members the forces of law and order are speaking in unison. That should clinch it.'

Forsyth underlined the message.

'We security professionals stand together in our determination to instil discipline and allow this country to recover its pride. Anything else?'

Higgins slipped into on-the-ball mode.

'You need to square the Party. They're so well entrenched at local level that their support is essential if the country's to remain calm.'

'Suggestions?'

'Arrange a Special Congress immediately after Cabinet has approved Chandler's appointment as PM. Delegates were disappointed when the last one was cancelled. It's a nice trip to town for them, an opportunity to fiddle expenses. Get them up here, arrange a few extra perks. My office could start preparing the paperwork now. If Congress approves, the Parliamentary Party will fall into line too.'

Forsyth was pleased.

'I hoped you'd give me that advice. Now, send for forces chiefs. They're across at the Ministry of Defence, expecting your call. Also Frank Fleming and Wendy Millar. You'll find them at New Scotland Yard. We'll meet here, a sort of unofficial national security committee which will ensure everyone's pulling together.'

Higgins looked up from his notebook and nodded, looking dazed – perhaps appreciating for the first time how thoroughly the Intelligence general had prepared. Forsyth dismissed him.

'Go to it, Harry. We'll work well together in the difficult months ahead, very well. By the way, your man Forbes is actually my man Forbes. He'll keep me posted on developments in your office. And I want him to sit in on the security committee.'

He enjoyed the surprise that flickered across Higgins' plump face.

'We'll meet here. I love the atmosphere of this room. Perhaps you'd have Forbes bring the others in when they've all arrived.'

The Cabinet Secretary backed out without a word, unwilling to leave this hallowed shrine to the none-too-tender mercy of an interloper. Forsyth didn't give a damn what Higgins thought. He got up, walked round the table and stood behind the prime ministerial chair – running his fingertips along the red leather top of the high chair back in imitation of Ken Stanley's gesture at the Cabinet meeting where he had outmanoeuvred Godfrey Cornwell.

It was done.

Alan Forbes was still amused by his brief encounter with the Cabinet Secretary. Higgins had accosted him and hissed 'You two-faced bastard,' before stomping off to his room. Once there, he must have studied his *THINK!* motto – a minute later he'd been on the phone.

'Sorry, Alan, we're all under a great deal of strain. General Forsyth would like you to take the minutes at his *ad hoc* security committee in the Cabinet Room. We're expecting Brigadier Kyle plus Joint Chiefs of Staff and two Chief Constables. Kyle's already gone in but perhaps you'd show the others in when everyone has gathered.'

Peacemaking mission. Forbes could afford to oblige. Committee members had been waiting in the foyer in a splendidly uniformed group, looking around with interest as he ushered them to the Cabinet Room.

Now, sitting beside General Forsyth and Brigadier Kyle, he was perfectly placed to observe the action. The assorted leaders sat across the table in two groups. To one side – Air Chief Marshal 'Shorty' Lecomber, Admiral of the Fleet Clive Forester and the army's Field Marshal Jimmy Jones. To the other – Chief Constables Frank Fleming and Wendy Millar.

General Forsyth had taken the PM's chair. After crisply describing Ken Stanley's recent arrest, he restated the salient point.

'Remember, I have irrefutable evidence that Ken Stanley conspired with the Americans in the matter of Derek Minton-Briant's assassination. To be more specific, with Vice-President Tidyman, acting without official US government backing.'

He paused. Forbes saw that only forces chiefs were surprised. So the Chief Constables were in the know. After allowing the uninitiated to absorb the news, Forsyth continued.

'As Deputy Premier, Field Marshal Chandler will become Prime Minister, subject to ratification by Cabinet, which meets in this room later today. You'll be attending, Frank, and I think it would be a good idea if our distinguished military colleagues also joined the meeting. Questions?'

Not yet. Forbes assumed forces chiefs were the target – Forsyth had the police in his pocket. Wendy Millar's fine-boned pale face was impassive, and Frank Fleming could hardly contain his satisfaction. It was the Commissioner of the Metropolitan Police who answered, his reedy voice in surprising contrast to ageing matinee-idol looks.

'So far so good, Bob.'

Forsyth smiled, as though he hadn't doubted the committee's reaction for a moment.

'I'll finish what I have to say, then throw the meeting open. Things were going wrong long before Minton-Briant's murder. The economy was collapsing, people were getting restless, the country was losing impetus and pride. I think everyone here believes the decline must be reversed. Britain needs order, discipline, a new sense of purpose . . .'

In the messianic pause that followed, Forbes reflected that the rhetoric was always the same. Every government talked of putting the Great back in Britain, refusing to accept a once-mighty imperial nation's decline into mediocrity, none willing to acknowledge a more mundane desire to manage the massacre their way. Forsyth resumed quietly.

'That is our task. This committee will be formally constituted with the present membership, and take a lead in meeting that challenge. We will discuss key issues and provide the advice Cabinet needs in order to set policies which will make this great country of ours strong again. Internal security will be a priority, of course, but there's more, which brings me to the Joint Chiefs of Staff . . .'

Jones, Lecomber and Forester tried not to look too interested, but failed. Forsyth didn't disappoint them.

'Our armed forces have been shamefully treated since the peace dividend was cashed. We're still flying thirty-year-old aircraft, the army would get lost in Wembley Stadium and you can float the navy in a bathtub. You need state-of-the-art technology, the latest hardware, more well-trained personnel. Think of the stimulus increased military spending would give to the economy, and of course it would also mop up a lot of youth unemployment.'

Forbes watched the Joint Chiefs of Staff as their pay-off was dangled. Eyes narrowed as they mentally compiled wants lists like kids promised an unexpected trip to Toys R Us. The next contribution came from an unexpected source.

'Or to put it another way, the forces represented in this room can pretty much tell anyone how to behave and there isn't a damn thing they can do about it. And that includes Cabinet, the Party and Parliament.'

Brigadier Anderson Kyle's deep voice somehow managed to communicate amusement and cynicism simultaneously. Forsyth looked at his deputy, annoyed by the indelicate interruption. Field Marshal Jones broke the awkward silence.

'It's true the armed forces have been shamefully treated since Options for Change gutted us. What sort of extra spend are we talking here?'

Maybe life wasn't so unfair, after all. Candy Paretsky was

feeling pretty pleased with the way things were swinging along. She was getting on great with her new friends, who turned out to be regular guys and a pleasure to do business with.

The writers were staying at the Plaza Hotel, and the night before had treated her and Randy to a meal at the Anaqua Room. The elegant atmosphere and attentive service made her feel like a movie star. After dessert, Gene Zarubica and Frankie Clifford went for a stroll in the courtyard, tactfully providing time for private discussion.

Randy was as high as she was. They'd agreed she'd call in sick next day, while he went to work as usual. Candy had already convinced the eager reporters that her story was worth hearing, done a good deal. She'd stuck out for fifteen thousand and settled for twelve in cash, plus all she could buy in half an hour at Mill Store Plaza out at New Braunfels. She loved that brick-built mall with its classy factory stores, and often persuaded Randy to take her out there Sundays, though they never had any cash to spend on the designer merchandise.

After the meal, they had driven back to their apartment to drop Randy off and pick up a few things for her. Gene had taken rooms at a Rodeway Inn out by Fiesta north of the city, explaining they wanted to keep her out of sight until the story broke. They drove into the motel's half-empty parking lot after midnight and went straight to their rooms.

Without complaint, Candy had shared with Frankie, understanding that these tough cookies needed to keep a close eye on their investment. She immediately fell asleep, waking early like a kid at Christmas in anticipation of the promised shopping trip.

Now, she had to deliver. Candy looked across at three new leather suitcases piled on the luggage rack in the corner. The contents must have cost five thousand dollars or more, but she could have used more time. Maybe she should have held out for the full fifteen thousand plus an hour at the Plaza. Frankie, who was setting up a tape recorder beside the TV set, caught her glance, misunderstood and smiled reassuringly.

'Nice work if you can get it. This better be good.'

On cue, Gene came in with a flask of coffee from the restaurant in one hand and silver metal case in the other.

'Could be a long day, ladies. You sit on the end of that bed, Candy, right beside the recorder. Frankie and me'll use the other bed, if you take my meaning. We fire questions, you shoot back the right answers. You're a clever girl, I'm sure you hear what I'm saying. So earn yourself some big money.'

Candy Paretsky heard what he was saying, and realized that a little creative embroidery might be necessary. When the coffee was poured and they were settled, Gene reached down to the briefcase, snapped the catches and opened the lid. The inside was full of bills, still wearing their paper wrappers. He reached over and started the tape.

'Gene Zarubica and Frances Clifford, formal interview with Ms Candy Paretsky. Let's start with what happened in the hotel the night Maria got herself killed, Candy. Tell it in your own words and tell the truth.'

He winked. Candy thought for a moment, then started talking, eyes still fastened to the money.

The committee meeting finally broke up. There hadn't been much of substance to discuss, because the chosen few couldn't fault Bob Forsyth's tempting logic. The rewards were obvious – and if that meant accepting the Intelligence general's emergence as their leader, well, nothing worth having came without a price. Instead, they focused on detail – the very process of discussion serving to establish and cement a powerful new relationship of common interests.

Brigadier Kyle played little part, content to act the loyal number two. He wasn't the only one building profiles of the participants. At one point he glanced sideways and saw the Cabinet Secretariat's young representative was equally intent. Alan Forbes became aware of the scrutiny and met Kyle's eyes. If asked, he would surely have agreed that Forsyth had pulled it off – the excitement that charged the conversation testified to that.

Eventually, he was free to go. Everyone else barring Wendy Millar would remain at Number 10 for the Cabinet meeting, only fifteen minutes away. Cabinet would do what was required. As Kyle had said so bluntly when Forsyth was explaining his plans, what choice did they have?

He left the building with Wendy Millar. She wore a waxed cotton coat over her uniform, and though the top of her head was barely level with his breast pocket Kyle was aware of the woman's poise. When he set off for his car, she fell in beside him.

'I walked over before the meeting, but all things in moderation. I'm at the Savoy. Is that on your way?'

Kyle looked down, sensing there was more to this than convenience.

'I'll drop you off.'

His white Vauxhall estate was parked at the Horse Guards end of Downing Street. He opened the front passenger door and she slipped in, putting her briefcase on the floor. As they started off, she spoke casually.

'I got the impression you weren't altogether happy in there, Brigadier.'

Kyle glanced across. Her head was high, the clean profile serene. He thought carefully before replying. This was an intellect to be respected, but also a calm presence that invited confidence.

'Andy, please. Yes, I sometimes wonder if we get carried away by our own self-importance, and forget we're supposed to serve.'

'A treasonable thought. Perhaps we'll be able to discuss it some time. I'd like that. There are so few people one can really talk to about the things that matter.'

The rest of the journey passed in silence, though Kyle felt they had established a rapport. After turning off the Strand and dropping her at the hotel entrance, he waited until she was lost to view, striding purposefully through a door held open by a commissionaire. She didn't look back, but Kyle would see more of this self-possessed lady.

He started the car and drove out of Savoy Hill, heading for New Centre Point. Forsyth would be occupied at Downing Street for some time, and there were arrangements to make.

Although he chose to occupy the Prime Minister's chair at the earlier meeting, General Forsyth had vacated it for Cabinet, though he pointedly occupied Field Marshal Chandler's place. Neither did he intend to impose his will as he had on his fellow-professionals. Did the organ-grinder dance?

It was an unusual gathering. There were notable absentees in Security Minister Chandler and Home Secretary Cornwell, not to mention the Prime Minister. But three armed forces bosses and one Chief Constable were sitting in. This made Cabinet uneasy. News of Ken Stanley's arrest – and the shocking reason – had thrown them into confusion. They watched the newcomers warily, evaluating the implications of this massive security presence. Even the Prince Regent, lurking at the bottom of the table, looked subdued.

The Cabinet Secretary rapped the table, stood up.

'The PM is not with us. Most of you know why, but for those who've heard nothing I'll make a short statement. Ken Stanley has been arrested under the Emergency Powers Act. He was deeply involved in the conspiracy to assassinate Derek Minton-Briant. That operation was planned with the Americans to put him into Number Ten. He was their man. This all seems incredible, but Intelligence has prepared a dossier which includes photographs, tape recordings and other proof. Copies will be made available after the meeting.'

Forsyth observed the dismay on every face – another trauma to absorb, more evidence that their comfortable world might be crumbling. Higgins went on, delivering his lines perfectly.

'The Security Minister was overtaxed by yesterday's meeting, and as you know the Home Secretary has been shot and wounded. General Forsyth will therefore speak on behalf of the security services. Happily, he will be able to assure you that the conspiracy has been exposed. There will be no more attacks, no more nasty surprises. I'm sure you'll be fascinated to hear the full story, before considering the decisive action we must take to stabilize this drastic situation.'

Forsyth looked up. For the moment, he was content to project a non-assertive image. They'd understand soon enough.

'Thank you. Firstly, I must welcome Field Marshal Jones, Air Chief Marshal Lecomber, Admiral Forester and Metropolitan Police Commissioner Fleming. Old rivalries have been set aside, so all those who can assist in the maintenance of public order can speak with one voice. Let me assure you that as of now we *are* speaking with one voice . . .'

To judge by their expressions, some Cabinet members were getting the message already.

Calling from Downing Street, Forsyth sounded cool and businesslike, though Brigadier Anderson Kyle suspected he was anything but relaxed.

'Get on to Granger and tell him to release those tapes I made earlier. I want Media to pull out all the stops on this one. I'd suggest a Public Information Broadcast at six o'clock to replace the early evening news. Saturation coverage. And Andy, congratulations.'

Kyle guessed what was coming.

'Congratulations?'

'We won. Cabinet bought the whole package. Couldn't have gone better. The weaklings rolled over like toy poodles. Chandler's PM, I'll become Security Minister as soon as a parliamentary seat can be found. In the meantime I speak for the government on security matters. When I get officially kicked upstairs, Intelligence is yours.'

A reaction was expected. Kyle tried very hard to make it enthusiastic.

'That's great, Bob. Now we can really start to get things sorted.'

'Dead right. I've got to finish up here with Harry Higgins, then I'll go home and tell Chandler his good news and come on to the office after that. Will you be around? There's so much to do.'

Forsyth's euphoria was showing. Kyle managed to respond dutifully.

'I'll be here. That was some achievement. See you later.'

If Forsyth noticed the lukewarm effort he didn't comment – signing off with a terse instruction.

'Get those tapes out now, Andy. I don't want any silly stumbles at the final fence.'

Kyle did as he was told – phoning Joe Granger and relaying the instructions. The hyperactive colonel couldn't wait to get him off the line and get on with the job, so Kyle left him to it. He sat at his desk for what seemed like a long time.

When he picked up the phone and asked the Duty Controller to contact Captain Roger Nolan of the SIS and tell him to expect a briefing within the hour, the gold hands of his Omega stood at five-fifteen. Kyle stood up, stretched like a massive cat and left the office. The Armoury had been notified of his requirements. Five minutes later he was in the basement car park, stowing a long case made of toughened PVC in the back of his Vauxhall estate. Out of habit, he covered it with a blanket.

Kyle drove up the ramp and into the late afternoon traffic scrum. The journey to Hamilton Terrace took twenty minutes. He parked under a pollarded tree and looked up at the foliage, already turning autumnal brown. He couldn't identify the species – but then he'd been a city boy all his life. He locked the car and strolled up the glass-roofed walkway to Kinnock House. The lion's-head knocker was answered by a male orderly who looked more like an all-in wrestler than a committed carer.

He stood in the carpeted hall as the man silently disappeared into the rear of the building through a baize-covered door to fetch Alistair Whittier. A moment later he returned, accompanied by the bluff psychiatrist. Kyle extended his hand.

'Good to see you. How is he?'

Whittier's handshake was firm. They were old friends.

'Restless, but ready to play. He's suffered the legacy of many years' repressed emotion. I don't know how these covert operators survive for so long. Sheldon seems to have been deeply affected by killing Mendlebaum. It's as though that was the final act among many which caused him to feel something akin to normal human remorse.'

'Do you have a TV lounge? I'll see him there.'

'I'll take you. Sherman, bring Sheldon to the TV room.'

The orderly rose from the reception desk and lumbered up the wide staircase – tank by name, tank by nature. Whittier led him to a room off the hall. Perhaps it had once featured a dining table where Victorians exchanged

bigoted views and swapped gossip, but now the contents
were designed for comfort – wide sofas, deep armchairs,
side tables bearing magazines and newspapers. A large flat
TV screen hung above the ornate fireplace. Whittier went to
tall double windows that faced the street and closed heavy
curtains. He turned to Kyle.

'This do?'

'Fine. How do you switch on?'

Whittier handed him a remote control unit.

'You press buttons. Don't ask which ones, but I expect a
clever fellow like you will work it out. Ah, Donny.'

Sheldon stood in the doorway, looking at them blankly.
Whittier went over, took the American's arm and guided
him towards Kyle.

'Donny, this is Brigadier Kyle. He wants a chat.'

He left. Kyle indicated a sofa facing the screen. Sheldon
shuffled over without protest. Kyle fetched a ladder-back
chair and sat down.

'I'm Andy Kyle from Intelligence. We have met, though I
doubt you remember.'

Unblinking eyes swivelled towards him, though the sallow
face remained devoid of expression.

'I know who you are.'

The accent was American. After years of skilled mimicry,
Sheldon was returning to his roots. Kyle spoke softly.

'Someone has taken advantage, Donny, used both of us
and a lot more people besides. Minton-Briant's murder, the
business at Nottingham – all part of this man's plan. You
could say he was responsible for Mendlebaum's death. I'm
going to tell you all about it, show you his face. Perhaps
suggest something that might appeal to you.'

He was rewarded with a flicker of interest. Kyle hit a button. The screen came to life – the back end of a commercial
for a national chain of funeral parlours. Kyle spoke over the
station jingle that followed.

'Let's watch TV, Donny.'

The announcer was an attractive woman who managed to
look – and sound – as though the world was about to end.

'We take you over to London for a Public Information
Broadcast. News at Six will follow in approximately ten
minutes.'

They sat back to watch General Forsyth addressing the nation.

That morning, Vernon Lustbader had returned to the cabin at Vandercook Lake. The Vice-President had agreed enthusiastically when he made the suggestion.

'Great idea. You've had a tough few days. No TV set up there, right? Get away from politics, catch a few fish, recharge batteries. Campaign's hotting up and I need my number-one strategist in good shape. Use my chopper. I'll have it fetch you Friday afternoon and we can spend the weekend trying to pick holes in the endgame. And Vern, thanks for hanging in, I appreciate that.'

So Lustbader had gone. Since arriving, he hadn't done much – just sat at the outside table watching changing cloud patterns reflected on the water. It was a peaceful place to analyse the immediate past and consider the future. But Lustbader had made his decision. All he needed was a little time, for the rationalization he needed to live with it.

He'd stick with Tidyman, because if they won the election he'd get to contribute to the many necessary and positive things Errol would attempt. If Errol was fighting dirty, did that make him different from any other politician? And he was black. Nobody ever handed him anything – what he achieved had to be taken with the strength of his being.

Lustbader turned on his battery radio. Pat Stark's troubles had brought the presidential election to life. With the result predictable and nothing new to say, the media had been slowing down. Now they were on turbo-thrust. He found a station carrying Errol's recorded press statement.

Hearing the Vice-President's voice was eerie. It sounded so familiar, yet Lustbader had just been thinking he didn't know the man he thought he knew so well at all. He listened for a moment.

'. . . disassociate ourselves from this circulation-building nonsense. Neither I nor anyone who speaks for me will comment on these unfounded allegations. This election must be decided on the issues that are vital to the future of the American people in . . .'

He switched off. Whatever else, Errol was sharp. Lustbader stood up, stretching his spare frame to ease stiffness. Maybe he'd go out in the Jon-boat, to see if those cunning but greedy carp were in a feeding mood.

He'd seen his polished performance on television. General Robert Forsyth felt the euphoria of a gambler who finally hits the big one – counting and recounting winnings, scarcely able to believe the elusive crock of gold is finally in hand.

Armstrong parked the Rover in a convenient slot. The driver slipped out. Only when he was satisfied no threat lurked did he open the passenger door and accompany his master to the clinic entrance. The man's caution was rather touching. Protection was his job, but Forsyth was no longer at risk. He stopped at the enquiry desk.

'General Forsyth to see Beth Highsmith.'

The receptionist was wearing a white starched cap perched on streaky-blonde curls. She glanced up in surprise, light catching large designer spectacles.

'I'm sorry, General, I thought you would have been informed. Miss Highsmith discharged herself earlier. Yesterday's operation went very smoothly and there's nothing to worry about, but if you'd like a word with her doctor, I think he's still in the building.'

She looked concerned. It was the sort of place where the merest hint of a problem started alarm bells ringing. Forsyth shook his head, rather more vehemently than intended. The last thing he needed was another medical lecture.

'That won't be necessary. Besides, some of my men are protecting Godfrey Cornwell and I want to check security. As I'm here I'll wish him a speedy recovery. Would that be possible?'

Relieved there wasn't going to be a scene, the receptionist picked up the phone. Forsyth waited while *sotto voce* enquiries were made. She replaced the instrument and treated him to a dazzling smile.

'You can see the Home Secretary. He's still very weak after surgery but is conscious. His room is on the second floor. One of your people will come down and fetch you.'

'I know the way, I was here yesterday.'

He turned to Armstrong.

'Phone my wife and tell her I'll be home shortly and need a session with Field Marshal Chandler.'

Forsyth strode to the lifts. As he arrived, doors slid open. A uniformed Intelligence lieutenant started out, stepped back with a hurried salute. Forsyth joined him.

'Cornwell's been kept incommunicado?'

'As ordered, sir.'

They rode up in silence. A private was guarding the lifts, two more stood outside Cornwell's door. Forsyth entered. Godfrey Cornwell was propped on white pillows. His eyes strayed to the visitor. Forsyth stopped by the bed.

'Hello, Godfrey.'

'Bob.'

'I gather you're going to pull through. I thought you might like to know we disposed of the animals who did this to you, and also brought the man behind them to book. We've arrested Ken Stanley for conspiring with the Americans to murder Derek Minton-Briant.'

The fallen Home Secretary regarded him thoughtfully, but didn't seem surprised.

'I guessed it had to be Stanley. Or you. I suppose David Chandler will take over now.'

'That's the general idea. You'll find there have been major changes when you finally get out. We're creating a merged security force under unified command. Always an ambition of Chandler's.'

Savouring victory, Forsyth watched the reaction to his understated revelation closely. He was disappointed.

'You've come out on top, then. I wanted to win so badly it hurt, so I've been lying here wondering why I don't give a toss any more.'

Forsyth sat on the bed. Cornwell went on, his voice low but steady.

'I've lost Alec Ambler. We'd been together for six years. Oh, I know that probably fills you with disgust. But we are what we are. Even so I didn't realize how empty everything would seem without him. Ambition which consumes your life seems pointless if there's nobody to share the rewards with.'

'I see.'

Forsyth didn't. Not that it mattered – Cornwell wouldn't be allowed anywhere near the centre of power, even after his recovery.

'I don't suppose you do, but what the hell? I'm finished. That's a fact of political life. I hope you never discover what I'm talking about for yourself. I can't recommend the experience. Now, if you'll excuse me I'd like to rest.'

Cornwell closed his eyes – his mind presumably filling with memories of the dear departed. Forsyth stood up.

'I'll call by again, Godfrey.'

There had been something disturbing about Cornwell's sincere declaration. He was still thinking about it when he arrived back in the reception area. Armstrong stepped forward.

'No reply from the house. I've tried three times.'

'That's odd. We'd better get over there and see what's going on, I must talk with Chandler. Go round by Beth Highsmith's place. I want to check that she's okay before we go home.'

'Right you are, sir, I'll lead on.'

Armstrong sidled towards the doors.

She tucked the tartan rug around her father's knees. He flapped his arms, attempting to push her away, but Alex could tell he wasn't angry. On the contrary, he was pleased to be in his beloved gunroom armchair, a solid piece in battered green leather inherited with the house from his own father.

For the first time since returning from hospital, David Chandler was starting to relax. The weathered red-brick Queen Anne manor outside Stockbridge always put him at ease. He took dark glasses off and dropped them on to the polished pine floor beside his chair, revealing white pads covering ruined eyes.

'Bloody specs make my nose itch, hate wearing them. Time for a Scotch. Before you get it, fetch one of my Purdeys.'

Alex opened a steel gun safe concealed in an antique yew-wood cabinet. There were six double-barrelled shot-guns to choose from, but she'd been shown the prized

Purdeys often enough to make the right choice. Although she had no interest in shooting, she could appreciate the superb craftsmanship of the London-made weapons with their intricate engraving and highly figured stocks. She lifted one out and took it to her father.

He ran his hands over the gun, then flung it to his shoulder as though addressing a remembered bird. He set the Purdey down across the chair arms, stroking oiled metal and polished walnut.

'Number three. It's two ounces heavier than the other two. Full-choke right barrel for grouse shooting. These guns were built for your great-grandfather, and they're still as good as the day they were made.'

She knelt beside him.

'Yes, Dad, he collected them in September 1898. You have mentioned the fact, usually in conjunction with a none-too-subtle hint that it's time for me to produce a son and heir for you to hand them on to. Well, there's not much chance of that. We didn't say anything, but Bob and I haven't been getting on too well lately. For quite a while, actually.'

He reached out clumsily, found her and rested a light hand on the crown of her head.

'I did notice. Not my place to interfere, though. Hoped things might improve. Can't say I'm altogether sorry if they don't, the way everything's worked out. Perhaps I'd better spit it out. Your husband has been playing a game of his own since Derek's murder, may even have had a hand in the killing.'

Alex couldn't accept that, dislodging her father's hand with an angry shake of the head.

'Impossible. Bob may be many things, but not that. He believes in everything the government stood for.'

Chandler raised his rejected hand defensively.

'I agree, but he accused Ken Stanley of the same crime and is going to arrest him. That's equally improbable. I haven't a clue what really happened, but do know one thing. Your husband is about to seize control in my name but there isn't a damn thing I can do. We only got out of London because I gave the minders a direct order. They'll stop me contacting anyone with influence. Bob's about to

become the most powerful man in the country, using me
as the lever.'

Her father's hands tightened around the shotgun. Alex
tried to take in what she had been told, felt angry on
behalf of the damaged old man beside her. She jumped
to her feet.

'You wait till I get hold of him!'

The threat was meaningless. Chandler knew it.

'What will you do, Alex? We'll probably never learn the
truth, and I don't delude myself. Bob's talk of a significant
rôle for me is hot air. If I go along for the ride I'll be a
figurehead. If I don't, I lose any chance to influence events.
It's a hard call, and I haven't made up my mind which way
to go. I blame myself. He's only doing what I taught him.'

Alex sat on the chair arm and pushed an arm behind his
shoulders.

'I love Bob, but he's having an affair and our marriage
has been dying. I've often thought he only stayed with me
because he was afraid a split would damage his career.
Right now I'm on your side, Dad. We'll stick together, see
how things work out. I'll be here for you.'

Her father leaned his head against her.

'We haven't been as close as we should have been, and
I've never been much of a hand at saying that I love you.
But I do. Always have, from the first moment I saw your
wrinkled little face. Bob's a fool. He doesn't realize yet, but
he's chosen a very lonely place.'

Alex stood up, brushing at her eyes.

'His problem. He's made the bed. Let him lie there alone,
or with his fancy woman. I'll get that Scotch. Tomorrow
morning we can go down to the river. You may not be able
to cast a fly to those brown trout any more, but it's still the
most peaceful place on earth.'

Her father sought and found her dangling hand, squeezed
hard.

He considered using the doorbell, giving her a moment to
compose herself, but decided to use his key. The moment
Forsyth walked into the studio's stillness he knew the
apartment was empty. He stood inside the door, drinking
the atmosphere as though Beth was in the air. Cornwell's

emotional outpourings had unsettled him. Perhaps, like a Catholic, he needed to confess and be forgiven, but feared she would be unable to grant absolution.

As a final irony, her sacrifice had been unnecessary – a crippling premium for insurance that wasn't needed. George's contribution hadn't been essential after all, and certainly wasn't worth the price Forsyth was now paying. More than anything he wanted to hold Beth in his arms, soothe away their pain, make everything right. Guiltily, he reminded himself that it hadn't been him who had paid.

He walked into the room, which was tidier than usual. The scatter of paperbacks and videos was gone. The bed was neatly made. There were no suitcases beside the long garment rack, which had gaps. He'd seen the signs before and recognized them now. The only difference was that more often than not he'd been there when Beth was preparing for a trip – sharing the sadness of parting and the mutual anticipation of pleasure which would follow her return.

This time was different. The sense of loss rolled over him even before he spotted the letter on the television set. It was addressed to *BOB* in her large, childish handwriting. He turned the envelope over – unwilling to face the message contained within paper walls.

Forsyth ripped it open, took out a single sheet and looked at Beth's words, his mind recreating her voice as though she were standing beside him, reading aloud.

Bob, I've decided to leave London for a while. Greg Browne is working in Paris this month and I'm going along for the ride. Paris in the autumn – must be a first! I have to believe you didn't know how the George thing would turn out but the fact is it turned out badly. Please don't try and contact me. I need time to work this out, some space of my own. I hope to be back soon, but can't pretend this is going to be easy. All love, Beth.

Forsyth stood stock-still. Something shrivelled inside. He needed Beth and she wasn't there – and wouldn't be back. Dropping note and envelope back on the television, he took a last look round. He'd spent many wonderful hours in this place. He wouldn't see the studio again. He didn't blame Beth. How could he? Perhaps he'd been foolish to hope.

Leaving his key on the top of the letter, he went to the door, turned off the lights and left. He'd go home. Have a coffee and share the day's triumph with Alex and the new Prime Minister.

The deadly duo of Gene Zarubica and Frances Clifford were not the only ones on the case – they'd wrapped up their end of the explosive Pat Stark story, but the *Enquirer* was chasing down other angles. One of their reporters reached Capitano Arturo Pulido less than twenty-four hours behind Mary-Jo MacInnes. A second-generation Hispanic from California, he spoke fluent Spanish and was able to be much more generous than Mary-Jo with regard to the Police Benevolent Fund.

Cumulatively, the effect was dramatic. Captain Pulido made a number of phone calls, voice urgent and commanding, before producing a bottle of Southern Comfort and two glasses from his desk.

They didn't wait long. Two drinks later a return call caused the captain to listen intently, ask quick questions and finally nod in satisfaction. He grandly informed the reporter that Guillermo Martinez, father of Linda aka Maria, had been located in a *cantina* behind Mercado Juárez, where he awaited their pleasure. He, Captain Pulido, would personally conduct his honoured guest to meet the man, in his own late-model Mercedes Benz automobile.

The *cantina* was the sort of place that has tourists backing out one second after walking through the door, wisely deciding the pursuit of local colour has its limits. A uniformed cop stood beside a table in the far corner of the dark, warm room, ensuring that Guillermo Martinez did indeed await their pleasure. The half-dozen men at the bar and scattered round tables studiously ignored the newcomers.

Guillermo was a small, worn person. He slumped over a *cerveza*, one hand clutching the drink. Yesterday's newspaper lay on the stained table-top. An unfiltered cigarette smouldered in the corner of his mouth. He looked up as they approached, and the reporter saw that the Mexican's black eyes were quick, in marked contrast to his downtrodden appearance.

Captain Pulido made the introductions, explained no harm would come to Guillermo but that it would be much to his credit if he were able to be of assistance to the important *americano*, who had simple questions to ask. The captain and his man discreetly withdrew to an empty table on the other side of the room, allowing the reporter to sit down and go to work.

He soon discovered that Martinez was nobody's fool. Stubbing out his cigarette, Linda's father began to talk. Alerted by the visit of the woman from the USA to his brother's house only the day before, Guillermo had understood that his beloved Linda's death was somehow of interest to the great American public.

The loss of a daughter was a tragedy, especially so soon after the death of his niece Maria. Linda was bright, had a great future. Naturally the family would grieve. But with elderly parents, four more children and two grandchildren to consider, including a son sent back from *el norte* . . .

At that point, Guillermo reached inside his frayed blue shirt and brought out an envelope, which he laid on yesterday's newspaper. The reporter, who had been listening to the recital with every appearance of sympathy and thinking his trip might be a waste of time, suddenly became interested. He gave the Mexican an interrogative look. Guillermo nodded. The reporter picked up the envelope.

Posted in San Antonio, TX on 20 August, the day before the night when Linda aka Maria Martinez was brutally killed. Addressed to Stefanie Martinez in Juárez. He turned the envelope over, and the name L. Martinez jumped out above the San Antonio return address. Savouring the experience, the reporter reached inside the torn flap and extracted the single sheet within.

He skimmed the letter – passing chit-chat about work, stopping at the words 'Next President of the United States' which were written in English, noting the enclosure of two hundred unexpected dollars. He mentally translated key phrases from Spanish and liked the result: 'really interested in me'; 'admired my looks'; 'asked what a pretty girl like me was doing working in a hotel'; 'said I should be in the movies'. The signature at the bottom was small and orderly, like the writing. It read 'Your respectful daughter, Linda'.

The reporter moistened his lips and looked up, finding Guillermo watching intently. The negotiation was swift and mutually satisfying. The reporter offered three thousand dollars, Guillermo asked for five, they split the difference. He could probably have got the letter for less, but as he would happily have paid five times as much, the reporter wasn't going to quibble.

As he finished counting out money, shook the calloused hand of Guillermo Martinez and locked the damning letter in his case, the *Enquirer*'s reporter reflected that Pat Stark wasn't dead yet.

But the prognosis was terminal.

This time, there were no sandwiches waiting in the kitchen, and no message from Alex scrawled on the work surface. General Robert Forsyth was surprised to find he had the Chelsea house to himself, apart from Armstrong – no Chandler, no wife, no bodyguards. Then disappointed. He'd been looking forward to talking through the day's dramatic events with the old man, sharing his excitement with Alex.

Puzzled at their absence, he called Headquarters and asked for Andy Kyle, worried that Chandler might have been taken ill. His number two came on the line, guessing what the call was about.

'If you're back home and wondering where the Field Marshal is, I'm afraid he's skipped off to Hampshire. The bodyguards reported in and I tore them off a strip, but they could hardly refuse his direct order.'

Forsyth wasn't pleased.

'What's he playing at, Andy, any idea?'

'He's less than overjoyed at today's developments. You may have pushed him too far. That's the impression I got, anyway. I had a word with him, before he left.'

'You did *what*?'

'Had a word with him before he left, mentioned that the evidence against Stanley might not be all it seemed.'

Kyle seemed almost indifferent. Forsyth couldn't believe what he was hearing. He felt his temper rising.

'You stupid bastard. If Chandler turns against me this

whole thing could still unwind. What the hell possessed you to say that? Get on to those minders. Order them to put the old fool into a car and bring him straight to Headquarters, and don't listen to any nonsense from my wife about him being unfit.'

Andy Kyle didn't reply. Forsyth couldn't understand what his deputy was playing at, spoke angrily.

'Do it now, dammit!'

Silence. Kyle had disconnected. Slamming the dead phone into its cradle, Forsyth turned and stormed towards the front door, brushing past Armstrong's protesting arm.

'Come on, back to Headquarters. You'd bloody well think Andy Kyle was the one person I *could* rely on to get it right, wouldn't you?'

He hadn't been able to take advantage of the first opportunity. The car came fast. After it stopped, a minder had emerged from the front, alertly checking for danger. From over a hundred yards away he seemed to look directly into Sheldon's eyes, but was merely identifying and studying the most likely location for a sniper.

Eventually he opened the rear door, hurrying Forsyth into the house with a protective arm around his charge's shoulders. He knew his stuff, placing himself on the target's right to obstruct a shot from the tall building that worried him.

The American was disappointed, but not concerned. These things were rarely easy. Back home, as a young man, he would remain motionless in cover for twelve hours or more, trip after trip, patiently waiting for the right whitetail buck. In the end, he always got his trophy.

A dank smell of curing concrete pervaded the Edwardian apartment block, which was being refurbished. Bags of plaster and tools cluttered Sheldon's lofty sixth-floor room, suggesting there was some way to go before the flats would be fit for the nation's finest. The workmen were long gone for the night, leaving the stately building quiet and still.

Creeping cold stealthily invaded his body, but Donald Sheldon was indifferent to discomfort. With hunter's intensity, he watched for movement in the killing ground, motionless in the kneeling position that allowed him to keep the rifle muzzle rock-steady. His elbows rested on a borrowed plastering table, far enough back to leave him hidden in darkness, free to shoot through a gaping rectangle yet to be filled by a replica sash window.

The streetlights came on, but his image-intensifying laserscope gave a bright, clear picture of Forsyth's front door. Sheldon pushed a button on the night-sight, causing a red dot to glow on the brass letter plate at which he aimed. Satisfied, he switched off.

He regretted his inability to check the rifle's zeroing. Still, Brigadier Kyle was also a professional, and whatever the man's motivation he would hardly have supplied a weapon that didn't shoot straight. The big Intelligence officer had been persuasive – maybe to ensure Sheldon's co-operation, perhaps feeling a need to establish his sincerity, probably seeking self-justification for extreme action.

His story of Forsyth's treachery was convincing, might be true. On the other hand, it could be some kind of trap, or Kyle might be using him to further a hidden agenda. Donny Sheldon didn't care. There was nothing ambiguous about the opportunity to avenge Mendlebaum, make some sense of his life. In the end, everything came back to doing what you were put on earth to do.

Down below, a wedge of light jumped into the street. The door was opening. Sheldon's finger found the button on the scope. He pulled the rifle butt into his shoulder and took a slow breath, holding cold air deep in his lungs.

Two men came out – target first, heading for the car. Followed by the minder, who ineffectually plucked at Forsyth in an attempt to get him back inside. Forsyth wasn't interested, pulling sharply away. His expression was angry, distorted, but it was unmistakably the face Sheldon had seen on television not three hours before. He decided on a body shot and nudged the button.

The deadly red dot appeared on Forsyth's coat, and the optics were so good the nap of tan suede and gleam of brown leather buttons were clearly visible. In a tiny passage of time during which he exhaled, moved the dot on to the left breast pocket and took first pull on the trigger, Sheldon saw Forsyth look down.

As he fired, he knew that Forsyth knew.

The high-velocity bullet knocked the target backwards. As he fell on the threshold, the crack of the shot came back from buildings opposite and the ejected shell case clattered to the floor. The minder vanished. An arm emerged, tried to pull Forsyth's dead weight into the house. Sheldon took careful aim. The second shot hit Forsyth in the right temple.

In the following silence, a sound that should not have been there came through the open door. They were close – had probably been in the building all along – and now they were coming for him. Sheldon polished the rifle's blued action with his sleeve, stood the Browning against the wall beside the empty window aperture and spoke very softly.

'It's not your fault, old friend.'

With fierce pride, Donald Sheldon had served his country well for all his adult life, but now he was tired. So very tired. He took two decisive paces forward and stepped into the only future that made any sense.

AFTERMATH

Ken Stanley and Godfrey Cornwell were playing a childish game as though the future of mankind depended on it. They sat at a picnic table in the grounds of Chevening House, staring into each other's eyes. Stanley's fists thumped together for the third time and his right hand flashed out, palm open.

'Paper!'

He nodded in satisfaction as he observed Godfrey's extended fist, which remained clenched.

'Paper wraps stone. That's me leading twenty-seven twenty-four.'

Cornwell wasn't worried.

'First to fifty, Ken. Besides, I won yesterday.'

Fists thumped again. They both came up with scissors – stand-off. Ken Stanley caught the evocative whiff of an autumn bonfire and looked around the immaculate grounds. Chevening was a jewel in the green Kentish countryside. A gardener heaped dry leaves on to the fire, stepping back as flames crackled up. Not bad, as prisons went, but nothing could compensate for the loss of position and influence.

The former rivals had become close since their house arrest, finding consolation in painfully shared experience. Actually, life was tolerable. Access to newspapers and television was permitted, there was a superb library and they were even allowed to write apolitical letters to old friends and colleagues in government. The concession provided ways of filling endless time. The younger man caught his mood, divined his thoughts.

'Where did we go wrong, Ken?'

The former Prime Minister gave their usual answer.

'In our own ways, we did what we believed to be right – for us, for the country. Our mistake was natural. People aren't supposed to behave like those clever bastards. We simply didn't understand the game. Speaking of which, mind if we don't finish this one? I fancy a coffee. Care to join me?'

'No, I think I'll hit a tennis ball with that strapping young thing that calls itself a physiotherapist, work up an appetite for lunch. Catch you later.'

Cornwell got up and wandered away, setting a meandering course towards the tennis court. Ken Stanley gazed after him. Where exactly *did* they go wrong?

George sat on a sea-front wall, watching graceful white motor yachts on serene blue water. Girls, servants, champagne, freedom – they had the lot. Life was miserably unfair. It was impossible to live decently on the pitiful pension he collected each Friday morning from the local Credit Lyonnais.

To add insult to injury, he'd seen Beth Highsmith driving along the coast road in an open-top Ferrari two days before, hair blowing in the wind, accompanied by some macho type wearing a straw hat. George himself drove an ancient Renault Clio.

Beth was the cause of his troubles, along with that half-caste bastard Andy Kyle. The remembered humiliation of being forced to sit through that repulsive video – and the subsequent expulsion from the country of his birth – made his flesh crawl. How dare they? Old Minton-Briant would never have allowed it. Ran a tidy ship, did the old man, for all that they'd had their disagreements.

Still, Beth hadn't got off scot-free. Pleasurable memories of their encounter stirred his groin. George's wandering eyes fastened on a topless sunseeker, jiggling by in search of a cold drink, a man, whatever. He whistled. She stopped – gamine face turning, blonde hair swinging, alertly evaluating him. Not in the first flush of youth, but she'd do. He waved her over. A moment later she was sitting beside him. Saying nothing, she pulled a shirt out of her shoulder bag, put it on and buttoned up.

Even in reduced circumstances he still had what it took to pull the ladies. George jerked his head by way of invitation, vaulted the wall and started to walk.

'My place is just round the corner.'

She raised plucked eyebrows – perhaps understanding English, perhaps only the universal language of sexual attraction – but followed. Typical little beach bum. Didn't stand a chance.

His apartment was three minutes away. Inside, the single room was musty. She looked around, clutching her bag as she took in a litter of dirty clothes round the unmade bed. Beside her, a corpse-speckled flypaper turned in air disturbed by the closing door. George knew she would be easy, but fun.

He went to the cocktail cabinet – a wall cupboard containing two stolen glasses bearing the blue and yellow Ricard legend, a nearly-empty bottle of Cutty Sark whisky and an opened litre of *vin ordinaire*. Scotch for him, wine for the girl. Her reply shocked him.

'*Mille francs.*'

Her tone was practical. George took a pace towards her.

'You expect me to pay? That *is* rich – I've never paid for it in my life and don't intend to start now.'

He reached out and grabbed a handful of cotton shirt. She didn't move. Without letting go, he slapped her face with his free hand. She was knocked on to the bed, shirt buttons tearing free as she went. George's palms went clammy as she bounced back up. A fighter, but out of her league.

As he drew back a fist to smash her arrogance to pulp, her right hand blurred out of the bag she'd never released. He felt a blow in his side. They stopped, face to face. Her exposed breasts heaved, but the urchin face was set hard. She spat words, turned and went.

'*Nique ta mère, espèce de salaud.*'

The door closed, but he couldn't turn his head. His body went numb. George swayed, clutched his side and fell to the bed. He contemplated a bloody hand, stared wonderingly at a spreading stain on the grey blanket. The bitch had stabbed him.

He whimpered until his throat dried. The sound of flies was loud in the airless room. After a while, pain hit him. He could hardly move, but forced himself to make the supreme effort needed to reach for help, the bedside telephone.

Then George remembered he'd postponed payment of the bill once too often. The treacherous Frogs had cut him off.

Far below, a moving cloud of disturbed sediment neared Lustbader's bait – a pellet of bread pinched on to a barbless hook. Eyes straining through polarized glasses, he could make out the refracted dark shape of a large carp with its nose down, hoovering across the lake bed. Suddenly, the white speck was gone. He struck, a second too late.

Even as his rod started to whip upwards the bait reappeared, blown out before the hook was driven home. The bread swirled free, detached by the force of his strike. The fish turned, fleshy lips sucking in the now-harmless morsel.

Vernon Lustbader glanced at the shore. The woman sat at the table in front of his cabin, watching as she drank coffee from the flask he'd left for her. She was persistent – an old-fashioned reporter who wouldn't quit on a good story – suspecting she'd been manipulated, meaning to get her own back however long she waited.

Mary-Jo MacInnes had started it a year ago with the article that ultimately derailed Stark. Her revelation of the link between the murder of a Mexican maid and the Stark campaign had started a fire that ultimately consumed Pat Stark's ambitions. By the end, the gutter press was openly suggesting The Candidate's fingers had closed around the dead kid's throat.

If Stark hadn't resisted temptation, and left evidence within the victim's body, he would probably be sitting in Bexar County Jail right now. But still the damage was too severe. Errol Tidyman's victory was the closest since 1960, when Kennedy scraped home 51–49, but he won the race. And now Lustbader had learned exactly how he did it.

At first, he'd lived with suspicion. President Tidyman had started to implement policies that offered hope. But Lustbader was compromising principles once held dear – not because he believed the end justified the means, but because he was a lonely old man. The relationship with Tidyman had brought shape and purpose to an emotional void.

Lustbader's resignation as Secretary of State – for health reasons – had caused a sensation, coming within six months of inauguration and the triumphal agreement with the Brits. Speculation had run from bizarre to ridiculous. But without credible alternative, the official line had held.

Except for this determined young woman from the *Washington Post*. She'd been camping on his doorstep for two months, staying on after the pack departed in search of easier pickings. In truth, he no longer minded. After ignoring her for weeks, dialogue had developed. He'd warmed to her directness, seen the person beneath the hard-bitten exterior.

He started the Evinrude. Her editor was no fool, setting a young turkey-hen to catch a rooster. Well, he was ready. He'd finally put the last piece of the jigsaw in place, with the name of a long-time Tidyman lieutenant and photograph to match.

The former Green Beret was on the books of Tidyman Inc. as a management consultant, but nobody recollected ever seeing him around any of the corporation's offices or plants. Now, Lustbader had found evidence that proved the man who'd already killed for his country never really changed his line of work.

Lustbader had mailed a bulky package to Mary-Jo MacInnes at her office that very morning, driving into town on the pretext of getting bait. It was all there. The responsibility for what he had done was truly awesome, as would be the consequences for President Tidyman. But as the Jon-boat picked up speed and curved in a wide arc towards shore, the former Secretary of State felt content. He would send her back to Washington, leave the rest to her. With the ammunition he had provided, it shouldn't be hard. She'd find herself on top of the biggest story since Watergate – and that didn't have dead bodies littered about the place.

Greg Browne lay on the private beach, propped on an elbow, studying his sleeping companion. She was having a passionate affair with the Riviera sun. Her flat brown stomach rose and fell, dusted with grains of silver sand. She had an ethereal quality, remoteness that consumed him with desire.

But no one had possessed Beth Highsmith since the ferocious assault that scarred her mind, though physical reminders had long vanished. The photographer accepted her lack of sexual interest without complaint. They were constantly together. He did his best work with her in the viewfinder. Only her. For her part, she needed both undemanding companionship and their demanding professional relationship.

They were snatching a well-earned break between a hectic run of top assignments, after a brilliant session for *Paris Match* at a château up in the hills. Greg relived every shot, revelling in the certainty that they'd created great pictures. He'd been lucky. Without Beth, he might never have been better than very good.

He hadn't told her how he felt, but she knew. Sometimes, when emotion was hard to contain, he was tempted to tilt up her face and take her lips, sensing she wouldn't resist. But her striking grey eyes contained a warning and a promise, and he pushed temptation away.

A rush of warm seawater curled around his toes. Rolling over, he entered the water quietly. He started threshing, shouting for help. Beth woke uncertainly, raising her sunglasses in an attempt to see more clearly. When she realized what was happening, she ran into the sea and splashed down beside him.

She laughed spontaneously for the first time in twelve months. Her arms wriggled round him and she kissed him full on the lips.

The man stood in shadow, against the trunk of a solitary pine which stood tall a few yards from the landing stage. He watched the boat turn, studying the hunched silhouette in the stern through miniature binoculars. The guy was on autopilot, oblivious of his surroundings. Lustbader had been doing too much thinking lately, asking awkward questions, throwing stones into the pool. The dumb bastard didn't know when to leave well alone.

Up at the cabin, the girl had disappeared, following a pattern observed on the two previous evenings. She went inside to make fresh coffee for the returning fisherman, maybe a bite to eat. That was good. The window of the kitchen area looked over the back yard. He couldn't touch her, she must see nothing.

Nobody would be surprised that a tired, sick old man stumbled as he stepped out of an unstable boat. Struck his head on the landing stage. Fell face down in the water. The man lowered the glasses and shook his head sadly.

The country churchyard was cool, splashed with sunlight which filtered through tall beech and chestnut trees. Wood pigeons conversed lazily. Somewhere over the fields, a tractor was working and a distant dog barked monotonously.

Alexandra Forsyth stood motionless, her back to the squat Norman church. She looked at the simple white stone which a year's grass already threatened to engulf, glad that Bob was resting in the countryside where he grew up. The old rendered farmstead with its thatched roof and flanking barn conversions was less than four hundred yards away, across water meadows where he played as a child. This was a peaceful place.

As if to dispute the thought, chattering magpies invaded, first one pair, then another – arguing noisily, flashing black and white against autumnal foliage until they finally came together in the skeletal branches of a dead elm tree. One for sorrow, two for joy, three for a girl, four for a boy.

The chiselled inscription was simple – *ROBERT FORSYTH*. No date or epitaph. A Red Admiral hovered, alighted on warm stone. Clumsily, she stooped. The butterfly fluttered away. When she straightened, nine red roses lay on the grave, one for each year of their marriage. She stayed for a moment, then turned and walked heavily between lichen-crusted monuments to forgotten human beings. Her eyes were bright with unshed tears.

She paused by the church porch in unspoken farewell, taking a last look around the neglected graveyard. She wouldn't forget, but neither would she return. Her life lay ahead, with the baby that slept snugly in the sling against her chest. Moving towards the waiting car, she held her hand against Bob's son, pulling him even closer. She talked to the child as though he could understand.

'I'll tell you all about him one day, Young Bob. But now we'd better get home to Grandpa. He's afraid I'll drop you on your head, so he won't have anybody to leave those wretched shotguns to.'

Their convoy was approaching Chequers. The faithful house had been fully restored, once more serving the nation's leader as a relaxing retreat where important guests could be entertained in style. Field Marshal Anderson Kyle watched the wooded countryside flash past the speeding Jaguar.

'Penny for them.'

He turned to his companion. President Tidyman smiled.

'Sure is beautiful out there, Andy. Reminds me of New England in fall. But maybe you have other things to think about.'

'I was thinking how clever your tame shrink was, that's all. Those poor sods all behaved just as the script suggested, though there were a couple of tough moments. That bastard Carney ran out on me without finishing the job, but Donny Sheldon made a good substitute. And I nearly died when young Dexter found that tape with my voice on it.'

The President winked.

'Still, we pulled it off. The top men were too busy watching each other to look over their shoulders. Never did see us charging up the inside track.'

'Forsyth didn't appreciate my influence with Intelligence officers, most of whom I'd trained. He was the hardest to live with, a friend, and I can almost believe he thought he was doing the right thing.'

'Don't we all? But it still bothers you.'

'Forget it, Errol, we must look to the future. You may be the world's most powerful man, but it'll cost you.'

'I guess it will, at that. But a deal's a deal. You won't find us mean-spirited. Fifty per cent on top of the agreed figure, plus a fifty-billion line of no-strings credit with the World Bank.'

Kyle fiddled with his watch band. It was the first occasion they'd been alone since Air Force 1 had arrived at London

Heathrow, but he couldn't broach the subject that was really on his mind. Instead, he steered Tidyman into safe business talk.

'Any problems your end?'

'Nothing I can't handle. Old Vern Lustbader cut up rough, which ain't altogether surprising. Vernon believes in the ends, just feels upset about the means. But I'm tackling some real serious problems back home, making progress, doing good things he wants to see done. He won't be making any more trouble. You?'

'We need your dollars to help with economic reconstruction, but everything's cooled down. The new political parties are starting to get their act together, we'll hold elections in two or three years. Chandler's a great President. Not in your league, but then we're a young republic. There are no flies on Prime Minister Higgins, either, and I've also got a damn fine Home Secretary in Wendy Millar. You'll meet them all at Chequers.'

Kyle returned to his vigil, feeling unaccountably depressed, then blurted out a question.

'Louise?'

There, it was out. Tidyman threw back his head and laughed.

'Thought you'd never ask. She's fine, sends her best regards. I nearly persuaded her to come over with me, but she couldn't lick a sneaky feeling you were using her to reach me all the time.'

'I thought it might be the other way around, that our meeting when I was in New York was no accident.'

Tidyman patted his arm.

'You kids must sort that out yourselves. I know you been pussyfooting around on the telephone, but there ain't any substitute for working these things out face to face. She's coming to England next month to front a documentary on the changes for NBC.'

As the car passed through the main gate of Chequers, Kyle found he was whistling *Rule Britannia* – somewhat tunelessly, but with great verve.

He wandered around the house, visiting rooms that were no longer familiar. Most of the contents were in storage, leaving only essentials. He would soon be quitting this place which had been a part of his life for so long – returning home to Hill Country, where there was space to breathe and being alone seemed natural. But the going wouldn't be easy.

His mind looked at well-loved pictures, but his eyes saw naked brass hooks above lighter patches of wallpaper. The phone rang. He walked through to the empty den, feet echoing on bare boards, and found the phone in a dusty corner. He thought about letting it ring, but he was still a cop. Just.

'Schneider.'

'Hey, Loot, you still in business?'

It took him a second to place the voice.

'Not for long, MacInnes. They're throwin' me out end of the month. I got too creaky to chase crooks. You still alive?'

'Churning out the words, trying to live down that Martinez fiasco.'

'We was both shafted real good. So what's new?'

'I'm looking at the photograph which matches that description you got of the Martinez killer, with a name on the back. Plus information on this cool dude, including his special service record and cancelled cheques which show who's been picking up the tab for services rendered. I also have the phone number of a cop up in Michigan who's looking into the mysterious death of one Vernon Lustbader, ex-Secretary of State in the Tidyman administration. Last, I see a first-class air ticket for San Antonio which just arrived by messenger. Interested?'

Lieutenant Richard Schneider felt like the Frankenstein creation when the switch was thrown.

'Maybe I am at that, MacInnes. What time does your flight get in?'

'Nine in the morning, if I can wake up in time to catch the plane. On second thoughts, I won't go to bed. We're talking Pulitzer Prize here, not that I'm in this business for glory, no sir. See you at the airport.'

'I'll be there. We may even get to visit an old friend of yours. Remember David Turrow? He's our new DA down here. Billy Ray Brandon got caught with his greedy mitt in the cookie jar, thanks to a little shrewd detective work by one of SAPD's finest.'

'That right? I sure hope you never bear me any grudge, you vengeful bastard.'

Schneider got up from his awkward crouch. He hardly noticed the ache in his left thigh. To his surprise, he realized he was more interested in seeing Mary-Jo MacInnes than what she was bringing with her – though she was right about one thing. He *was* a vengeful bastard. It would be a real pleasure to close the Martinez file before he turned in his badge.

He wandered into the bedroom and looked at the big wooden bed where he must have spent more than fifteen thousand nights. Maybe the world wasn't such a bad place to be alive in, after all.

Nothing stirred in the Chiltern Hills. Honeysuckle and clematis crowded the twin lodge gates of Chequers, smothering intricate ironwork that barred a long-disused approach to the Prime Minister's country residence. The scent of an English Autumn was fragrant on still air.

Inside the brick-and-flint lodge cottage, Sergeant Terence Seymour flicked off audio switches, lit a cigarette and settled his stocky body in the swivel chair. Sophisticated electronics seemed insignificant beside moted sunlight striking through the diamond-pane window.

Idly blowing smoke at a spider that was lowering itself from the cracked white ceiling on a gossamer lifeline, Seymour reviewed his unsatisfactory circumstances. He should never have slept with the ruddy girl, let alone married her. Then she lost the kid, if there ever was one. Fancy falling for that old scam. Joy Christie as an unfulfilled ambition was one thing, Joy Seymour in married quarters rationing sex and running his life like a company sergeant-major was something else.

He thought about Lizzie Pike. There was a real woman. But she'd left when reconstruction work on Chequers was completed – not bothering to say goodbye, gone without leaving a phone number. Pity, they'd been good together.

Gratified by the spider's rapid retreat, Seymour reloaded, dragging deeply on his cheap cigarette. He glanced at the instruments. Nothing. The Yank and the other big shots were safe as houses. He puffed another plume of smoke at the spider, which curled up tightly in self-defence.

He checked his wristwatch – ten grand's-worth of gold Rolex, a surprise wedding gift from Joy. The provenance might be dubious, but Terence Seymour loved that watch. Two more hours before his relief arrived.

God, the job was boring.